Praise for the Novels of
Bestselling Author Kris Radish

ANNIE FREEMAN'S FABULOUS TRAVELING FUNERAL

"Move over, Thelma, and make way, Louise! Annie Freeman's raucous and heart-tugging journey to eternity will put Kris Radish on the map—in a red Cadillac!"
—Jacquelyn Mitchard

"[For] readers who relish the idea of women forming bonds when their mettle is tested and finding power and self-actualization in grief, sharing and love."
—*Publishers Weekly*

"The book's themes of sisterhood, loss and love [will] have wide appeal."
—*Cleveland Plain Dealer*

"Deftly blends laughter and tears ... Readers ... will be anxious to embark on this new Radish journey. And, like Annie's funeral, it's sure to attract more along the way."
—*Albuquerque Journal*

"I wish I could buy a copy for every woman I've ever met. I am so in love with this book, the women's stories, and their relationships with each other."
—Susan Wasson, Bookworks, Albuquerque, New Mexico

"A rallying cry for the empowerment of women, Radish's novel is also a celebration of the strong bond that exists between female friends."
—*Booklist*

"A group of women, meeting informally for years, have shared secrets, joys, heartaches, losses, and pain. When one confesses she is pregnant and that the baby is not her husband's, the confession draws the women into a life-altering step that affirms the bonds of female friendship."
—*Booknews* from The Poisoned Pen

"[Kris Radish's] characters help readers realize they are not alone in the world and their struggles have been or will be experienced by other women."
—*Albuquerque Journal*

"A story of friendship and empowerment."
—*Library Journal*

"A message of hope, renewal, and the importance of female friendships."
—*Duluth News-Tribune*

Also by Kris Radish

The Elegant Gathering of White Snows

Dancing Naked at the Edge of Dawn

Annie Freeman's Fabulous Traveling Funeral

And coming soon from Bantam Books

Searching for Paradise in Parker, PA

1. the
2.
3. Sunday
4.
5. List
6.
7. of
8.
9. Dreams
10.
11.
12.
13. Kris Radish
14.
15.
16. Bantam Books

THE SUNDAY LIST OF DREAMS
A Bantam Book / February 2007

Published by Bantam Dell
A Division of Random House, Inc.
New York, New York

Bantam Books and the rooster colophon are registered
trademarks of Random House, Inc.

Library of Congress Cataloging-in-Publication Data

Radish, Kris.
    The sunday list of dreams / Kris Radish.
        p. cm.
    ISBN: 978-0-553-38398-0 (pbk.)
    1. Self-actualization (Psychology)—Fiction. 2. Mothers and daughters—Fiction.
3. Lists—Fiction. 4. Dreams—Fiction. I. Title.

    PS3618.A35S86 2007
    813'.6—dc22

                                2006024428

Printed in the United States of America
Published simultaneously in Canada

www.bantamdell.com

BVG   10 9 8 7 6 5 4 3 2 1

Dreams are the lively and lovely desires of the heart, soul, mind and body that should propel us through every moment of our lives. The Sunday List of Dreams is for every woman who wishes and lusts and laughs and yearns and wonders and imagines and who dares to make her own list.

Don't just write it—live it.

Acknowledgments

Getting *there* is never easy to do alone.

What are you thinking? That *there* is more than doable but writing a book alone? Well, my sex-toy store in the literary world is a wonderful maze of people who hold on to the very edges of my life so that I do not fall over and hurt myself any more than I already have.

And let me tell you, the research for a book about empowering women to exalt their sexual selves as much as they have every other part of themselves was sheer hell. I had to go to sex-toy stores, watch videos, read sex books, travel to cities and towns to talk with women about sex and ask them intimate questions, and then ponder my own sexual self in ways that were, believe me, trying, sometimes laughable, but terribly rewarding.

Sigh. Sometimes it's hard to stop writing a book like this.

But when I did, and then looked up, several Sunday heroines rose to the surface, and one hero, who I pray has not been maimed for life.

My hat, and anything else these wonderful women want, is off to Keely Newman and Kelli Savage, co-owners of Tulip, a luxe toy gallery based in Chicago and expanding across the country. Their openness, accessibility, and trusting hearts gave me a full view into their professional world and the women they work so hard to make happy. They were indispensable and patient in their explanations, demonstrations, and endless hours of interviews and thank the goddesses they have great taste in wine.

Parts of this novel take place in New Orleans, and I was there just weeks before the tragic storm. In this novel I remain true to what New Orleans was before and what, I think, it will always be. The men and women who helped me, gave me a flavor for the real spice of Louisiana life, and remain a true and special part of the book—thank you.

Countless women shared their sexual souls and stories with me during the writing of this sometimes spicy book. Their openness and trusting hearts gave me safe passage into secret and very private places that helped make this book real and true. You know who you are and I will always be grateful.

My agent, Ellen Geiger, is a woman who gets women and who knows that those of us on this literary track cannot stop ourselves. She has made so many parts of my life easier and her trust in my vision is all the light I need.

The support I receive from my Bantam Dell family often astounds me. Kate Miciak, Barb Burg, Shawn O'Gallagher, Elizabeth Hulsebosch, Cynthia Lasky, Irwyn Applebaum, Nita Taublib, Theresa Zoro, Carolyn Schwartz, Rachael Dorman, Gina Wachtel, Loyale Coles, and every soul under the Random House umbrella—you are all the air under my wings, and every single thing you do for me I appreciate.

My daughter Rachel, and my partner, Madonna Metcalf, are wild and generous female hearts who continue to fertilize my life, my work, and my heart in ways that would fill up another entire novel. They help me write and create in numerous ways.

And my son Andrew, a gentle, kind, and patient soul, deserves a special thanks for keeping his head above all the swirling female energy and for guarding his lovely testosterone with charm and good humor. As he leaves the nest and flies toward his own destiny and dreams, one of my main hopes is that I have given back to the world a boy turned man who addresses life with openness and acceptance.

I know I have succeeded, and, Andrew, no matter what I write, what I create with my words—you will always be one of my two greatest accomplishments.

One

1. Stop being afraid.

Connie Nixon's house starts talking to her at 9:51 P.M. on a Wednesday.

She has just finished pawing through her heart and examining the long lines of desire that parade through her body like an endless roll of string and tangle in a knot inside her chest. Her left hand is holding the knot, loosened briefly by means of the pen in her right hand that has translated her dreams into the list. The 48th list. Connie Franklin Nixon's list of dreams.

Connie's list-making tonight has been assisted by one and then two glasses of red wine—a really nice dry cabernet from Australia—and she is trying to decide if she should have another glass. This would push her way over the halfway mark, as far as her usual alcohol consumption goes, and into a semi-critical "what the hell" state that she associates with the early stages of drunken folly, Saturday nights on her sister's back porch and the good old days, which did not last long enough.

Three seconds of hesitation is enough and Connie Nixon rolls over, lets the pages of her list fold against each other, drops the pen, grabs the gorgeous dark red bottle off her book-laden nightstand and pours the wine into the rounded, clear glass so close to the top that she has to lean over and sip it before she can actually pick up the glass.

That exact moment is when she hears the house speaking.

"What?" she whispers out loud. As if she is answering the walls that seem to be speaking. "What did you say?"

She pauses. Her top lip is swimming in wine and her bottom lip has wedged itself against the smooth glass, her breath in a holding pattern. Six years alone in this house have left her on more-than-intimate terms with every squeak, roof sway, late-night foundation-settling creak, gutter birds, falling limbs, and an assortment of other sounds that are as familiar to Connie as a rushing waterfall might be to someone on an enchanted vacation. Even before those six years, when the girls were still romping through the house, climbing in through unlocked windows after curfew and sliding their tricycles, bicycles, cars and motorcycles into the garage door from dawn to dusk, there was a rhythm to the sounds, a symphony of life, a ballet of movement that signaled a house settling in around its family, the arms of the walls wrapping them close and keeping the rain and snow off the beds and dressers and the kitchen table.

The sound Connie hears now, however, is a distant voice, a faint indistinguishable rumble that tangos itself into a kind of hum. It is highlighted by a hint of music, as if someone has left a radio playing at the far edge of the basement. It echoes and sways as if it is about to snuff itself out and, when Connie pauses, unmoving, not frightened but a bit confused about its origin, the sound does not change or grow or stop or turn into something else. "Maybe," she speculates. "Maybe the list has started to speak."

Connie drinks half the glass in one gulp and swings her legs off the edge of the bed. Accustomed to sleeping in whatever she happens to be wearing at the moment she falls into bed, Connie makes certain that if she has to avert disaster she can do so with at least partial dignity. When she looks down, she sees that she has on an old navy-colored t-shirt that will at the very least come to her knees when she stands up and, peeking out from the left side, where she has her foot raised, a pair of cotton underwear, original color unknown, present color something just this side of an old gray sock, frayed like hell along the edge of the stretched elastic.

Peril, disaster, trauma, the unknown—none of those things totally frighten Connie Nixon. She adores silence, most unexpected events, the way the simple shift of the wind can change everything. Death rolls into her hands on a daily basis at her hospital—she says "her" as if she owns the place and indeed she has worked there as if she has owned it for 33 years, night and day, tirelessly, with passion and compassion. Her real fears, the ones she has acknowledged, have been translated into the list she now holds in her hand.

"Ha," she thinks, standing quietly at the side of her bed

and totally focused on the sound she hears. "What could this be?"

She pauses there, unafraid, hands on hips, listening. The whisper of sound returns. Connie smiles to herself because she thinks the walls may be singing. When she lifts her head, she can see her reflection in the mirror that has hung above the old black dresser for 28 years. "I'm not dead and just imagining this," she tells herself out loud. Mystified by the now-constant humming, Connie listens hard. She decides to check every corner of the house.

First she leans across her nightstand, missing the lamp and maneuvering past the books, places her hands against the wall, and then turns her head to press her ear flat against it. She listens. Hears nothing.

Stepping over stacks of books, a pile of magazines, three empty water glasses and last week's wine bottle, Connie manages to get to the door of her own bedroom without falling over a box or impaling herself on a coat hanger, one of her ex-husband's leftover baseball trophies, or what she has decided to call "the endless stacks of shit."

"It's a lifetime of shit," her best friend Frannie O'Brien has told her 16 times since Connie started making huge donations to the local Goodwill store six months ago. "This purging isn't going to happen overnight. Get used to it."

Connie counts on Frannie, or O'Brien, as she prefers to be called, to say it like it is no matter where they are, who is in the room, or whose feelings might get hurt. A psychiatric nurse who refuses to quit smoking even as she passes Connie's intensive care unit and its coughing patients numerous times each week, O'Brien has worked with Nurse Nixon, as she loves to call Connie, for 26 years, swears like a Hells Angel or a high school junior, and plays poker with her nephews, the neighbor boys and six guys at the senior center three times a month. "Remember," O'Brien is always quick to add, "even if it's a lifetime of shit, it's still shit and you need to get rid of it." This from a six-foot-tall Afro-American woman who married a short Irishman named Daniel, throwing the entire redheaded Catholic Irish family and the entire blackheaded Catholic Afro-American family into parallel cultural comas; who attends church herself more religiously than her rosary-saying mother-in-law; who produced two strapping Afro-Irish sons; and who has definitely not thrown away so much as a toothpick or plastic bag in the last 15 years. "Shit," O'Brien is quick to say in her own defense, "is shit only if you don't think you will ever use it again."

The baseball trophies are obviously shit, Connie decides, as she pushes one over with her toe and turns into the hall at the end of her now trendy 1960s ranch house. "Go figure," her real estate broker told her when she dropped off the papers five weeks ago. "Young couples love these houses. They turn them into art deco retro masterpieces and they want to live just like you did—you know, the June Cleaver kind of deal—when you first moved in here. They add a bathroom in the basement, get a Weber grill, and have another baby."

"June Cleaver, my ass," is what Connie wanted to say. "June Cleaver didn't put herself through nursing school by working full-time and trying constantly not to get pregnant. She didn't suffer through the night shift for five years so someone would always be there with the kids, probably never mowed a lawn or shoveled the driveway in her life, and never realized until the mid-'70s that the Beaver was destined to be gay. My God, the kid wore patent leather shoes, parted his hair on the side and carried his books to school in his arms. Today the Beav would be on 'Queer Eye for the Straight Guy.'"

The house murmured her out of the 1960s and into the short hall—nothing unusual there—past the two smaller bedrooms where more boxes of shit sat waiting for transportation to their new destinations, into the living room that was still untouched so Connie could make believe one part of her life was still intact. Connie went through the dining room, which she'd enlarged herself one rare afternoon off when, sick of the tiny kitchen, she had walked into the garage to find a sledgehammer, knocked a hole through the plaster and announced to her then-husband Roger, "Now will you knock out the wall like I've asked you to for the past three years?" Connie laughed whenever she stood in the spot where the wall used to divide the kitchen and the dining room. Sometimes she stood in that spot eight times a day and she laughed every single time. Sometimes, when she just needed to laugh, she stood there, too, and it always seemed to work.

It wasn't long after the wall-bashing incident that Connie realized she could have set up a couple of strengthening beams and knocked out the wall without asking for help from a single person, especially her husband. It was less than a year later, when she ripped out the old carpeting one Saturday night while Roger was fishing, as she was kneeling on the bare floor with carpet nails jammed between her lips and pounding in the new padding, that she counted up the hours she spent with her husband and without him. Something that felt like the size and weight of a bowling ball moved through her heart and lodged in her stomach. "Sex," she told herself, spitting out the nails into her hand, "is the one thing left I thought I needed a husband for these past few years, but I can probably figure out how to do that myself too. He's never even here, for crying out loud." The rest of that afternoon, pounding, ripping, and working as a mother-referee to three teenaged daughters, she thought of nothing but her marriage and how it seemed as if she had suddenly passed through some kind of narrow tunnel that only had room for one person—just her.

The demise of her marriage was not really quite that simple. "No divorce," her therapist told her, "no matter how uncomplicated or seemingly agreeable it appears, is simple. It's a life-changing decision, Connie. Along the way it will hurt like hell, leave a few scars, melt your resolve, leave you breathless and terrified and Roger will keep fishing and you can knock down your own walls or build a few new ones. It's all up to you."

Standing at the lip of her old dining room, wondering if the humming walls were not some left-over, unsettled business from that momentous decision 13 years ago to divorce, Connie places her hand on the dent she refuses to plaster over from the flying pot Roger threw at her when she demanded that he leave the house. The dent had grown smooth over the years and she'd repainted it three times because she often stood there, as if the spot held some magic power, rubbing it with the palm of her hand and remembering how she'd willed him to throw something so she could threaten him with a police visit that would guarantee his departure. "Power," she said out loud now, with her head tilted towards the ceiling. "I loved the feeling of power."

He did leave. Eventually apologized for being a crappy husband, a sort-of-okay father, and he even made a brave and fairly decent effort to be more a part of his three daughters' lives ... until he got remarried to a much younger woman and started the whole process again. Connie now called Roger a friend, an exclusive and very meaningful title in her world, and once she'd even asked him to help her when their first grandchild arrived. But now, with two toddlers of his own, she was pretty certain his fishing boat had not moved from behind his garage in several years and if they spoke once a year it was close to a miracle.

Connie leans in to put her ear against the kitchen wall, smiles as a flood of kitchen memories—birthday parties; the night Frannie danced on the counter; the week her sister Kimberly's four kids camped under the long oak table; the times her own girls, Jessica, Sabrina and Macy, ate, worked, slept and lived there and told all the whispered secrets that circled throughout the room on a daily basis. The wall is quiet but there is still a voice somewhere, and Connie, glass in hand, throws her rear end onto the kitchen counter, dangles her short legs over the side, sips the wine and wonders if it just isn't her leaving it that has the house talking.

Most people know that Connie is planning on selling the house as soon as she gracefully slides through her retirement party the following week, makes it through her last days of work the week after that, and then ditches what she is calling the first half of her life for the second half. But only O'Brien knows how scared she is of all the changes that seem to have collided and are now whispering to her.

Beyond the seemingly bold and broad boundaries of her life, Connie remains frightened of doing what she has promised herself she would do for so many years she cannot bear to add them up.

Connie Franklin Nixon is terrified to stop writing and rewriting her list of dreams and to start living them.

That's why Connie is not calling 911 for help, even though her house is speaking to her, which might seem like a reason to panic for most people. She thinks the sound is the house urging her to begin something that has been in a holding pattern for what is now more than half of her life. The house, she thinks, trying to come up with something that

seems only partially insane if not logical, is simply leaking
out nearly thirty years of stories and swearing, parties and
fights and girls sneaking in the back window and all the sex
that apparently happened in hallways and bedrooms and
even the bathroom when she wasn't looking. The house is,
for one last time, saying good-bye to Connie herself—if only
Connie can bring herself to actually leave the physical house
and the memories that seem to be leaking out of it now in an
almost constant song.

The welcome-home-from-college parties, two bridal
showers, new in-laws' footprints. The three horrid dates
she'd had in 13 years. A few of those damned basket parties
and one of those surprise marketing level meetings that
Connie thought was supposed to be a candle party. Lots of
laughter, tears enough to irrigate a field for one season, and
increasingly more laughter than tears as the years wore on
and the pace of life settled into something routine but pleas-
ant, right and pretty damn wonderful. Connie listens, kicking her feet back and forth, and decides to forgo traipsing
into the basement, which she has already pretty much gutted, because she knows there isn't anything down there besides a water heater, furnace and the requisite Midwestern
dehumidifier. In her Indiana town—a community of 48,000
noteworthy only because it is close to something else—an
entire house can rot from the basement up if you don't have
a dehumidifier in the humid 20-second summer months and
a humidifier in the dry winter months that make up the rest
of the year.

When she realizes it's closing in on midnight and that
she's already waltzed herself out of an hour of sleep because
of the humming house and two extra glasses of wine, Connie
decides to go back to bed. She has a full load in her intensive
care unit, three new nurse assistants to finish breaking in,

and a young doctor who needs a lesson in bedside manners, respecting battle-weary nurses, and the importance of kindness as a therapeutic tool. And there is also the training of a new clinical nursing director, community liaison, and ICU head nurse. Her left hip starts to hurt just thinking about her last week of work as she hops off the counter and smiles at the murmuring kitchen wall.

When she tumbles into bed, with the soft whispers of singing voices blending in a chorus of confrontation, Connie reaches for her tattered list. She rests its cold leather cover against her cheek and tries to remember when she last cried. Connie pulls her knees towards her chest and remembers one patient and then another before that who died in her arms, their last breaths of life a soft curl of air against her face and her tears falling like slow drops of warm spring rain into their hair.

And before that, how long before that did you cry for *yourself*? Connie asks herself this question as a rising wave of unexpected emotion washes through her. Was it when Jessica left? Was it the last time a man touched you? Was it the day you divorced? How long, Connie? How goddamn long has it been?

Connie cries so quietly and for so long that the walls become silent and the center of night turns a wide corner towards morning. Her unexpected emotional dive paralyzes her with a kind of fear that has grown into something huge, something terribly frightening and real, and just before she finally drops into sleep she promises herself, promises the walls, promises anyone or anything who might care, that she will start tomorrow.

She will.

Tomorrow she will start living the list of dreams.

She will.

TWO

2. Let go. Stop holding on to things so tightly. Loosen your grasp. Be honest.

3. Get rid of SHIT. Start with the garage.

The house sounds continue with an occasional pause—as if the voices are taking a breath—the next day, the day after that, and throughout the weekend. The noise has pushed Connie to do something she has put off for so many years. She reminds herself that her house started speaking because it was time for her to take action, to stop dreaming, and to start living.

Start living the dreams.

"So easy to say," she says aloud. "Not so easy to do."

Nurse Nixon now carries the first three items on her list in her front pocket. Numbers one, two, and three are on a white piece of paper, written in black ink. She takes the paper out of her pocket 15 times before she leaves for work that day, swallows the words, slips the paper back into her pocket, and thinks right away that she may have to switch from the top to the bottom of the list or maybe to the middle if she is going to get anything done.

Nurse Nixon works part of the second shift on Saturday night when someone calls in sick, then comes home, hears the walls talking and leaves the house for a few minutes to see if there isn't a power line down, or some strange meteorological phenomenon, or a neighbor boy perched on a telephone wire with a hanger in one hand and a Geiger counter in the other. She sees nothing. She decides to cruise over to Frannie's house to tell her about the talking walls—which she is beginning to answer on a regular basis.

"Nixon, did you find one of the girls' hidden stashes of dope when you were cleaning out their rooms?" O'Brien asks her when Connie finally tells her about the talking house. They are leaning against the long counter in the center of Frannie's huge and gloriously organized kitchen.

"My children never smoked dope," Connie declares with a make-believe British, aristocratic accent. "All three of them are nuns and working in hospitals, churches, and third-world countries."

"You are mad, woman," O'Brien bellows back. "Do you want me to ask the Irishman to drive over with us and take a look?"

"I kind of like it," Connie admits. "The sounds make me happier. It's terrific company."

"But don't you want to know if you are losing your mind just days before you retire and get into that new life and all those plans you have? I mean, we know all about this. Aren't we the ones who take care of people who have a heart attack the day after they retire or go crazy three days after their fiftieth wedding anniversary on the way to the Hawaiian Islands?"

Connie tells O'Brien she feels fine, never better, is ready for the blue horizon, only has the garage and the living room and part of her bedroom left to sort through, and is way too afraid she might miss something to let herself dip into mental illness or to begin hallucinating at this stage of her life.

They decide that O'Brien will hop into Connie's car, ride back to Connie's house nonchalantly, like she has about three thousand times, and then listen to decide if a band is playing or there are dwarfs living in secret passageways in the walls. If none of those things are happening, O'Brien will then rush her friend back to the psych unit at the hospital where she will install her in a private room, preferably facing the inner courtyard and the hospital gardens.

"Give it a second," Connie cautions as they quietly open the door from the garage after turning sideways to get through all the boxes. "And for God's sake, stop laughing."

O'Brien cannot stop laughing.

"I feel like I'm in a movie," she says, snorting into her hand as she slinks into the kitchen with Connie. "We've done some pretty lame-ass things, Nixon, but if this is any indication of what lies ahead of us in your golden years, count me in, baby."

The two women stand with their hands on their hips in the center of the kitchen-dining room and hold their breath so they can listen.

One second.

Another second.

Five more and O'Brien turns slowly towards Connie and mouths the words, *Holy shit, I can hear it.*

Three more seconds, and into the first few lines of what sounds like a slow blues tune, they both exhale at the same moment and cannot shut up.

"I told you!"

"What could it be?" O'Brien asks, narrowing her eyes and looking around suspiciously.

"I knew I wasn't nuts."

"Let's not get carried away. 'Nuts' is a relative thing, believe me. I hear something. But it's just a noise to me. Something mechanical. Did you look everywhere?" O'Brien asks as she starts opening cupboard doors.

"Almost, but I had this weird notion that I wasn't going to find anything so I didn't go into the basement or rip the paneling off the walls."

"Did you say you were drinking Australian wine that night?" O'Brien has opened the cabinet below the kitchen sink and runs her hands under the edge of the counter as if she is a homicide detective.

"What the hell are you doing?" Connie asks her, starting to laugh all over again. "Do you think this is 'CSI' or something?"

O'Brien glares at her friend and keeps moving, hands roving as if she is searching for ticks on her mother's ancient cat, until she has finished inspecting every inch of the kitchen.

"Half of what I do at the hospital is detective work, you know that," O'Brien tells her friend Connie. "I go through pockets, look for signs of drug abuse, run my fingers across arms to feel for old scars, search under mattresses. You never know. Someone could have slipped in here and done something weird to your house. Stranger things have happened. The world is full of fruitcakes."

Connie drops to her knees and then rolls over, laughing into her hands. She is on the floor, inches below the dent in the wall from the night of the pot-throwing incident.

"Frannie," she giggles, "I'm 58 years old, have not had a date in 8 years, I've let my hair go gray, I could care less what people think of me, I need to start a whole new life, I'm trying to pack up and leave my house, at least two of my daughters think I need to look and act like some grandmother they've seen in a magazine at the dentist's office, and I'm about to embark on a retirement adventure that could end up maiming me, killing me, or validating what those two daughters think about me."

"Well, there's always Jessica, the good liberal daughter who will probably never marry, so that's something cheery to focus on," O'Brien retorts as she pulls her head out of Connie's oven. "That is if you ever see or speak to *her* again for more than five minutes."

Nurse Nixon looks at her friend and feels a wound, never healed, widen just below the edge of her heart. The mere mention of her third daughter makes her ache all over. Jessica. The daughter who has managed to lose herself in New York City, who no longer has time for her mother, who has a life of mystery, a closet full of unshared stories and a load of secrets that she is unwilling to share with her family.

"O'Brien," Connie whispers, "I have to tell you something else. It's big, baby, really big."

Her friend raises her hands, palms up, at the same time she raises her eyebrows. She waits. Could something be bigger than a house that talks?

"I started the list," Connie confesses. "The night the house started to talk, I had a little nervous breakdown, kicked myself in the ass, and look . . ."

Connie digs into her pocket. She pulls out numbers one, two, and three without actually letting Frannie see them. She looks like a kid showing her report card to her mom.

O'Brien walks over to Nixon, puts her hands out without saying a word, and Nixon reaches up like a child and is yanked to her feet before she has a chance to shift her weight. She springs up like one of those little rubber balls attached to a paddle.

Frannie laughs and tells her she'd better get used to rough landings and jumping and moving fast and weird noises and running naked into the desert and, she adds, "maybe making love" as if she is swearing and her mother is about to catch her.

Connie is silent. Glaring. Nostrils flared, she takes a step back from her friend.

"Did you peek at the list?"

O'Brien does not hesitate.

"Of course I didn't peek at the list. Are you kidding? That would be like . . ."

She stammers, trying desperately to think of something that would be as horrid as looking at the list before Connie was willing to share it.

"Stabbing a baby," she finally sputters. "Sleeping with your husband's brother. Slapping your mother. Come on, I'd never peek at your list. We've talked about your list for years, Connie. We've talked about it all. I don't have to actually *see* it."

Connie Nixon looks into the dark eyes of the tall, strong woman standing across from her and thinks that she has never in her life trusted or loved anyone like she trusts and loves O'Brien. They have fought and disagreed and kissed and battled and made up and held hands through weeping sessions. They have traveled roads of friendship that some unfortunate women never get to travel. And she knows, just as she knows her house is speaking to her, she would die for this woman and she is suddenly compelled to tell her just that, without even having the correct number from the 48th draft of her list that suggests professing her love to those who deserve it rambling around in her pocket.

"You know I love you," Connie whispers, totally reversing what O'Brien thought she was about to get. "If anyone ever hurt you, or bothered you, I'd kill for you. I'd throw myself in front of a train or truck or bus for you."

"If this was a movie, we'd kiss now," O'Brien says, not able to stifle her wit, even at this precious moment when the house is singing and her best friend is voicing the exact same thoughts she's thinking. "I love you too, even if you live in a house that speaks to you. Aren't you glad it's not speaking in French or German?"

Frannie redeems herself by opening her arms and bringing Nurse Nixon into the space, her "inner sanctuary," as she calls all the inches within arm's reach where she likes to think she protects everyone and everything that comes there. They hug for a moment and Connie feels the heat from her friend rising towards her, the fragrant smell of her earthy perfume, the patterns of her breathing—and the familiarity of every inch of Frannie O'Brien makes her smile.

"Honey," Frannie whispers into her tangle of gray hair, "We've talked about that damned list of yours, I know what you are up to with it, where you keep it, what it means to you, but I've never once even touched that ratty thing, let alone read it."

"I know," Nurse Nixon whispers back. "You know me better than I know myself, but I had to ask."

"You've got this space of time coming up and I was afraid you'd just shutter the house, keep writing down stuff on your

list you want to do but never will, and turn into an old, divorced, and retired nurse who still walks around in her stinky
work shoes," O'Brien says. "It's about time you did something besides write the damned thing."

"'The damned thing' is right," Connie agrees, closing
her eyes just as Frannie closes hers.

The list, they both think at the same moment. *The list.*

three

3. *Get rid of SHIT. Start with the garage.*

*T*he list. The well-worn book of Connie's dreams and thoughts and wishes that she has worked and reworked for the past 30 years. A scratched-up, tatter-edged, brown leather-bound notebook that has been Connie's Sunday salvation before, during, and after her attendance at the traditional religious gatherings that she abandoned about the same time as she abandoned her marriage. The list was and remains Connie Nixon's Prozac. Her unending bottle of champagne. Her escape. Her salvation. Her daily life raft. Her way to live in the present, to survive every part of the reality of now, and throw her climbing rope towards the future.

The list of dreams, as O'Brien has taken to calling it.

The little brown book fits into Connie's hand like a favorite glove, molded into her palm, an extension of her arm, her heart, the invisible paths of her mind and the winding road of her soul that has changed directions, traveled through rough terrain and clicked into gear time and time again. The ride of her life, most days, is a challenge of accomplishment, survival, change, and the hard-earned right to pace herself however she wants—slow, fast or totally in neutral, idling however she wants to idle.

"Maybe I really am finished writing in this book," Connie says aloud as she picks the list up from the ancient rocking chair and walks down the hall and back towards her friend. No more Sunday night musings, no quiet time on the chair or burrowed into her bed with her precious list like a frozen dog, no throwing her imagination into overdrive, no seemingly insane dreams and then wondering when she will actually get to them. And while she walks, the book resting in her hand as if it were a delicate heirloom, the house serenades her.

"The queen has arrived," Connie shouts to the kitchen, the talking house, and her pal O'Brien.

"Sit and drink some royal wine, my darling," O'Brien tells her, patting the dining room chair. "Let us discuss The Book of Lists and the grand noise that, I do confess, needs addressing in a professional manner."

Professional manner, she begins explaining to her friend, because in the back of her own mind she has the wisp of a memory that reminds her of Connie's talking-house story. A

woman or a family or an entire apartment complex, O'Brien
tries to remember, who also heard a house talking and the
noise ended up being some kind of freak electrical problem
that could have blown the entire place to hell and back again
if they had ignored it and not called in the noise busters.

"Really?" Connie asks. "Are you making this up?"

"Nope," Frannie responds, looking around the house as
if she is frightened by the mere sight of the place. "I think
we should call the Irishman. Really. He'll check the wires,
and anything else you can use a screwdriver on, and he can always call his friend Al, the electrician. He's into us for about
five grand. He'll come running."

"Can we wait a little bit longer and sit inside the sere-
nade, just you and I, for maybe an hour or so? It's weird but I
have this goofy notion that the house is speaking to me."

"Maybe it's your list," O'Brien tells her. "Your list telling
you to hurry up or slow down or to include your best friend
in these adventures."

Adventures, Connie admonishes her, is hardly what they
are called. *Dreams*, she emphasizes, saying the word just a little too loud, as if it had been stuck in her throat and had suddenly pried itself loose. "They are dreams. Wild dreams,
O'Brien . . ."

"Dreams can be adventures," O'Brien fires back. "Just
simmer down, drink some wine, and tell me the story one
more time before we call Mr. Husband and check this out. I
am worried, you know."

Worried, Connie thinks. *Worried* is surely not the word
she associates with Frannie O'Brien—the wild poker-playing
black woman who has melted the hearts of grown men and
savage patients, and the snarly attitudes of so many other
human beings it's impossible to remember half of them.
Frannie O'Brien who helped her waltz her three daughters

into adulthood, who helped her learn how to live alone.
Frannie, who kicked her in the rear end when she slowed
down or whined. Frannie O'Brien who sat with her during
her father's funeral and helped her direct the dismantling of
the family home in North Chicago. Frannie at funerals and
weddings and through one crisis after another at work.
Frannie laughing her way up the front sidewalk, walking with
her through twenty summers at Indiana Dunes National
Lakeshore, bravely helping her set up the tent each one of
those twenty summers so they could camp out and her girls
and Frannie's boys could wake to the sound of waves. And
Frannie's "in your face" laugh, the one that erupts like a cap
under pressure and sounds like a machine gun inside of a
metal barrel. O'Brien's tears, the size of golf balls, that are
not plentiful but arrive to celebrate passion and loss and
grieving and love during moments that are sweet and true—
the heartache of losing her own mother; the patients who
cannot seem to go on no matter what O'Brien and her doctors do; those burly sons, Ryan and Peter, who still ask their
mama to sing to them and cook them lasagna, chicken, and
cinnamon rolls when they cruise in from their lives in San
Francisco and Chicago; her Achilles' heel—a temper that
flares like a rocket and can annihilate men bigger than the
running backs on her favorite and occasionally awful and then
suddenly brilliant football team, the Chicago Bears; that remarkable well of courage that allows her to walk through the
halls of the psych unit as if she can cure the blind and heal
the lame and soothe the fears and worries and terrors of
every single person who has ever had to take shelter in its
facilities.

O'Brien, who knows that Connie, in spite of her own often swaggering demeanor, is terrified of living her dreams,

of what she might discover, of who she might become, of where the list she has been making might take her.

"Focus," O'Brien tells her, snapping her fingers and throwing her legs up onto the table. "The list."

The list.

Connie closes her eyes and pushes through the tangled mass of memories that are much dimmer towards the back, where the list was born. Years ago. A night before the first baby. A Sunday night, home alone. House dark. Sitting in the same rocking chair that is now about to fall into 45 pieces in her bedroom. A one-bedroom apartment only blocks from where she has lived ever since. Terrified out of her mind because of what she knows as a nurse about having a baby. Husband working second shift as a patrolman. Three years into her job as a hospital nurse. No mother. No Frannie O'Brien. No true friends since the move from Chicago and the university and the closeness of her now scattered family.

"Gnawing at your leash," her sister Kimberly told her when she would call crying, lonely, scared. Kimberly with three kids in five years, a husband with an exploding career at IBM in Rochester, Minnesota, and no time for any sympathy for a baby sister who had a tendency to "be too liberal and want it all."

"Up yours," Connie told her sister, whose next bit of advice that night was to tell her, "This is just how it is." Their relationship never swayed from that point and when Kimberly's husband took off one miserably cold winter day when they had three kids in high school at the same time and that darling little oops baby in fourth grade, Connie almost bit a hole in her lip to keep from saying, "He must have been gnawing on that leash a *really* long time."

Frannie sits silently through the telling of this story. She has heard it only twice. Once when two of Connie's daughters were home just last year, as Connie was beginning her retirement plans. Connie's youngest two daughters—Sabrina, 27, the suburban Chicago mom, and the baby, Macy, 25, a "way too young" married mom herself who refused to work, lived in Indianapolis with her graduate student husband, and who had made a hobby out of criticizing her mother—had come to visit for the weekend. The impromptu gathering did not include their older sister Jessica, who never even returned a phone call asking if there was any way she might make it home for two days. Connie and Frannie had huddled in Connie's bedroom, listening to Sabrina and Macy's voices rumble through the tiny house, and that night, while her daughters caught up, Connie shared the story of the list. And again six months ago, during a long quiet weekend when the Irish husband was out of town and Connie and Frannie had a slumber party.

The telling of its creation sounded powerful and beyond poignant but it was that night, nine months pregnant and rocking alone, wondering how the course of her life had veered so far to one side, afraid, angry and wanting to stop the forward movement of time, to push it in a new direction, that Connie Nixon claimed the right to create her list. She rocked and wrote and as she did so she placed her life—all the hard parts, the giving, the wanting, the sacrifice, mistakes, unspoken words, inappropriate reactions, lost chances, expected behaviors—every single thing that she regretted, into a deep cave that was temporarily inaccessible from her position on the chair.

And she rocked and the only thing she took with her on her rocking chair voyage was a brown leather notebook, a pen, and every dream she could capture. Connie wrote until her ankles, already the size of large, ripe tomatoes, swelled

another inch. She wrote until her back tingled and her baby
shifted so that her weight was directly on top of Connie's already minimized bladder. Sometimes, during her two-hour
dream ride, she closed her eyes and imagined that she was
doing exactly what she wrote about. Some things simple,
some complicated, some hilarious, some selfish, some just
an exercise in physical, joyful abandonment.

> *Sleeping in without an alarm clock.*
> *Never cooking dinner at the exact same time every single*
> *   day ever again.*
> *Having the entire bed to myself.*
> *Moving into a real house with a backyard.*
> *Having the perfect baby.*

Sometimes one idea covered an entire page and included
wild drawings, scraps of food, drops of wine, milk or tea. Sometimes a page just contained one word—*"sleep"* or *"exercise"*—
and sometimes it detailed in precise form how something
would happen—*"Sleep in very late. Walk through the house without stepping on anything and notice immediately that a maid has
been in to clean the entire place—TOP to BOTTOM."*

Connie Nixon kept the book for a long time in a drawer
that no one else bothered to open. Sometimes, when her
one baby had turned into two, and then two became three,
and when she realized that the burdens of married life, because of her husband's rotating police work schedule and his
addiction to fishing, would keep the division of family labor
tilted towards her side of the ledger, she would simply open
the drawer and touch the brown book, as a lover would touch
the arm of a partner in passing, and then keep going.

And there were always Sundays.

The only day of the week, at first, when she reserved a

small space of time, sometimes only fifteen minutes, when she could fall into her own dreams, see what they looked like when they turned into words and imagine the reality of what she would do someday when they danced to life. And the list changed as her life and needs and own direction changed.

> *My own bathroom.*
> *One lesbian daughter so I do not have to worry about boys ever*
>   *again.*
> *Make that two lesbian daughters.*
> *A trip to New York City.*
> *A convertible the color of Paul Newman's eyes in* The Hustler.
> *A place to be alone where no one can find me.*
> *At least one of my daughters to be my friend, my real friend,*
>   *someday.*

Sometimes, when the house was a crowded maze of kids and friends, Connie would spend an hour in her bedroom and write only one item for the list. Sometimes she would doze off and wake up hours later to realize that no one had died, the house had not burnt down, the fish were still biting and her daughters were figuring out how to live one moment, and another one and the one after that, without her. There were weeks when she could not retreat into the bedroom and work on her list—work schedules, kid schedules, exhaustion, a vacation, or someone was ill. And there was the period of time before, during, and after the divorce when the tone of the list changed to reflect loss, yearning and a sweet desire for simplicity.

> *One day without yelling.*
> *A maid.*

> Someone else to drive the two girls who do not have driver's
>   licenses to the three thousand places they need to be every
>   single damn week.
> Just one daughter telling me that she has decided to remain a
>   virgin and dedicate her life to saving orphans, the sick,
>   lame, and poor of the world.
> Someone to say "sorry"—so I don't have to.

O'Brien smiles while Connie tells her this part of the list story because she remembers each one of the dreams. She remembers because Connie would talk incessantly about what she wanted, how she was counting the days until the divorce was finalized, as if something magical would happen at the very moment the judge ruled that the marriage had been irrevocably broken, pounded the gavel and sent the newly divorced couple on their separate ways. Nurse Nixon, she also recalls without saying so, was exhausted during those months. Exhausted from the idea of change, from facilitating it, from managing the girls and work and the trembling and frightened heart of a husband who had grown accustomed to a life that was guided by the lifting of a single finger, his occasional presence, and the automatic depositing of his check into the family bank account.

And then the list really changed. It became wilder and bolder as the many arms of possibility showed themselves to Connie, as they often do to every woman once the grown babies begin flying away, life descends into a hum of predictability, and the edge of the horizon seems so much closer than it ever has before.

Connie smiles while she talks about this part of her Sunday list. She fills their glasses with more wine, places her elbows on the table, props up her head and goes away, her upper body moving as if she is indeed swaying to the orchestra trapped inside of her dining room walls.

Rafting the Colorado.
Having a real love affair with any man. To love, to feel lust
again—to dance until dawn, to wake up in someone's
arms, to want so bad that my vagina aches. To smell like sex
when I go out in public, to glow in the dark, to unearth all
the passion so deep inside of me that it may require a very
long expedition to uncover it again.
Not giving a shit about the 15 pounds that will apparently never
go away.
Voice lessons. I want to take voice lessons.
Early retirement.
Driving up the northern coast of California in that damn blue
convertible.
Connecting with all the people I let slip away.
A spa weekend. Oh my gawd—make it a spa month.
That one daughter to be my friend. I still want that.
New patterns. Change. Lots of change.

Connie Nixon is breathless when she finishes. Her face is the real horizon, Frannie thinks, adorned with gorgeous laugh lines, freckles from all those years in the sun, and something fierce and yet fine—determination, survival, the elegant grace of a woman who has come into her own and who is very nearly ready to push through the last barriers she has set in front of her own life.

"Let's run naked through the neighborhood," Frannie says, charged from the conversation and moving her feet off the table so she can reach in and touch Connie's hand. "Are you ready?"

"Sure, but are the neighbors ready?"

"Good point. We'd end up having to do CPR on all of them, and some of them would die, and then we'd have to write detailed reports, and there would be lawsuits. Oh, shit, just forget it, we'd better call Daniel before we blow ourselves to hell in this singing house."

"Can you just have him come over tomorrow?" Connie asks, squeezing her friend's hand. "I want one more night of this ear candy. I love the house whispering to me like this, and it's been good company, maybe even inspiration."

After O'Brien leaves, Connie sits in her kitchen for a long time, listening to the faint line of music and smoothing her fingers across the list, the first three numbers, that she has spread out on the table in front of her.

1. *Stop being afraid.*

2. *Let go. Stop holding on to things so tightly. Loosen your grasp. Be honest.*

She gives herself a B-plus for numbers one and two, decides that #1 might be in her pocket for a very long time, and then turns her attention to #3.

Get rid of SHIT. Start with the garage.

Connie's laugh overtakes her musical house, floats through her gray hair, wraps itself around her ankles and seems to fill up every inch of a home that she honestly—see #2—can admit has become a lonely haven for a single, middle-aged woman, who often acts like the shit—see #3—but is indeed scared shitless.

"Cleaning out the garage," she says, still laughing, "is going to be the easiest thing I have written on this whole damned list."

Four

2. Let go. Stop holding on to things so tightly. Loosen your grasp. Be honest.

$2^{1}/_{2}$. Do not apologize for keeping this one on the list.

The orchestra in the walls turns out to be the upgraded cable service, installed by a man who should not be let out in public with a screwdriver. Somehow he has managed to cross wires and pipe a 24-hour international radio station into every speaker that has been hammered into place throughout Connie's house by her daughters' boyfriends during the past 20 years. Although the wiring is not dangerous, it has to go because Connie Nixon is beginning to answer the songs, which are often muted by the walls, plaster, and the boxes of junk stacked against them.

The Irishman, Daniel, and his friend Al are so intrigued by the wiring, loops of cable wrapped up in string, tape, and in some places yarn, that they spend hours crawling around Connie's house with pliers and drills in their hands as they unscrew vents and talk as if they have discovered buried treasure.

"Al, get over here, this one is looped around a gas pipe," Daniel shouts excitedly from the bathroom. "It's sitting behind the plumbing and I can't figure out how in the hell they got it back so far into the wall. It's kinda cool."

The men laugh as they work and Connie watches them while she drinks coffee, works on her five-minute retirement speech, and shocks herself with an unexpected slice of pleasure.

She likes seeing men crawl around her house with their butt cracks showing.

Daniel hears her laughing in the kitchen and as he walks past he leans over, sets his hands on the table, and asks her what is so funny.

Frannie O'Brien's husband and their two boys have been Connie's handymen for years. They have jump-started cars, installed gutters, helped her put up and take down her window screens, trapped mice and squirrels and one time a wild cat in the basement. They have pretty much been on call since Connie's ex-husband got sidetracked with a new wife and more kids, and Connie made a conscious decision not to replace one man with another.

"It's nice to see your ass and Al's ass while you crawl through the house," Connie admits as she drops her head into her hands and blushes.

Daniel laughs almost as loud as his wife.

"You think we're hot?" he manages to ask, swaggering a bit and hoisting up his pants.

"Hot is a bit much, honey," Connie says, lifting her eyes and laughing at the strange sight of a testosterone-motivated Daniel. "Truth be told, dear friend, it's been so long since I've seen *any* skin, besides my own, a gorilla could crawl through here and it would excite me."

"You slut," Daniel says, leaning in to plant a kiss on top of her head. "You know, Connie, you are sweet and smart and attractive. You should start dating again."

Connie's heart stops at the mere thought. Today the butt crack, tomorrow the whole banana; it's not going to work for her no matter what is on her list.

"All this because I saw the top half-inch of your white butt? Honey, imagine what would happen if I held a man's hand. Go," she orders him. "I'm focusing here. And for God's sake, keep your pants on your fine ass and tell Al to do the same thing."

The Irishman has thrown Connie temporarily off course. She is tempted to make Al and Daniel leave immediately so that the singing house, which has given her great courage, will continue to push her forward. She knows there are items on her list about sex, and men, and love, and Connie cannot imagine when in the hell she'll put those numbers in her pocket and start living them. It took her nearly three glasses of wine to even *write* those items on her list of dreams; actually *living* them makes her want to roll back into her bedroom with a very sturdy eraser.

Frannie has already mentioned that it was not the house that started Connie moving towards living her list, but her well-rounded and -designed plan to retire early. That way,

Frannie reminds her, she can begin sorting through all the other "shit" in her life.

"Not just the physical shit either," O'Brien had admonished. "You are so take-charge at work, and with at least two of your daughters, but you do have some other shit going on, baby."

Like Connie didn't know. Until the house started singing, she had been unmoved, terrified, and content to just plan her simple retirement party and procrastinate selling the house, which would force her into moving more than just a few boxes. She'd have to move the rest of her life as well.

By the time Al and Daniel hoist up their pants and leave, Connie has worked herself into a panic. Men. Sex. The unfinished speech. An old job and a new job. Days and weeks and months of unstructured time. The numbers in her jeans pocket from the list that seems to be laughing at her. Whimpering, she calls O'Brien and tells her she needs a house call.

And, of course, Frannie O'Brien makes house calls.

They talk for a long time and O'Brien makes Connie lean back and remember the parade of decisions that actually brought her to the kitchen table, the retirement speech, the singing house, and the men with the lovely butt cracks. Frannie pushes her, asks her to just talk, to simply process the journey. Even in friendship, Frannie O'Brien's skills as a psychiatric nurse flood to the front of everything she does, everything she is, everything she hands to the people she loves.

Connie remembers and is embarrassed by her frightened heart.

Frannie leans forward as if she is waiting for something

that she has never seen before to fly out of her friend's mouth—an African snake, three blue pigeons, naked dancing men, ancient explorers, Annie Oakley.

What comes out instead involves a new hospital administrator, a series of horrid deaths on the unit, her aching ankles and the discovery that she could indeed afford to retire and work part-time if she downsized, if her life really did change.

"And . . . ?" O'Brien presses, impatient, eager for this part of the story to unwrap itself.

"And I'm almost retired. I've got a new part-time position at the Midwestern nursing facility as a roving consultant. And these three months. Three free months stretching out in front of me, following the damn retirement party, to do what I want, to tackle my list, to live a few of these dreams."

"Come on," O'Brien coaxes. "The best part. Bring it on, sweetheart."

Connie laughs and at the same time wonders if she would have done any of this without her co-pilot, her sometime navigator. She imagines her life as it has been—predictable, unchanged, rotating at the same speed and level and with the same flavors it has always held in its mouth for another year, three more after that, and maybe another 10 after that. Her stomach turns. She keeps smiling and sends a signal skyward to the goddess of friends, the delightful queen who sends women exactly the most perfect and fine best friend in the universe.

"No one but you knows the whole story," Connie answers slowly, savoring the words like fine wine before a feast, a cup of coffee on a long trip, a kiss from a long-lost lover. "I'm locking myself in here for a week or so and then taking off without any serious obligations until my next job starts in three months. And I'm going to do whatever in the hell I want to do whenever I want to do it."

"That was easy once you got into it," O'Brien said, pleased. "Stop being so scared, sweetheart. The span of time you have in front of you will fly. You'll have a glorious time and I'll be jealous as hell."

"Once I get through the rest of this crap, the retirement, once I really lean into the list, I will focus on what I'm going to do the day after that and the next day."

"Which is not very many days away, is it?"

And it wasn't and the days suddenly moved like rockets.

Connie finished her retirement speech and then decided to throw it away two days before her party at the best restaurant in town. She had started playing CDs in her bedroom really, really loud to replace the singing house, and so that she would stay focused on moving forward and not slouching backwards. It was a concert of noise and action she needed to hear.

She thought about being spontaneous. The word was not on her list, which she had taken to reading not just at night but at least three times a day. When Connie placed her mind on the word "spontaneous" and on how she had lived for almost 30 years—schedules, kids, work, the necessary demands of life—it occurred to her that acting on the moment had been absent. There had been no room—she had made no room for dancing with a moment. She'd decided that the entire theme of the list could be centered on the word *spontaneity* and that's what had prompted her to tear up her one copy of the speech—which she had reasoned was really part of #3 and getting rid of shit—and then immediately regretted it.

But it was too late.

Macy and Sabrina came to the party, left their husbands and babies at home, and informed her, as they were leaving for the restaurant, that they couldn't spend the night because of their kids and husbands, and as they rambled into their confessions Connie simply held up both hands, said, "This is fine," and showed them the dozen roses that had come with a simple card from their sister Jessica that said, "*Congratulations Mom,*" and she added, "At least you two showed up," which made her two youngest daughters laugh.

Sedated with cocktails, Connie managed to brave her party with the grace and style her co-workers had been accustomed to throughout every single year of her career. Her speech ended up to be an unsentimental remembrance of the old days and a challenge to always remember what the medical profession was all about. It lasted three minutes.

Her gifts included a bright pair of funky white tennis shoes for her new job, a hilarious photograph of Connie sitting on an old-fashioned bedpan at the last Christmas party, a plaque with a mannequin's hand on it to celebrate Connie's special way of "touching" people, a dizzyingly expensive bottle of champagne, and a round-trip airplane ticket to any destination in the United States.

Connie stayed up until 2 A.M. following the party. She was alone and bravely hanging on to the edge of her new list-driven life as she set the champagne bottle in the refrigerator, placed her new photograph on the dresser she hoped to sell sometime very soon, opened up the back door and threw her old nursing shoes against the tree by the garage, and slipped the airplane voucher into the back of her list of dreams book.

Then she wrote.

She took out a piece of paper, jotted down her numbers for the next day, the real first day of her new life, and fell asleep thinking that tomorrow she could do whatever in the hell she wanted to do.

Or not do.

Five

3. *Get rid of SHIT. Start with the garage.*

5. *Stop setting the alarm clock.*

11. *Watch all the movies you have clipped out of the review section for the past—what?—thirty years.*

13. *A span of time to indulge myself in any damn thing I want. Eat. Drink. Be merry time. Turn off the phones. Maybe lie about what I'm doing. Minutes. Seconds. Hours. Days.*

Connie Franklin Nixon wakes at 9:57 A.M. and wonders what the bright light is that's shining in her eyes. When she realizes it is the late-morning sun, she rises up out of bed as if someone is lifting her towards the ceiling with a very fast crane.

"Shit," she says, jumping straight up. "I'm late."

And then she begins her well-practiced "Get Ready for Work Dance." She lunges for her watch, looks desperately for her schedule book which is not where it usually is, and rotates her head in a circle to crack her neck into place.

It is only when she turns and sees the small pile of papers beside her pillow that she remembers it is the day after her retirement party. Connie sits back down on her bed with a sigh the size of her entire right lung, reads each one of the three pieces of paper she wrote on seconds before she fell asleep, starts laughing, and slips them inside the pocket of the baggy t-shirt that someone else might call a nightgown. Before she passes through the doorway she turns on her CD player for company, for encouragement, for inspiration, and just in case.

"My God, I picked a mess of easy stuff to start with," she says, stuffing her feet into her pink slippers that look like half-dead and dyed kitty-kats and wandering into the kitchen.

The day—what is left of it for a woman who often rises at 4 A.M. and who has worked every shift and been at work every hour of the day for most of her adult life—is such a gift, such a glorious span of time, that Connie almost starts to cry.

Almost.

Connie remembers the champagne and kisses her own hand because she also has orange juice in the refrigerator. Brilliant move, Connie, absolutely brilliant.

Connie Franklin Nixon, the retired nurse, the retired administrator—for 90 days, anyway—is feeling celebratory, light, and bold, even before her morning mimosa. She fills up the largest glass she can find and parades through her house.

Finally the singing walls are resting. There are no men crawling around with sagging tool belts and smiling ass moons. There are so many damn empty rooms, diminishing signs of life, a house in retreat, that Connie ponders turning

the CD player on high when she cranks it on. Time, then—
maybe past time—to pass on the reins of this once lively
dwelling to someone who can change its face, set a new
heart inside of its kitchen, guard its parameters with a different set of rules.

When Connie looks out the back window she sees that
her old nursing clogs are lying next to the tree like wounded
soldiers waiting for an airlift. She decides to leave them
there. It looks as if someone has climbed the tree and
dropped the shoes from the first branch. It surely looks
spontaneous to her and also a bit funny. Funny is good and so
is the champagne.

When she walks by the telephone she pats her t-shirt
pocket as a salute to #13 that is resting on one of the white
slips so very close to her braless bosom, picks up the phone,
and sets it on its side so it will turn off in a few moments. In a
rare act of total abandon she also turns off her cell phone.

This is big. Really big. Connie, the mother of three
daughters, the official stepmother of O'Brien's two boys,
the mother hen of dozens and dozens of nurses, unit man-
agers, doctors and hospital administrators, has not turned
off her cell phone since the day she bought it. What if there
was an emergency? What if one of the girls needs her? What
if O'Brien has a crisis? What if all hell breaks loose and they
need a triage expert?

Connie holds the phone for a few seconds, drains her
glass, and then drops the phone into the top drawer of the
desk near the front door.

"O-h m-y G-o-d," she says, sounding out the letters of
each word as if she is just learning English. "I'm doing it. I'm
actually doing it."

Giddy from the power of free time, and from the glorious

champagne, Connie keeps walking through the house, and
then makes herself a second mimosa about the same time
she would normally be poring over stacks of reports from the
third shift. Then, very quickly, she decides to watch two
movies. Two movies right in a row. One after the other. No
turning the phones on. No pause for a bath. No break to
drive over to the gas station for a newspaper, a donut, or one
of those slices of pizza with huge jalapeno peppers baked
into the crust.

"Forget about the shit," she says out loud. "Sit."

She doesn't get dressed, which in the old days might
have resulted in a public whipping. Connie gets a little tipsy
after the second movie, a holiday sleeper called *Pieces of
April*. The movie keeps her plastered to the couch and she
consumes half the bottle of champagne, which tastes much
better without the orange juice, and goes astonishingly well
with a late-morning meal of popcorn that fills up a bowl the
size of a very large puppy.

Besides being a bit tipsy, Connie is also lost in her day.
She has not looked at a watch, answered a phone call, bothered to read a newspaper, or worried. When she gets up from
the couch just before 3 P.M. to use the bathroom, make a
sandwich and take a peek at the spontaneous shoes, she realizes it was probably the champagne that made her not worry,
so she decides to keep drinking it and watch something else
on television.

And then she chugs through two Oprah reruns, watches
an incredibly detailed show on the Discovery Channel about
finding murderers, and decides, without having gotten
dressed or turning the phones back on, that she is simply going to go to bed and read. And she doesn't read the list. She
barely gets through three pages of a novel before she turns

off her CD companion and falls asleep with her fingers resting on the pocket where her little slips have been nesting for
the entire day.

By the next morning Frannie has left her six phone messages, there's a turn in the weather and it's suddenly 62 de-
grees in Indiana in early spring, Connie is out of champagne
and almost out of her mind with restlessness. By 9:14 A.M.
she hops out of bed, rolls her tongue around her mouth, and
for a mere three seconds wonders how in God's name they
are getting along without her at the hospital.

*"You have either suffocated yourself with your own list or
you're in a drunken stupor and can't answer the phone,"* O'Brien's
first message sings. The five after that get a bit longer and
louder and include a gentle reminder that the Irishman and
his wife are going to be gone for four days visiting son
Numero Uno and the wife would like just one call from
Connie so she won't worry when they are on the road.

They play phone tag while Connie shuffles through the
house in the same dingy and terribly comfortable t-shirt,
makes a very large pot of coffee, tosses out the champagne
bottle, and shudders when she looks around the garage.

"Number three, I hear you," she says out loud as she
drops the bottle into the blue recycle bin and realizes that
she is going to lose her mind if she doesn't keep moving.
One day on the couch has not only made her rear end sore
but it's also made her anxious. Three months is 90 days.
She's only got 89 days left.

The last message Connie sends O'Brien via her cell
phone is a tiny whimper of hopeful action.

"I've got to do something," she whines. "I'm going to
start dismantling the house again and browse through my
list. I'm fine, baby. Go have fun with Mr. Nice Ass. I'll see
you next week."

Connie goes down the hall to her room, throws on a jogging bra, a pair of black sweatpants, and a t-shirt with the
sleeves ripped off that's left over from the last breast-cancer
walk, and heads for the garage.

The garage is a formidable mess. A disgusting tangle of
shit with a capital S. Mountains of boxes, some of them actually hers, are stacked against both sides and up against the
old workbench on the back wall. Every single box needs to
be looked through and Connie guesses there might actually
be one or two items she wants to keep out of the entire col-
lection. At least half a dozen of the boxes are Jessica's. She'd
had Macy drop them off three years ago before Jessica left
for New York and for what she called "the manufacturing opportunity of a lifetime." Jessica took off with her business
degree and six years of marketing and managerial experience in her portfolio and Connie has not seen her since.

And not much before that, either.

Simply looking at the boxes with her oldest daughter's
name on them brings Connie to a dead stop. Her heart races.
She will touch them last, when her courage is at an all-time
high. She will touch them when the patron saint of hopeless
causes brushes his shoulder against hers, or later in the day
when everything else is finished—whichever happens first.
Connie purposefully walks past Jessica's boxes and, in a
show of control, to convince herself she can do it, she kicks
open the garage door and starts on the SHIT.

And there is definitely shit. Years and years of shit that
has been stacked in corners, piled on top of the totally dor-
mant workbench, hanging from the rafters like loose ends of
a life that needs to be tied together to form something new,
anything new. A car has not been parked inside of the garage
since . . . when? Maybe just before Macy got her driver's license, before the world started turning sideways, the father

left, and Jessica left, came back and then left again, so it
seems, for good.

Connie has pawed at the boxes and broken pieces of furniture on and off for months but the garage needs a serious
and final assault. She knows that to get to #31—signing the
final house papers—she has to purge, push, and pull. Fortified
with an entire pot of coffee, more sleep than she's had in
years, and the terrific advice from the Oprah show that she
watched hours ago about reorganizing your life, Connie is
determined.

By mid-afternoon she has called the local St. Vincent
de Paul Store and begged for a truck to come clear away what
she thinks is "most of the good stuff" and when the truck
shows up the workers are not disappointed. They score a
lovely but beaten dining room table, a not-so-bad floral
couch, three lamps, 12 boxes of paperback books that Connie
kisses good-bye right in front of them, eight bags of used female teenage clothing and six boxes of "assorted" shit that
includes Halloween costumes, flower vases, mismatched
glasses, and some doodads Connie thinks may have been
from her ridiculous wedding.

And the garage is still not finished.

Connie is so proud of what she has done, so excited
about almost getting number three off of her damn list, that
she goes to bed early. Putting on the same t-shirt that she has
slept in for two nights, she fingers the pieces of paper in her
pocket, and decides to give it one more day. Tomorrow, the
88th day, she'll finish the garage if she is dauntless. She'll
wash the t-shirt and get on with the list.

The plan starts out fabulously. Connie hoists open the
garage door the next day only to discover that the 60-degree
weather has cranked itself back down to 40. The door closes
and she gets a sweatshirt. The first two boxes she picks up

are photos. All the photos she took during the past three thousand—so it seems—years and then jammed into these very same boxes thinking like an ass that one day she'd make really beautiful photo albums and later some of those lovely scrapbooks made by women who did not have to hold a catheter in place when someone's veins ruptured, raise three daughters almost alone, and keep a house from falling down around their ears by begging friends to help. She carries the boxes into the kitchen, deciding that she'll simply divide the photos in three piles, give each daughter a box filled with them—even Jessica—and be done.

What's mostly left then are Jessica's boxes. Two are obviously filled with old clothes with pilled sweaters falling out of the top; another is loaded with her old college textbooks. Connie pushes these towards the edge of the garage. She'll give Macy a call and see if she wants to store them. Then they will be gone. There is no room left in Connie's life or garage for Jessica's shit.

Three of the last boxes, Jessica's boxes, appear to be filled with papers and documents. Connie brings them into the house, sets them on the table, and then goes back out to sweep the garage which, when she is finished, is about as good as it is ever going to get.

"Hot damn," she says, standing with her hands on her hips and smiling into the fabulously uncluttered space. "You could park a car and a half in here now and still fill up the side wall with more boxes."

Connie celebrates by opening up a bottle of wine. Her ridiculously small wine rack has five bottles in it, all dry reds, and she picks the best one—a lively Syrah from California that she lets breathe a bit while she washes off her face and hands, grabs her numbers out of the pocket to prop them in a line on the counter, and then takes her first drink.

Before tackling Jessica's SHIT, she decides to sort out the photographs. This is not on the list, she realizes, and then she remembers that there is a place for change, for adding new numbers, and she does it in her head. "Number whatever—Sort through the photos."

And she begins.

Babies and Girl Scouts.

Family reunions.

Camping trips.

The first day of school.

Prom. Twirp. Homecoming.

Tennis matches. Track. The three weeks Macy lasted in soccer.

Drinking beer on the roof.

The last trip to the lakeshore.

Connie sits at the table and runs her fingers over the photographs as if she is touching the real faces of her daughters. Her left thumb brushes against glossy braids, a sunburned arm, the flushed curve of a cheek, legs that look like spring twigs. As she lays out a series of photos she is suddenly overcome by a crashing wave of emotion that she knows can only be called love.

Babies growing into young girls. Young girls growing into teenagers. Teenagers turning into women. Grown women. Women who make love and cry into their own glasses of wine and who have stretched the connection between themselves and their mother long and hard and, in Jessica's case, very near the breaking point.

It takes her two hours and more than half a bottle of wine to sift through the stacks of photos and as the three piles grow she wraps the stacks with rubber bands. And she wonders, as she imagines she will wonder on and off for the rest of her life, if it was okay. Was she okay? Where did she fail them, frighten them, make them want to run and hide? Will they remember the good parts, the moments captured in the photographs? Will they? Will she? Will you, Connie, ever be able to forgive yourself for the mistakes of motherhood that come with the first set of baby booties?

When the last photo has been stacked, Connie sits in the quiet of the kitchen, realizing for the first time since she started the project that her bedroom music has stopped, and she finishes her glass of wine in the quiet. Then she kisses each stack of photos and places them inside a box, sets the box by the front door, and faces a serious challenge.

Jessica's boxes.

Thank God for the wine.

"Now or never," Connie says as she contemplates the first box. She pushes aside the half-empty wine bottle with the edge of the box, takes a deep breath, and cracks open the cardboard carton.

Files. Documents. Sketches.

"Sketches?" Connie says out loud as if she is talking to the walls once again. "What the hell are these?"

It takes her 15 minutes to sort through the box and, halfway through the papers, files, and artist renderings, she sits down on a chair, pulls over the bottle of wine, and finishes what is left of it in one long drink as if it is tepid water, without bothering to put it into a glass. She wonders if anything she knows about life, her daughters, the world, her own fingers that are holding sketches of items she barely recognizes but could surely not name, is true. Connie Nixon feels like an idiot, someone who is the last to know—the wife who wakes up and finally realizes her husband is unfaithful, the woman who doesn't know about the hidden stash of money in Bermuda—and then she goes numb from the rush of wine, from what she has just discovered in her daughter's

box of shit, and because of what she is already thinking
about doing next.

Her daughter, Jessica Franklin Nixon, lives in New York
City; this is true. She is a marketing and manufacturing
executive—in fact, she is at this very moment part owner of a
business that manufactures, sells, and distributes a fascinating array of products and apparently makes lots and lots of
people, mostly women, very happy. This is all also true.

Jessica is CEO and part owner of Diva's Divine
Designs—one of the most successful sex-toy stores in the
United States of America.

Connie cannot breathe. It feels as if someone has low-
ered a rope into her chest through her open mouth and has
tied off her lungs.

She stands up, puts both hands on the table for a moment
to steady her heart, looks quickly through the other box that
is loaded with business plans, more papers, letters from
banks, phone numbers—secrets from a world so far away
Connie thinks she may not even be able to visualize it, to
find it, to locate its name on a map.

Then suddenly, the quiet house is screaming, but what
Connie hears is the sound of her own voice. A voice mixed
with anger, regret, and a yearning so deep that it buckles her
knees. It is the voice of loss, the voice of a wounded heart,
and Connie stretches her mind back to a succession of moments that helped build a wall between her and her oldest
daughter.

Arguments. Questions about boys and girls. Those moments when Connie wondered about her daughter's sexuality, about her honesty, about aspects of her life that Jessica
said were none of her business. A mother's seemingly simple
worries that piled up and turned into hills and then mountains. And the weight of the world Connie often put on her

oldest daughter's shoulders and then could not seem to remove.

The night shifted inside of Connie like a painful and very
physical ache. She paced, drank more wine, stood by the
window looking out at the spontaneous shoes until the sky
was littered with spring stars, and then she closed up the
house and went to the rocking chair in her bedroom.

It was not so far from dawn when she finished tearing
apart strips of paper and then writing on them, not in pencil
like all the others, but in ink. Not so far from dawn when she
rose from the rocking chair, lined up the slips in an even line
right next to the bedroom telephone, and wondered if she
could honestly do it. Not so far from dawn when Connie
Franklin Nixon stood with her hands on the old bedroom
dresser and peered into her own eyes to see if there was one
thing that she could recognize in the mirror. Not so far from
dawn when Connie fell asleep with her hands locked like
claws on her list of dreams, wishing like hell that she had
never let the Irishman silence her encouraging and terribly
inspirational house.

Six

2. Let go. Stop holding on to things so tightly. Loosen your grasp. Be honest. (And try to work this number off the list before the end of this decade.)

7. Recapture Jessica. Find Jessica. Hurry, Connie, but start slowly. Find your baby.

20. Time in New York City. This city scares me but I dream about it. I want to walk on the streets, sit in a café, meet people at a bar. New York City. I want to own the damn place.

Savage packing.

Savage traffic.

Savage parking.

Savage ticket line.

Savage two-hour O'Hare International Airport terminal wait.

A series of suddenly savage moments turns the ordinarily quiet, yet far from mild, Connie Nixon into an urban Amazon who is ready to rip the throat out of the next person who says, "That will be $35.98 please," or, "I'm sorry, you can't park there." Or, "You can't get the super discount, just the regular discount because you missed the deadline by 13 seconds." Or, "I'm sorry, we are out of that." Nurse Nixon has had it. She's whiplashed world-class surgeons and spit on the shoes of senators who tried to derail patient-needs funding and grabbed post-op professional football players by the throat, and tackled more than a few of O'Brien's would-be escaping psych patients. The airport personnel, parking lot attendants, and assholes who think the plane will leave early if they cut in line in front of Nurse Nixon are looking like easy prey to her. She snarls back at everyone. Holds her ground. Moves through the lines and gates and check-ins and check-outs and past the security point of no return without looking back or physically assaulting any men, women, or children. It's a miracle.

Connie has suddenly dipped so deep into her list of dreams that she is running on pure adrenaline. Unable to sleep following her discovery of Jessica's biggest secret to date, armed with her latest slips of list numbers, and possessed like only a mad mother can be possessed, Connie rose from her bed, grabbed her retirement airline gift from the back of her list of dreams book, made a reservation to New York with an open-ended return, and within three hours had packed, closed up the house, downed four cups of tar-like coffee, and headed straight for the airport lest she lose courage.

Halfway to New York City it hits her. She has not made friends with the garlic-breath man who is sitting next to her in the extra-wide and very fine Midwest Express seat because he's had his face buried in his computer since the airplane leveled off. So when she says, "What the hell am I doing?" out loud he looks up as if he's been slapped at a cocktail party for staring at someone's breasts.

"Are you talking to me?"

"I'm just talking but it could be to you if you want," Connie answers, feeling a bit cocky from her terminal experiences.

She's wearing beige sandals, a fairly hip pair of jeans with flared legs. Her list numbers are riding in the left front pocket of those jeans, next to a tank top and an old navy blazer. She looks normal and this throws off Mr. Computer, who is used to judging a book by its cover. Looks normal. Sounds goofy. He wavers and Connie, still more than pissed off about the chain of traveling events that seemed destined for a time to derail her spontaneous trip, decides she really does not want to talk to this man or any man at all.

"Sorry," she says, touching his hand in a way that she knows totally disarms most humans—softly, with her hand skimming the top of his wrist and then gliding off towards his fingers in a sensual push that makes his entire body shiver. This is not sensual for Nurse Nixon. It has everything to do with control and she's used the wrist move on so many patients they gave her a plaque with a hand on it as part of her retirement party.

The retirement party.

Days ago.

Hours ago.

Connie turns away from her now-breathless companion and gazes into the face of a cloud. This time she asks herself, and no one else, what in the hell she is doing and she teeters on the edge of that very fine line, as thin as thread, that could make her either laugh or cry, try to scramble out the window or order a stiff drink, take the man into her arms and kiss him, or pretend that she has forgotten she is on an airplane and headed for an unknown terminal in a city that is as foreign to her as the Panama Canal.

Connie smiles. She touches her own wrist, feeling what the man just felt, and instead of letting her fingers drop, she holds her own hand, fingers across her wrist, thumb to thumb and she steadies her emotions, checks her balance and decides that if she did tell Mr. Computer her story he would ask to switch seats.

"Well, I just retired and I was going to watch movies, clean the garage and then have this series of adventures, dreams really—kind of like making my dreams come true one at a time, no rushing, but then I discovered this box in the garage. That changed everything because I found out my daughter makes, well, she makes sex toys and I thought she was some big executive in a manufacturing company and so I dropped everything and I am rushing off to New York . . . to . . ."

"To what?" Connie wonders. "To run into the store and throw myself on top of a vibrator? To grab her and try to figure out who she is? To find out what possessed her? *What? What am I doing?*"

Reckless is not a word that anyone would use to describe Connie Nixon. She knows this and as she entwines her fingers, lacing them together as if she were praying, she imagines what it might be like to own that word. She wants to own it. She doesn't want to admit that a part of her is frightened, not only because she is going to a city that is so huge and wild and loud she wonders how she will survive even the first thirty minutes, but because she knows her approach into this world of her daughter's has to be smooth, and maybe even gentle, and she has no idea how she is going to be able to do that. To land without screaming. To march into the store, place her hand against a display case of funky implements of sex and nonchalantly say something like, "So, honey, what's new?"

Being afraid is not a bad thing. Connie Nixon knows this better than half the world. She knows what it's like to be around people who are scared to death all the time. Cancer moving from one breast to the next. Diabetes crawling up the side of a leg and eating it from the inside out. A heart that wants to stop beating inside the body of a baby who can barely hold onto the pinky finger of her terrified mother. Teenaged girls and boys with arms and faces and legs mangled from car crashes. The newlywed who discovers a rare kidney disease before he can return the tuxedo. She knows this kind of fear.

And the fear of loneliness, of being alone, the weight of *that*. The fear of waking up in the middle of the night when you hear a noise and knowing that whatever caused it could rip your throat out or cost you thousands of dollars—a burglar or a broken furnace. Knowing then that the weight of your life, your decisions, your next moment is all driven by your very own hands and not another's. The weight of that. No one to throw the grenade if you forget one. No one to remember change for the tip. No one to hold the daughter who screws up the ACT test and decides to forget about college and have a baby instead. A few good friends to cover your ass but no one there *always*. No one to curl around your back in December when the worst storm of the year pulls against the gutters, strands you inside for 38 hours, and the girls, all three of them, are trapped someplace else. That ache just to have someone want you. The paralyzing fear that you may have once been beautiful and never knew it. Maybe also, maybe someone you know wanted you, wanted to run his fingers along the inside of your thigh until you jumped on top of him and rode him like a pony. What if you missed that because you were afraid you might miss it? What if you forgot to look up and see if he was watching you because you were always too damn busy? Wondering if you stay alone and when you turn 45 who will help you with your canes, who will adjust the hearing aids? Who will drive you to the liquor store for the Syrah? Who will buy you the occasional, and deeply loved, Saturday night rum-laced cigar?

Connie Nixon knows about being afraid. She knows what it's like to spend months imagining life without him, wondering if the girls will be permanently damaged by the blight of yet another divorce, another broken family, the seemingly common surrender to the statistics of failed marriage. Will they read the local paper that shows up like an insurance bill so regularly and quietly one afternoon after volleyball practice, choir rehearsal, and hanging out at the library and say, "Holy shit, you guys, look! Mom and Dad's divorce is in the paper!"

Will the car make it another year? Will anyone come home for Christmas? Will I really be able to pull off my expedition into the list of dreams I have been nurturing all of these years? If I screw up, will everyone still love me? Will I ever *not* be afraid?

The trenches of her own world have turned Connie Nixon into a soldier who has no more space for the Purple Hearts she has won—even as she prepares for another battle. Even as she closes her eyes and imagines rolling into the clouds without the cover of an airplane. Even as she wonders what she will say, where she will stay, what will happen next, she also knows that in two months, a week, or even a few hours later she will look back on these moments of hesitation and self-doubt with the mature knowledge that somehow everything will be just fine. Somehow there are still lessons to learn and pages to read and places to see. Life,

Connie knows, from seeing it slip through her hands hundreds of times, never ends or begins at one particular time. It is a succession of chances and change and challenges that ripple through your life in waves that, thank God, sometimes give you another opportunity, another moment to catch your shallow breath, another view of a terrific beach, another unexpected experience that can change the direction of the very air that courses through your lungs.

And without warning it happens to her. Just like that. A crashing wave that sneaks up when Connie is passing a cloud that she has decided looks like a turkey riding a pig. The man with the computer pushes himself out of the chair, stands, looks towards the back of the airplane, takes a very fast glance at Connie, and then gathers up his computer and leaves. Connie figures he needs to spread out and she is about to do the same thing when a woman drops into the seat beside her as if she has fallen out of the overhead bin across the aisle.

"Thank God," the woman says, flopping back in the seat and then looking at Connie as if she knows her. "Did you hear the frigging coughing? There's a guy up there who must have escaped from a TB ward."

The woman's blonde hair is about an inch long except in the front where it dips into her eyes. Maybe about Sabrina's age—27-ish, maybe a bit older. Light makeup, silver jewelry everywhere, blue cowboy boots, a red tank top with a white cardigan sweater and a pair of jeans that are faded in just the right places. She reeks of self-confidence and Connie imagines this woman's life. New Yorker. Party girl. Artsy. Doesn't take shit. Gets free drinks at the bars. Travels without a suitcase. Smokes dope on the weekends and loves to flirt with men and women. *Hip.*

She's a hairstylist.

"No, really?" Connie says as a question-statement, as if her new friend Mattie has just told her she is in a traveling circus and has a spare body part tucked into her back pocket. "You look, well, artsy."

"What I do is art, Connie baby. I get $125 for a 30-minute haircut."

"No kidding?" Connie mouths in shock.

"No shit, it's art, all right. I can take anyone and turn her or him into a flaming goddess," Mattie assures her. "By the way, thanks for letting me sit here. If you get sick I'll give you a free haircut."

"Could you fix this?" Connie asks, grabbing her hair, suddenly totally distracted from her perilous mission of visiting her secretive oldest daughter by the disarming woman who leans over without hesitation to feel her hair, push it around between both hands and all her fingers, and then pulls back to imagine what she would look like "fixed" in New York.

"You need color. It will take 15 years off you, sweetie," Mattie promises. "I'd highlight it, trim back the sides. What I'm thinking here is that you'd be borderline *hot*."

Connie snorts.

"What?" Mattie demands.

"Hot? That's the last thing I'd ever think about myself."

"That sucks. You have a great figure. Wonderful skin. Life can't be all bad, for crissakes. My gawd, woman, half my clients are over 50 and they are something. I mean it. Age is nothing. I bet you are, what, 53? Sexy has nothing to do with age. It's style and grace and what comes out from the inside. And you've got it. But your sexy is a bit camouflaged."

Connie buys Mattie a drink. She wants to marry her.

Then Mattie buys her a drink and Mattie, who is booked six weeks in advance, tells her no matter what, to come by her salon tomorrow at 6:45 P.M. and she'll bring out her inner sexy. Then Connie tells her why she's going to New York and it's Mattie's turn to snort.

"Oh, my fucking gawd," she says and then apologizes for using the F word.

"What?"

"I love Diva's," Mattie admits. "I go there all of the time. My salon is just three blocks from the store. Shit. Is your daughter Jessica? My God. You look like her, or she looks like you. I've been trying to fix her Midwestern hair for three months. How absolutely cool is this? Her store is pretty popular. I can't believe you didn't know this. How could you not know this?"

Connie doesn't know what to say. She's never even seen a dildo, and now she has a daughter who not only sells them but apparently designs them as well. How did she not know? How could she let Jessica slip away into a world and life that seem as foreign to her as Antarctica? Should she have asked more questions? Hired a private detective? Kept her locked in the back bedroom? Turned her into a female eunuch before she reached puberty? Tried harder to climb over the huge mountain separating them?

"Shit happens, isn't that what they say?" she finally responds.

"You never visited? Did she think you'd be mad? Did you two have a fight or something?"

Mattie spits out these queries as if she is on fire.

"These are good questions, Dr. Hairstylist," Connie fires back. "That's what you are. Hairstylists, bartenders, and nurses like me, we're all psychiatrists. We listen and ask questions no one else dares to ask, especially if we have scissors, a shot glass, or a sharp needle in one hand. That's why I'm on my way to New York City. I guess I want to know the answers myself. I want to know how the hell this happened."

Mattie takes her hand and Connie squeezes it.

"You're cool, Connie," Mattie tells her. "Most mothers would just call and scream. Well, my mother would call and place a large order but most mothers—really, they'd freak."

Why? Connie wonders while they sit and sip their drinks and she can feel the plane start to lower its belly towards earth. Why is #7 from the list so important? Will it make everything else easier, the dreams closer, the numbers in my pocket sing louder? What is it that makes mothers go wild like this? Why do they freak out if their kids, who they have hopefully raised to be productive citizens of the universe, change course a bit?

And that goddamn insane love of a mother for a child.

"Do you have children?" Connie asks her new friend.

"No. I have absolutely no desire to bring another human into the world. I would not be a good mother. It's something I've always known. I can nurture hair and faces and run the show at work, but babies and this instinctual thing women are supposed to have, well, it passed right by me."

"Good for you," Connie tells her. "For knowing, I mean."

"You make me want to cry," Mattie says softly.

"Why?"

"Most people freak when you tell them you don't want to be a mother. It's like the third question at every frigging party. What do you do? Are you married? Do you have children? It's how society defines us and it pisses me off. You are the first person who ever responded in a positive way when I said I didn't want to be a mother—well, except for my own mother and about eight hundred men who just wanted to screw my brains out and didn't want to have to worry about me wanting them to be a father."

Nurse Nixon has a parade of bad mother stories in her head that kick off and start running. Bruised arms. Burned fingers. Empty tummies. Mothers on crack. Unwanted pregnancies. Little children who have been molested and tell you it's okay if you want to touch their pee-pees. Even in Indiana, land of flowing cornfields, basketball heroes, home-baked bread and the Christian brigades, babies cry and suffer and lurch towards adult insanity because so many women become mothers without the credentials of the heart and soul.

"Nothing really prepares you anyway," Connie tells Mattie. "You think, especially if you have been medically trained like I was, that you'll jump right in and some magic thing will happen and you will know how to become their everything overnight. But it's almost impossible to be ready. And then there they are, this thing, this person, this *face* resting below your left breast and two things happen."

"Two things?"

"First of all, you are scared shitless," Connie tells Mattie. "Even if you've had other babies and can bounce one on your leg while you write poetry and cook dinner and save the whales. Then, you look at them and see this wonderful pathway into the universe. This transforming tunnel that is like an electric charge that turns you into a raving maniac, a protective lioness, someone who could push over a car, rip off the face of a stranger, kick ass from one end of the world to another, to save your baby. You go mad. Mother mad."

"That's it then," Mattie tells Connie, clapping her hands to congratulate herself. "*That's* why you are going to New York."

"Why?"

"You're mad."

"I suppose. I have to do this. I've missed Jessica. I so want to know who she is, why she is, what she is, everything about her."

"Look, she's still your baby. For crying out loud, my mother still makes me lasagna every year for my birthday and sends me towels, and asks if I've had a flu shot. If it snows in Milwaukee, where she lives, she calls to make sure I'm not driving."

"I get all that." Connie shakes her head. "Shit, I can't believe I'm talking to you like this, but what the hell. Part of me, well, part of me is totally embarrassed that she didn't tell me, embarrassed and maybe a little pissed off, and I feel a weight around my heart that needs to let go so *I* can let go. I'd also like to see if we can figure out how to forgive each other."

Mattie reaches over to touch Connie on the arm as if to hold her back.

"You look pretty damn loveable, except for that shitty hair," she tells Connie. "She probably doesn't know who you are, just like you may not know who she is."

Connie shrugs and turns her back to the clouds. This hair artist, she thinks, is totally correct. Connie Franklin Nixon has no idea who Jessica Franklin Nixon is. She knew her once, could predict what she would eat off of her plate, how she would stand in the doorway, what her grades in math class would be. She has this view of Jessica, her daughter, as that—a daughter. A girl still, one who rushes in and out of her mother's life, has a cardboard box filled with secrets and, apparently, ran screaming from Indiana to New York City with a dream that she never once shared with her mother. Her own mother.

"I hate you," Connie says, smiling, moving across her

seat so she can whisper the next sentence. "I'm sure she never uses any of the sex toys she sells."

The two women, unlikely companions on a journey through a slice of life that Connie sees as a thin line connecting her to something ... something new, something frightening, something beyond what she imagined just hours ago as she boldly attacked three major numbers from her list at the same time.

It is female communion. That astonishing crossing of cultures and ages and time and place that wraps women together and makes them one. It is a holy moment, a sacred sharing of estrogen, a remarkable gift of love. It can happen in a public waiting room when a stranger asks another woman to hold her baby—her beautiful baby—when she needs to go to the bathroom. It can happen when you see a woman on a street corner and two guys are hassling her and you open your car door and she gets in without hesitation. It can happen when you see a woman at the grocery store crying because she is a dollar short and you pay her bill and carry her groceries to the car with her kids and then slip her another 20 bucks. It can happen when you are at a play and that woman you saw arguing with that asshole man won't come out of the last stall of the bathroom until you hand her some toilet paper and then she cries into your shoulder and you give her the phone number of the women's shelter. It can happen when your mother tells you about her first love and your heart stops because you realize your father was her second choice. It can happen anywhere—this female communion where women feel safe and close and absolutely as if they have touched a piece of heaven because of you.

It can happen on an airplane on the way from Chicago to New York.

"See, you look sexy when you are sad and I can't help but

imagine you with a light color, some dark tits, oops, I mean tints." Mattie laughs as the plane dips lower and New York spreads itself out on either side of the plane as if it were doing its own Broadway dance. "Oh, look, there's my city."

Connie looks. She pushes her forehead against the window and watches the edges of the city grow like a fan until New York is an enormous palette of brown and silver and green below her. Massive lines of cars moving like snails across bridges, and the surge of blue when the plane dips towards the Atlantic makes her stomach rise with excitement. The city glows. She has only been to New York City once before, on a quick two-day trip with a group of friends from the hospital, but she's never really *been* to the city and she surely has never imagined that this is why and how she would get there.

When she turns back towards Mattie, her new friend— who is young enough to be her daughter and wise enough to be her mother—is smiling. She has written her cell phone number on the back of her business card.

"Wait till you get your feet down there," Mattie says, pressing the card into Connie's hand. "I love the action, the sleeplessness of it all, the constant surge of life that makes you feel as if nothing, not one single thing, is standing still."

"I live in Indiana," Connie replies flatly and they both laugh again.

Connie looks at Mattie, her temporary muse, a modern crusader for the individual rights of a woman, artist to the masses, friend to traveling and confused mothers, and she feels a bizarre sense of security. She slips the business card into the back pocket of her jeans and knows, like a mother would know, that if she called this woman, if she said she needed help or directions or a ride, Mattie would come to rescue her in a second. More communion.

Before they get off the plane, Mattie cannot help herself.

She leans over and pulls what she can of Connie's hair in some kind of funky new direction, the left side to the right and the right side to the left, and reminds her that she has an appointment for the following evening.

"I'm serious," she insists, hugging Connie as they move into the terminal. "If you don't come I'm going to find you at Diva's and chase you through Manhattan with scissors and a bottle of dye in my hand."

Connie kisses her on the cheek and then stands in place for a few seconds, not just to look around but also because she isn't sure what she is going to do next. Get a taxi, obviously—but then what? The airport is a whirl of business travelers, men and women walking and talking on cell phones, people sitting in chairs and working on computers, restless children being yanked through the narrow hallways and past stacks of candy bars, potato chips, and magazines. Connie watches it all, a little mesmerized by the hurricane of activity, wondering where everyone is going, who they are when they take off their polyester jackets and, when they land, how exactly do they do it. "How will I do it?" Connie asks herself.

Fighting the urge to call O'Brien, who might order her right back onto the airplane or encourage her to become a Rockette, Connie follows the signs at La Guardia and wanders to the main floor where the taxi signs point her towards the sidewalk. She stops and fishes out of her pocket the address of Diva's that she found in Jessica's files, realizes that if she is going to show up at the store before it closes, she'd better stop hesitating and get moving.

When it is her turn for the taxi, she gives the address to the driver, a tall African-American who is almost too beautiful to be a man. Connie says, "It's called Diva's," and the driver winks, shakes his hips seductively, and opens the door for her as if he is ushering a goddess into the back seat of his yellow cab.

"What the hell am I doing?" she asks herself again as the taxi pulls out into the pre–rush hour traffic that is already beginning to snarl and snap to a chorus of beeping horns which make her laugh.

And so Connie Nixon, nurse to thousands, mother to three, friend to many, murmurs "What the hell," as her yellow taxi eventually slides to a stop in the long shadow of Diva's Divine Designs. She sucks in her breath and walks forward as if she knows exactly where she is going.

seven

1. Stop being afraid.

7. *Recapture Jessica. Find Jessica. Hurry, Connie, but start slowly. Find your baby.*

Connie Nixon wants a cigarette. The craving rises inside of her like an unseen volcano erupting with a surge of unexpected want, pushing against her lungs, riding her like a cowboy in Bozeman, Montana, forcing her to focus as if she is about to commit a crime and needs every ounce of her strength not to do it.

"Shit," she whispers as she paces like a nicotine junkie outside of Diva's. Actually, Connie is just to the left of Diva's, behind a series of newspaper boxes and a light pole, and under cover of a long umbrella that has cast a shadow large enough to hide every cowboy in Montana, not just the ones in Bozeman, as well as a confused, slightly dazed, and incompetent-feeling mother from Cyprus, Indiana.

Nurse Nixon is trying to think. She is trying to figure out what to do, how to do it, what to say, when to say it. She hasn't had a cigarette in 23 years, except on those occasional drunken nights with her friends at their favorite bar and restaurant or when she made the girls try them when they went camping, thinking that smoking a cigarette with a parent is the same as smoking it with your friends behind someone's garage. But what she suddenly remembers as she is gasping for a solid fill of air is the comfort that the cigarettes gave her, the sense of evenness when the smoke hit her lungs and the nicotine surged through her bloodstream and jolted her with a nar-cotic fix. She wants to feel that way right this second, now, before she walks into the store that her daughter not only owns but runs and where both of them will undoubtedly feel so uncomfortable that one or maybe both of them will want to close her eyes, open them, and be on another planet.

Wonder-nurse and super-mom Nixon knows her behav-ior is not only ridiculous, but probably unwarranted as well, but that doesn't change her uncertainty, the way she imag-ines every possible outcome of what is about to happen. While the news-addicted New Yorkers buy newspapers, six women go into her daughter's store, five come out, and ab-solutely no one looks her in the eye.

Connie decides a cup of espresso to keep herself from fainting will help. She discovers a small bodega around the corner, orders her poison, and then unzips the side pocket of her travel bag to retrieve her list of dreams book.

For a second she considers throwing it into the garbage and racing back to the airport but, as she lifts the book, a photograph falls out and catches her off guard. She's saved the photograph from the stack on the kitchen table and she is astonished to realize that it is the fuel that will make her take the next step. It is a photo of Jessica at her 14th birthday party. Her hands are on her hips, she's looking away from the camera, and she's laughing at the Barbie doll birthday cake that Connie has made for her as a joke.

More than anything else in the world Connie wants to find that Jessica again, the girl in the photograph. She wants to take her daughter into her arms and start over, retrace steps, forgive and be forgiven. She wants to run her hands along the back of her oldest daughter's neck, kiss her on the lips, unlock the door and pass right through the very tall mountain separating them.

As she scans down her list of dreams, flipping pages as if her fingers are on fire, Connie Franklin Nixon realizes that the most important number on the list, the one that means more than anything, the one that will solve every other riddle, her biggest dream, is #7.

Recapture Jessica.

And then she gets up. Her mother-madness is screaming so loudly she turns to see if someone else hears it and then remembers she's in New York City, where people wear dogs on their heads and dance publicly in their underwear.

After what would have been enough time to chain-smoke four cigarettes, Connie decides she simply has no choice. She waits on the sidewalk a few more seconds, frozen like a hunk of quartz, hoping that all the customers will come out of Diva's so she can be alone with her daughter but then realizes that the woman she sees through the window could be in there for hours and then eighteen more women or men could follow in right behind her.

She cannot put off this encounter any longer.

One step inside of the store and Connie cannot breathe. The word "seduction" seeps into her mind, holds every inch of her brain in its sexy hands, and keeps her pinned against its lusty arms. She cannot move and lets out what Jessica will later tell her is a groan and, at that exact same moment, Connie catches the eye of her daughter who looks up from behind her desk to see who is having sex in her store before purchasing anything.

"Oh my God," Jessica shouts, grabbing the edges of her desk to steady herself. "Oh my God," she repeats as if she can't remember what she has just said.

Connie does not want to stop looking at the off-white and sky-blue lighting, the way yards of silver material are draped from the edges of the wall and onto the tops of shelves, as if the entire room is one giant waterfall. She doesn't want to stop listening to the wind and the water she hears rushing from the 27 tiny speakers that are hidden throughout the store and she wants to follow the rocky path that has been created on the floor with pebbles and mid-sized rocks and one very large boulder as if she were in the middle of a forest adventure.

But there is Jessica, looking as if she has just swallowed something the size of a small handbag that has lodged halfway down her throat. There is Jessica, looking beautiful and wise and so New York in her low-cut white shirt, very short black skirt and shoes with three-inch heels the color of a Mexican sunset. There is Jessica, watching her mother surrounded by vibrators and condoms and leather wrist cuffs with silver studded links.

"Hi, sweetheart," Connie says, striding forward, her voice quivering with emotion.

Jessica lets go of her desk and discovers that she fits just as she has always fit in the grooved spot below her mother's chin. She lets her arms move around her mother's shoulders, and when she does this, she can feel her mother's heart beating as wildly as her own, and she takes comfort not only in the embrace, but in the knowledge that her mother must be as terrified at this moment as she is herself.

"Mom," she whispers into Connie's ear.

The sound of Jessica's voice is like a hammer. It pounds back from this very moment to all the moments before it when Jessica whispered in her ear, cried in her arms, coughed into her hair, laid her hands on her face and told her a hurt, a wish, a secret. Jessica's voice. The voice of a woman that resonates with all the Jessicas within her—baby, girl, young woman, not-so-young woman. Every syllable a link to a moment, a memory, a time that will never, could never be erased from Connie Nixon's internal electrical system. Jessica's voice.

The last customer has made her way to the front of the store, arms filled with Diva's delightful products, and Jessica pulls away, says "Just a second, please," and walks to the other side of the store.

Connie uses her second to watch her daughter move and smile and sell and stand and converse and she cannot remember ever having seen this before. Jessica the businesswoman. Jessica, the adult. Jessica, the woman of the world. Jessica, especially, without her mother as a significant part of her life.

And Jessica is praying for a torrent of customers. She wants a tour bus to pull up outside, unload 300 people, sweep them into the store and then accidentally take her mother with them when they depart. Shit. Just shit. She inhales, throws back her shoulders, and feels like kissing the customer who has temporarily distracted her on the lips.

"What in God's name are you doing here?" Jessica asks

Connie when the woman finally leaves. "I almost had a heart attack when I saw you."

Connie takes in a huge breath, the last puff of her imaginary cigarette, and makes an instant decision to save that answer for later, maybe much later, because she isn't sure what to say. She is sure that she is stunned by the store, by the apparent success and grace and panache of the young woman who once moved to the backyard tree fort for two weeks because she was protesting her allegedly excessive chores, always hated to shave her legs, and pierced her own belly button during freshman orientation week in college.

Connie decides to go with the truth, most of the truth, a small taste of the truth, just to get warmed up.

"I found your boxes in the garage. The ones with all the papers for the business. I was cleaning. And I sort of freaked out, wondered who the hell you are and made a decision last night to find you, see you. So I hopped on a plane. And here I am."

"Are you angry?" Jessica asks, crossing her arms in front of herself, ready for battle.

"Not angry at you, angry at me for missing something, for not knowing who you have become, for setting up some kind of roadblock so you felt as if you couldn't tell me, couldn't see me, couldn't be in my life."

It is Jessica's turn to take a breath, to hold it and let it stop everything for just a second so she can focus. But she cannot focus. A small part of her, a piece of skin the size of a long envelope, wants her mother to touch her again. How long has it been? Three years? The rest of her, the parts that are confused, suddenly wandering around in the past like a blind woman in the middle of a maze, want to throw this woman out of the store.

"Look," Connie starts to explain, acknowledging with

her soft voice that the mere sight of her may have put her daughter into the early stages of shock. "There's more. There's lots more to tell you and it might seem absolutely stupid and ridiculous to see me standing here, to just show up in your life like this, but here I am."

"Mom, your timing sucks. I'm in a bit of a mess here. As you can see, I have my own story to tell."

"What? Are you in trouble? Did something happen?"

Jessica begins to explain and after the first sentence realizes that the explanation will turn into a two-hour-long story. She mentions something about New Orleans, new products, crooked politicians, staffing problems, and then stops herself, looks at her mother standing in front of her with a bag in her hand, a pair of jeans she recognizes from five years ago, and a look of terrified exhaustion blinking on and off in her eyes like a stoplight.

Connie follows Jessica through the store, the mother–student to daughter–teacher as Jessica walks through Diva's closing procedures out loud. Connie follows behind, listening, helping to lift boxes without being told, shutting the back windows, straightening shelves and smiling to herself when she locates something—which is pretty much everything—that she has never seen before. She marvels at the interior design and tries to avert her eyes from stacks of lustily adorned videos, magazines covered in whips and chains, and a selection of garter belts that are not only beautiful but provocative as they hang suspended in front of a wall of floating silver material.

"Now what?" Jessica asks as she looks over Connie's shoulder lest she has forgotten one small detail.

"Let's have dinner. Is that okay with you? If you don't have any plans, and then—you might not like this—but I need to sleep on your couch or have you get me to a hotel."

"I don't have a couch, Mom, but we'll figure this out as we go along. And, of course, I don't have any plans tonight. I usually stay here and work late into the evening."

"No social life?"

"Work, this business, the company—it is my life. Right now it's my entire life."

"I had no idea," Connie reminds her, skidding right into pissed-off mother mode, but then catching herself. "I just knew what you told me and I guess I just assumed certain things. That's not necessarily a good thing to do."

Jessica stops outside her door, sets the alarms, and only then turns back to respond.

"Mom, this isn't easy. I never expected this and I don't have time for this in my life right now, but here it is. Here we are."

Jessica pauses and her throat tries to close up. She's fighting back tears, pushing her top teeth tight against her bottom teeth, her jaw forming a steel cliff, stranded for just a few seconds in an emotional oasis that seems like an isolated, dangerous, and very tiny island.

"Mom, listen, just listen for a second," she stammers, edging towards her words slowly, afraid that she will say the wrong thing, insult her mother, throw the entire past hour into a tailspin that will crash and burn and never be able to fly again. "I thought you wouldn't understand this. I thought if I just told you I was in the manufacturing business, which is true, that you'd just accept it and move forward and not worry. A part of me, maybe, thought you had already worried enough for about 25 lifetimes. And then of course, it's not like I'm selling Tupperware."

Connie tries to say something but Jessica puts a hand up to stop her.

"There's the other stuff too, Mom," she explains. "All

the crap from high school and college and the same old unspoken knowledge that I've held onto all these years that no
matter what I do it won't be good enough for you."

Connie puts her hand out. She touches Jessica on the
arm to steady herself, and then tightens her grip, so that
Jessica will go no further, so that she will stop right where she
is, so that she knows if she says one more thing, what might
happen between mother and daughter might not happen.

And they pause.

They pause as everything Connie wants to say backs up
against the top ledge of her heart. Jessica may be a wise
woman of the world, a city legend, a sex goddess, but rushing this, saying what comes to mind before a pause, before a
breath, before wine and dinner and the lovely balance that a
public room can bring to a discussion that has the potential
to blow doors off of hinges is a necessity.

This from the mother. The wise mother. The mother who
has mourned the loss of a daughter every single day since the
last day, the last embrace, the last phone call. And Connie
knows that they both have things to say, things to forgive—
how she hopes Jessica can forgive and she knows if she can
get Jessica to the second bottle of wine that it will pry open
an emotional lid that will allow the frantic and lovely movement of reality—two worlds of reality: one Connie's and the
other Jessica's—that will hopefully push back time and chance
and whatever reasons might propel them to say or not to say
something.

The weight of her mother's fingers is a long-buried signal to Jessica to stop, just stop, and Jessica bites into her own
tongue and wonders what will happen next and how in the
living hell this, her mother showing up in her sex-toy store
and in her world, has happened just now. Just now when so
much is happening and about to happen. Just now when her

rear end is in a sling with deadlines and problems and just
now when the last person, the last problem, the last relative
she ever expected to see is her mother.

"Mom . . ." Jessica speaks because she cannot stop herself, because as always she wants to hurry and solve problems
and get it over with.

"Can it wait?" Connie asks. "Can we just wait?"

"Are you upset about what I do? I can wait but I have to
know before we take a step, mom. I have to know."

Connie wonders if she did not grip her daughter's arm
hard enough.

"Here it comes," Jessica thinks. "She wants to know if I
am a lesbian or if I have some kind of freaky sexual appetite
or if I've been arrested yet. She wants to know for sure if my
sisters know about my real life or if I ever mentioned it to
her sidekick, O'Brien. She wants to know if I love pain and
have fallen and hit my head."

"What, Mother? What are you thinking?"

The pause is long enough for the traffic light to change,
for them both to walk into the intersection across the street
from the restaurant, for a heart to pass three gallons of
blood through veins that have temporarily seemed to stop.

"Is there a family discount?"

Connie says it without blinking, while looking into her
eldest daughter's eyes, where something shocking lodges
the moment the words hit Jessica's lively brain and she realizes that her mother is just as shocked.

Eight

7½. Recapture Jessica. Again and again until it really happens.

Jessica and Connie are laughing so hard when they get into the restaurant that every single diner looks up as they stumble into the lobby and the hostess asks them if they are all right.

"We are fine," they both say at the same moment and then begin laughing all over again simply because they are in sync.

At the bar they sit and order their first cosmo as if they

are drunks waiting for a fix. Jessica keeps looking at her mother to make certain that she is real, and that what is happening is real as Connie asks her if she is okay. Okay, yes, Jessica says and then does not say that she is shaking on the inside, wondering if the long moment of laughter will get them through what surely must come next, what she must say, what her mother must also say.

And what that is neither one is certain of and while the first drink settles against the empty lining of their stomachs they talk about the neighborhood, about the flight, about the retirement party and everything but themselves until they are seated.

Jessica tells her mother about New Orleans while they sip the first drink at the table, to get it out of the way. How a plastics manufacturer, settling back into Louisiana following the hurricane, has been helping design and manufacture a signature line of Diva products and how suddenly there is a problem, just weeks before the huge "mostly planned" release party for these Diva products and an even bigger announcement about Diva stores multiplying across the country.

"Some jackass local politician from Jenko County has appeared like Jesus and I have to get down there fast, hire some new employees, plan this huge party—well, shit, Mother, and now you show up," Jessica explains, temporarily emboldened by the booze.

Connie, who is constantly brushing her hand against the list numbers in her pocket, does not say a word. She considers this tongue-biting exercise to be a ticket to paradise, a free drink when she needs one, a kiss from a handsome stranger.

After they order a huge-ass dinner—pasta and fish, mega

salads and a basket crammed with delicious carbohydrates—
and are well into the second bottle of wine, Jessica, in the
restroom, calls her business partner, Geneva Wheaton, a
lovely, brilliant, lesbian Hispanic accountant, to warn her
about her mother's arrival. At the table, Connie seizes the
moment to grab her own cell phone and call Frannie O'Brien.
Both phone calls are a swirl of questions and answers, uncertainty, excuses, and unintentional hilarity. If Jessica had ex-
changed phones with her mother, the two women on the
other end of each line might never know it.

Jessica: *"What the hell? She just showed up. What am I going
to do with her? Of course I never told her about the store. And now
I have to go to New Orleans. . . . Go ahead and laugh. It's not funny.
You know my apartment is the size of a pinhead and I have not
cleaned in like a year. Do you think she even knows what a vibrator
is? Well, no, she didn't freak out. What do you mean I'm the one
who is freaking out? I am not the one who is freaking out. Where is
your mother? Very funny. Invite her ass up here from South Carolina
for tea and see how you like it. Help? What could she do? Shut up,
Geneva. I am not drunk. Just a little tipsy. It's the pressure. I've got
to go. Tomorrow."*

Connie: *"How the hell was I supposed to know? There were
two other kids, you know, a mortgage, I was worried about shit all of
the time. I have no idea. She seems okay. I'll stay there for a day or
two. Christ, O'Brien, I am flying by the seat of my pants here. All I
know now is that Jessica in so many ways seems like the same Jessica
she has always been and I don't mean that way. The plane ride? Oh,
gezus, I met a hairdresser. She wants to do a makeover on me tomorrow. Maybe I'll go. Shut up. Of course I have no idea what I am doing. Have I ever known what I am doing? Oh, listen, quick—before
she comes out. No, she can know I called you but just be quiet for a
second and listen. Call the girls. Just tell them I went to New York.*

Yes, come on. To visit their sister. They don't call much anyway but I want to cover my rear end. No, let the goddamn plants die. Pick up the mail if you think about it. I'll call you tomorrow. I love you too, you big asshole."

"Mom," Jessica begins after she puts her phone away, "I know it must have been hard for you to show up here and I don't want you to ever think it was all you all these years because it wasn't."

Connie listens, half-suspended above the words, watching the moment play out in front of her, and decides to hold back her own transgressions, her own misgivings, her own not-quite-there understandings. She puts them back inside of her soulful pocket, closes the zipper, and thinks that her life would have been chaos, empty, a wasteland of ignorance if she had not thrown her book of lists on top of her ratty Jockey cotton underwear, gotten on the airplane, and headed through traffic as thick as an Army brigade on its way to the next Republican war in this slice of New York City.

"I didn't mean to hurt you," Jessica concludes. "I just charged forward, I was done with Indiana, ready for this phase of my life, removed, even emotionally, from most of my past, even you. I don't even know if that's wrong but it is the truth."

"Things happen," Connie Nixon tells her daughter, trembling a bit from the edge of her elbow to the fingers that are holding onto her glass as if it were a life raft. "We'll work through it. It's what happened, what you needed, where you were headed."

"Doesn't this freak you out at all?" Jessica asks, pointing in the direction of Diva's. "Your daughter is creating a sex-toy dynasty, for crying out loud. She's had lunch with porn stars and ordered sexual objects from businesses in Europe, demonstrated how to use all this shit and obviously— well, obviously I believe in what I sell and I use what I sell."

"Freaked is putting it lightly, Jessica, but my first glimpse this day, of what you are doing, well, we are sitting here talking, are we not? And we have laughed and if I think about how much I have missed looking into your beautiful eyes, I'll start crying and never stop."

Then without speaking Jessica reaches out, touches her mother's hand and smiles the exact same way she always did when she knew her mother was on to her.

Later Connie Nixon is not stunned or embarrassed or shocked by the size or condition of her daughter's apartment. She has seen and lived in worse. The apartment, she can tell immediately, doubles as an office, conference room— Diva Central, she begins calling it right away.

Both women are exhausted, one inch away from the kind of drunkenness that could give birth to terrible headaches in the morning. They have covered the sisters, O'Brien, the retirement party, just one small slice of Connie's plans for the next forty or fifty years. Really, just the part about the new job and taking some time off and the revelation from Connie that the house will be on the market soon and that she's "open" to change and life. Sort of.

"Sort of?" Jessica asks, brushing her teeth in the doorless bathroom.

Connie ignores the question and asks if she can help her hang up the bathroom door in the morning. "Do you have the door?"

"Yep. Never needed it. I don't have many sleepovers."

"What a shame," Connie scolds her, insisting that she skip the floor and sleep in the bed with her.

"I can't believe you're here," Jessica tells her, promising not to drool.

"You always drooled," her mother reminds her. "You also used to grind your teeth. It drove your sister Sabrina out of her mind."

"So that's how it happened."

"Stop it."

Jessica laughs, turns over, and is an inch from sleep when Connie opens her suitcase, uncovers her toothbrush, and accidentally runs her fingers over the nicked and battered leather book that holds her list of dreams. She picks up the book, turns to make certain that Jessica is not looking at her, closes the lid on the toilet and then sits for what she thinks will be just a few seconds as she turns the pages, not to read them but just to look at them, just to feel them brushing against the skin on the tips of her fingers, just to see the building blocks of her words, her dreams stacked against each other on page after page.

Jessica turns once, twice, and then quickly falls into the exhausted kind of sleep that is enhanced by alcohol, emotional trauma, confusion, and the mere thought of having her mother barge into her life and then pause there as if she may stay, as if she may peek in her underwear drawer, as if she might find another secret that she doesn't even know she possesses and a few dozen that she totally claims as her own.

Connie leans forward from her throne and sees her cheek pressed against the sheets, long hair splayed across the pillow, hands curled under her chin, and she closes the book. When she rises she slips it back into the bottom of her bag and then she climbs into the bed, focusing on nothing, absolutely nothing at all but her first dream, her biggest dream, the most important dream of all.

Jessica.

Jessica Franklin Nixon. CEO to the masses, sexual goddess extraordinaire, New York hipster and, even after all these years, a drooler who still loves to push her cold feet up against her mother's legs, sleep on her left side and crank the pillow around her head as if she is the queen of the bed and the pillow is her crown.

Nine

7. Recapture Jessica. Find Jessica. Hurry, Connie, but start slowly. Find your baby.

6. Take yourself to Confession. Make the penance easy.

What the hell?"

"Are you awake, honey?"

"How could I not be awake, Mother? It sounds like you are slaughtering a cow in my make-believe kitchen."

"How's your head?"

"What head? I feel like shit. How much did we drink? I can't remember a damn thing from the time I hit the pillow. Did I drool?"

"Yes, sweetie, it was a flood."

Morning in New York is hilarious and unlike the se-
rene scene in Cyprus, Indiana, where the paper shows up
at 4:43 A.M., the coffee kicks in unabashedly promptly at
5:05 A.M., Connie's feet hit the floor—or did up until about
a week ago—at 5:15 A.M., the shower goes on three minutes
later and Matt Lauer rests easy inside the old Panasonic television for his morning debut seven minutes after that. New
York, on the other hand, is loud and *fast*. There are apparently no walls in between the cheap apartments in Jessica's
building. Tenants sneeze, use the bathrooms constantly, and
argue. Horns honk without stopping and when someone
speaks on one end of Manhattan you can hear them plainly
on the other side of the island. It is one noisy-ass city.

Connie, so charged by the kinetic energy, by the noise,
by the city cycle of life that in one day seems like an endless
circle of vibrancy, feels 20 pounds lighter, bewildered,
stoned, drunk and frightened halfway to Tennessee and back.
Her initial reunion with her estranged daughter has given
her hope and the past night's reading of her list of dreams in
the doorless bathroom has given her courage. She keeps
moving because she wants not only to blend in with the action and the noise and the people and the very sidewalk below the apartment, but because she is afraid if she stops
she'll realize what she has done and, then, in the ensuing
moment, that she has no idea what will happen next.

Jessica wants to get out of bed but the thought of any
movement other than breathing makes her stomach roll into
her throat. She speaks slowly and with great agony.

"Mother, what in God's name have you been doing? It
smells like food in here. There was no food in this apartment
last night, or the night before that."

"I couldn't sleep. New York is too damn loud and so I
went for a walk. I bought food. I met people. I cooked. I

started to hang the door. I read three newspapers—imagine that, three newspapers all in the same city—and I met this guy who wanted to take me out when I was at that little grocery store, I think about four blocks away, and you were totally asleep."

Jessica groans. She wonders for a moment if she is still drunk. She wonders the next second how her life has gone from the crazed place it was in just hours ago to this—her mother cooking eggs and toast in her ridiculously small kitchen, a half-hung door, a very close-to-intimate conversation over dinner, some vague memory of a hair appointment, the family home going on the market and oh, yes, the silly little problem in Louisiana that she needs to fix. And then there is the small problem of what to do with her mother while she restocks sex toys and trains two new clerks during the next 15 hours.

"Mother ..." Jessica tries to say, sitting up, and then falling back over.

"You need some water, baby," Connie says, mostly to herself because Jessica has the pillow pulled over her head. "Here," Connie says, sitting on the edge of the mattress and pressing a glass of water into Jessica's limp hand. "Drink this while I get the coffee."

"Coffee," Jessica manages to murmur as she finishes the water and sets the glass on the floor. "Coffee in my coffeepot and not from the joint by the subway. Mom, how do you make coffee?"

Overjoyed by the perfume of high-octane caffeine, by the warm cup she can feel in her hand, Jessica forgets for a moment about her immediate and seemingly perilous future. And as she rises to accept the cup, the princess lifting her head from the pillow, she realizes the last time anyone served her anything in bed, besides a fast-handed condom,

was probably about six Christmases ago when her mother
did this very same thing.

"Jesus . . ." Jessica whispers.

"Honey, is the coffee that good?"

Jessica looks at her mother, really looks, and holds back a
stream of memories—some bad, some good—that could
flood her right out the door and into the elevator. Reams of
kindness. Yelling. Her father pounding on one side of the
door while her mother pounds on the other. Curling up tight
at the end of the hall when she got sick in fourth grade.
The summer she couldn't go to camp because there wasn't
enough money. The sound of her mother walking from room
to room—no matter what time it was, no matter what day, no
matter how many hours she had worked—to make certain
everyone was in bed, tucked in, breathing. The screaming
fights over boys and bras and college. All the things unsaid
when Jessica zipped a bag over her mouth and heart and her
entire life when she slipped away not just to New York but
before that—when she lied about something terribly important and lied about studying over Easter break when she
really went to Paris—glorious Paris—and the look, the sad,
hurt, crushed look on her mother's face when she told her—
how many times?—that no, she would not be coming back
for Thanksgiving, or Christmas, or maybe ever, if she could
help it. There are barges filled with memories that have been
awakened with this simple cup of frigging coffee. Jessica
pushes them all back, levers each one against a place three
steps closer to the front of her mind and heart, and then
quickly steps away.

"Mom, you are, like, freaking me out."

Connie takes a step back, hands on hips, and agrees with
Jessica that, yes, a mother uncovering some of your secrets,
showing up at the door, making you breakfast in a virgin

kitchen, and flirting on the street corner is probably a fairly good reason to freak out.

"I am a little freaked myself, Ms. Sexy Diva, but we've already had part of this conversation and I bet you have to get your sorry ass out of bed and go to work," Connie bickers back. "I probably should have taken notes last night so we can move right along."

"Right along to where?"

"Good question," Connie tells her daughter with a laugh. "I haven't thought much beyond breakfast and that hair thing tonight."

"Hair thing? What hair thing?"

Connie looks at her daughter, who has one leg under the covers, the other on the floor, her hair sticking up in a classic hospital-head style, and she wishes she had a camera. She has one camera planted inside of her head, the same one every mother has, every woman has, who wants to seize a moment and put in a place so that she will never forget it.

"I don't suppose you remember the part last night about me being a traveling hooker who works out of a tattoo parlor in Cyprus now that I'm retired," Connie says, moving to get the rest of breakfast. "Get up, use the bathroom, young lady, eat and then—don't you have a business to run?"

"You act like my mother," Jessica says, obeying her and wishing that her mother had managed to hang the entire door as she asks Connie to turn her head and then comes out with the screwdriver in her hand.

Connie has the door up in ten minutes and, when she turns around to congratulate herself, Jessica is sound asleep and looking as if she could sleep for a year.

"Now what?" she asks herself as she sits down gently beside her daughter and removes the warm coffee cup from her hand. She sits on the cheap sofa bed, unable to move, unable to decide what she should do next or right after that or the week following.

Connie's touchstone—her rope to a reality that she is creating every moment—is the feel of the white slips of paper in her pocket and a stolen moment, while Jessica slept, to read through her list of dreams book. Beyond that she is winging it, flying without a compass, hovering in New York City—which she is thrilled to say is #20 on her list.

There is also the reality of Jessica's life and the lingering promise from her daughter to tell her a very important story. But first Jessica must get to her Diva office and apparently must make arrangements to travel to New Orleans. During the course of their alcohol-laced marathon meeting, Jessica mentioned training new clerks, budgets, her home office, some major problem, expanding, her business partner Geneva and life in the fast lane. Connie places her hand on Jessica's hair, a soft reminder of a long-ago ritual when Jessica had gone through her nightmare stage and could only fall asleep if Connie was stroking her hair and sitting right next to her on the bed.

"You have to close the closet," Jessica would insist with the covers pulled over her face.

"There's nothing in here," Connie would respond almost every night, and then she'd push through the hanging clothes and sometimes actually crawl through one side of the closet and out the other to prove her point.

"Only I can see them," Jessica would explain patiently. "They're *my* monsters."

Occasionally, as the monsters screamed on from one month and into the next and then into the third and fourth, Connie would lose her patience. One night she let Jessica cry until the door rattled with her anguish and then Connie, filled past her eyebrows with guilt, raced into the room, pulled Jessica out of bed and carried her into her bedroom where she held her until the sun rose and apologized every three seconds for abandoning her and leaving her alone with the bogeymen.

The monsters finally departed for good, as they always do, and Connie braced herself for the other monsters that would eventually move into Sabrina and Macy's closet and she'd lose her patience again and no one died and the monsters did not eat one single daughter.

Connie can still see a glimpse of the baby who was terrified of monsters when she touches Jessica and she cannot stop herself from running her fingers from the tips of Jessica's hair to the side of her daughter's face where her hand lingers and her heart stops. Connie then imagines her daughter's monsters since the days of the permanently closed closet. What could they be?

School. Friends. Lovers. The impossibilities of the still male-dominated business world. That guy Jacob who called incessantly for months even after he knew Jessica had moved to New York and Connie had stern instructions not to share her phone number. And this Diva stuff. Sex toys. Some hidden desire to physically please, Connie assumes, the sexually unfulfilled women of the world. Finding a store. The business partner. The stares of people who still think sex is something you do once a year to fulfill a marital obligation. The tangle of city codes and laws and the charming personalities of the zoning and health inspectors. Probably a crippling wad of guilt because of what she has not shared with her mother, but apparently with her siblings. And this New Orleans problem. Franchise expansion. An apartment that has just moments ago been christened with its first cup of real coffee.

Oh, Jessica, Connie thinks. Oh, my baby.

"Your monsters are still there, aren't they?" she whispers so quietly that the breath from her words is as faint as the breeze from a butterfly's wings. "Monsters everywhere you look, bogeymen the size of Army tanks. Oh, sweetheart, where did you go? I had no idea. I had no idea how much I missed you—or how much I have missed."

In those minutes while Jessica sleeps, her mother wonders if she couldn't make Jessica's small apartment sing to her like Connie's house sang to Connie. She wonders what will happen tomorrow or next week, and at the tail end of that thought is also the knowledge that it does not matter. It doesn't matter if she stays here in New York for a week or a month or maybe for the rest of her damn life. It doesn't matter because she is here now and Jessica is here, too.

She wakes Jessica after that. Connie wakes her sweetly with her fingers dancing through her hair and then onto her face, across her lips.

"Hey, baby, what time do you have to get to Diva's?"

Connie's voice is a semi-foreign noise that rides itself through the corridors of Jessica's brain and out to the ledge of her woozy consciousness. She remembers as she stumbles awake. She remembers strips of the past 24 hours as if she is watching a cartoon being put together. The champagne. The phone call. Her mother standing by the purple dildos. Dinner. All the damn booze. A conversation that would have stunned her into oblivion if she had not been stoned on the grapes of Santa Barbara. The bathroom door. Coffee. And now . . . her mother touching her face and this feeling as old as her heart that she will soon, very soon, call a love as fine as life itself.

"Jesus, Mom, I can barely move. I have been so damn busy I'm not even drinking anymore."

"How sad is that?" Connie whispers again, this time a bit louder.

"What time is it?"

"It's close to nine. What time do you open?"

"Not until 11 today, but I have to get my sorry ass in there and set up and I'm training the new clerks at noon."

Connie's brain flashes into mother mode. In less than five seconds, she smiles and forms a plan for the day. It could be 15 years ago when all three girls got the flu on the same day and she was scheduled to give a lecture, head up a conference with three administrators, and meet her insurance agent for an update after work.

"Listen," she says, trying to act nonchalant. "Let me take care of your arrangements for the New Orleans thing. You get up, shower—you will notice there is a bathroom door now so don't walk through it—and eat if you can."

Jessica grabs her head and thinks: "This is what heaven must be like. Someone helping you through a rough passage. Coffee that smells like a street in Paris. And a bathroom door. A lovely bathroom door."

"Okay, Mom," she manages to mumble. "That would be terrific. You have me at a very weak moment. Save me some time later today. I have something else I need to tell you. We might as well get everything on the table and see if the damn thing tips over."

The second Jessica pulls herself together and manages to leave the apartment, Connie swings into action as if she has just been released from a chain gang. She cleans, makes the bed, and then plops down in front of the computer to get airline phone numbers and to email O'Brien, Sabrina, and Macy. Her emails sound like an ad for someone who is considering increasing her Prozac dosage.

"Sabrina and Macy—*You will never believe it but I decided to start my time off by visiting your sister in New York. As you both know, it's much different than Indiana and I can now spend some time traipsing through the city like I have always wanted to do. Your sister, as you also know, is busy with her business, so I will steer clear of her and see the sights. We are also speaking to each other which, as you know, is really something. No yelling—just speaking—so far, anyway. You have my cell phone number and I know you are in touch with Jessica, so call if you need me—otherwise watch the newspapers—maybe I'll get a stint in one of the Broadway plays.*"

Her note to O'Brien is more to the point.

"*Love it here. Staying for a while. Don't feed the cat. I don't have one. I'll call you this afternoon when I know you are not chasing crazy people.*"

While she is on hold with the airlines, Connie stands and moves to the tiny window that looks out over a busy street, the name of which eludes her. With one hand on her left hip, and the other on the phone, she doesn't feel like a mother or friend or nurse or even a woman. She feels simply *powerful*. Ready, excited, new. Connie Nixon feels *new*.

When the phone finally clicks and she gets a live human being on the end of the line—always a miracle—she reserves two seats on the Saturday flight to New Orleans—not one but two—and she does so without hesitation because New Orleans is now on her list, it's always been on her list, and Connie knows she has to go there.

She *has* to go there.

Jessica doubts her hiring expertise the second she looks up and sees Meredith and Kinsey enter Diva's for their first day of training. Talk about colorful opposites.

"Shit." She whistles to herself as she pours her fifth cup of caffeine and sizes up the outfits and personalities of her two in-store employee selections.

Meredith Rojas is 28, Hispanic, beautiful, and pierced in her nose, ears, eyebrow and most likely numerous other places—one in particular which she mentioned during her interview to prove that she was not only sexually aware but could relate to the intimate problems, questions, and concerns of Diva's customers. An NYU graduate in psychology, Ms. Meredith is in love with the hippie renaissance and with Manhattan, where she has held a succession of jobs while she tries to "stay focused on her cosmic abilities, desire to experience life, and passionate need to make certain women are sexually satisfied." To help herself with that last little goal, Meredith has tried to sleep with every woman in the five boroughs and Jessica figured if she hired Meredith all seven thousand of her successes to date might become customers.

And Meredith is sassy, bright, fun, and has tons of retail experience, what with her psychology degree, nine years of waitressing, stints at two shoe stores, a bakery and one upscale jewelry retailer—and there's little doubt that she already knows the products. Her first day of work at Diva's and Meredith shows up in a scarlet miniskirt, white flip-flops, a white spaghetti-strap tank top with a black lace nightie-looking top and a grin that is as eager as it gets.

Then there is Kinsey. Lovely Kinsey Barnes. A tall, thin white boy from Cleveland who is one of the thousands of Broadway star wannabes who have immigrated to New York and who can also handle lots of the day shifts when he is not auditioning for off-Broadway plays, taking voice lessons, or riding his bicycle into the side of moving taxicabs. Kinsey is outgoing, in a goofy kind of way that might make anyone buy something from him. He has spent way too many years as a bartender in a sleazy side-street saloon and is more than willing to learn how to usher lovely ladies and divine men up and down the aisles of Diva's, where he can also use his technical skills to manage the website, keep an eye on the storeroom, and call one of his barroom thugs if anyone gets out of hand.

Kinsey arrives at Diva's this morning wearing a pink shirt, red tie, gold vest, and jeans. He is so adorably anal that he straightens the leather whips, nudges a window sign closer to the edge of the sill, and looks as if he's ready to take over not just the business but the entire city on his way to the front of the store.

Jessica sighs. She says good morning and then she has a brief moment when she wonders if she should not run screaming from her store and all the way back to her apartment where she can plop into bed, ask her mother to make more coffee, and sleep until the books are balanced, the assholes in New Orleans have been spanked, and the store shelves have been lined with Diva's own signature products.

Her mother and what lies ahead is a topic Jessica decides to ignore.

Jessica jams on her CEO hat, grabs a stack of training documents she has prepared, and launches into phase one of her Diva training program with a chorus of tiny hammers pounding against her temples. She wishes, as she hands employment papers to Meredith and Kinsey, that she could have a beer or a Bloody Mary to feed her narrowed blood vessels so they'd stop slamming around in her head. She takes her new employees into the back room so they can fill out forms, and fights off any uncertainty about what is happening.

And it begins.

And there is no time to blink. The phone rings. Half of

New York has decided to visit Diva's on this particular day. Jessica has a hangover, her mother is probably rearranging her apartment at this very moment, and a bunch of shitheads in the Big Easy are trying to shut down her manufacturing shop.

"Geneva," Jessica whines into the phone as she scoops it up and tries to straighten up the mess which has accumulated around the cash register. "It's a madhouse here and I've got Meredith and Kinsey lurking around all day. I hope to God this training program I devised works out."

"You were born to do this, baby," her partner encourages from the desk of her "real" job as an accountant on the other side of Manhattan. "I'd come in but as you know I have absolutely no vacation or sick days left," Geneva tells her. "At least *you* can lie down on the floor if you have to. If I do that here, some other accountant will jump on top of me."

"You know I'm going to New Orleans tomorrow for crisis number 55, right? You have to open, close, and work with Meredith all day. And then you get Kinsey on Sunday. So follow the damn instructions I wrote down and don't invent anything new while I'm gone."

"What are you going to do down there?" Geneva asks. "Do you have a plan?"

Jessica considers answering that the best plan would still be to run screaming from the building as fast as possible but she takes a breath instead and tells Geneva that she does not have a definite, well thought-out, organized assault, but she will surely have one by the time the plane lands in New Orleans.

"Great. You get to traipse around Bourbon Street while I show Fritzina and Harry, our new hired hands, how to make us rich," Geneva says, mocking Jessica. "Tough work if you can find it."

"Want to trade, Wheaton?" Jessica asks her. "Some southern jackass will probably try to kill me and I'll be staying at the same Motel 6 I've stayed at the last 10 times and I've never been to Bourbon Street in my life."

"You are such a baby," Geneva informs her.

"Hey, when you cruise by during your lunch break, bring every single file from New Orleans that you have at your office. I do have to throw something together before I get down there. I swear to every plastic god in the universe that we have our bases covered, but I want to call our attorney and make certain they can't throw an injunction or some work-stop clause at us."

As she hangs up the phone, Jessica, a slender blonde who was such a brainy geek in high school that she was the president of the chess, political, and computer clubs at the same time, wishes that Geneva could go with her. Geneva, a track and soccer star in high school and college, saved her aggressiveness for athletics, financial figures, women's causes and her live-in lover, a gorgeous Latino woman who moved with them from Chicago and is now fully entrenched in her own life canvas—teaching art to grade schoolers at an experimental school and working on her own paintings when Geneva and Jessica are working at the store, which is pretty much all of the time. Geneva—who could get a below-market-value deal on gold, could negotiate leases and manipulate men and women with a wink or a nod but who hated social interactions if they didn't have anything to do with her business—was no match for Jessica's ways of the world. The Diva partners are perfect professional dancers: they moved in the same direction but listened to two totally different tunes at the exact same moment. No two women could be more opposite or more equally matched.

Although she likes a good battle, Jessica is also grace under fire, embraces poise as a pattern of life, and can plan a
party, store opening, or marketing campaign to knock the
socks off of men and women who would walk ten miles to
buy her products even in the dead of winter—without their
socks. She and Geneva had met in graduate school, thrown
their own dreams into the same barrel, and were inches away
from opening up a Los Angeles store, another in Chicago,
and hopefully blowing their small list of competitors out
of the water while at the same time enhancing the sexuality of women from one end of the universe to the next. The
future, when they remember to think about it, is beyond
intoxicating.

The connecting link, the last piece of their workaholic
obsessions, the passageway to phase two of the Diva Plan, as
they love to call it, is the delivery of the order from the
manufacturing plant east of New Orleans. Diva's signature
line, products with a purpose, sexual stuff, sensual pieces of
life's feminine puzzle, life-enhancing articles of amazement
that no woman should live without, objects of tremendous,
trembling joy—all this is a main part of the dream that is very
close to the finish line.

At this moment, Geneva and Jessica don't even get to the
mother part of Jessica's life. Connie Nixon. Former nurse.
Mother to the sex goddess. Coffee-maker extraordinaire.
New York City street-walker.

Back at the apartment Connie is slamming through the
tiny rooms like a human vacuum cleaner. Organizing. Grabbing
what she assumes is her daughter's travel bag and throwing
it on the bed, loading up the tiny, apartment-sized washer,
and then sorting through the few pathetic items of clothing
that she managed to put into her own bag before she left.

Shoes, slacks, jeans, a sweater, an old beige skirt, and not one thing dressy or professional enough to wear to a shout-out in Louisiana.

While one load tumbles, and the other washes, Connie races to the small boutique she discovered when she went food shopping. She slips inside and into a world that is so far from Cyprus, Indiana, she almost wants to ask for a map so she can find her way around the store. When she's finished buying a gorgeous turquoise blue linen suit, two blouses, a pair of leather dress sandals that cost more than every garment she's purchased in the last ten years, a tailored pair of dress slacks and a tight-fitting denim blazer, she races back to Jessica's apartment as if she just purchased a weekend stash of drugs.

She can't help it. She leaves what she thinks will be a distraught message on O'Brien's answering machine but instead it sounds as if she's just robbed a bank and no one cares.

"I just spent hundreds, let me repeat that *hundreds* of dollars, on clothes. I think I've lost my mind. Maybe something happened when those walls were talking. Oh, one other thing, O'Brien. I'm going to New Orleans in the morning. Now I bet you will call me the minute you get off work tonight."

When she hangs up, Connie says, "I'm sassy," to herself, folds the last load of wash and pauses just long enough to close the lid on the toilet, sit down and motivate herself by pulling her book of dreams out of her bag and simply touching it. "Please let Jessica not be mad. Please let me keep my mouth shut. Please help me find my way to the store. Please help me not to turn back, not now."

As Connie begins walking towards Diva's, nothing and everything makes sense to her. While she maneuvers through the crowds and dodges cars to cross streets, she feels as if old air is being sucked from her lungs. Connie bounces through several intersections, and fights all her old urges to plan, to prepare, to always be ready. She has no idea what she is going to do when she gets to Diva's. She has no idea what will happen in New Orleans or if her daughter will politely and then not so politely refuse to allow her to go. She may end up at a hotel tonight and even that does not matter.

And she misses Frannie O'Brien. While she waits at the last traffic light, Connie thinks that if someone asks her if she is married while she is in New York she will say, "Yes, I'm married to this truly wonderful woman and her husband. We do everything together—well, almost everything." And then she wonders if she's ever too much for Frannie. Frannie, who calls her just as much and who often plans her days and weeks in unison with Nurse Nixon's. We are good, she reaffirms to herself, but maybe I need to be an Indiana hermit for a while.

Maybe.

Or maybe not.

And she's suddenly thinking about sex.

Who wouldn't, with make-believe penises and whips and chains and clothing that make you want to shudder just looking at them flashing in front of you as you enter Diva's?

Who *wouldn't* think about sex?

TEN

1. Stop being afraid.

C onnie is saying, "Who wouldn't?" as she pushes open the door to Diva's with one hand clutching a bag of bagels she picked up at the coffee shop, and a carafe of coffee and some cups in the other, correctly assuming that Jessica has not bothered to install a coffee center in her own store.

"Mother . . ." Jessica mumbles under her breath, as if this is the first time she's seen her in years. "You're back."

"A snack," Connie says, holding up the bag. "And some willing arms if you need some help this afternoon."

Jessica freezes. She's a rock. Frozen in place. Unable to think. Dumbfounded.

The new kids, Meredith and Kinsey, are in the back room stacking shelves, there are five customers roaming through the store, both phone lines are ringing, and there is a delivery guy pounding on the back door.

"Mom," Jessica says a little louder, with her teeth clenched, as if someone were pulling the words from her mouth. "You know we sell sex toys here. This is not a hospital emergency room. Sex toys."

"I've figured that out, Jessica," Connie replies, looking around the store. "It looks like you're busy. Why don't you let me help you?"

Jessica feels like a trapped dog. Her mother? Selling sex toys?

"Wait here for two seconds," she orders sort of politely, and then gets Kinsey to handle the delivery and Meredith to handle the customers. Handling her mother will take half an army, she's certain of it.

Connie obeys and remembers her promise to try and keep her mouth shut. It is not an easy promise to keep. When Jessica returns and they head into the back room, Connie cannot stop herself. She sets down the coffee and whispers into her daughter's ear, "You should get some terrific coffee in here. And some Diva cups. People will want to keep shopping while they drink your coffee."

Jessica looks at her mother as if she has just witnessed a miracle. She's never seen this woman before. She has no idea who she is.

"You were a nurse, Mother, but maybe there is some carry-over into this profession," Jessica says as she writes down *buy coffeepot and funky coffee,* and adds, "What the hell" to her sentence, almost as if she were speaking to herself. "Set up the coffee out there and let me think for a few minutes. Is that okay, Mom?"

Connie is so happy to be doing something she almost drops the bagels as she turns to maneuver her way through the store. And Jessica watches her mother introduce herself to Kinsey and Meredith, greet two customers, and begin passing out coffee.

Her mother.

Jessica stops and places her right hand on her desk. Her left hand goes to her heart. For an instant a frozen thought parades into her mind, pushing through the debris of her day, the New Orleans fiasco, the 37 things on her "to-do" list, and she is a prisoner. She remembers.

Her parents' divorce. Her mother working odd shifts as a supervisor. Jessica, 17, who now has her driver's license and a boyfriend and her own brand-new, almost-adult responsibilities, grows weary with supplementing as her mother's assistant and tells her mother to go to hell. Her mother. The woman who has packed her lunches, rubbed her back through 47 menstrual cycles, gone up against the inappropriate English teacher, supported the family on wages that frequently seemed criminal given the level of her responsibilities, carried the load when the grandparents were ill, and sacrificed her personal time and any potential relationships because the girls—her three daughters, her life—had to come first.

"All this driving Sabrina and Macy and picking them up and making certain they are where they're supposed to be is so not fair!" Jessica had screamed. "What about my life, my time, my dreams . . . what about them? You can go to hell, Mother. I've had it."

Her mother is so wounded by Jessica's vicious attack that

she stumbles against the refrigerator door as if she has been pushed there by the weight of the world.

Her mother's face. Jessica will never forget her mother's face, which instantly became an acre of pain, an ocean of torture, a universe of sorrow as she dropped to her knees and wept quietly into her hands.

That was Jessica then, and Jessica now cannot move. A line of anguish cruises through the very veins that rested against the side of her mother's womb before she was born. Veins that glided through her stomach, and into her own heart and then up through her throat and into her neck and towards the very brain that has occasionally made her selfish, rude and ignorant.

Her mother pauses on the floor all those years ago and lets her anger ride itself out through the front door, into the tiny front yard, and onto the roof of the first car that passed by the house so she could watch it disappear. Then she looked up at her daughter, the girl-woman who looks so much like her that they could, on a really, really good day, pass as sisters, and she let her heart settle so she could say one of the most powerful and poignant things that she has ever spoken.

"You are my dream, baby. Beautiful. Strong. Wise. Sometimes a pain in my ass, but I have held you close and tight and I have let other things go, but never my dream. My dream to see you grow and go and build your own nest of dreams. Get them. Get your goddamn dreams and ride them until you hop on a new one. But never let them go, no matter how much it hurts."

Jessica takes a cleansing breath, a purging announcement to her lungs, her heart, and especially to her soul that she remembers everything. She remembers how her mother apologized for all the responsibility, for all the empty nights and days when she was not there because she had to work, for the anguish of the divorce, for all the things they could not afford but never, not once, for living her own dream, for wanting to be happy, for knowing she could be happy.

And then Jessica sees Connie move towards the vibrator aisle, raising her hands to touch the flowing fabric as she walks, and then leans in to ask the gorgeous woman who is holding something that looks like a rabbit if she'd like a cup of mocha java while she shops. Jessica watches and she knows now, immediately, before anything else happens or changes, that she needs to tell her mother the real story of why and how Diva's came to be, the real reason why she finally pulled away, a story that is intimate and a story that desperately needs telling.

First, she orders a trial by fire for her new employees. "My mother and I will be talking back here. Handle everything," she orders. She then asks Connie to sit, tells her before they can go anyplace else, before they can *really* move forward, Connie needs to hear the true story about the beginning of Diva's, about the woman Connie once accused of being a bad influence on Jessica, about the girl-turned-woman who is her daughter.

And then Jessica begins and Connie listens, unmoving, barely breathing.

Jessica Franklin Nixon is 19.9 years old the first time she has sex with a man. Well, sort of a man. His name is Ricky, or Rocky, or did he say Ron something, and he's in her economics class at the university and he is also 19 and they both know Fowler Jackson, the university basketball star from Kentucky who is as famous for his parties as he is for his extreme height and the way he rockets the ball into the net no matter where he is standing or how hungover he is at that exact moment.

Jessica is drunk. Ricky is drunk. Fowler is always drunk. Everyone else is drunk or stoned and a few people in the back room are snorting or eating something and someone mentions that those particular drug freaks have been in the room now for 21 hours. Jessica knows Rocky Ricky is a mistake even before he tries to kiss her in the backseat of his father's Buick but she does not care. She wants to get this over with. He's not unattractive. He has not tried to rip anything off her body and she suspects he may also be a virgin and wanting to enter into the secret society of "I did it" before another second passes, and he's also bright enough to have a condom in just about every pocket.

It's pathetic from the beginning but she does not stop. She does not stop even as he immediately slumps on top of her and she has to shake him so she can move to pull up her jeans.

She keeps trying. Jessica Nixon is dauntless. She sleeps with five more men and it gets a little better. Ben Jacobsen is the best because she nearly falls in love with him. This helps but even Ben—who must have taken lessons from romance novels because he reads poetry to her, tries unique positions, leaves a rose petal trail at her apartment door, and licks wine off of every inch of her body—does not rouse her to passion in a way that makes her want to crawl through a building to see him naked, have him touch her, let herself slip inside of him in a way that lets her breathe fire at the same time she is a captured sex slave.

During a retreat as part of her woman's studies class, Jessica, who identifies as a heterosexual but never closes any doors, lets Romney Switala seduce her. It is one of the loveliest weekends of her life. Women know how to please women, Jessica decides, as Romney locks her cabin door and undresses her in a way that makes her feel so sexy and wanted and beautiful that for the first time she cries when she makes love. While Romney, who is a tall, blonde woman who models on the weekends and will eventually become a vascular surgeon, rolls her onto her stomach and touches her, *every* single inch of her, Jessica realizes that this is exactly what she wanted. Intimacy, someone to look at her, someone to touch her, someone to be soft, to focus, to give, to see her—really see her—as a woman, a sexual being, and this is when she cries for the first time. Romney is not selfish but, eventually, during the weekend, Jessica wants her to be. At the retreat, they miss so many meetings they end up having to write three extra papers and explain their behavior, which they do without blushing, or hesitation, or excuses.

And they go on. Not because Jessica is in love or because she desires women but because she feels safe, because she is more sexually satisfied than she has ever been, because she feels desire, because she has this wild line inside of her that started from a place or a person or an event or from an ancient goddess ancestor who says to deny even one part of who she is and wants to be and what she craves would be wrong. Even when Romney asks for more, even when she thinks that maybe Jessica could love her the way she loves Jessica, even when Jessica touches her lover's cheek and says no without saying a word and feels a surge of tenderness that is as close to deep love as she has ever been.

"But . . ." Jessica finally tells her. "There is something."

Romney, who could have any woman or man on campus by turning her head the right way. Romney, who is so smart that Jessica can hear her brain snap and pop like those buzzers that try and kill mosquitoes. Romney, who loves to please Jessica not only physically but also socially and mentally. Romney, who will hold on to her notion that Jessica will one day turn the corner and see another beautiful woman and feel the sag of her heart towards her knees and the quiver in her stomach and the stab of pain from breath that wavers and makes her almost faint on the sidewalk—that Jessica will realize that she was born to love women and come back to find her. Romney will do anything when Jessica says, "But . . ." Anything at all.

But, Jessica tells her, *but,* she says, there is just one thing.

"What?" Romney asks her, panting, wondering, pleading. "Anything. What is it, honey?"

"I miss a penis."

A penis.

Jessica says the word "penis" as if she has a wad of gum in her mouth the size of Georgia. A penis.

Jessica hesitates. She is waiting for Romney to slap her and grab her clothes and take her beautiful self out of the door, out of the apartment complex, out of the state, out of Jessica's life.

Instead, Romney smiles a slow smile, the sun rising on Christmas morning, sweet smells from the sea all those miles before you see it against the blue Pacific sky, something you want really bad rolling like silk through your fingers, holding the baby for ten minutes and then the lovely feeling of not having to take her home to feed her, bathe her, raise her, send her to college, watch her fall in love with the wrong person.

"A penis."

"What?" It's Jessica who asks this time.

Romney smiles.

"Do you hate me?" Jessica asks.

Romney laughs and Jessica is instantly disarmed. She has worked for a long time to convince herself that she did not, could not, really love Romney. She has worked on that thought like a poor woman in a village linking together the broken threads of string to make the socks last just one more winter. Just one more week. One more second.

"I can get a penis," Romney tells her, clearly in control, knowing that she has this woman she loves for at least another month, maybe longer, before she begins medical school on the other side of the country and Jessica begins her business internship and resumes her hunt for a man—*the* man.

"Get dressed," Romney orders, slapping Jessica on the ass and strutting through the tiny bedroom to find her own clothes. "And I will get you a penis."

Jessica is no sexual dunce. That's what she tells herself as Romney orders her into the car, smiles at her sideways and drives through the center of Madison, Wisconsin, as if the rear tires are on fire. She turns the car towards Lake Mendota and then misses the clutch on her Toyota for the first time that Jessica can remember, and the car stalls in mid-traffic.

"Excited?" Jessica asks, knowing that they are headed for a tiny sex-toy store that she has frankly never taken the time to go into, had the need to see, or had the nerve to enter.

And, yes, Romney is excited. And, yes, Romney is a sex-toy expert. And, yes, Jessica blushes in the store as Romney tells the little man behind the counter that she doesn't need any help and that they might be there for a while so that he will go back to his book and his dish of granola.

They shop.

Jessica is speechless.

Why she never imagined such a place or has never been to one is almost as astounding to her as what she sees and holds and unabashedly wants to try.

What Jessica Franklin Nixon most remembers from the day, from the trip to the sex-toy store, has nothing to do with dildos and sexual pleasure and her lover's need to please her, to try to keep her, to make her happy—which is what a true lover is supposed to do. Jessica, even now, remembers the way the sun stood for an unbelievably long time on the very edge of the lake as she walked back to the car that day with Romney. She remembers how she simply pushed on Romney's arm, as if to say, "Stop, please, for just a second," and how Romney stopped because she knew what she wanted without a word. They stood there, at the intersection of two streets, one curving towards something unseen, and one straight that ended along the usual path. They held hands, not caring who would see them, and they clutched the bag with the dildo between them and watched the sun move sweet, soft and slow until it fell off the edge of the sky and into the dark lip on the other side of the lake.

Jessica remembers feeling alive, sure, wanted, beautiful, courageous, and so frigging *empowered*. She remembers stretching her hand out so that if someone had taken a photo, just then, it would have seemed as if she were holding the sun between her fingers. And then Romney let go of a breath, a wish that she had been holding, and leaned against her and the warmth from her shoulder melted into her and moved through her arm, touched her heart and then skidded along the road that curved and disappeared into the night, black and intoxicating, with an unknown end.

When she finishes her story, Jessica looks up and her mother begins sobbing into her hands. "Mom," she says. "Are you okay?"

Connie stands up, takes a step forward, and then opens her arms.

"I may never have been more okay in my entire life," she says, moving to embrace her daughter so that she can say she understands, that she too has more secrets to share, and so she can especially say she is sorry for never understanding when Romney was in Jessica's life all those years ago and why Jessica disappeared and turned into a Diva.

And when Connie Franklin Nixon speaks, it is with a voice that is totally sure and unafraid.

Eleven

6. Take yourself to confession. Make the penance easy.

8. Do something with your damn hair. Everyone looks the same after 47. Take a deep breath and hand the scissors to someone else, for crissakes.

10. Buy a convertible. Something flashy. Red or blue. Put the top down and drive someplace without thinking. Just get in the car and take off.

2. Let go. Stop holding on to things so tightly. Loosen your grasp. Be honest. (Accept the idea that this one may never come off the list.)

Connie remembers to check her cell phone for messages just after midnight when she is huddled for protection in Jessica's bathroom, thanking her dead grandfather for teaching her how to hang a door, and wondering what in the hell she could say to her oldest daughter to get her to shut up already about the fact that her mother is going with her to straighten out the politically misaligned faces of the good ol' boys.

"What the hell?" Jessica says not so softly about a minute

before Connie has locked herself in the bathroom pretend-
ing to have to use it for something besides a safe harbor.
"Mom, you can't just fly into my life like this and take me by
the hand and think that you can join in the fun and games as
if you've always been there. I said get *me* a ticket, not get *you*
a ticket."

"I could help like I did this afternoon," Connie replies,
not at all oblivious to the fact that she and her oldest daughter have completely switched roles, and that she is begging
just a bit. She knows she sounds like a teenager who wants
something she knows she might not get. "It's not like I am
some kind of ignorant ass who has never dealt with the
public."

Connie *had* helped. She'd helped so much in fact that
Jessica had wondered what she would have done to survive
the day without her. Her mother had no idea what she was
selling, no clue about what the difference between a vibrator and a dildo was, looked a few times as if her mouth had
been permanently propped open when a customer asked her
for something Connie had never heard of. Jessica was certain
that at least two couples, one a lovely man and woman and
the other a lovely man and man, had been stunned to see
someone who looked remarkably like their mother running
around the store with coffee cups and a whip hanging out of
her back pocket.

And Connie, even after dipping into her pocket to read—
Stop being afraid.—a good ten times, could not bring herself
to tell Jessica she had purchased two tickets to New Orleans
until moments ago. Moments she wishes she could somehow exchange along with the damn tickets.

"Mom," Jessica snarls, partly out of simple frustration
for the disruption her mother has brought to her life, "it's
sex toys we're talking about here. This isn't a hospital. This

isn't a post-op patient recovery room, you don't dress in one of those perky pink surgical costumes, unless of course a customer wants you to special-order one because they have some kind of funky medical fetish and love to put Band-Aids on people. I do this stuff alone. Geneva handles the store when I'm gone and I'm going down there to kick some ass and it might not be *pretty*."

Connie suddenly longs to slap her and say, "I'll show you ass-kicking. I'll show you *pretty*." But instead she makes believe her hands are around her own throat so she cannot speak, says in a monotone, "Excuse me for just a second," and departs swiftly to the restroom which she hopes will provide some kind of answer to the seemingly short but extremely complex question, *What now?*

The cell phone leaps into her hand. There are 23 messages and most of them are from O'Brien, one from each of her daughters, three from the real estate agent and two from her former co-workers who called during a staff meeting and left the speaker phone on so she could hear what she was missing—a power play for the final say on patient discharge protocols; a discussion on where the garbage can should be located at the nurses' station; a rather spirited debate about who would organize the fall picnic; a few stifled laughs when someone asked why Dr. Lambrinski allowed his dog to slink into the waiting room three times in one month while the good MD ran into his office to grab files, talked to staff members, and stole a drink from the lounge fridge.

Connie turns on the bathroom fan and calls O'Brien, who she prays to God will answer the phone. While she waits, she goes from being pissed off to thinking that maybe she really did lose her mind when the house started talking to her. Maybe, she tells herself, there was nothing wrong with the wiring and everyone was trying to protect her until

they could get her out of the house and into some kind of se-
cure environment where she wouldn't hurt herself or anyone
else—especially her eldest daughter. Maybe she snuck out
and got on the airplane to New York just in time and totally
screwed up the plan. Connie feels as if she will take a giant
step backwards unless she can hear O'Brien's voice.

"The plan, hell," she utters out loud just as the fan kicks
in. "What about my list? What the heck am I doing?"

"Jesus, Nixon, what in the hell is going on?" O'Brien
shouts into the phone on the fifth ring. "I leave you alone for
a few hours and now you're selling sex toys, getting make-
overs, flying to big cities and making the one daughter you
desperately need to have a relationship with hate you even
more than she already does. I'm jealous as hell."

Connie suddenly feels like a fool, and an ass, and that's
exactly what she tells O'Brien as through the closed bathroom door she hears Jessica fling God knows what in the
space that serves as her living room, dining room, porch,
basement cellar, bedroom, and the corporate headquarters
for Diva's.

"Imagine how you would feel if your mother showed up
while you were unpacking cartons of condoms and lubricat-
ing gel, sweetheart," O'Brien admonishes. "It's not like she
runs a flipping daycare center. And she's also used to being
alone. You upset her routines, her schedule, her life balance,
and, apparently, made her wonder what the hell happened to
her *real* mother."

"I'm the same. I haven't changed," Connie protests,
stung.

"Tell me what you look like right now."

Connie was not the same and neither was her daughter—
physically and mentally. They had both, with more than a
bit of cajoling and badgering and finally the appearance of

Mattie at the door of Diva's with a blow-dryer aimed at Jessica as if it were a gun, turned into Divas themselves. They had become new women—at least from the neck up. Haircuts, dye jobs, a parade of brushes and wands and scissors and a takeout order of Chinese, almost two six-packs, and 3.5 hours later and the two Nixon women were definitely saucy and Connie had not even written #8, the hair dream, down on her pocket list yet.

"Shit," Connie admits over the hum of the bathroom fan. "I'm sort of a blonde now."

"See," O'Brien says, trying not to laugh, "Jessica probably doesn't even recognize you. No wonder it's thrown her into some kind of frantic realization that her mother is an adult, she is also an adult, and everything has changed. Don't start baking chocolate chip cookies and reading her *Goodnight Moon*, for God's sake, or you will screw up everything."

"Tomorrow, shit, Frannie, in like *five* hours we are supposed to fly to New Orleans and I had this idea that I could help and she doesn't want me to go and I don't know what the hell to do," Connie moans, hands on her knees, ass on the closed toilet, and the fan blowing on her bare neck where Mattie had shaved off all of her hair.

O'Brien lets her have it for a good three minutes. Just go to New Orleans, for crissakes, she tells Connie. You've got the ticket, you've wanted to go for years, if Jessica doesn't warm up just go to a different bar in the French Quarter every 15 minutes until she's finished. Go see a swamp. Stop treating her like a daughter and just treat her like a woman. Gezus, Nixon, you ran an entire hospital, raised three kids pretty much on your own, and you don't usually take shit from anyone. Don't back down. Get pissed off yourself.

While O'Brien tries hard to motivate her, Connie wonders if Jessica might be afraid of failing, of dipping backwards

into her own fears, into that place where not making it seems
predestined. Connie thinks that if the New Orleans trip
works out, she may be able to cross out number seven. And
number seven, she reminds herself, is the real number one.

Connie listens and then has so much to say that she
needs to take a breath before she starts, but Jessica pounds
on the door just then and yells, "Mom, get off the phone and
come out," and Connie does just that, thinking the fight will
resume. But Jessica really needs to go to the bathroom, and
probably make her own "What the hell?" calls, Connie thinks.
And as tempted as she is to stand by the door and listen, she
cannot bring herself to do it. In the next 15 minutes, instead,
Connie finishes packing, checks to make certain the tickets
are tucked into the pocket of her new jacket, runs her fingers through her very short and very blonde hair, and then
drops into bed imagining the early morning smell of New
Orleans—a mix of serious coffee and lightly baked beignets,
she fantasizes, a perfume seeping through the cracks of the
very old, very well-restored, and very hip bed-and-breakfast
hotel room she has reserved on the second floor of a building encased in antique wrought iron on Dumaine Street in
the very heart of the French Quarter.

"And you have done harder things," she reminds herself
in a whisper. "So many dreams, so many are so damn close."

It is possible, Connie Franklin Nixon discovers, to do some
serious traveling with a partner and not speak to her. You can
sleep in the same bed, get dressed, eat a bagel, hail a cab,
check in, sit right next to her on the plane, pass her a note
that says *Geneva called while you were in the shower*, order coffee, and then slink away into your own world, all without saying a single word.

Silence is like a delicious appetizer to Connie, who has decided to ride out the silent storm and enjoy the scenery.

"Call it mother's revenge for the secrets of the daughter," she tells herself, "but I am not excited about arguing and my good intentions need to be recognized. Christ," she adds, silently of course, "I paid for the plane tickets and this spicy suite. A little jazzy decadence, wild fun and 24-hour street dancing . . . I've wanted a slice of The Big Easy since I can remember."

And remembering goes way past those days when Ms. Sex Toy Diva who is now sitting beside her on the plane was a baby and Connie was lucky if she had the time to read a page in a book, and when reading a whole book would be like having an illicit affair, which she admits she would not have known how to have anyway. So page by page, month after month, Connie would read and finally finish a book—mostly when she was in the bathroom because it was absolutely the only place in her house where no one would bother her.

"Mommy is going potty!" she would yell out to one of the girls while sitting on the toilet but not for the usual reason. "Go play with your sisters until Mommy is done!" And for every time Connie said that, she would have to have had six bladders and a urinary tract infection every month for seven years but it was the only way she could finish books and make believe she was traveling to exotic places like New Orleans, places that she doubted she'd ever actually get to see in person, with or without a cranky, pouting, and very silent daughter.

When they start the approach into the appropriately named Louis Armstrong International Airport, and Connie looks out the window from her aisle seat to the expansive green blanket of lushness called Louisiana that seems as if it is opening its arms to the plane, she catches Jessica's eye for

a moment and starts laughing. Connie cannot stop and Jessica
sets down her notebook, glares at her mother and waits for
her to say something. Connie's laugh is not the sweet, "on an
airplane" laugh that might come squeaking out of a short-
haired, middle-aged blonde woman who is reading women's
magazines. Connie roars. Wild dogs would have run. Janis
Joplin would be offended. Harley riders would be insulted.
Jessica decides her mother has lost her mind.

"Mother," she finally says, looking totally disgusted.
"What the hell is wrong with you?"

"It was the bathroom," Connie giggles, "when you were
a little girl and I always told you I was going potty—"

Jessica is trying hard not to grab her mother and tell
her she is sorry, except she isn't quite ready for that yet because she is still trying to figure out what to do later in the
day when she meets with the boys from her manufacturing
company and the assholes from Jenko County. Jessica Nixon,
the MBA entrepreneur who has stabbed the odds in the
back, is at a self-confidence standstill, a professional pause,
an unforeseen roadblock that was definitely not covered in
economics class, business logistics, or any of the other goddamn MBA classes she took that cost her close to $50,000
and three of the best years, so she thinks, of her life.

Add to her professional panic the near-constant presence of her mother, a woman who was not a stranger just
days ago but surely estranged, and Jessica is on the edge of
exploding.

"Mom, you sound crazy," she mumbles, turning towards
the window and trying desperately to be tough, brave, and
everything she is not at that exact moment.

"Jessica, just listen to this," Connie insists. "Remember
when I used to hide out in the bathroom?"

Connie explains, remembering the sound of padded pajama feet in the hall, the tapping of tiny fingers on the bathroom door; a terrific paragraph; rising to leave and then sitting back down again abruptly because she cannot bear to leave the women in her book; hoping all three girls will just lie down where they are so she can finish the chapter, and hoping deep in her heart as she hides in the bathroom to read that her girls, her babies, will love books and the world books bring to doorsteps, bathrooms, and tired lives as much as she does.

But Jessica cannot be bribed by her mother's sweet attempt at conversation and when Connie stops talking, Jessica plunges back to her immediate problem, something more dangerous, more imminent than the surgical process of stitching back together her relationship with her mother.

She has talked to the lawyers, she's rechecked her files, she knows she has every permit and ordinance and signature that she needs to knock Jenko County back on its ass but what she doesn't have is the experience of bullshitting, playing the game until you are ahead and standing in just the perfect spot so that you can piss first when the duel starts. Jessica has the looks and the brains but the singular battles have eluded her. The confidence that comes from many battles has not yet forged a smile of satisfaction on her face and her business sword is short—so far, everything has been pretty damn easy.

They skid to a halt. The southbound plane. Mother and daughter. The Franklin Nixon women and their baggage. It's a wonder the plane can perform a controlled landing with the heaviness of it all, but land it does, and Jessica and Connie do not so much walk as race to the terminal, pulling their luggage and the threads of their last conversation.

Neither of them is ready for the late spring heat of a city that makes even frigid men and women hot. A city that really never dozes. A city that makes New York look like a mere training ground for 24-7 people. A city that leaps into your arms and expects you to carry it because there is no way in hell it is going to carry you—unless of course you are a big tipper, have access to an exotic float builder, can go without sleep for three days in a row, and understand the importance of the word "fun."

Fun—if Connie can just manage to hold her tongue firmly in check and use her once lively mouth only for breathing and not for speaking.

The taxi ride starts out with a bump that seems insurmountable for as long as it takes Nurse Connie to clear her throat, put back on her "I'm-not-backing-down-and-I'm-here-to-stay" hat and forget for five seconds that her daughter would like to slit her throat.

"Where *are* we going, Mother?" Jessica doesn't so much say as spray.

"It's not the Motel 6, sweetheart," Connie spews back with a hint of anger. "It's called Sally Rutherford's. It's a bed-and-breakfast place. Upscale and in the French Quarter, untouched by the disaster, and it's an early birthday present for you, and part of it's for me too."

"How the hell am I going to get to the meeting at 3 P.M. out at the factory?" Jessica snarls, pushing herself against the side of the taxi and speaking loud enough to make the driver shift in his seat and adjust his mirror.

Connie pauses. She's itching to reach over and try her magical touch on Jessica's hand but she is too angry to move.

"You should get out more, Ms. CEO," Connie seethes. "I rented a car. I have a map. I have lots more than that if you can give it up for three lousy seconds and take off that shitty mask you put on last night. I get that I'm from Indiana and a hick and your damn mother, but there are a few things *you* don't get."

It's hot. Connie is exhausted from trying, from lack of sleep, from the river of her own self-doubt that cascades through her every single time she brushes her hands against her pocket and feels the small ridges from the slips of paper she is carrying—today's list numbers, which seem to be crashing into each other constantly.

Before Jessica can respond, the driver begins speaking in clipped English, hardly a Creole or a Frenchman, more like a transplant from the West Indies, and says something about the cemeteries, the heat, and three other things that fail to register with either woman, and then, just as Jessica is about to let go of her temper, they are parked in front of Sally's. She lets out a huge ball of air, climbs out of the cab and walks into the lobby as her mother pays the driver.

"Holy shit," she says before Connie gets there. "This place is like a museum. It's absolutely . . . beautiful."

"Holy shit," Connie echoes behind her as she walks into a lobby that is almost beyond a step back in time.

Before either of them can move, or say another word, a concierge steps in between them, takes them both by the elbow, and says, "Everyone is stunned by the magnificence here. My name is Salvatore. Are we lucky enough to have you two beautiful women—sisters, I presume—staying with us tonight?"

"We are staying here as mother and daughter," Connie tells Salvatore shyly, sort of flirting but not even realizing it, and Jessica decides that if the suddenly constant presence of her mother in her life gets any more constant, she is going to run upstairs and jump off the balcony. "What an absolutely astonishing building."

"Just wait," Salvatore cautions as he ushers them past a room filled with antique chairs, under several huge chandeliers, across carpeting that feels like a spring meadow, and towards a low, dark oak desk that sits in front of an open window that is backed by a garden seemingly transplanted from the center of Costa Rica. It is the Garden of Eden. Springtime in the Rockies. A slice of heaven in the middle of a city.

Both women are temporarily speechless and both women decide this is a very good thing.

Salvatore shows them to their room and departs with a broad smile. The balcony of their small suite looks out at the same lobby garden and they discover that the garden also contains a tiny swimming pool and an outdoor bar. Connie pushes open the street-side window and immediately exposes the room to a swirl of noises—honking horns, horses' hooves, people yelling, laughter pealing up and pausing on the windowsill from every direction—and she can barely bring herself to turn around and face her daughter.

Her daughter. Connie Franklin Nixon freezes for a second, trying to pull a moment of past grace from the combined life of a mother and daughter.

"Jessica," Connie finally says, turning to face her daughter, who is still slamming her personal objects as hard as she was in her own apartment before they left New York four hours ago. "It's no more than a 60-minute ride from here to your factory. No rush hour traffic this time of day. Let's call a temporary truce. Gather up your books and we'll go down into the courtyard for lunch. We have two hours. What do you think?"

"Fine, if we can eat and you can let me focus," Jessica responds. "I have to figure this out. I have no idea what in the hell will happen."

Connie almost bites a hole in her tongue. She thinks of something hard, something hellish. She thinks of the months when Jessica was a baby and Connie was in nursing school and she had no idea how she was going to make it through a day without sleep and then the doctor called to tell her another baby was already boring a hole into her heart from the inside out. "You're pregnant, Connie," he said, as she sank to the floor. She thinks of the night Sabrina's appendix almost ruptured and she sat with her fingers resting on her daughter's forehead and trying to imagine what one second of her life would be like without this child in her life, her arms, her heart. She thinks of the way her stomach twisted when she took her girls, one at a time, into the bedroom and told them their daddy was no longer going to live with them. Connie thinks of all this and then she lets it go. She lets it go because she knows Jessica has her own version and form of hell, her own ideas of what the word "hard" means, and her own way of surviving life's blows and surprises.

Jessica's cell phone bleats halfway through the jambalaya and it does not sound good to Connie, who keeps eating, sips on some iced tea that she knows would taste much better if it had at least one shot of vodka, and wonders if Jessica will ever reach the "maybe Mother can help me" point in her Southern adventure.

"I did not, let me repeat that, *not* invite that commissioner to meet us today!" Jessica shouts into the phone.

"No, Justin," she fires back as Connie pops a biscuit into her mouth to keep herself from grabbing the phone. "What do you mean you can't do anything? This contract is worth thousands of dollars to you. Think of something, for cris-sakes." She frowns. "I'm the boss, you say?"

Jessica gets to her feet. Her face is now the color of the small tomatoes that are sitting in her Cajun salad.

"This is your turf, Justin. You have the rulebook down here. You had better think of something. I'll try and get there early. Yes. Justin, can you tell I am pissed?"

Jessica hangs up, throws down the lovely off-white cloth napkin that she has been clutching in her left hand, not so much places as flings her cell phone on the table, then turns to her mother.

"I have to go, like, *now* and I also have to make about a thousand phone calls," she explains. Then she groans, and covers her eyes with both hands. "You know I hate to do this but will you drive me, please, so that I can handle the calls and *focus* before I meet these jackasses?"

"Yes," Connie says without blinking but raising a silent "yes" fist into the air in her mind as she gets up, hands her credit card to the waiter, ushers her daughter up to the room and asks for the rental car to be pulled around to the front of the hotel in 15 minutes.

During those 15 minutes, Connie braces for a continued storm of emotions and, as Jessica scrambles to get her papers together, Connie slips into the bathroom, barely has time to throw on fresh makeup, and then flips through the pages of her list of dreams book that she has tucked into her carry-on bag as if she is an addict who needs a hit before she can go out in public.

twelve

19. Moments with my daughters that are real and open and where all four of us can be who we really are.

Jesus," Connie breathes as she drives, during that one second when Jessica is not on the phone to Geneva, or her attorney, or some other legal expert on the West Coast, or hopefully some burly wide-ass man she knows who likes to beat up people who get in his or his friends' way. "Are you sure *Deliverance* wasn't filmed someplace around here?"

"Mom, it's rural Louisiana," Jessica explains. "It's no different than rural anywhere."

"Not," Connie responds firmly as Jessica punches in yet

another number and turns to glare at the blurry skyline and what she seems to think might be impending doom, the demise of her dildo dynasty, and possibly a set of broken fingers once the commissioner shows up.

Connie has taken them south of New Orleans, along the edge of Lake Pontchartrain and towards what she assumes will be a long-deserted field where men in pickup trucks sit and whittle while they wait for unsuspecting women from the East to try and tell them how to do things. While she drives, Connie tries hard to let go of the wild notion that perhaps she can be more than a chauffeur. She is instead possessed with the idea of visiting a bayou, of snaking her hand into the first few inches of its murky and very warm water, water that cradles crocodiles or alligators or whatever large scaly things live in these mysterious backwaters of a part of the country that is so alive with history and ethnicity that the entire state smells like hot sauce.

There is not the imagined long-lonely field when they finally turn off of the interstate and wind through a tight residential area until the road curves around what Connie can only guess is a misguided and extremely weedy tributary of the Mississippi. This part of Louisiana, ravaged in so many places by the hurricane disaster, has sprung alive with rebuilt businesses, new housing developments carved in and around huge piles of debris, masses of tangled trees, and water marks on the buildings that remain standing. A curving stand of industrial buildings that look abandoned greets them as they turn into Chasse Industrial Park. Three weed-filled vacant lots, a line of battered buses, and a heap of scrap metal stand like sentries as Jessica directs Connie to a back parking lot.

"How in the living hell did you ever find this place?" Connie asks, just slightly astounded by the location.

Jessica smiles and feels just a tinge of pride. "It's a long story about a woman searching for a not-so-timid American manufacturer who does quality work, cheaply and on time."

"I'm impressed, and just a little frightened, honey." Connie gets out of the compact car and gasps just as a blue convertible shoots into the parking lot about three inches from where she is standing.

"Jessica, who the hell is this?" Connie wants to know, bending over to lean into the car so Jessica will hear.

Jessica is suddenly pale. She groans and says, "Shit, it must be the commissioner and he's looking at your ass, Mother." She grabs her notebooks, places her phone in her hip holster as if she is strapping on a gun, and gets out of the car.

Connie takes a step forward just as the man swings around the side of his car and walks directly towards her. The man leans into Connie, who decides that she is about to meet Burt Reynolds's twin brother—a gorgeous, dark-haired man with Burt's moustache, gray hair at the temples, teeth that look as if they glow in the dark, and shoulders that could not be wedged into a space smaller than four feet if his life depended on it.

"Michael Dennis, Jenko County Commissioner," he says, pushing up his sunglasses and stretching out his hand to clasp Connie's.

"Connie Nixon," Connie manages to say.

"I'm Jessica and I think you came here to see me." Jessica moves to stand protectively beside her mother.

The studly commissioner turns for just a second to acknowledge Jessica with a smile and a hello. Then he turns back to Connie so fast it's a wonder his neck stays in place.

"And you are?" he asks, leaning so close Connie can

smell his cologne, see how close he shaves, and that the lines in his eyes curl up from smiling and not from frowning.

"I'm Jessica's mom and the driver," Connie tells him. "I'll just hang out here while you two go inside and take care of your business."

"Nonsense," he declares, boldly putting his arm around Connie's shoulder. "Come in. Justin, the CEO, has a nice room we can sit in and maybe you will want to see the plant. It's actually kind of interesting. Some day this plant is going to be on the map for more than these Diva products. Justin's scientists are doing some remarkable things with plastics."

Jessica's eyes have never been this large in her entire life. "Jesus Christ," she whispers as she follows the happy couple in through the side door of the plant. "This guy is flirting with my mother. Holy hell, my *mother*."

Connie works to get Jessica's attention as they move through a long corridor and into an office that has a couch, some chairs, and a very narrow window that offers an interior view of the plastics-manufacturing plant. Desperate for some kind of an exchange with Jessica, and obviously emboldened by the commissioner's attention, Connie swings into action. She whispers, "Watch this," into Jessica's ear as the commissioner picks up a phone on the desk to call Justin out of the factory. She plants herself directly in front of him. She's flirting too, big-time. Jessica is just an inch from being paralyzed and, before she can say anything, Connie takes over as if she just inherited the entire Watkins's plastic manufacturing business, half of Louisiana, and every four-star chef in the French Quarter.

In the back of her mind, in a place that never really grows totally weary, a place that is filled with flying daggers to protect the weak, rows of fresh flowers, and arms as wide as the world—a place cultivated by every mother on the earth, a place that can never be erased—Connie Nixon Franklin also feels her armor fall into place.

She cannot help herself. Warrior mother, charge nurse, and also, rising like a splash of heat from a warm spot, almost dead, almost forgotten just a bit south of her pubic bone, Connie feels a wave of sensual *heat*.

"Michael," she begins, busting right past the formality of the word "commissioner" and reaching out to put her hand on his arm, "what is this confusing meeting all about anyway? Jessica has her permits, this is a private business, and last time I checked the absolutely gorgeous state of Louisiana *is* part of the United States of America."

Michael, clearly taken aback and captivated at the same time, tells Connie he agrees, which makes Jessica want to weep with joy. And then she gets mad.

"Why did you tell Justin he had to shut down then?" she asks, unable to control her obvious anger. "Why are we here? I am totally confused."

"Sit," Michael tells them as Justin walks in, introduces himself, and perches on one end of the couch. "Let me talk to you two about the politics of Jenko County for a second and then you can ask some questions. Please don't be angry. You might think, Connie, that Louisiana is part of the United States, but Jenko County is often its own entity. I've been trying to bring the place into this century for the past five years. It's no easy chore. I had to make a big deal out of what Justin is manufacturing for you," he said.

Connie stops him by putting the famous handhold on his arm and says, "Sex toys, Michael. You can say it and your lips won't fall off. They are sex toys and don't worry, it took me a while to work up the courage myself. Don't be scared. I'm not even sure what half of them are for. Some of them look like things the kids used to play with, or car parts, for crying out loud."

"Okay," Commissioner Michael Dennis says, smiling with relief. "The sex toys you are manufacturing are not the usual product of this part of Louisiana, Jessica, but Justin hired new people for this job, it's terrific business for him and, in the long run, as a businessman I can see what this will do for the people in this county who need jobs, and an economy that needs all the damn help it can get. Even so, when word got out about the sex toy products, I had to make a scene. Do you understand this?"

Connie understands it like she understood how one doctor always had to pull rank, and why even though she ran half the hospital someone else always took the credit, and why she often teetered on the edge of a very thin line that could be called insubordination, survival, or prostitution, depending on how you looked at it.

"I think so," Jessica says doubtfully. "So we really don't have anything to discuss and I have been freaking out for nothing and the sex toys are about ready to be shipped to New York?"

"Yes," Justin assures her. "It's just part of the game, Jessica. I'm sorry but I couldn't tell you. Down here people still tap phone lines, eat without silverware, and sleep in pajamas instead of in nothing or boxers."

"So we're done already?"

"Not really," Justin adds. "People know we are having this meeting. You have to hang out here for a while so they think we are arguing. So let's take a tour of the plant, mostly so your mother can see what we do here, if she doesn't mind, have a cup of coffee, and then we will release you."

By the time that happens, Connie has cemented a morning

date for a swamp tour with Commissioner Michael Dennis that does not include her fine, beautiful, and extremely dazed daughter, who will, instead, spend the morning in product development meetings with Justin's design staff who have come up with an idea for a new toy that they know from personal experience and experimentation could make lots and lots of women very happy.

Three hours later, drifting back towards New Orleans, Jessica, who has been fairly speechless since they peeled out of the factory parking lot, turns to her mother and asks her if she has lost her mind.

"I thought you'd be happy that you can still make your toys, honey," Connie replies, turning to look at Jessica, who is leaning up against the car door as if she is trying to escape.

"Mom, you are going to a swamp or bayou or whatever in the hell you call it with a man who has been married at least twice and who just tricked us into a trip here to save his own political ass," Jessica says, accelerating her voice along with the engine. "I ask you again: Are you out of your mind?"

Connie's throat seizes up. She can actually feel something moving up from the base of her heart and towards her mouth. It is something old. Something she has never spoken out loud before. Something she now decides could change everything and—no matter what—it's something she has to share with her daughter. A daughter she has lost, a daughter she so wants to reclaim, a daughter who needs to know where her mother has been.

Right now.

Connie pulls off less than a mile from the freeway and parks the car at the edge of a dirt road facing a stand of tangled bushes. Jessica looks frightened but Connie lets her have it anyway. And *it* is nothing Jessica expects.

"You told me your story, your sexual encounter with

Romney, why you have launched into this business, why you pulled away, how my seemingly rash judgments of you and your sexuality made you distant, made you leave my life," Connie explains, at first looking right at Jessica, and then looking away as she begins her own story, a story she has never before shared with anyone. "Now it's my turn. Can you listen to this?"

Jessica nods with the slow movement of someone who is terrified and compelled at the same time.

And Connie begins.

The man she was dating said he was ready to try.

Connie was way past ready. Nurse Connie was so far past ready that she was afraid if John McCorde simply rubbed up against her she'd experience such a great swell of sexual pleasure she could just send him home and call it a night.

It was so far past time to have a physical encounter with the man she had been dating for almost nine months that Nurse Nixon was on the verge of begging. She was ready to crawl, to cry, to assist in any way physically, medically, socially, and spiritually possible.

"Your kids would even tell you that you need to get laid," her friend and co-worker Kim Ratton told her about 23 times. "I know you think you are from the old school, honey, but this is all about *you* now. It's time to get on with a bit of pleasure."

"Pleasure?" Connie had said at first. "It's been so damn long since I've had *that* kind of pleasure, I'll be lucky if I know where to put everything."

"Everything?" Kim, a saucy little redhead who apparently could co-author a sex manual, had asked her, laughing. "What do you think he's going to bring along?"

"Jesus, Kim," Connie had admitted while they gulped their tea during a shift changeover, "it's been ages since I've been intimate with a man and I'm scared to death. You know that. I launched into babies when the rest of the women my age were out running naked on the streets, smoking dope, and sleeping with 12 men in one night."

Kim took her hand and smiled.

"You can't even say the word 'sex,' honey," she tells Connie, her smile growing larger. "Think of what you do here, what you've seen, the conversations you've had. Your kids are teenagers and then some, for crissakes, Connie. I know you and it's pretty damn hard for me to imagine that you're so . . . virginal. That's it, so *virginal*."

Connie gasped, dropped her head and was quiet for a few seconds. Virginal, she was thinking, might exactly be the correct word to describe her. And that realization made her want to roll backwards and leap right out of the window and go hide someplace where no one would discover her deep, dark, not-so-wild sexual past.

"Kim—" Connie began, trying hard to look into her friend's eyes, but Kim interrupted her.

"Connie, you're not embarrassed? You're not *shy*?" Kim asked, more than a little shocked that the head nurse, the wild leader of her unit, the woman who would not hesitate to slap a doctor upside the head, threaten a nurses' walkout, who had personally tackled more than a handful of nutso patients, counseled gaggles of nurses and comforted two-plus decades of grieving relatives, patients and the professionals who could not save them was embarrassed about her not so sexually exciting past.

"Yes," Connie admitted, softly.

The sassy, liberated, single, 31-year-old Kim, who didn't so much date as sleep around, was obviously young enough to be Connie's daughter and that meant, in the part of Connie's mind that screamed "mother," that her own three daughters could be as sexually liberated and educated as Kim. This idea floated around right next to her embarrassment, near what she now realized must seem like the hurried realities of her introverted, limited, and terribly uneducated sex life. "I'm a nurse, for crissakes," Connie told herself. "Nurses are supposed to be physically savvy, worldly, sexually aware, a step ahead of the next societal trend, we're supposed to know things—lots of things. . . ."

Connie Franklin's first kiss was a peck on the lips when she was 17.3 years old and her first and only prom date, Hank Martinelli, who almost had to stand on his toes to reach her lips, kissed her for two seconds and then ran to his car so fast he dropped his keys, banged his head on the window, fell into the seat and let his head drop onto the horn, which was not a really good thing in her neighborhood. It was a neighborhood riddled with large men who would be perfectly happy if their daughters never dated, kissed, or touched someone of the male species at 2:15 A.M.—or ever, for that matter.

A year later—just before she met husband-to-be Roger Nixon—she had what at the time she thought was a wild evening with a guy who most likely had a name but after three shots of tequila, four beers and her first taste of marijuana there was no way in hell Connie could ever remember what it might have been. Mr. Smooth Move "let's go into the bushes," was, from what she could remember, adept at removing a blouse, a bra, one pair of cutoff shorts, a t-shirt and finally her lovely light blue cotton underwear—that honest-to-God were stitched in pink with the word *Thursday*. Connie Franklin's first total sexual encounter left her with pine needles stuck up and down her legs, bird shit in her hair, the immediate feeling that she could have handed him a tight glove and he would never have noticed the difference, and a stoned hangover that carried her from living hell to purgatory and

then back to the light of the living over the course of three
entire days.

Then came Roger Robert Nixon.

Connie Franklin was barely into her second semester of
college when Roger walked past her on the way to a math
class as part of his policeman's training program that was as-
sociated with the city of Indianapolis and then, for some
unknown reason, he stopped right in front of her, turned
sideways, looked at her and declared, "God, you are gorgeous."

That single, luscious, brilliant moment could have been
as great as half the sex she ever had in her entire life. Connie
felt her knees soften, her uterus shift, her breasts swell, her
heart stop, drop, and roll right in front of this policeman-to-
be and then her heart slowed so quickly that she felt dizzy.

Connie wanted to throw him down right there and dip
her entire body inside of his blue eyes, run her hands
through his Germanic blonde hair, and straddle him like a
racehorse until the cops showed up. Lust. It was such pure
lust and such a new sensation that Connie wondered for days
if someone hadn't slipped some kind of narcotic drug into
her Coke during her English seminar break. But when she
saw Roger two days later and he asked her if she felt the same
way as he did and he took her to his ratty apartment on their
first date, kissed her hungrily and then threw her down on
his bed—which was a piece of foam rubber that he had scavenged from behind a couch factory—she confused her lust,
her primal sexual urges, a woman's right to own the lines that
connect her mind to her breasts and to every single inch of
skin, every blood vessel, every muscle, every cavity below
her waist—for love.

And that was it.

Lust for Roger Robert Nixon.

Sort of.

There were wild nights here and there after they'd had a few bottles of wine or when one of Roger's buddies would say something like, "I took my wife to a motel this weekend and I wish we could move into the damned place. It's amazing what something like that will do to loosen up a woman." And then Roger would buy flowers, pull back the covers, and quickly forget that some of the guys told him sex could actually last for hours and hours and not just minutes and minutes.

Romance, Roger, Connie wanted to say.

Seduction, Roger, Connie wanted to say.

Foreplay, Roger, Connie wanted to say.

And she would have. Connie would have said it.

Then, of course, Connie got pregnant. Connie got pregnant three times.

"And, honest to God, Kim, that was pretty much it," she confessed in such a rush of words that Kim almost missed what she was saying. "That was *it*."

"Oh, you poor baby," Kim moaned. "That was it? Tell me you're lying. Tell me that the woman I hold up as a goddess, a woman that I revere as the model for all liberated women who do not take shit, has never really let go in the bedroom? Tell me my entire life is not a lie. Tell me, Connie. I'm begging you. Please tell me you are not my mother, who I think had sex twice, got her kids, and then sewed something very useful shut."

And Connie went on to explain, while the tea got cold and just outside their little hideaway they could hear the next shift grumbling about the full load of patients, that shit happens. Shit happens, Kim. Like you fall in lust, and then work your ass off to make it seem like love, and then life does not stop and large hunks of the lust break loose very quickly.

You have a baby and you never want a man to frigging touch you again. You have to finish school and get your nursing degree to help support the baby and then before you can even step into your new white nylons and spongy nurse shoes, you miss a period from having sex, goddamned sex, and then you work all those months while your feet swell and your mother yells at you for not quitting your job and your husband occasionally wants to get frisky and you really want to cut off his wiener with a dull hatchet. Then you get tired, Kim. You're a beautiful, young, liberated woman who lives in a different time and place and space than I did, even though the media makes it seem like every woman over the age of 50 screwed her brains out and knows how to have orgasms while brushing her teeth and wearing a jogging suit or simply breathing.

Not.

You get tired.

And then this thing happens where he slips over from wanting to bounce on you every 15 seconds to sleeping in the chair every single time he sits down, and you notice that his hair is falling out along the edges just a few inches from his big hairy eyebrows, and he doesn't move as fast and he doesn't want to play baseball any longer. He's done. He's done unless you say, "Let's go fishing." His little pee-pee has reached its peak and those three greatest peaks are now entrenched in grade school and middle school, Girl Scouts, soccer, band practice, basketball, dance classes, and birthday parties for every goddamned kid this side of the Mississippi and you do not have time to go to the bathroom let alone think of ways to have a grand romp in the hay—or the bedroom or any room at all.

And then you pick up a *Seventeen* magazine or God help you, *Cosmo*, or something your daughter leaves under her stack of unwashed clothes, and you see that your own sexual

peak could be years away and that you are supposed to be lur-
ing men into your stylish boudoir and making love as if there
is an aphrodisiac hooked to your stretched-out brassiere.

Sometimes though, Kim, you actually do feel sexy. Just
for a second or two, or maybe even an entire minute, when
you look into the mirror and you see your grandma's beautiful fine skin that will wrinkle only about 15 seconds before
you die. You see that your lovely breasts that were small in
high school have now filled out and will most likely never descend more than a few centimeters, you are a nurse who
never sits down and there is not an inch of fat on your thighs,
and when you touch your own breasts you close your eyes
and wonder what it would be like to have someone else
touch them in every damn way they can. Someone who is not
the man snoring on the chair.

"But," Kim interrupted. "There is so much stuff—books
and toys and movies. . . . You didn't do *anything*?"

"Kim, Kim, Kim, oh, the blessed innocence of the child-
less, unmarried, hot women of this decade," Connie told
her, raising her head and feeling a rising tide of missing, the
loss of something so unfamiliar to her she cannot bear to
find a name for it. "There is and was never time for that.
Thinking about sex was so low on the list I'd need bifocals
just to see it. Roger and I had sex twice the year before we divorced. Twice."

"Holy shit," Kim mumbled. "I want to cry. I just can't
imagine living without it."

Connie thought about it with John, her second date in
the eight-year span since she had divorced Roger. She liked
John. He was kind, handsome, and frisky, but he was a gentle-
man, as her mother would have said, six years older than she
was, widowed . . . and extremely impotent as she was about
to discover.

First they met for dinner at the Starlight in a suburb of Chicago where John had rented a hotel suite and decked it out with champagne, flowers, three cards placed strategically in every room, a beautiful hand-crafted gold bracelet, and every single thing that might scream romance except his very own libido.

Connie, who had not taken her clothes off in front of anyone for almost nine years but her pal O'Brien's dog, Reckless, a lively Irish setter when she dog-sat, was beyond devastated. John was humiliated. He confessed that he had tried everything including Viagra, had no idea how to sexually please her without a penis, and left Connie with his Visa card, a sobbing apology and the words, "It's not your fault."

Connie did not cry. She drank the champagne and took her fingernails, the ones she had painted a light shade of mellow red and let grow just a bit so she could run them down the sides of John's glorious back, and used them instead to dig an invisible trench around anything that even might appear or taste or smell or look or feel like lust or sex. Goddamned sex.

"I don't care anymore," she told herself for the next six hours in that hotel room, never sleeping, watching some old stupid-ass reruns, refusing to cry as she played with the bracelet that John had hooked onto her left wrist when she had walked into the bedroom after putting on a long silk robe that she knew matched her dark blue eyes. A robe that made her feel beautiful, sexy, ready to inhale every inch of John. Simply—ready to make love.

Kim could have helped her reach at least some sexual plateau but then Kim left the hospital because she was sick of cold weather, and Connie lost her sexual muse.

And then college, romantic and career crises erupted times three with Jessica, Sabrina and Macy.

And then Roger got remarried.

And then Connie got promoted.

And then the years stumbled over themselves.

They stumbled into what Connie would eventually tell her granddaughter was a "quiet pause of personal and physical reflection" and then laugh and say honestly that she had yet to discover a piece of herself, a buried third arm, her own natural and glorious yearning for sexual pleasure and release that every woman deserves.

Connie, the smart, sassy, attractive divorced woman from Cyprus, Indiana, who should have known better, who could have talked to a hundred friends, fifty professionals, her own educated and sometimes—at least before they were married—promiscuous daughters, her best friend Frannie O'Brien, and any high school or college girl/woman within a fifty mile radius—did not.

She did not.

Connie Franklin Nixon, the daughter of a hardworking carpenter and a grade-school secretary, a woman who could seize the reins of her own life in almost every imaginable arena, rolled over that night in the suburban Chicago hotel that had a sweeping view of a city that she loved, and she gave up.

And she never told a damn soul.

Not one.

Until this moment on the highway with her daughter quietly crying behind her hands, the heat from the southern landscape rising between them, and a confession like nothing she ever imagined when she wrote down #7 on her list of dreams.

thirteen

1. Stop being afraid. (Here we go again.)

29. Look at yourself naked—physically and psychologically and spiritually. Figure out how to salute what you might see. Shit—this has been on the list, I think, since it started.

14. FORGET IT—I CANNOT EVEN WRITE THIS ONE ON A SLIP OF PAPER RIGHT NOW.

The scent of water—fleshy, rich and hot—is a dark wave of narcotic sensuality that washes over Connie Franklin Nixon the moment she drifts off the blazing hot spring Louisiana freeway with her boyfriend of two days, Commissioner Michael Dennis.

Connie is riding in a blue convertible with the Burt Reynolds twin. Her hair is too short to blow in the wind but she can feel its recently dyed edges dance just a little like a baby ballerina's. She's listening to Michael's life story while she keeps peeking into the side mirror to make certain she's alive and hasn't been stabbed to death by her daughter who is convinced her mother is just this side of nuts to be heading out to a swamp with a man who lured them to the Deep South because he is afraid of a political institution he's trying to bust like a wild teenager from a country farm.

Michael is taking her to the bayou, his bayou. He closes his eyes when he says the word "bayou" as if he's just had a sip of the most exquisite Scotch ever produced this side of heaven. "I was raised in the backwater," he told her. "My God, Connie, it's a treasure chest of life and love that few people ever get to see or experience." He's showing her the other side of New Orleans, he says, the one that stretches and meanders and saunters its way for hundreds and hundreds of miles through parts of Louisiana that have yet to see the bottom of a human foot and he's so sincere and real and interested in her that Connie wants to throw him down and rip off his shirt every single time she looks at him.

Connie has no idea what to do with the rebirth of this feeling, with the easy way she said "yes" when Michael asked her if she wanted to see his world, and with the tentative— make that malicious—manner in which her daughter has reacted to the fact that her mother may have anything beyond maternal instincts, feelings, urges and drives.

The newly launched relationship with Jessica has hit a brick wall, so Connie has decided to walk around the wall and let it rest, at least for one day. The temptation of Burt and a swamp was too much, too delicious, too intoxicating to ignore and even that astounds Connie. "What is happening to me?" she keeps asking herself.

"Some people think I'm a slick shyster," the commissioner had explained in the parking lot of the manufacturing plant as he tried to convince her to head south with him for just part of a day so he could show her his boyhood neighborhood—a place, he explained, where the simple magic of basic survival blended with a bit of wildlife, a touch of swamp-water moonshine, and an uncle who had a singing voice that sounded like heaven.

Connie had imagined for about 2.3 seconds what it might be like to be back home in Cyprus—simply fingering her list of dreams and not actually doing anything about it. She'd be packing boxes, watching 19 more movies, calling out for a veggie pizza with extra green olives, taking 10 more calls from the nurses who missed her, and then driving her car to the sandy ledge of her favorite Lake Michigan cliff for the 200th goddamn time—and she said, "Yes, Commissioner, sir," with barely a breath to separate those three words.

But then there is the first drink before noon. Way, way before noon.

"Maybe I am nuts," she tells herself as Michael pulls into a small parking lot at a place that has a huge sign about as big as an operating room in Indiana that says FROZEN DRINKS.

"Connie, I want you to stay calm now, but this is a part of New Orleans just as much as Bourbon Street and those gators we're about to see," Michael tells her. "My mama raised a polite boy and don't think I am trying to get you liquored up so I can take advantage of your sweet northern naïveté, darlin', but this is a drive-thru daiquiri store and you have to experience this."

"You pig," Connie says, laughing. "Drive-thru drinks? Drinks with booze? Does this have anything to do with that lively tour yesterday?" And then she remembers where she is, what it took to get her there and how being in the car with an almost unknown man, a daughter waiting to tear her into shreds, and a list that has suddenly gone from one number to another way too fast, and she turns to Michael and says, "Get me a large, please."

Michael laughs so loud and long that Connie wonders if she should drive or get out to make certain he is okay. And just the mere mention of the tour of the factory makes her start laughing, too, so that they are both doubled over and look as if they are sick.

The tour was a blessed event that took them through the research department, to the moldings wing, and out into the heart of the factory where men and women worked to build and mold and then probably pray over the vibrators, dildos, plugs, and an assortment of attachments that would eventually make their way to the Diva warehouse and then to the store in New York City. The tour, directed by Justin and assisted by one Jessica Franklin Nixon, was a serious affair that pretty much launched the bayou rendezvous of two middle-aged people, both divorced grandparents who had at one point in their lives thought they had seen and done everything—but that was before what they were now calling the DT—dildo tour.

"My favorite part of the DT was when Justin held up The Cowgirl and proudly explained that it was a Diva signature product designed exclusively for my daughter's company and that she had an entire line in the works to honor every wonderful profession occupied by women," Connie recalled as she and Michael sipped their slushy, sugar-filled drinks out of cups the size of bird feeders. "Michael, I'm a nurse for God's sake and I've seen just about, let me repeat that, *just about* everything. But this, this tour with you and my daughter and Justin and all those, those—"

"Sex toys, darlin'," Michael said, interrupting her with

what Connie thinks is a sexy southern twang. "They are sex toys. Don't be afraid to say it."

"You kill me, Michael," Connie says, laughing. "You absolutely kill me. You know we thought you were going to be a royal asshole. And here we are boozing it up on the way to the bayou."

At first Connie could not explain her attraction to Michael, beyond the immediate physical pull she felt from seeing any handsome man. The way he touched her arm, paid attention to her, the way he smelled, and what he wore, and even the damn way he talked made her want to stand next to him and pant. Had this ever happened before? Had she ever before let herself feel this way? Could she jump over the vicious looks of her daughter and just have a day with a handsome man who made her feel rich, attractive—and almost beautiful, sweet and fine?

The answer came following a very long conversation, while she and Michael leaned against boxes in the storage room and Jessica and Justin, a seemingly perfect anal and business-minded couple, discussed shipping procedures, labeling, and the glorious differences in communications systems, hiring procedures, and the future of independent and risqué enterprise.

The facts in Connie's mind were hard to ignore. Commissioner Michael Dennis is nice, she told herself—working hard, she will eventually admit, so he can usher her off to some backwater wonderland. He's damn nice. He's witty, funny, and fierce in his love for this land where his roots are so deep that they meet the rising tides at the end of the Mississippi. He meant no harm, he told her, in giving her daughter such a difficult time with the factory.

His first wife had left him for another man 22 years

before. He left his second after she took to tending bar at one of their restaurants, fell in love with Jack Daniels, Ms. Smirnoff and Bloody Mary, and refused his offers, his pleadings, his cries that she admit herself to one of the best treatment centers in the country. He has two kids, both adults now with their own babies, but he raised them and was glowingly proud of their successes. Overwhelmed by his honesty, Connie said, yes, yes, Michael, show me the swamps and let's have us a day.

Before that happened, however, Connie had to endure a fight with lovely Jessica. Alas, she'd thought Jessica would be jubilant about the dildo production victory, the news that her breakthrough products were about to be released from captivity in Louisiana and sent out to the willing and waiting masses, the oh-so-very-tiny interruption of her mighty Diva development plan, the nice commissioner, but she leapt off the other side of the bridge instead and wailed about the injustice of politics that was a tarnished blade of the past. A man who played a game she refused to play. A county that allowed her to make her dildos but also made her want to vomit.

"Shut up," Connie finally told Jessica as they parked the car and walked into their hotel and Connie found herself wondering how in the hell this raging creature had come out of her. "The world is not some book you read in school, sweetheart. You want to exist and survive and flourish, then sometimes you have to play the game the way the guy in charge says you play the game."

Jessica, spunky and not so forgiving, retorted that she wanted to make her own rules and play her own game. Their conversation lingered and rose and fell over dinner at a restaurant just two blocks away that made Connie's heart swell because the food tasted as exquisite as the restaurant looked. Everything hot. Everything spicy. Everything fun. Not that she could actually enjoy it with Jessica breathing down her neck like the heat in a bottle of voodoo hot sauce.

"And running off to the swamp with this guy, Mother," Jessica scolded, dipping her head while she looked at the two shrimp that were left on her plate. "I never thought you'd do something like this. I just don't get it."

Connie paused. She looked at the long part that ran all the way from the front of her daughter's blonde head to the back and realized that she had most likely created the permanent line because she had kept Jessica's hair parted and in braids for most of the first 11 years of her life. *So much of what I did, what you saw, is who you are now,* Connie thought before she said anything. *"Like mother, like daughter" is very true.*

"You poor thing," she said instead.

Jessica looked up at her with wide eyes and a stunned expression. "Don't you think it's possible that we barely know each other, Jessica?" Connie asked, instead of launching into some long discussion about childhood angst, religion-induced guilt, and the backwards glances everyone seems to make to determine if a decision, a thought, a gesture, a way of life had really been the correct path to choose. There was not, Connie decided, enough time or wine to handle *that* particular long discussion in one short evening.

"You're my mother, of course I know who you are," Jessica acknowledged, pushing back in her chair as if she was ready to jump up and launch into a physical fight at the very mention of one wrong word.

"Oh, Jessica," Connie sighed, exhausted from trying to hold back. "Are you ten years old? I'm not *just* your mother. I am a woman, a friend, I've been someone's lover, I'm a nurse, and—dammit—I'm starting the rest of my damn life."

Jessica gaped at her as if she had just announced she was

going to have a sex-change operation in the middle of the
restaurant right after dessert.

"I'm just going to spend part of a day with a nice man,"
Connie said, backing off from a deep and very passionate desire to whack her oldest daughter upside the head in what
would be the girl's first physical assault of her life from her
mother. "Let's just call it living. I'm *living*, Jessica."

"Mom, you are a dreamer," Jessica said, looking disgusted.

Oh, baby, if you only knew, Connie said to herself, thinking
about her list of dreams, the years she saw spanned out in
front of her like Tarot cards, like the choice of direction she
had come to know that even uptight little Jessica Franklin
Nixon had made in her own life. And she began wondering
what Jessica's list of dreams might contain—soft strains of
hope and laughter? Or the pull of regret, of reconciliation,
of yearning?

The women called a truce after that because Connie was
afraid she truly might flip out and because Jessica was exhausted from what was obviously her second passion in life
these days—worrying—and together they walked back through
the terribly lively streets and to the hotel with Connie managing to say, "Tomorrow night we are going out—I mean
REALLY going out—so get your work done and when I get
back from the swamp you and I are going to see the French
Quarter. I am not going to sleep here without exploring
every street. So don't lift any heavy sex toys or you will be
too tired in the morning."

That was, Connie was thinking as Michael pulled out of
the liquor barn with a Jamaican Red slushy in one hand and
drove back onto the state highway, if she ever came home
from the swamp. . . .

The morning drink buzzed through Connie's veins as if she had inhaled an illegal substance. Michael reassured her that he could handle the convertible, drink slowly, and get them to the swamp safely. "I've been doing this since I was 14 years old," he said, smiling, and with total confidence. Connie believed him. She knew she would believe anything he told her. "The car flies." *Great.* "We are never coming out of the bayou." *Terrific.* "Sixteen swamp rats will meet us with torches and take us to an underground cavern that leads to a magic kingdom." *Sign me up.*

Instead, they drive south for three more miles and then Michael turns off the road at some invisible marker with such swift movements, never spilling a drop of his Jamaican Red, that Connie thinks the car must know the way or this man has been down this particular gravel road more than a few times.

"There's bumps and a few potholes for the next ten or so miles," he warns her, gliding through a dip in the road like a professional dirt bike rider.

"*Ten* or so?" Connie asks. "Won't we hit the ocean or something before then?"

"God, you are fun, Connie." Michael beams. "The world from here on in is going to be damp and very lively."

"How lively?"

"Well, sometimes I have to pull over and let a gator pass or someone trying to get home for dinner barreling through at about 60 on this gravel gut-wrencher, or—"

"Stop!" Connie yells as they take a rough corner and a grove of huge oaks sprouting from swamp water appears inches from the side of the rocky road. "Just let me get out and *smell*. Turn off the car."

Michael obliges. He moves the car off the edge of the

road in case someone really does come roaring up behind them, but the instant they get out of the car they are over-whelmed with silence. In the distance Connie can hear birds speaking to each other in their secret ornithology language and the fast-fading ricochet of a truck speeding miles away on the highway. The sun caresses her arms and face and the perfume of the swamps, an earthy wet soil laced with a multitude of sweet smells—late-blooming spring flowers, she assumes—is utterly intoxicating.

Michael says nothing but he is watching her. He knows where Connie comes from. He knows the flat, wooded forestlands of the Midwest have their own charm and the magnificent sky over Lake Michigan is breathtakingly beau-tiful, but the commissioner also knows that an introduction into this world, extreme, seemingly dangerous, and so for-eign to someone who lives mostly with concrete under her feet, can be a charming or a deafening interlude. Watching Connie's face as it moves from the sky to trees and back around again makes him smile.

"I love to bring people in here," he tells her, speaking softly so he doesn't break the spell.

"Bring a lotta women here, do you?"

"I wish," he replies, laughing. "I actually cancelled about 45 meetings and postponed two major appointments to bring you down here. You're good people, Connie Nixon, and the last person I expected to see on a DT in the middle of Louisiana. I also happen to think you are beautiful."

Nurse Nixon cannot respond. The last time she felt at-tractive was so long ago she sees a hazy image of a young medium-sized woman in tight shorts with hair down to her shoulders, firm breasts, flesh unrippled by time and turbu-lence, and a smile as innocent as Christmas on her face.

And then she looks at the man seated beside her and she

smiles without speaking because what he has just told her—
that she is beautiful—must settle deep and firm inside of her
before she truly believes it. It must lodge itself in between
her last two dates, a marriage that was beyond bland, and the
closely held notion that no one would ever want her, touch
her, make her heart beat like this, goddamn it, just like this,
ever again for the rest of her life. And also because she might
not let him.

And so Connie freezes the moment, the way he looks,
the damp, rich smell of the swampy world around her, so that
she can digest it in her own time, and then she leans over to
touch Michael's hand in that magic spot where she can control him and just maybe the entire world for one more astonishingly beautiful moment.

Connie stretches out on the car hood beside him and
they begin talking about the land, how Michael traveled
back and forth to his grandparents' bayou home on a regular
basis from Wisconsin, where his parents lived, and how he always felt lucky to live in this place. Connie will remember
these 30 minutes parked on the side of the gravel road as a
moment suspended in time.

"My mother was a nice German girl from Milwaukee
who met my father just after the Second World War, when
he was deployed out of the Great Lakes Naval station in
Illinois," explains Michael. "My dad was a Louisiana boy
through and through, raised right down at the end of this
gravel road, who knew every inch of this country better than
anyone."

Connie thinks about chance as the commissioner tells
her about his grandparents, both now deceased, and about
his parents, who shared the rich history of their French
Canadian past as their ancestors were forced from their
homes in the mid-1700s for practicing their Catholic faith.

Many of them settled in the south Louisiana swamps and bayous where they could live as they wanted to live. "And they did it with gusto," Michael tells her, blending their French dialect with the country and its resources they came to claim as their own.

"Their persecuted past, being forced to leave their homes and wander up and down the East Coast all those years, gave them a reason to celebrate in ways that perhaps others find a bit much, but no one enjoys life like the people in southern Louisiana," he tells Connie as clouds bump and roll overhead, revealing a sky the color of the ocean Connie swears she can smell from the car. "Cajuns have a rule about working hard and playing hard and we are all very good at it."

In the moments of silence, when memories of his family stir themselves to the surface of his mind, Connie imagines Michael's mother brushing her shoulder against his wild and happy father at the bus terminal on his way to Chicago and how one glance changed both of their lives forever.

"I suppose," she says slowly, "we all need to take more chances. I was a breath away from saying, 'Hell, no, I'm not going into the swamp with a guy who looks like a movie star and who is king of Louisiana's dildo production,' but here I am and look what I might have missed."

"Just wait," he tells her, swinging off the car and motioning for her to hurry up and get back inside.

The end of the road is a good ten miles away and when they come to a clearing, pass several wooden houses and edge out along a river that Michael tells her is part of the bayou, they veer off onto yet another dirt road that seems to loop along the very edge of the bayou, which to Connie looks pretty much like a wide river. They stop at the first house, a one-story wooden structure, that appears as if it is tended by someone who cares for it with a toothpick and toothbrush. It is immaculate, with a long garden stretching out to the left side, paths off of either end, and a wide porch the entire length of the house that sits almost directly at the edge of the water.

Connie raises her hand to her heart, just like in the movies, and tells Michael it is beyond charming.

"My father still lives here," he tells her as they walk around the side of the house, and Connie smells something that makes her mouth water. "I bought the house when my grandparents died. And then when my mother died, my dad moved back out here and I spend as much time with him here as I can," he confesses as he pushes open the door and they enter the simple cottage.

"In here," someone bellows from a direction that takes Connie closer to the glorious smell which she is about to discover is the famous Dennis gumbo, bubbling on the stove in a kitchen that looks as if it has come right out of a page in a 1933 *Good Housekeeping* magazine. A giant white porcelain wood stove is glowing in the center of the back wall, wooden cabinets painted in bright blues and greens line every wall, and, just like at her grandma's house, a huge wooden table that appears as if it was once dragged behind a covered wagon is the centerpiece of the room. Nicks and dents and slash marks instantly label it as a survivor of countless fine meals.

"Come here and hug me, young woman," Michael's father orders. "I have to keep stirring or these little crayfish buggers will swim right out of here. They call me Baboo. Long story having to do with children not being able to say Robert when I was growing up and now I'm Grandpa Baboo to every alligator this side of the Mississippi. Welcome, Miss Connie. You are definitely keeping bad company today."

Baboo talks nonstop, and with a hint of the French accent

that pervaded his life as a youngster but has been washed away by his years of living and working in the Midwest. He is beyond adorable and he shoos them back out the door and to the dock before Connie can say more than a polite, "Thank you."

And the bayou is stunning.

Michael sits at the back of the flat-bottom boat, a duck boat she tells him is what they'd call it on the Indiana lakes, and they curve past a cluster of houses with porches that hang over the water. Ramshackle by some standards, Connie can see that they are brimming with the kind of life Michael has described to her. Fishing poles and old grills fill every porch and every cottage comes with what seems to be a requisite junk pile so that anything can be fixed at a moment's notice. A few men whistle to Michael, who whistles back, and one holds up a catfish longer than Connie's thigh and says, *"Joie de vivre,"* which Michael quickly translates for her as "joy of life" and Connie totally agrees.

On the way back through the bayou, after showing Connie the backside of elephant ear plants, turtles sunbathing on every log, an owl sleeping behind an enormous oak, numerous jumping fish, three alligators—one that Michael touches affectionately and calls Jessie—and an expanse of trees so thick it looks like midnight, he orders her to simply breathe during the 45-minute ride back to his father's home. No speaking. No sudden movements. Feel the wind in your hair, he tells her. The rush of warm air against your face. The scent of a peoples' journey still as vibrant and real as the water you can feel snaking off the sides of the boat. Just *be*, Connie. Whatever it was, whatever it might have been, whatever it is, just shove it away and feel this part of life and the world.

"This is a patient and kind place," he tells her, skimming

the boat across water that is already warmer than any July lake in Indiana. "People think it is wild and rough and frightening down all these passageways, but it is beautiful and rich. Like anything, it is what you make of it."

Connie tries hard. She thinks about #29 on her list. She shuts her eyes and lets go of Jessica and of the cell phone she'd left at the bottom of her purse in the car. She lets go of her real-estate agent and her fear of strange men who look like movie stars. She lets go of her doubts about what kind of mother she has been, what kind of friend she could be now, what kind of trouble she is already creating for the legions of friends and family members who at this moment think she is on a quiet, motherly New York visit. She tries hard to let go of every dying patient, every asshole doctor, every mean weirdo who has pushed up against her life for years and years. And she feels the ancient hand of a French woman touch her face and when she quickly opens her eyes she sees that Michael has steered the boat under a low tree and a small leaf has brushed against her cheek. Connie Franklin Nixon thinks about letting go of her fear of lost love, missed chances, lust and love. She imagines herself sliding across the top of the water just as the boat is doing, just as Michael is doing, and just as she would really love to do.

But then she can't help herself.

"Michael, do you ever think of your mistakes?"

"All the time."

"Does this help?"

"All the time."

"Are you happy?"

"Right now I am terribly happy."

"What would you change?"

He hesitates and pulls the boat against the side of the wooden steps leading up to his father's house. Connie waits for his answer as he turns, ties up the boat, holds out his closed hand, and then, without speaking, opens it as if to ask her to sit on a bench that faces the water.

"Beer?" he asks as he dips his hand under the dock and finds some hidden liquid jackpot there. The family treasure chest.

"Yes," she says, her heart throbbing from the ride, the air, and the stretch of time while she waits for his reply to her question. *What would you change?*

He sits next to her on the bench with both hands clasping the brown bottle as if it is holding him in place.

"I have so much," he finally says. "I lost a lot, made mistakes, the kids are terrific, but, Connie—the truth is I'm lonely. And lately I wonder if I will ever fall in love again. I'd love a life with someone, but only if it's full of passion. I love what I do but I miss . . . well, I miss *passion*."

"Are you proposing?"

Michael laughs so hard she has to reach over to steady the bottle that nearly falls out of his hands.

"Wouldn't it be hilarious to just get married and then go back and tell your daughter and my kids what we did?"

"Michael," Connie responds, laughing, and then imagining it for just a second in her own mind. Jessica flipping out. O'Brien trying to have her committed on the spot. Sabrina and Macy sobbing in their husbands' arms. Dogs barking wildly across the United States. Spinsters weeping into their napkins. Men standing on porch steps with their shotguns balanced on their hips. "This is the most wonderful and insane few hours I've had in a long time. You—Well, I've never met a man who is as honest as you are this fast."

"What do you mean?"

"Oh, Christ, Michael, most of this stuff is a game. People talk and flirt and move the chess pieces of their life into places where they think they can win and unless I am a total ass you are simply sharing this wonderful day with me, and sharing your heart, too, and you've totally taken me by surprise," Connie admits, fingering her own bottle. "I'm not used to it. I gave up on men quite a while ago."

"Well, maybe we should date for a while then before we get married."

Connie slugs him and then, without any warning, Michael leans over, grabs the back of Connie's very short hair, and he kisses her.

Commissioner Michael Dennis tastes like salt and heat and like a fast wave of life. His Burt Reynolds moustache dances against her lip and Connie instinctively moves her arm around his neck, tilts her head, and moves against him so that her neck slides against his and their hips touch. Then her breath takes a nosedive into the far bank of the bayou and it is as if a soft hand has reached inside of her and pulled out something old and hard, something that has been hidden for a very long time in a place much deeper and darker than any bayou.

It is a very long kiss that costs them both an entire beer as the bottles drop onto the pier and then roll into the bayou where they sway like happy dancers until the soft currents of that south Louisiana waterland carry them towards the center.

The center, as Connie Franklin Nixon liked to tell her recovering patients before she retired, is a very fine place to be, because from there you can see both sides and select the best way home.

Fourteen

7. Recapture Jessica. Find Jessica. Hurry, Connie, but start slowly. Find your baby.

7½. Open your heart wider, Connie. New Orleans is a chance. It may be now or never. Do not let her get away again.

Music not so much drifting as slamming into the hotel room jolts Jessica awake, as if someone has jumped on top of her face and is blowing a whistle in her right ear. She is drooling, too, and this does not please her. She rolls to one side, feels an ache wind its way across her hips and down her left leg from lifting boxes, pulling plastic sheeting out of huge packages, and bending over long tables with drafting designs stuck to them as Justin explained what he laughingly called "the ins and outs" of sex toy development.

Jessica turned to him once during his discussion that included angles, lengths, widths, and surface bumps, and left her body for a brief moment. Justin, from that position, was just a nice-looking guy in faded jeans, a polo shirt, slip-on loafers without socks, a fine black leather belt with a small silver buckle and a simple silver watch on his left wrist. He wore a tiny gold band on the same hand and Jessica imagined that he was married, had two young daughters who had no clue what their father made for a living and a wife who had left a lucrative position as an advertising executive to marry him and raise their two children so they would not have to go into daycare.

Justin caught her looking at him and turned sideways to smile at her.

"Are you looking at my ass?"

"What?" Jessica exclaimed, startled and embarrassed because that is exactly what she was doing.

He laughed and straightened up, resting his hands on the drafting table, and told her that he wondered if anyone ever looked at his ass anymore.

"I work too much, don't get out very often, and I think the last time I had a date was more than a year ago," he told her. "How about you, Jessica? I bet your life is the same. You seem a bit possessed."

Jessica, in fact, could not remember the last time she'd had an intimate conversation with a man, or anyone besides her mother or Geneva, let alone a real date. She wanted to tell Justin that he did indeed have a nice ass but she could not bring herself to do it and so, within two minutes, she had steered the conversation back to business, which confirmed every single thing Justin thought about her.

She did let him drive her back to the hotel, left a message for her mother that she didn't need a ride, and then he asked if she wanted to have a drink or go out for dinner.

"I promised my mother a wild night in the French Quarter," she lied, because it was her mother who had promised her the wild night. "And we have to leave in the morning to get back to New York."

"Sounds like an all-nighter to me," Justin said as he pulled up in front of her hotel. "They have a terrific bar in here. I'm going to park and make you have one drink with me."

Jessica tried to stop him but he parked anyway, took her arm, let her stop at the restroom, and then paraded her into the bar where they had more than one drink and a really good time. And during the 90 minutes they spent together they mostly talked about everything *but* the production of sex toys, which made Jessica more nervous than discussing whips, crotchless panties, sensuous massage oil and implements that come with or without batteries.

Thus the semi-drunken nap on the bed that was induced by three glasses of wine, a polite handshake from Justin, who said he would really—with an emphasis on the word *really*—look forward to her next trip to Louisiana.

Jessica spun into the room, fell on the bed, and before a clear thought could pace itself through her mind she fell dead asleep.

And then the band arrived.

"Shit," she complains, rising with a raging thirst. "What in the hell is that?"

That, she discovers, is a band of six, walking itself down the street in front of the room. It might have been hired specially to announce the arrival of her mother, who flies through the door with a touch of sunburn on her nose and cheeks and a fine glow in her eyes that startles Jessica.

"Mother, it's almost 7 P.M. and I was getting worried," Jessica lies.

"My good gawd," Connie drawls as if she has a southern accent all her own. "I had the most remarkable day and we talked so long that I ended up going to a committee meeting with him and we got your message late because I had my cell phone off and so we went back—"

"Stop!" Jessica shouts, putting her hands up. "Food. I have not eaten in hours and I had a few drinks with Justin."

Connie wants to jump and clap her hands at the same time over Jessica's news but, instead, she washes her face, looks in the mirror, as if she is 14 and has just had her first kiss from some short bozo on the playground, to see if she looks different, and then takes a moment to calm her fast-beating heart and change out of her shorts.

When her slips of paper fall out of the shorts pocket, her morning list of dream notes, Connie thinks about how easy it would be now to lose her way. How easy to run off with the first man she kisses, how easy to forget about the most compelling, the most important number on the list. Jessica. Number seven. Connie pulls on some slacks and leans into the mirror again and quickly adds 7½ to her list. She writes it with her mind, pins it to the top of her heart and makes certain that it sticks. This is a big night. A possible last chance. Connie looks into her own eyes one more time, takes in a huge breath, and softly says, "*Yes.*"

Then she hustles her oldest daughter out of the room and towards the restaurant Michael recommended.

And what a recommendation it is.

Seafood that fairly dances as it is eaten, thick homemade buttermilk rolls, a martini that seems to sing a soft jazz tune as it goes down her throat, and then another, as Jessica surprises her mother and orders a bottle of very expensive wine and they compare notes about the day. They launch into a conversation that both of them will wish for the rest of their lives they had captured on tape and film and audio and with someone who was a color-crayon artist, if such a person existed.

It starts with the kiss.

"I kissed Michael," Connie whispers across the top of a blue-cheese–stuffed olive.

"What the hell?" Jessica whispers back across her own olive. "Mom?"

Connie closes her eyes, smiles, and says, "Oh, Jessica, it's been so long, so very long since I felt, well, sexual, alive, attracted to something besides getting home early when I worked second shift."

"Look, Mom, I've had three glasses of Chablis, one and a half martinis, and there's a bottle of Burgundy in front of me," Jessica said. "I may need to drink everything in sight to complete this conversation."

Connie takes a sip and reaches out to put her hand over the top of Jessica's hand that is resting with her fingertips on the bottom of her glass. She can feel the early weight of the drinks tiptoeing through her own blood, accelerated perhaps by her own astonishing afternoon. It is now or never and Connie is feeling suddenly more powerful than she usually does and is in no mood to accept the word "never." She wants Jessica in her life, wants to be a part of Jessica's life, wants to cross that rare bridge between a mother and daughter that allows them to be friends in a way that demands openness, spontaneity, and a soulful connection going way beyond weighty familial boundaries.

"Listen, kiddo," she says, pushing away her plate and pouring them each another glass of wine. "Why should it be so hard to talk about physical emotions with your mother? I never once shied away from talking about sex with you, and I admit that my own sex life sucked."

"It's hard to think of a mother that way, " Jessica admits. "It's also . . . easy to assume things," she concludes uncomfortably.

"Well, shit, honey, think about it. Your father made three babies and fished. I worked and most of what I learned was from my girlfriends at Girl Scout camp, and later from reading *Our Bodies, Ourselves*," Connie explains. "The sexual revolution still has not caught up with me, baby, and I'm beginning to think that truly sucks."

Jessica smiles and squeezes her mother's hand. She leans in just a bit, closes her eyes, shakes away thoughts of her mother tucking her into bed, reading to her the week she got the flu, grounding her for climbing in the bedroom window way past curfew one too many times. When she clears as much as she can away from her memory bank, she opens her eyes again and looks at a woman named Connie. Not her mother, but Connie Franklin Nixon.

"I'm so sorry," Jessica says with such sadness in her voice that Connie's breath catches in her throat. "It's hard, even if you are my age, to think of your mother as a sexual being."

"But isn't that what your business is all about?"

Jessica pauses. She's teetering on the same brink of uncertainty that her mother has been balancing on since she wrote the invisible number seven-and-a-half on her list and, for a second, before she answers her mother, she thinks about how hard and painful holding back has been. She thinks about the times she wanted to pick up the phone and call her mother, the hours she wondered what her mother would think, how Jessica would fail her again and how goddamn much she has missed so many parts of their early relationship.

Jessica finishes her second martini, moves on to the wine, and tells Connie something bold, something she has wanted to say for days, something she knows she must say before she too can move forward.

"Mom, I so want to be over this. I so want to forgive you, forgive myself, and have you be a part of my life in all the ways you have not been a part of my life," Jessica says. She's running her words together because if she stops she may lose courage. "I've missed you, Mom. And there have been a hundred times when I knew you could help me, help the business, be a part of my life, and I just could not do it."

She goes on like a rocket. Recounting the boyfriends, the weekend in the cabin with Romney Switala, the months of sexual fulfillment, her inability to open her heart, her last date, and the tremendous idea to merge her passion for business with the notion that women must claim their sexual selves and do it every possible way and with the help of 100 Diva's, if that's what it takes.

Throughout the telling Connie does not blink, move her fingers off the table, lower her eyes, or think at any moment that she is going to have a heart attack. She does think that she is in the midst of one of the most remarkable moments of her life.

"Do you hate me, Mom? For all the secrets I've kept from you?"

"I'm Connie now, remember. Your mom is home baking bread and cinching up her chastity belt."

"It's a bit much, even for a hipster like you," Jessica reminds her.

Connie is quiet for a second and decides that it really is now or never. She moves her hand to her heart, touches the very sacred place where she has placed number seven point five, and then she slowly peels back the layers of what lies below it, all the sections of her own heart, every inch.

"It's not a bit much and your honesty right now is the greatest gift you have ever given me, Jessica," Connie tells her daughter. "I cannot tell you how I have grieved over our relationship, how I have replayed our arguments, how I wish I could go back and change who we were, how we acted, what our lives were like."

Jessica has occasionally imagined this conversation and to suddenly be in the middle of it is a breathtaking pause of reality. Her mother is rambling through her life, pushing through a wide barrier that has been held up by both of them, and is detailing her own version of why Diva's is so necessary.

First the drunken guy at the party and the sad news that sex, a generation prior to Jessica's generation, that generation which was on the cusp of the great sexual revolution, was not as widespread as some 30-somethings like to think.

"We learned most of what we knew from each other at slumber parties, from library books, and from a few consciousness-raising meetings we may have drifted into in between home economics and babysitting," Connie explains. "Imagine my life after that—three kids coming out of me like rockets—and your father fishing and working every possible shift and where do you think the sexual revolution ended up on my priority list?"

"I never thought about it, Mom," Jessica admits. "I never thought of you as a sexual person, as someone who sacrificed so much."

"It is what a mother does," Connie tells her.

"Do you have any idea how many of us there are, honey?" Connie whispers. "How many women have made babies and run businesses and saved lives and changed the world and who have not yet been sexually fulfilled? You

think you know but I'm telling you there could be a Diva
store on every corner and there still wouldn't be enough
equipment to make us all happy."

Jessica has wine in her mouth and she cannot swallow it.
She cannot move.

"Jesus, Jessica, I have no idea what I was selling in your
store," Connie admits. "I didn't know but I did know that I
loved handing one of those things to another woman and
knowing that she is going to become very happy because of
what she just purchased from me and it's made me think,
well, about a lot of things."

And then, she says, Burt Reynolds came out of nowhere.

"Christ, Jessica, in the past few days my life has been
flipped over and rotated as if I was a car getting an overhaul,"
Connie tells her daughter, filling their glasses again. "Coming
to find you, having a man tell me I turn him on, kissing like
I have not kissed in so long it's a wonder I didn't fall off
the pier."

"He kissed you on the pier?"

"For starters."

"*Mother.*"

The two women laugh. They acknowledge that coming
to this moment has taken more than enough time. The sharing has created a mutual wave of forgiveness that feels like
baptism, a beginning, the chance to have what both Jessica
and Connie want. And there is the gentle shifting of something felt but not seen, the pages of Connie's Sunday list
of dreams changing course, turning in a new direction, blazing a new trail of unexpected chance, change, and discovery.

"We all think we know things about each other and life
and we surely don't know it all," Connie tells Jessica. "I sure
as hell have a lot to learn, especially about sex toys, dreams,
and taking new chances."

Finally Connie turns back into a mother and tells Jessica that she has been a pain in the ass to be around. Stuffy, too businesslike, afraid to let her heart lean out of the top of her dress—it's as if she's missing dessert every frigging day of the year.

"You are the one who should be out on the pier kissing the boys," Connie suggests. "Honey, maybe you are really not interested in boys. It seems to me that a good portion of the women who come into your store are lesbians. Have you given this idea some thought? Have you ever thought about tracking down Romney?"

"Jesus, Mother, why don't you just hit me over the head with a bag of rocks?"

"Listen, as long as we are getting crocked and baring it all, I'm just going to say exactly what I want to say."

"Like that's something new."

"Ouch," Connie mumbles. "Actually, I've pretty much bitten a hole in my lip, not just during the past two days, but way before that, if you really want to know the truth."

For just a second Jessica imagines what it would be like to create a war zone inside the fancy restaurant and slide backwards—again. She would grab one table, tip it over and hide behind it while her mother runs to another table, drops it on its end and then starts hurling glasses and dishes at her, and long rambling insults as well.

Jessica can't help it: she laughs.

"What the hell is so funny?"

"We are," Jessica sputters. "We're talking about sex, lies, shattered dreams, dreams in motion, and I just suddenly want to giggle. We don't have to fight anymore, Mom. You're right. I am an uptight, asexual bitch who sometimes hides behind her own sex toys because she is terrified."

"Terrified? Of what?"

"I'm not even sure. Commitment. Finding out the truth about my own sexual orientation, giving it up to another man who has no idea how to make love to a woman. It's as if I am on some kind of mission to save all the women of the world and the entire time I'm drowning myself."

Oh, baby, Connie thinks. *My poor, poor baby.* Connie forgives Jessica then. She forgives her for being an ass, for not telling her about her dreams, for slipping away to hide behind her business desk, for shadowing the life her mother showed her as Connie waltzed through her own celibate days and nights.

Connie pushes back her chair, stands up, and walks over to put her hands on her daughter's shoulders.

"Get up and hug me," she orders.

"Okay, Mom," Jessica says, surrendering. "My white flag is up. I'm all yours. Save me, please save me."

And Connie whispers into Jessica's ear that salvation comes from within. Giddy with delight, with the waves of burning grace from her own salvation, she quietly explains to her oldest daughter that her personal penance surely must now include a *very* wild night in the French Quarter.

Jessica kisses her mother on the lips, finishes her drink, and the penance begins.

Saffine has the premier spot in the read-your-palm, tell-your-fortune section of the French Quarter. He/she has set up shop near St. Louis Cathedral at the edge of a gorgeous wrought-iron fence and just in front of a bar where Connie and her daughter, who is now acting like Boom-Boom Nixon and flirting like mad with men, women, and stray dogs, have purchased a couple of New Orleans Hurricanes to go as they wander throughout the Quarter totally seduced by their dinner conversation, the charm of a city gone wild, and a night that is warm, sultry, and sensuous.

Actually, everything is sensuous to Nurse Nixon and her totally uninhibited companion–daughter who is two drinks from being snookered and having the time of her life.

Before they decide to turn left or right they also decide to be responsible for five minutes and make two quick phone calls. Connie calls O'Brien, who does not answer the phone, and says, "Oh, my gawd, honey. I'm in the French Quarter about to expose my breasts with my daughter. I kissed a man. I'm horny as hell and I may never come home. Call me in the morning when I'm sober and by then I should have about twelve more stories to tell you. Bye-bye, baby."

Boom-Boom calls Geneva, who does answer and who immediately considers getting on the next plane to Louisiana.

"Geneva, we're going to flash people in the balconies."

"Who is this?"

"It's me. I've been drinking since like three o'clock. Oh, I forgot to tell you. Everything is fixed. Dildos coming. Oh, my God. That's a pun. Isn't that funny?"

"Jesus, Jessica. Are you okay?"

"Oh, sure. My mom is here. Oh, guess what? She kissed the commissioner and now she has the hots for him and everyone else she sees."

Geneva laughs. Part of her thinks whatever is happening is very, very good for uptight Jessica and the other part is just a tiny bit worried.

"Are you two all right?"

"We're getting smashed. Having a ball. We had the most unbelievable conversation. We'll catch the plane, don't worry too much. Keep the skip floating. I mean the ship."

"Don't forget we have the women's festival in three weeks, and there is a ton of work to do and we don't even know yet who is going to handle the booth. So get back here."

"Oh, Geneva, we are going to have our fortunes told. Got to go. See you tomorrow."

Jessica lurches towards the edge of the street and scans the crowd until she makes eye contact with a fortune-teller at the very beginning of a line of men and women who have set up tables and chairs and umbrellas and signs and flying flags to try and lure customers. The fortune-tellers, readers, visionaries of the future have a rich history in New Orleans. They jockey for positions along the edge of this city park every single night and day of the year.

"Oh, Mother, Mother, Mother," Jessica shouts, starting to run down the lovely brick courtyard adjacent to Jackson Square. "She's the one. Look at her. At least I think it's a her. This is perfect."

Connie, not as buzzed as Boom-Boom, catches her arm and says, "Well, this is perfect for you now that you are in this state of hetero–homo limbo. Let's do this. How fun could this be?"

Lots of fun. More fun than they will even be able to describe the next day, a month later, or next Easter. They sit on rainbow-striped lawn chairs and look into the ravishing blue eyes of Saffine who tells them in two seconds that she's working hard so she can finish her sex-change operation. Connie and Jessica turn to each other, say "perfect" at the exact same moment, and then put their hands on a deck of well-worn tarot cards and prepare to hear their futures while sipping on their Hurricanes.

Connie holds her breath and whirls herself back to Indiana for a moment behind her closed eyes while Saffine

shuffles the cards, crosses her long legs, pulls on the neck-
line of her off-white t-shirt, and asks them if she can smoke.
Jessica talks about the cards, engages Saffine in some
pre–fortune-telling conversation, and Connie wonders if
she ever imagined this moment.

Did she?

Did she imagine one night, one lovely Sunday night,
tucked away in her room, rocking away while she worked on
her Sunday list of dreams, that one day she would be three
sheets to the wind, sitting in a lawn chair in the very heart of
the French Quarter with her drunken daughter who sells
whips and feathers so that people can play with each other's
bodies? Did she imagine that she would have confessed her
deepest secrets, her abandoned longing for lust and love and
passion, to her daughter? Her own daughter? Did she even
think of writing this in her list of dreams? Did she, could she
have wished herself to this sultry spot, a lingering kiss plastered to her psyche and a longing for something more that
started at the tiny spot below her knees and wound its way
through her loins, past her stomach, through her heart and
lodged itself right in the front part of her brain and made it
so she could think of nothing else?

Did she imagine that the discovery of a box hidden
among the debris piled in her garage would parachute her
into an adventure that seems to be expanding and multiplying every single second of every day?

The travel. The daughter. The man. The expanse of time.
The swift turn in a path that she thought she had already
paved and planted and then trimmed to fit dreams that had
cascaded through her whirling life for all those years. Years
and years that often belonged to everyone, so it seemed, but
herself.

Connie sets down her drink and leans towards Saffine.

Saffine has her legs crossed and is bobbing the top foot up and down so fast somebody will get hurt if she moves it wrong.

"Concentrate, honey," Saffine urges. "Let your mind race forward a bit and brush your hands across the cards."

Jessica turns to look at her mother and she too is suddenly wondering if she could ever have dreamed of this moment. Half drunk before 6 P.M. in the middle of the week. Watching her mother sell Diva products to her customers. Discussing the intricacies of her latent sex life with the woman who used to ground her for banging the old motorcycle against the garbage cans along the side of the garage.

Jessica wants to laugh at the sudden absurdity of her world. She wants to throw herself down on the tiny card table, right on top of the soiled doilies and the Kmart candles and the vividly colored cards, but Saffine turns abruptly and begins shouting at a man who is perched behind her and has leaned over to touch the back of Saffine's chair.

"Goddamn it!" Saffine snarls, totally disrupting the cosmic flow of her reading. "I told you to stay away from here and not to touch anything! Get the fuck out of here!"

When she finishes she turns back to Connie and Jessica as if nothing has happened and starts fingering the cards, totally oblivious to her bizarre behavior. Connie grabs Jessica's hand, squeezes it at the same moment Jessica gently kicks her leg under the table. Connie thinks Saffine couldn't get a good reading if she had a cell phone connection to the future but says, "That's okay, honey" so Saffine won't think they are offended by her Tourette's syndrome–like behavior.

"People hate me," Saffine declares, launching into her own story instead of getting on with the card-reading. "It's not my fault I have this gift. People get jealous because everyone wants to come to me."

If Connie or Jessica were impolite, either one of them would have leaned forward, grabbed back the $30 they had given Saffine that was still sitting on the edge of the table, and said, "What the hell?" But neither one of them wants to miss this moment.

"It just came to me, *whoosh*, like that," Saffine explains, waving her hand in the air flamboyantly. "My friend Reg was reading me and then all these images and people came into my head and I just knew I had it and that was that."

"Wow," Boom-Boom responds with one elbow on the table, imagining what it would be like to live in Saffine's world. "So now what? What's up with the sex-change?"

"Oh, honey," Saffine says while she continues to shuffle the cards and cocks her head sideways to make certain the bad man won't intrude again on her territory. "My life could be a book. I'll get to that someday."

Then, while Connie and Jessica sit back, cross their own legs and let the moment happen, Saffine tells them her life story. Her mama raped her. Her daddy raped her and she fled to the streets of Atlanta to sell herself to the highest bidder. Lost her soul for years to the slavery of drug abuse, lived until recently with a male lover who was helping to pay for the beginnings of the sex-change operation.

"Want to see my titties?" Saffine asks.

Even for nurse Nixon, this is a new one. Without turning to look at Jessica, who has not moved since the beginning of Saffine's horrific story, Connie says, "Oh, please, that would be nice."

Saffine lifts her shirt and exposes a very tiny but lovely right breast. It's as if Saffine has just launched into puberty and has budded out before the final hormone rush that will make her breasts swell and turn into glorious mounds of female flesh.

"They are quite nice," Jessica manages to say. "When will you be able to finish?"

"Well, I'm working my tush off doing these readings and saving like crazy and as you can tell I surely don't eat much and sometimes I just live on the street, so I'm hoping soon, sweetie, really soon."

Oh, baby, Connie thinks. If ever a man was born to be a woman, it is Saffine with her blonde curls and blue eyes and the gestures and heart of someone who has tangoed this far in time on a tiny male shoestring.

And then, finally then, Saffine looks down at the cards and launches into her rendition of the futures of Connie Franklin Nixon and Jessica Franklin Nixon.

"Do you have a control issue?" she asks Connie. "Just let it go, honey. Let it go."

"And you," she continues, looking at Jessica. "Honey, you need some lovin'. You really need some lovin'. Can you do it?"

The women are momentarily impressed and then the bad man comes back, lurking in the background, Saffine launches back into her "fuck you" routine, her little rainbow flag dips towards the table and the two women rise and leave Saffine for her next unsuspecting customers.

"Holy shit," Connie says as they lurch away from their fortune-teller. "Wasn't that something?"

"Jesus, Mother, think about her life. Do you think there's any joy in where *she's* headed? What she has to do to get there?"

"Here and there, baby," Connie says, grabbing her daughter's hand. "Just like our lives—here and there, but don't you think it could be more here than there?"

The Nixon women wander up one street and down another, stopping once at a tiny hole-in-the-wall to get another drink lest they lose their perpetual New Orleans buzz, and then they follow the sound of music until they come to a street where a small group of men are playing a banjo, a guitar and a trumpet. They sit and listen and fall into the rhythm of a city that feeds itself on the soul of life—music, love, fun, the wild connections to the heart of life the way it was meant to be lived.

Connie turns after a while to Jessica and says with a slight, rum-laced slur, "Do you know this was on my list and it just dawned on me."

"What list?"

Connie wonders if she would tell this story to her daughter if they were both not tipsy and hundreds of miles from their real life. She knows, even with the rum cascading through her veins, that she would never have told her this in her kitchen in Indiana, from a phone in the back bedroom, during a conversation when Jessica flew home for a 20-minute visit. But now, in the street with their feet dangling in the gutter, men playing songs from their souls, the heat of the late spring night wrapping itself around them, and the knowledge that she and Jessica have finally passed through some unseen barrier, she tells her daughter, her oldest baby, the woman who is now Boom-Boom, about the list. The list of dreams.

And Jessica cries.

"Oh, Mom, I never knew. I never thought about you giving up your dreams for us, and I so fought against so many things that you did and were," Jessica tells her. "I feel like such an ass."

"Oh, honey, it's nothing to feel bad about," Connie answers. "After all, I didn't know about your dreams, about the passion you're trying to find. It's what happens but, really, it should never have happened."

Jessica falls into her mother's arms and feels something as familiar as her own breath when Connie wraps her arms around her and touches her hair the very same way she touched her hair all those years ago when she was a baby, a child, and when she occasionally allowed her mother to touch her as a teenager. She smells her mother's smell—rich and warm, like the sweet smell of a Cyprus summer—and then she asks her mother to forgive her for wandering away without leaving an address, for losing touch.

"Listen, Jessica, it's what we do," Connie tells her. "You need your own life and place and space and it took this time for us to weave our way through our own shit, through worlds of hunger and schedules and finding the right trail which, you know now, is a trail that shifts and changes and here we are now, baby. Let's hang on to this."

And they do hang on. They hang on as they visit a voodoo temple and sip pungent red wine with a priestess who launches off on some tangent about women and their periods and the cycle of life. They hang on as they put dollar bills on her temple altars and giggle on their way out the door and then walk back up to the infamous Bourbon Street that is as awake at 1 A.M. as it is at 10 in the morning. They both look up at the same moment and see men and women dangling beads the colors of a rainbow from a balcony.

"Jesus, Mom, should we?"

"Honey, both of us have put way too many things on hold and I for one refuse to live like that any more. Yes, we should."

And they do. Connie raises her shirt, stretching out her favorite bra, exposing her very fine and still-firm breasts as a waterfall of beads drops onto her head and then Jessica follows suit—not for as long, but she does it—and then the two women dress themselves in the beads and walk hand in hand back to their hotel. Connie thinks that she has not felt this happy in a very long time and Jessica thinks, *I did it, oh, my God, I did it!*

And the world does not stop but it does tilt for just a second as the Nixon babes swagger into the lobby, Connie reaches over to pinch the ass of the stunned doorman, and they laugh themselves into bed for a measly five hours of sleep.

Fifteen

37. Make certain the list changes. Give yourself that option. Keep some. Throw some away.

Kinsey Barnes has his hands on his favorite wide leather belt, which is holding up his straight-leg black jeans. Kinsey's head is bent towards the floor, his feet are pointed at the lovely display case that is cradling beautiful boxes of scented, flavored, and colored condoms, and he feels deflated, depressed, lied to, totally out of his league, the entire ballpark, and male humankind altogether.

"Meredith, honey," he whispers just loud enough so his

co-worker can hear him. "I feel as if my half of humanity has done a huge disservice to the other half."

"What is it, sweetheart?" Meredith asks as she slings a box of vibrators onto her sturdy shoulder. "Did you see an old girlfriend in the store?"

"I could have. The planet is probably littered with unhappy women who have known me," he responds glumly. "I'm just stunned."

Meredith and Kinsey are opening the store alone on Monday morning. Their boss Jessica is giving them time to settle in, to see if they can do it, to tie or untie themselves with the Diva ropes. She's a phone call away and it's minutes before opening after a wild weekend of record sales, baptism by sex-toy fire, and a promise from Geneva that she will never ever again be as bitchy as she was Sunday afternoon.

"I hate this shit," Geneva groused as she'd locked the door 30 minutes late, totally exhausted and overwhelmed by the apparent success of a weekend without Jessica bossing them around. "Customer service is not my bag. Jessica better get her ass back here and, as for you two—I'm buying you both dinner and drinks after this kick-ass day."

Dinner and three pitchers of beer did nothing to calm Kinsey, who had fancied himself a sexually alert and astute male. A man who knew women. A guy who could listen. A big boy in the bedroom. But nothing had prepared him for the parade of women who came into Diva's with tears in their eyes and a longing in their loins that astounded him.

"After all the discussion last night I have to tell you that I'm, like, numb about the numbers of sexually dissatisfied women in New York," he tells Meredith as she turns to face him on Monday morning. "New York is a hip city and I feel

terrible for women everywhere who still think sex is something everyone else has or does."

"Baby," Meredith says, walking to him with her arms
open. "I've been doing my part for years but it's places like
Diva's that can really create a groundswell."

"I keep thinking about all the women I know," he confesses. "I want to run through the city with a dildo in my hand
like the Pied Piper and say something like, 'Come with me
and you will come.'"

"You should feel good about what you're doing here,"
Meredith consoles him. She's trying not to laugh. "It's apparently not just a job to you but a life's mission now. Be
proud, son."

Kinsey pushes her away and laughs, but also tells her that
he's serious. He's serious, he says, every single time a woman
comes in and peeks at him from behind a stack of vibrators
and then shyly comes forward to ask him a question. He's serious, he tells Meredith, when he overhears a woman old
enough to be his own mother confess to him or Geneva that
she's never had an orgasm. He's serious, he says, when he
thinks about all the women in the world, and yes, even those
three sensitive men, who were around before toy stores like
Diva's were open and when sex was something the bad girls
did and only boys liked.

"Welcome to the real world, cutie-pie," Meredith applauds, punching him in the arm. "It's no different in the lesbian world that I inhabit. You'd think that particular group of
women would be free and would have this sex thing down to
a fine artful science, but I'm here to tell you even women
who love women need a little help and, well, some of them
need a lot of help."

Kinsey groans, "Oh, no, they were my last hope," and
then the day starts, as they have already taken to joking,

"with a bang." The phone rings precisely at 11 A.M. and both Kinsey and Meredith mouth, *It's Jessica*, before Meredith picks up the phone and then smiles as she, silently, says *yes* and the first customer not so much walks as sneaks into the store.

It's a woman. She's not smiling. She looks frightened and this is the part that Kinsey does not have down yet. This is when he looks up, thinks about his mother having sex with her second husband, or her first husband, or one of the boyfriends in between and he goes temporarily blind, deaf and especially dumb. This customer looks like she's in her mid to late 50s and she is as white as the drapes flowing behind the checkout counter. He looks towards Meredith but she's on the phone and busy writing. He looks at his feet and they are not moving. He shakes his head, desperately tries to slip into his actor mode, and walks towards the woman.

She takes one look at Kinsey and sees her son. She sees his pressed jeans and his fine belt and the way his hair moves in circles and waves and she imagines he tossed it like a salad, just like her son does, before he came in to work, moments before he knew he was going to sell sex toys to someone who looks like his sweet grandmother or mother.

"Can I help you?" Kinsey whimpers.

"Just browsing," the nice customer manages to say.

"Well, if you need any help just ask, okay?"

"Sure," she nods as she angles towards the edge of the store. "I'll do that." *Just as soon as an elephant flies out of my rear end*, she also says to herself.

Like hell, Kinsey thinks at the same moment. *She'd rather walk a frigid line right back where she came from* and that's what he tells Meredith who is busy making a nice, anal list of everything she has to do before Queen Jessica gets to the store.

"I can't talk to some of these customers," he seethes as quietly as possible through his teeth, his lips barely moving as he leans across the counter. "Women like that don't want to talk to some jackass kid who could be their son, and you, my dear, look like a punk rocker. She's not going to ask us how to stick a G-spot vibrator up her vagina."

"You did okay yesterday."

"I was behind the cash register most of the day, remember?"

"The guys like you."

"Most of our customers are women. The guys like me because I look like I'm gay, for crissakes. I'm an actor. I *have* to look like I'm gay."

Meredith looks up. She sees the woman dodging in between aisles, holding a package up to her face, and she decides that Mr. Kinsey might be on to something.

"What are you thinking?"

"It's too soon for me to retire. I like this place, even that ramy, hyper, slave-driving Jessica. But, well, remember when Jessica's mom was in here shuffling around last Friday, offering coffee, selling everything from whips to lubricant?"

Meredith remembers. Connie was like an older-chick magnet. Even the younger women were not hesitant to ask her questions. Connie looked pained half the afternoon but she managed to get the questions answered even as she admitted she'd never used, held, or discussed sex toys in her entire life—not even when she helped remove some of them from various parts of bodies in the emergency room during her nursing career.

"Well, isn't she, like, a retired nurse or something who has a new job?" Meredith asks.

"Something like that," Kinsey says. "But doesn't it make

sense to have someone like her passing out cookies and coffee while she helps them regulate vibrators and try on red leather harnesses?"

Before she can respond, they hear the door chime ring as the woman who kick-started the day slips out of the door without saying another word, asking a question, or spending one thin dime.

"Shit," Meredith yells. "I think you may be on to something, Kinsey."

"We need a grandma in here selling dildos and stuff," he says, grabbing onto his belt and hoisting it as if he just discovered gold and he doesn't want to get his pant legs wet in the Sacramento River. "Think of a way to lure Connie into the store today and we'll give her a crash course in sex toys when Jessica goes to her meeting with Geneva this afternoon."

"I'm on it, baby," Meredith promises as she grabs the phone. "Go stack some batteries like a good boy. Grandma is coming for a visit."

Connie Franklin Nixon is staring at a dozen long-stem red roses. She wants O'Brien to show up and slap her across both cheeks so she'll know that she's alive and back in Jessica's apartment in New York City and not floating in some Nirvana-like place that's shadowy and sultry like a fabulous dream.

"Mother, what the hell?" Jessica barked when the doorman brought up the flowers. "Did you sleep with this guy or just kiss him?"

"I should slap you upside the head, missy," Connie snorts. "I happen to be a *really* good kisser."

"Did you slip him your tongue?"

"Hey, that's none of your business. Do you want me to wash out your mouth with soap?"

"There's my answer. Mother, you little slut."

"A slut would have thrown Burt Reynolds down in the swamp, Ms. Know-It-All. It was just a kiss. An extremely nice kiss and then several more along the way home, and in the parking lot . . ."

"Stop!" Jessica yelled. "That is just too much information. I have to get out of here. Come by or call or whatever. Just sit here and smell the damn flowers all day. I'm gone."

Still exhausted from New Orleans, her emotional roller coaster with Jessica, the flight to New York, the newfound notion of romance and the distant thought that she should probably get back to Cyprus, Connie throws herself on the bed and immediately falls into a rose-scented sleep; within minutes, she has dreamed herself into someplace very cold. When she glances down she is standing on two huge and fast-melting sheets of ice. "Large ice cubes," she thinks, watching as they melt. Connie jumps to another set of ice cubes, watches these, too, melt, and then leaps to another pair. "What the hell," she shouts, laughing at the endless game, the endless sea of ice, the endless maneuvering to get from cube to cube.

Twenty minutes later her cell phone rings and jolts her from her perfumed dream of ice.

"Hey, Connie, it's Meredith. From Diva's. How was New Orleans?"

Connie shudders, feeling chilled from her dream, which lingers at the edge of her mind.

"Wonderful. The dildos are on the way."

"That's funny. Remember before this sex-toy world how

kids used to call each other dildo in, like, junior high school? Now, the real dildos are on the way. Hey, are you coming in today?"

Connie hesitates. In, she thinks, as *in to work*. Into the store. Into the wild blue yonder. Into more seconds, minutes and hours of her daughter's life. Into trouble and onto another iceberg

"I'm not on the schedule today, am I?" she asks, stalling.

"Nope. But it's helpful when you're here and I'm guessing Jessica didn't bother to get the damn coffeepot."

"Well, I'm going to try and get a flight back home," Connie finally says. "I really didn't plan on coming into Diva's at all today, sweetheart. I'm betting the place won't close down if I'm not there."

"You might lose that bet," Meredith warns darkly. "Didn't you like working here?"

Something is going on. Connie can feel a swinging door moving just slowly enough for her to peek into a hidden room. *Yes*, she can admit to herself, *I liked being at the store. It was fun and new and embarrassing as hell, but working at a sex-toy store is* not *a number on the list.*

"Meredith, I have this whole life going on someplace else and I need to get cranking on that," she answers slowly. "I think you are in pretty good hands with my daughter—even if she is a little uptight. Take out one of those whips."

Meredith is struggling. She's an inch from desperate.

"Listen," she finally says, going in for the motherhood kill, the stretch of words that will induce Connie into guilt. "I want to talk to you. Really. Can't you just come in for a while? I'll take a break about 1:30. Can you please come in then?"

Connie bites the hook and then swallows it. Meredith might look as if she's on break from the flying circus with her loopy and wild clothes, but she's smart, tough, fun, and maybe she needs a wise ear. Maybe that's just it and not some kind of trap that will keep her locked up in a pair of those studded wrist cuffs for the next year or two.

"Okay, I'll try," Connie says, surrendering. "I'll bring the coffee."

"Sure," Connie thinks. "What the hell. It will only take me 15 minutes to get a seat on the next plane back to Chicago. What's another two hours of smelling the roses? I can clean the apartment for the 12th time, go down to the corner grocery store and flirt and then go have coffee with the kids at the sex-toy store. Then maybe a stroll before an early dinner, say good-bye to Mattie, who created a Diva and a Burt Reynolds magnet with the new hair, and then back to my life. My *real* life. Not this blip on the radar screen that manifested itself because of a box of papers I found in my garage. Gezus. What was I thinking? What the hell, Nixon? Get a grip. Get out the list. Go sit in a chair and take a good hard look at it lest you lose your way—again.

That was it, then. A short plan. A map with a clear path back home, to her real home, where she could get on with the business of moving forward on her predetermined jour-ney towards the new job, the condo, and maybe the painting class—sedate #24—when she recovered from New York, New Orleans, and every other frigging new thing that had in-vaded her life since she'd had the bright idea to clean out the garage. Connie decides that she needs to pause more often and write on her slips, so that she can reach down and run her hand across her pocket every time she gets an offer that seems too good to refuse. She decides she needs to stay grounded to the list, to its numbers, to all those years of writing and planning and moving forward to this time, this time of the Sunday list.

Then there is just time for a hasty and gracious whiff of sweet roses as Connie buries her face directly inside the middle of the bouquet and puts her hands around the vase, transporting herself back to the bayou where the scent of the rich, damp land makes her wonder what it might have been like to make love to Burt, the commissioner, in his world of luscious and totally intoxicating sensuality. The mere idea that #14—the "Maybe Sex" number—could actually become a reality makes her think about it.

She closes her eyes and wonders for a few delicious moments. Closes them and drifts to the edge of the water where Michael has pulled the boat over near a nest of ferns. Keeps her eyes closed and her nose on the roses as he takes her hand and she turns without waiting to kiss him, to take charge just a little bit, to let him know that it is not all about him. Connie's mind goes red with passion then as Michael takes her down a path with no markings, no worn footmarks, nothing to guide him but his own feelings. When they turn past the stand of cypress trees they are in a forest of ferns and he grabs her there, right there, and gently pushes her down under a tree that he whispers will now stand guard over them while he makes love to her.

Connie sits down and does not take her hands off of the flowers while she falls into her imagined tryst. Michael kisses her neck and runs his fingers up the back of her head and then she pushes him over, straddling him around his waist and she starts to unbutton his shirt while he moves his hands across her back, down the sides of her rear end, and back onto her shoulders. Connie spreads open his shirt and slides her hands across his chest, breathing hard, as her fingers move to his belt buckle and she holds her breath.

And then the damn phone rings.

"Shit!" she shouts out loud, fairly breathless and just a bit pissed off.

It is Kinsey, also begging her to come in at 1:30. Not sooner or later but right about then. Could these two be any more suspicious? I'm coming, Connie tells him. God, she thinks, I was just about to have sex, which is so far down on the list it seems to have disappeared. The list. The list she is ignoring by going into Diva's.

Connie takes a breath, turns to look out the window, and clears her head of the rose residue, the icebergs, her sinful falling away from the list, and then her cell phone rings.

"What the hell?"

It is Sabrina. Daughter number two. The perfect wife and mother almost catching her own mother having make-believe sex as she smells roses before she heads off to sell sexual devices to whoever wants them. Connie shakes her head, touches her own hand in her Nurse Nixon way to steady herself, and tries to sound calm.

"Hi, baby," Connie says without the slightest hint of panic in her voice. "How is everyone?"

But Sabrina wants to know about Connie.

The conversation races at first. New Orleans. New York City. The store. Questions about her response to Jessica's job, Sabrina's acceptance of it as a business decision, and a surprising discussion about female sexuality. Connie bites a hole in her tongue, and then wonders why she does it, as Sabrina launches on about kids and a neighborhood meeting, and then the real reason for the phone call.

"Mom, do you think you'll be home by next weekend?"

"I should be home tomorrow, as soon as I get online and get a seat on an airplane headed west."

"Well, we were wondering if you could baby-sit for a

couple of days. Maybe just for the weekend, like Friday through Sunday. What do you think?"

Think? Connie thinks she wants to rip Burt's pants off his sweet solid ass and then ride him until the swamp sunset cascades like a waterfall across her face. Think? Connie thinks she should never have left New Orleans and she sure as hell thinks she probably, most likely, sort of made the right decision by leaving Cyprus, Indiana. Connie thinks, in the seconds it takes her mind to check back to where she can have a normal conversation, that she'd love to be drinking champagne or some really great dry white wine out of a golden slipper in Commissioner Michael Dennis's bedroom.

But that's not what she tells her daughter.

"Sure. I can babysit for you."

"Oh, thank God," Sabrina says. "I asked Macy but she's sick as a dog these early days of her pregnancy and it's just easier for me to get the kids to your house, unless you want to watch them at our house. . . ." Sabrina says, a sort of question.

Connie is not sure she can even remember where she lives. Does she own a house? What is her last name? How many grandchildren does she have? Will she drive to Chicago or have the children driven to wherever in the hell she lives? Is this woman really her daughter? And the roses . . . where did they come from?

"Yes," Connie says, four times in a row. "Yes, and yes, and yes again." They say good-bye and hang up.

And then, before she can get up to use the bathroom, turn in a circle, or rearrange her thoughts, the cell phone rings yet again.

Shit. Damn it. What the hell?

"WHAT?" she yells into the phone without waiting for an answer. "WHAT THE HELL IS IT NOW?"

It's O'Brien. O'Brien laughing at the rich sound of her friend, the irritating bob of the words, the way Nurse Nixon does not even try to be friendly.

"Jesus, baby, has New York got your underwear all balled up or what?"

"My underwear is wet," Connie says, fast. "I'm horny as a teenager, kissed a stranger, the kids want me to come down to the sex toy store, my daughter has become my friend, sort of, Sabrina wants me to baby-sit, and I suddenly cannot remember my last name or how I even came to be in this city in the first place."

O'Brien drops the phone, laughing. Nurse Nixon hears the phone hit something and then crackle, and then she hears what sounds like her best friend in the world coughing.

"Honey," O'Brien wheezes when she retrieves the phone, "have you come undone?"

"No. But I *want* to really, really bad."

And Connie tells O'Brien everything. The kiss, the date, the dinner, the roses, even details of her make-believe lovemaking session that had been interrupted by the damn phone call from daughter number two.

"Why in the hell would you come home?" O'Brien asks, seriously.

"What do you mean?"

"Think about it, you jackass. Look where you are, what you have just done, who you have met and kissed. Listen to me . . . *are you totally crazy? Are you that far off the list?*"

Maybe, Connie tells herself, *maybe I am crazy or I would not be here.* Maybe I should just call back home and have someone blow up the rest of the junk in the garage. Maybe I need to lie down for a week. Maybe I should not lie down because something sinful might happen. Maybe I suddenly have no idea about anything. Maybe I need to sit down and look at the list again.

"Are you there?" O'Brien asks. "Baby, I'm worried."

"Worried," Connie says. "Think of how I feel. Think about this wild, roller-coaster turn of events in my life and the last conversation we had when the house was talking and the discovery of my daughter becoming the queen of the sex toy world. Think about Burt Reynolds putting his tongue down my throat and me wanting to rip his pants off and these kids from the store calling me with mysterious questions and demands and my God, O'Brien, I don't even *look* the same."

"So what?" O'Brien tells her. "You big crybaby."

"I'm not a baby."

"So smell the flowers, then take a big, deep breath."

Connie takes a breath. She takes a breath while O'Brien briefs her on the past weekend which included two checks on her house, one call from the real estate agent, a frozen pizza, two emergency admissions to the psych unit—both women—a son who called to tell her by the way he was going to Egypt for Christmas, and a huge sale on chicken cutlets at Connie's favorite grocery store.

"See what you're missing, baby? See what you'd be racing home to?"

"Shit."

"Yes, shit covers it nicely."

And that's what Connie thinks about after she hangs up and fishes for airline flights anyway, puts one of them on hold until midnight, takes a shower with the bathroom door wide open, leaves a thank-you message on Burt's answering machine and then takes a right turn outside of her daughter's apartment building so she can pick up more coffee on the way to meet the kids at Diva's, where she knows she will definitely run into more shit.

Halfway to Diva's it finally hits her: this is the first time she has left the apartment, made a move, taken a turn in many days without first writing down a number from her beloved list and putting it in her pocket.

She stops. Takes a breath. Remembers bold-sounding #37 from her list. The number of change. The number of options. The number, so it seems, that would lead her towards all things made of chance. *"Make certain the list changes. Give yourself that option. Keep some. Throw some away."*

Spring in New York rises from every crack and corner and seems to leap from the amazingly blue sky. The air is warm, light, fresh, and Connie realizes, standing still in the midst of a place that never stands still, that she is no longer afraid of getting lost, of bumping into a criminal, of losing her wallet, or of meeting someone who might want to whisk her away to a side street café for a lingering lunch, a proposition of chance, a moment to just . . . pause.

Connie looks behind her. She hesitates only a second before looking at her watch and then she bravely moves forward and, as she walks, she makes believe she is tossing all the numbers on her list into the air so that they can blend together into something that would make #37 very, very happy.

Sixteen

1. Stop being afraid.

26. Mix up your friends. Do this with intention. Younger, older, whatever. Not just the ones who are convenient.

C

onnie misses Jessica by less than two minutes, which makes Meredith and Kinsey almost wet their pants.

"Holy crap," Kinsey whines to Meredith when Jessica lingers to restack a display. "If they run into each other, we are *dead*. Jessica will kill us, fire us, *and* I'll have to go and *beg* to get my last job back."

"Maybe she'd be fine with it," Meredith replies. "They just got back from New Orleans and they're still speaking to each other and no one is dead yet."

"Think about it," Kinsey hisses, as Jessica answers a customer call. "Would you want to be selling dildos with your mommy?"

"Honey, my mommy *bought* me my first dildo."

"You don't count. You skew the study I'm doing. You are not normal."

"Well," Meredith shoots back, as Jessica pauses at the door and frowns at both of them, like she's sure the store's going to burn down if she does leave it, "I happen to think I am normal and everyone else who does not embrace their sexuality and who did not have a generous and open mother like mine is not normal."

Ten minutes later, when Jessica has finally left and Connie breezes in with her coffee and muffins, she catches the kids still arguing. She sets down her treats and orders them to stop it or she will send each of them to their rooms.

"Where's Jessica?" she asks.

"A meeting."

"You knew this," Connie tells Meredith.

"Yes."

"You wanted me to come when she wasn't here? Why? Are you going to quit? Steal toys? Tell me a secret, as if there are any secrets left."

Connie looks at Meredith and Kinsey standing silently and not answering her questions and she can only imagine what must have gone on before she arrived. Some magical conspiracy by a couple of 20-something New Yorkers who would probably get lost in Indiana if they didn't go crazy 30 minutes after landing there. Meredith, who always looks as if she left the house in a hurry—long earrings in one ear, short in the other, just like her wild hair which also seems short on one side and long on the other—but a woman who struts and saunters as if the world is waiting for her arrival. And Mr.

Potential Movie Star, Kinsey Barnes, who is so in touch with his feminine self Connie would like a peek under his very tight zipper. Kids. Powerful, wonderful kids who could probably teach her a thing or two about not only sex toys but about their world as well. They are lovely and wild and kind and, sweet Jesus, she thinks suddenly, they could be #26.

"Can we have coffee first?" Kinsey asks her. "And maybe, Meredith, maybe you should just talk to Connie while I handle the customers for a bit."

Connie is suddenly reminded of a discussion that was almost exactly like this. A conversation that took place years ago, when middle daughter Macy came home, quietly asked for a private meeting in her bedroom, and then wanted to know if Connie would take her to the clinic or Planned Parenthood or someplace so she could get birth control.

Connie had tried to act cool. Connie had tried to act as if a conversation with her 18-year-old daughter concerning the staggering news that the latter was ready to have sexual intercourse, sex, SEX, was an everyday and totally acceptable occurrence.

"I'm ready, Mom, and Ryan and I discussed this, and we decided to just be up front about it and so I'm asking you for help," Macy said, moving her fingers back and forth so fast Connie wondered if her daughter was about to levitate.

A deep breath filled Connie's lungs before she spoke and, when she did, it was very slowly, lest she fall off the edge of Macy's bed, vomit, or call 911.

"This is a wise decision," Connie told her daughter. "Are you sure you're ready, honey? This is a pretty big step."

Macy said yes and now, standing in front of the sex toy checkout counter, Connie wondered about all the lesbians and gay men who felt as if they had to parade their sexuality in front of parents and relatives and neighbors and ex-lovers.

Why? she suddenly wonders as she trails thoughts of Macy's sexual awakening behind her.

"Meredith, why do people have to come out?" Connie asks. "You know, I don't recall sitting my parents down when I decided to have sex to let them know I was a heterosexual."

Meredith chokes on her coffee and a small stream of the black liquid runs down her chin—which Connie immediately leans over to brush off with her fingertips.

"Where the hell did that come from, Connie?" Meredith sputters.

"Thin air, I suppose, and thinking about the time my daughter asked me to get her some birth control," Connie shares. "I feel like you're about to tell me some secret just like she did then and it got me wondering."

"Actually, it pisses me off because I feel the same way," Meredith tells her. "I don't know why we have to come out. Maybe some people feel as if they owe it to their friends and family, so everyone will stop trying to set them up with straight people."

Maybe that's it, they both agree as Meredith takes Connie into the back room and suggests she ask Jessica for a job.

A job.

And now it's Connie's turn to spit out coffee and she wants to know if Meredith has been smoking crack with Kinsey on the job.

"Just listen," Meredith urges. "Do you use sex toys?"

"No, but I have to admit I've been feeling terribly sexual since I landed in New York and stumbled in here."

"Most of our clients are women and many of them are your age and, well, we think you'd be a terrific addition to the staff and we sure as hell need the help," Meredith rushes on. "And you were really fabulous the other day in here, and I could give you, like, a quick in-service and we could just see what happens."

Connie is laughing so hard inside of her loopy mind that she can barely sit up straight. Work at a sex toy store? With her daughter? Counsel women about sex? Stand up there and hold dildos and vibrators and whatever in the hell else is in all those boxes and sell them?

"Meredith, listen, I haven't even had sex in many years—"

"Which makes you perfect for the job."

"I have a job."

"Not for several months."

"I have a life back there—"

"Connie, life is everywhere. So you just try this and see what happens."

"Does Jessica know about this? You can't hire me. What the hell are you thinking?"

"Of course I can't hire you but I'm asking you to think about it. Jessica needs help."

Connie runs her right hand through her hair, or what is left of her hair, and sets down her coffee cup. She looks over Meredith's shoulder and stares into something that she's pretty sure is a harness—a seemingly impossible tangle of leather and silver. She has no idea how to put it on, what to do with it or why in God's name anyone would ever wear one. She turns and sees cardboard boxes with names on them like The Sage, Seducer, The Fox, and Twirling Heaven, and she gets a twitch under her left eye that cascades down her face, rolls into her lip, and lands right in the center of her stomach.

Meredith is silent. She is watching Connie think and she's sipping her coffee, already envisioning Connie Franklin Nixon in a black leather vest with her new hair, some nice red leather boots, and a glass of white wine, explaining, during a private party, how to use a variety of vibrators for a group of women who have recently thrown away their bridge cards.

She's also thinking about how much she likes Jessica's mother. Connie's not a bit like her mother. But Connie seems to be able to handle everything from a fast trip to New Orleans to the discovery of her daughter's blossoming business as if she was born for a trauma-induced life. Maybe it's the nursing, Meredith thinks, but maybe it's just Connie. Cool Connie.

"Look, Meredith," Connie finally says. "I have things to do and a list to follow and Jessica is never in a million years going to go for this."

"Well, Connie, Jessica might not have a choice," she whispers, leaning over to kiss Connie just below her left twitching eye. "She's totally forgotten that she was supposed to hire someone to go to this huge women's festival with me in 10 days and now that the new toys are coming in and the launch party is on the horizon, she needs you badly."

"What are you talking about?" Connie asks, bewildered.

"Too much work and not enough help. Jessica's totally on overload."

"I'm a nurse, for God's sake, not a salesperson!"

"Oh, I know, and you are the perfect age, and you are attractive, and just say you will think about it, give me a little time to talk to Jessica, and let me start you on my little Sex Toys 101 class right this second."

Connie closes her eyes and tries to remember what her backyard looks like. She sees a small stack of firewood, a broken door leading into the garage, a pile of junk leaning against the neighbor's fence that has been there since the day they bought the house and that's all she can remember. Everything else is hazy around the edges. She can barely remember the color of the fading siding that has needed paint for five years.

She looks at the tops of her hands, which are now resting on her legs, looks up at Meredith and she wonders what Meredith sees when she looks at her.

"I would have been cleaning out the rest of the garage today," Connie mutters.

"This could be much more fun."

Connie doesn't say anything but she knows #37 should be in her pocket and she moves her hand there and runs it over the very top, just below her waistband, slipping one finger inside so she can feel where the slip of paper should be, just for reassurance. She wonders what it might be like to say no, to ignore #37 and all the numbers that are before it so she can . . . What? Start over? Go backwards? Follow some line of descent that is only a ledge of safeness she has built inside of her own mind? Then she shakes her head up and down and not sideways. She shakes her head up and down and then into a little twist that only she knows could, with a bit of a stretch, look like the number 37. She squeezes her eyes shut and she thinks she should keep them shut and when she opens them up Meredith is sitting in front of her with a tiny, long blue thing that looks like a funky cigarette lighter.

"This is a waterproof vibrator."

Connie puts it in her hand, feels it vibrate through her skin, into her thumb muscles, through the bones in her 58-year-old fingers, and she wonders if O'Brien has remembered to shut off the porch light, grab the newspapers, and call the damn realtor. She's a very practical woman, sitting in a sex toy store in Manhattan that her recently unestranged daughter owns, with a blue vibrator purring in the palm of her hand.

"Oh, Connie, you're blushing," Meredith almost shouts. "They are going to love seeing you blush just like they do."

"Well, I hope to hell I am blushing," Connie says, turning one shade pinker. "Last week I would have tried to plug this into my dashboard."

"We've got one of those, you know—"

"Of course you do," Connie says, shaking her head and smiling. "I know right where it is. Right down the first aisle. I think I told someone last week it was a fish locator."

Meredith laughs so hard she bumps into Connie and they both drop to the floor at the same moment to pick up the cute blue waterproof vibrator and Connie would have given away everything she owned just that second for a photo of Meredith and herself crawling on the floor of Diva's, trying to catch a swift-moving vibrator while the rest of the world drove through traffic, turned on the oven for dinner, worked overtime or cried into a beer at the corner bar.

"This doesn't mean I'm staying," Connie says just as she snatches the vibrator. "I might not stay. Do you hear me?"

"Right," Meredith says, mocking her.

Right, my ass, Connie thinks as she laughs herself back into the chair and holds out her hand for the next sex toy, which happens to come in her new favorite color—beet red.

seVenteen

23. *Tell the people you love that you love them. Do it more.*

The bathroom on the fifth floor of Geneva's office building is like a palatial harbor for every woman who has discovered its location. There are three extra long and extremely soft couches, spotless sinks, wicker baskets filled with plush blue washcloths, scented lotions, stalls as wide as most Manhattan apartments, flickering candles that smell like the earthy forest after it rains in central Wisconsin, and a cluster of chairs that have doubled as Jessica and Geneva's office for as long as Diva's has been in business.

Jessica, unaware of what is happening at this very moment at Diva's with her mother, has claimed their usual meeting spot—the two big chairs next to a waterfall—an absolutely real and wet waterfall in the women's restroom. The first time she heard running water in the bathroom, and turned to see the floor-to-ceiling masterpiece, she wanted to strip down and jump right into the decorative display, reminded of the rippling sound of the waves along her favorite beach in northern Indiana, the beach her mother and O'Brien took her to so many times as she was growing up. Jessica loves the cascading sound of the artificial oasis. And sometimes, while she waits for Geneva to free herself from the chains of the numbers and figures that keep her partner tied to her desk in her accounting world, Jessica moves the big chair close to the pool and dips her fingers in and out of the water that tumbles down and then miraculously rotates right back up to the top of the falls.

"There's something sexy about water," she told Geneva the first time they claimed the room as their permanent meeting place. "It drives me wild."

"It's wet, for one thing," Geneva had suggested.

"I think it makes me want to let go," Jessica said, as she touched the falls for the first time. "Makes me remember being a kid, back when not much bothered me."

"What changed?"

"Life. A broken heart here and there, my parents' divorce, college loans. The usual stuff. Just like everyone else," Jessica answered, lost in the rise and fall of the water.

"You need to let go, baby," Geneva offered.

But Jessica had held on. She held on to her potent and remarkably powerful need for success in the business world. She held on to her notions of love and sex that were apparently much more freeing for her customers than for herself. She held on to a small box that was locked and sealed with her heart and inhibitions, and where she kept the key to that invisible box was a secret, even to her. She held on for a very long time to the notion that her mother would never accept her, that what she did would never be enough, that it was best to not merge their lives.

This day—with hours of work stretched out in front of her, with unsolved problems, the rising strain of staffing an upcoming festival and this wild party that is being designed to launch Diva's and Geneva and her into a new national orbit—the water makes her pause. She cannot stop herself. Jessica leans back, slips out of her lovely black heels, rests her head on the back of her chair and pushes her left hand into the water.

Then she groans with pleasure.

Her right hand is riding on her thigh, Jessica Franklin Nixon is smiling, her legs dangle like toothpicks in the wind and for the first time in a very, very long time, she is thinking about sex. Not her customers having sex, not her mother having sex, or Geneva or someone she sees on the subway— but herself.

A whisper of wind, a breeze from a slight movement right in front of her, makes her open her eyes. Startled, Jessica opens her eyes to see Geneva standing close, hands on hips, smiling as if she has just witnessed the landing of a vehicle on Mars.

"Geneva."

"Jessica."

"Where were you, baby?" Geneva asks.

"I was just sitting here," she explains. "Waiting for you."

"Jessica, did something happen in New Orleans?"

"Lots of things happened in New Orleans."

"Did you sleep with someone?"

"What the hell, Geneva? When would I have had the time? Are you kidding?"

"Girl, you have been nothing but a pent-up piece of work for a very long time," Geneva tells her. "You sell sex toys but I bet you never use them, and when the heck was the last time you had a date? And this business with your mother. How did it go?"

Jessica longs to jump inside of the waterfall and stay there for a year or two. She has not had a date in longer than she can remember, and when she thinks of dating it is men who make her turn sideways, not women, or maybe not women, and yet there is this unsolved canal that leads her right back to her old female flame, Romney. Why?

And her mother. Better. Getting better. Not the best. But a bridge she thought was uncrossable has been half crossed and Jessica has begun whittling away at the wedge she placed inside of her own heart to keep her mother away.

Geneva is studying Jessica as she shuffles several file folders from one hand to the next. She's waiting patiently for Jessica to speak even though she knows that Jessica has no idea what to say. She looks at her watch, feels the lunch-hour meeting time eating itself up, launches into her noon lecture.

"You are clueless, aren't you?" Geneva asks Jessica.

"What the hell do you mean?"

"For a woman so business-savvy and out there and attractive and feisty, you are like a 14-year-old girl, woman. What happened to you?"

Jessica sits up. A small fire ignites itself somewhere deep inside of her bloodstream and she wants to bop Geneva in the head, or maybe start a water fight in the bathroom they use as an office refuge.

"Tell me, wiseass, just tell me. Stop all this dancing around whatever's bugging you. We have a lot to do."

"Let me explain it with a story," Geneva says, kicking off one shoe so she can curl her foot underneath her. "If I said you were in heat and we just got on with our business here, you'd probably never speak to me again."

"How poetic," Jessica says sarcastically, stretching back to where she was before Geneva entered the picture. "So I'm in heat, am I?"

Geneva quiets Jessica by holding up her hand and then launches into a story about a friend of hers, Elaine, who discovered her sexual attractiveness one day sort of by accident. Elaine was on a business trip and, like Jessica, the woman was all business. She never paid any attention to the physically passionate part of her life, beyond a rare date or romantic fling that gave her about as much satisfaction as a trip to the dentist. And then one day she was reading a novel on an airplane and the book had a section in it about a woman just as sexually dead as she was.

Jessica looks up at Geneva with a mocking smirk. Her "get to the point" face does not make Geneva hurry. Geneva happens to think this is an important discussion and she happens to know there was some serious flirting going on in New Orleans—by Justin, the factory manager, if not Jessica. She also happens to know that being satisfied in every arena of your life is truly important and that Jessica has not been satisfied with a man, a woman, or with herself for a very long time. But she is getting close.

"The book made Elaine think," Geneva goes on. "She thought about missed chances, about rapture, about the fact that she might miss her sexual peak—as if such a thing is possible—that she might be attractive now and not the following year."

Jessica is listening. She doesn't really want to, but she is listening because this morning when it was her turn in the bathroom she had done that very same thing, just after she finished worshiping the new door that her mother had put up, a door that she was able to close behind her.

That morning, hands on the sink, totally naked, with absolutely no makeup on her face, before she hopped into the shower, Jessica Franklin Nixon looked at herself. She ran her fingers across her forehead, turned her head first to one side and then to the other, backed up so she could look at her ass, her flat stomach, the way her thighs and calves had miraculously held their athletic shape since high school, and then she ran her hands down the entire length of her body. "My body," she said aloud, as if she had never seen herself before, never felt her own skin under her fingertips, never dared to caress herself in a way that someone else might think was sexual.

"I am beautiful," she told herself, haltingly at first and then, after a few seconds of deep breathing, of reaching inside of herself, as if her body was a pillow and she was fluffing herself up, she said the three words again and she believed them. "I am beautiful."

And then she thought of her mother.

While she moved into the shower and washed her hair and kept her mind on a track that was as distant and unfamiliar as a wild kiss, she thought of the years her mother had given away. Years of sleeping alone, of no romantic involvement, of never addressing what must have been at least an occasional sexual desire. Jessica thought about that and she wept.

Jessica wept not just for her mother but also for her own missed chances. She wept for the years she had lost when she could have known her mother, called her a friend, put her own hand back inside of her mother's heart and life. She wept for not being ready for Romney and for walking away from other chances at love. She wept for knowing, finally knowing, what the ache inside of her—in that now hollow spot just at the top of her pubic bone—must be.

Sexual longing.

Desire.

The need to be touched.

The ability to let someone slip inside of her not only physically but any other way she wanted them.

Lust.

Every single thing she tried to help her customers embrace.

Jessica cried for having realized her loss before it was too late, before she missed a good year, before her hips swelled and her breasts fell and she could no longer harness her sexual and physical and mental power and then she stopped herself right in the middle of that thought and grasped the idea that her mother, pushing 60, was sexy and had just lured Burt Reynolds into the bushes. She thought about her last professor, a lusty woman of 69 who had two lovers, a trail of ex-husbands, and a list of men and women who would have loved her in a second if she would have them. She thought of her manufacturing consultant in downtown Chicago, a woman 55 years old, who had a lover of 23. And then Jessica cried some more.

She cried quietly, a steady stream of lovely tears that fell from her face onto her firm breasts and into the water that poured down her body. Jessica realized that her tears were like her shower—a cleansing—an awakening that collided with her sorrow for having put something so valuable, so real, so important, on a shelf for such a long, long time.

When she stepped out of the shower, dried herself off and looked once again into the mirror, Jessica saw someone new. She saw a 30-something woman who was sexy, hot, alluring, powerful, beautiful. She felt the way she did when Romney had held her, talked to her, simply looked at her, and she felt a surge of energy that seemed to change the color of her skin, the way she stood, how she knew she was going to attack the day and its multiple problems, how she moved and stood and even looked out the damn window.

Jessica Franklin Nixon was indeed in heat and she intended to stay that way the rest of her life. In heat and needing so much to tell her mother she loves her, that she is sorry, and that she gets the message she has been working so hard to share.

"So," Jessica says, smiling in a way that is unfamiliar to Geneva. "What happened to your friend?"

"Everyone started hitting on her," Geneva replies. "She put down that damn book, which we should probably sell at the store, and she took in a breath and she was a changed woman, a woman who embraced her sexuality, who knew she had it, who wanted it and so did everyone else who looked at her or came within a one-block radius of her sexually charged self."

Jessica throws back her head and laughs and Geneva says out loud, "Oh, yes, baby, just like that," and Jessica laughs again, heartily, and parrots her words, "just like that," and then she tells Geneva that she knows exactly what she is talking about, what her friend Elaine had discovered.

"Truth be told, baby, men *and* women have been hitting on me for a while now," Jessica admits. "If you stay long enough, and we don't switch back to our business discussion, you'll hit on me too."

"In your dreams, honey," Geneva shoots back, laughing. "I've got my hands and mouth and pretty much everything else full at my house. Besides that, you saucy straight girls are too slow, and you are *definitely* too short for me."

"Hey, Geneva," Jessica asks, scooting her chair forward just a bit and totally disrupting her business meeting seating chart, not to mention her usually business-driven, anal life, "Can you tell, really?"

Geneva likes the new Jessica so much she wants to dance around the bathroom. The two women have worked so closely for such a long time that there isn't much they don't know about each other. Jessica has been the mastermind planner and she's had fun driving to this Diva place, but Geneva knows more than Jessica does about balance, about keeping your pie plate full all of the time, about making certain all the corners of the world are filled.

"I can tell and so can every man who walks past you, darling," Geneva whispers seductively. "I told you—you are in heat—and I know there's a better way to say it but it's me and you here, baby. You are spicy, girl. Very spicy these days. It sort of coincides with the arrival of your mother now that I think about it, and I just hope you can keep it and, especially, use it. And your mom, Jessica—well, she's smart and sexy and when she's in the store, in case you haven't noticed, she sells more than anyone."

"My mom and I have collided in a good way. It's not over, but we are both trying like hell to make it work. Thanks for caring, Geneva. I needed a slap upside the head."

"Care, my ass. I've always cared. Let's just see what the hell you do with it. And just so you know, baby—your mother is hot but you still don't have a clue."

"What do you mean?"

"You have no idea?"

"What?" Jessica asks, totally mystified.

"Baby, women and men hit on you, and I heard you and you claim to be physically attracted to men. Am I right so far?"

Jessica nods. She's thinking. She's hot, but she can still think.

"The best sex you've ever had, the greatest love of your life up to this moment right here, has been with a woman, right?"

"Right."

"Which brings me right back to the clueless part."

"Maybe I want everyone. Maybe I'm into that polyamory gig where people have several lovers. Men. Women. Whatever."

Geneva loves Jessica. She cannot imagine her not in her life, in her world, living too far away. She'd throw herself in front of a New York bus for her and at this very moment she knows a hell of a lot more than Jessica knows.

"Jessica, why do you have to decide?"

Jessica shrugs and says it seems as if it would be easier.

"It's not like we're playing dodge ball and you're picking teams," Geneva advises. "Just go with it. Just flaunt your sexual self and see what happens. You've let go this far—why not just take off the entire shell and see where the hell you go?"

Jessica pauses. She wonders if Geneva is right. Wonders if she, for just the second time in her life, should let things simply happen. If she cuts back a bit on the use of the duct tape she's been using to keep her life in place, what might happen? Who might happen? When might it all happen?

"I'll try," she finally says, surrendering the last piece of camouflage that she has used to keep herself away from the wild dogs of the world.

Geneva applauds her, throws open her bag of folders and spreadsheets and numbers and the two women plunge back into the world of business as if they have been discussing what to make for the gang at the employee appreciation dinner.

And there is much to discuss and not every discussion has an answer that can be as simple as the word "sex."

By 3:55 P.M., Connie Nixon Franklin believes she has become a senior citizen sexpot. She has her AARP card and is wondering, as she occasionally runs into the back room to look at the notes she made during her crash course in the use and care of sex toys, if she is supposed to be having this much fun.

"Quick, hey, Meredith, what did you say again about batteries and plug-in vibrators and the differences in sensation?" she asks as she races into the back room while a woman waits by the counter.

Meredith tells her and wants to jump up and scream. She's created a monster. Connie is not only fun but she's also smart and she cares and the customers—at least the last 15 who have come in since Connie's mini–sex training class—seem to adore her.

And Connie is flirting with both the men and the women. She's flirting and she's selling sex toys and occasionally she'll rush past Kinsey or Meredith, who cannot stop smiling at her, and say something like, "How are you planning on sneaking me across the border?" or ""I want a raise" or "I had no idea" as she maneuvers past them holding a sexual device that looks as if it belongs in a baby's playpen.

And in a moment when she stops, pauses to regroup in between customers, Connie is not at all convinced that she is doing more than just filling in at her daughter's store for a few days. She's not at all sure she knows what in the hell she is doing. She is not at all sure that she should have left Indiana, kissed Burt, temporarily abandoned her list of dreams, forgiven her daughter for living in a world that she never even knew existed, and helped throw her entire life into a tailspin that has her parading around a city she was so scared of just days ago as if she knows what in the hell she is really doing.

Connie is afraid to look in a mirror because she may not recognize herself but she's also hanging on to #37 on her list so tightly that she tells herself she cannot afford to change directions—especially if it means going backwards. But pausing just around the corner from the desk-door, from the eyes of her co-workers, and with her hand resting on a long purple feather that is attached to a finely woven black leather handle, Connie Nixon Franklin doubts herself. She doubts her ability to sell like this, to keep up with the kids she works with, to rotate her life so quickly without even calling O'Brien, for crissakes. What could she be thinking? Has one kiss caused her to go mad? What if Jessica fires the whole damn bunch of them when she finds out about her whip-toting mama?

Then, as if someone has sent out an emergency call for a career/sex counselor, Mattie, the lively hairdresser, bursts into the store, not so much walking as floating. She's looking for Connie in the middle of a late afternoon coffee break, takes one look at her standing with her hands on her hips, at her perfect hair, her eyes focused on the billowing material against the far wall, and she thinks she's helped create her own Diva.

"Connie, you look fabulous!" Mattie exclaims as she moves in for a hug. "Actually, you're glowing."

"I got kissed."

"It's the hair," Mattie yells, pumping her fist into the air. "Actually, I have someone else for you to kiss. I came in to see how you feel about blind dates."

Connie cannot speak. If she said the word "fuck" as often as other people did, as often as her own daughter or most of the women she worked with back at the hospital, that is what she would say right now. But instead she says nothing. Nurse Nixon looks at Mattie as if she too has lost her mind and cannot find it.

"Connie, you are sort of shimmering here while you stand under the shadows of the lovely sex toys. I'm serious. There's this guy who comes in to my salon all the time and I told him all about you and he wants to take you for a drink or dinner and I already checked him out. He's not a serial killer or anything."

"Honey," Connie stammers. "Hold on. I just left Indiana, plowed into the sex-toy business, kissed Burt Reynolds, found out my oldest daughter's deepest secrets and now this?"

"Burt Reynolds?"

"Well, he looked like Burt Reynolds and let me tell you, if Burt Reynolds kisses like that you can call me a stalker," Connie shares. "But . . ."

"But what, baby?"

"Shit, Mattie, I just spent the last few hours learning about sex toys because Meredith confided in me that Jessica is on overload, and they have some kind of festival they might need me to go to and I just thought, 'What the hell?' and now I'm thinking for real, 'What the hell am I thinking?' " Connie says, not waiting for an answer, or a breath, or anything from her new friend.

Mattie grabs her and pulls her into the back room while holding up her right hand as a moving stop sign so that Kinsey and Meredith know to leave them alone.

"Sit," she orders.

Connie sits.

"Now listen, woman."

Connie listens.

She listens as Mattie drops her sex bomb. It is a bomb filled with years of sexual heartache from all of her clients. It is a bomb that coincides with every ounce of scientific and medical research—research that supports Jessica and Geneva and Mattie's contention that way more women are sexually dissatisfied than satisfied. It is a bomb that explodes with the reality that so many women, even now, even after all these years of education and experimentation and liberation, still do not know their bodies. It is a bomb that explodes with the very real and extremely sad news that many women still buy into the sexual and historical stereotypes that blast the world with the idea that men like and need sex and women do not.

Woman do not need it.

Women do not like it.

Women do not want it.

And the bomb explodes in Connie's brain as if she had been holding it in her own hand.

"You know this is true because this has been your life and the life of many of your friends," Mattie tells her softly, but forcefully, as if it was something she knew Connie had already thought about and held close but needed to hear from someone else. "I bet you have talked about this now and then with your friends, but I bet it's even hard for you, a woman of the world, a nurse who has seen and heard and felt and witnessed everything."

Connie wants to know how a hairstylist can be so smart but she is afraid to speak. Because every single word Mattie is saying is true.

"Do you know how many of my clients I send right here to Diva's after I warm them up with a shampoo and a neck massage and they begin to cry and tell me something like, 'I've never had an orgasm'?"

Hundreds, Connie imagines, but she knows Mattie does not want her to speak and she also knows she probably could not speak even if she was allowed to at this moment.

"My God," Mattie continues, putting her hands against her face. "It's so damn sad, Connie. So sad to see these beautiful, seemingly smart women trapped in this arcade of a life, and to know that they have never experienced sexual pleasure in a way that can set them free. Jesus. I'm tempted to quit and come over here to Diva's myself. I'm serious. I know Jessica wants to open more stores and I feel like it's saving womankind to offer services and classes and sex toys and a place to allow women to let go and learn."

Connie has a sudden urge to get up and run through the streets with a vibrator in her hand. She has heard the stories, some of the same stories that Mattie has heard. Women cradled in her arms who are sick and boozy with medication telling her their deepest secrets. Women holding Connie's hands tighter and tighter when their husbands come into the hospital or ER room and do not bother to touch them or kiss them or offer any words of love. Women, some of them her own close friends, who have been raped and abused, who have yet to cross over that very long bridge back through sexual recovery to their own selves.

"Connie, look at yourself, look at who you are, and how you've lived, and what you could bring to a place like this," Mattie urges her. "You are sexy and you are not a kid and you have all those years of administrative poise and tact just burning a hole in your pocket. Jesus, Connie, besides that, can you imagine anything more fun at this particular moment in your life than being your age, selling sex toys, and hanging out with really cool hairstylists? If you were coming in here, wouldn't you like to talk to *you*?"

Connie doesn't hesitate this time. She stands up and she grabs her friend Mattie and she hugs her and as she hugs her she thinks about Mrs. Cradow. Mrs. Cradow who, back in 1983, was in bed 12 on the surgery ward following a hysterectomy. Mrs. Cradow, who had given birth to nine children. Mrs. Cradow, who had lost five children during the third to sixth months of pregnancy. Mrs. Cradow, who was only 39 years old but who looked like a grandmother. Mrs. Cradow, who had already taken her 16-year-old daughter to Planned Parenthood when her husband wasn't looking. Mrs. Cradow, who had grabbed Nurse Nixon just below her elbow and pulled her with such force onto the bed and who then wept in her arms and said over and over again for 15 solid minutes, "This is the happiest day of my life because I will never have to worry about having another baby. Who needs a womb anyway? I have never once, not once, had sex for pleasure."

Connie Franklin Nixon turns her head just a tiny bit while she is standing in the stockroom of her daughter's sex-toy store and thinks she sees her old white nurse's cap drop to the floor and vanish under a shelf right under the stacked boxes of the new blue vibrators.

Then she turns her head back towards Mattie's ear and says, "No, Mattie, I cannot think of one thing more fun than being right here, right now. But what about Jessica?"

"Oh, Connie, all you have to do is let her know you love her! Just tell her, for crying out loud," Mattie answers.

"Jessica needs you here and in all places of her life just as much as you need her. Just tell her."

"I will," Connie promises, to her own astonishment. "The second she walks in here, that is exactly what I will do."

And then they both giggle as an entire carton of strawberry lubricant falls off the shelf when Connie leans in to hug Mattie and dozens of tiny red bottles roll against each other and sound as if they are clapping at the edge of a vast and endlessly enchanting stage.

Eighteen

17. Another camping trip. Don't call me crazy. I loved camping when I was a kid. I want to resurrect the old tent and do it. Fires every night. Burnt hamburgers. Cold mornings. Whiskey in my coffee cup.

10. Buy a convertible. Something flashy, red or blue. Put the top down and drive someplace without thinking. Just get in the car and take off.

36. Enough. Stop writing—Connie—Stop writing and start doing something.

I t could be a movie.

This same thought is rocketing through three minds at the exact same moment. Connie, Meredith, and a last-minute recruit who appeared as if by chance, Sara Hanson, a lanky 22-year-old casual acquaintance of Kinsey's who happens to be free for the days needed to drive a trailer loaded with sex toys, a tent, an assortment of camping gear, and three women all the way from Times Square to Michigan, attend the big festival, and drive back again.

Connie is the designated mother. The woman in charge. The official organizer, keeper of sanity, harmony, and the religious conductor of a schedule that appears by the time the fascinating group of traveling women reach the Ohio-Michigan border to be an insane impossibility. She has not even bothered to write down the glorious #26—the mixing of friends—and here she is in the middle of it so thick it may be impossible to travel in the proper direction.

"I cannot believe we are doing this," Connie says from the co-pilot seat as she sips from her seemingly perpetual cup of gas-station coffee. "How did this happen to us? I can't believe my daughter hired me."

A laugh from Sara—a dark-haired misplaced '60s flower child look-alike who wears long skirts and tank tops and the requisite Birkenstocks, and who is sprawled in the backseat of a van that is filled from top to bottom with Diva products—has everyone say in reply, "This would be a *great* movie!"

"No shit," Meredith laughs from behind her own coffee cup. "There's no turning back now."

No turning back.

Connie wrestles with this idea as she stretches her legs and realizes that in just a few hours they could pull up to her Indiana house, toss the sex toys into her garage, fire up the grill, pop open some dry white wine, and call it a day—or a week and a half.

O'Brien, of course, has not only encouraged this fasci-nating cross-country adventure but has run interference for Connie with her daughters, who Connie assumes may be wondering if their mother has lost her mind. "She's having fun and cannot tend the grandbabies," O'Brien told them, trying to get them to grasp the notion of a grandma peddling implements of sexual satisfaction at a women's festival. "After raising the three of you, don't you think it's just dandy if your mother has a little adventure, tries something new, kisses a few boys, and drives off into the sunset for a while?"

O'Brien had tried hard to stay with Connie's new life direction when Connie called to fill her in on the latest installment of the Nurse Nixon Story, which was unfolding daily in what was starting to seem like a comic parade of chance, change, and a flaming middle-aged crisis. Connie told her everything, from her sex-toy training session to the notion that she had been newly ordained to save as many sexually repressed women as possible and, try as she might, O'Brien actually could not discourage her friend.

"What do you have to lose?" O'Brien said, after hearing how Jessica never batted an eye when she heard about everyone's new plans for her mother. Jessica was just not totally prepared for this cross-country trip, not to mention the business at the store, the pending arrival of the new products, the final planning for the big launch party and the list of business-related activities so long that it was about to make her go blind. She had planned but not quite enough and, to Jessica, her mother was suddenly like an unexpected Christmas bonus.

"Mom," Jessica had confessed, when Meredith and Kinsey and Mattie told her their plans, "I need you and not just to fill a spot at the store but a spot in my life as well. I love you, Mom."

Connie never imagined it like this. She never imagined it would slide into a gorgeous embrace, a wall that seemed to collapse with the weight of the words, "I love you," and with the unexpected acknowledgment of mistakes made, forgiveness accepted, lost time to be made up, and a wild and joyful horizon of possibilities to be explored.

"I love you too, Jessica," Connie told her daughter. "That has never changed, it will never change. But this work thing—you and me, and me working for you. Is it maybe too much?"

"Yes and no," Jessica answered honestly. "From a business standpoint it's perfect. But from a 'Can I really work with my mother?' standpoint, I have no clue. . . . But let's try. Do the trip, Mom. See what happens. Let's do this one day at a time."

That "one day" philosophy is what Connie thought about when she sat in Jessica's bathroom as she packed for the trip and wrestled with her list, wrestled with the notion of the flashing #37. And then she realized that what she was doing, where she was going, and what might happen were all part of the dream list anyway. Connie convinced herself, as she wrote down numbers on her slips of paper for her camping pants' pocket, that she had not veered too far off the list after all and that maybe, well sort of maybe, it was all going to be just fine. "I won't lose anything," she whispered out loud, hoping the sound of her own voice would make her believe.

And O'Brien thought about losing Nurse Nixon herself. She thought about how she already hated driving over to Connie's house and knowing that she would not be there. She hated the empty kitchen, the quiet, untalking walls, the way Connie's newspapers landed against the side of the front door and then fell into the bushes as if they had totally surrendered and abandoned the house.

"What if you never come home?" Frannie asked her.

"How could that be possible?"

"Jesus, baby, look at where you're going. Anything is possible. You should know that now more than ever. You are headed to a wild music festival to sell sex toys with a couple of kids. Did you even suspect that was possible a week ago?"

"Hell, no."

"Well, then, maybe you will never come home."

"Maybe anything is possible," Connie admitted as she watched the New York traffic from the window of Jessica's apartment. "Maybe I was guilty of getting so caught up in a plan I thought I had to follow that I almost missed something. A whole bunch of somethings."

O'Brien knows she is right and she tells her that, as well as the truth that she misses her. Misses her like crazy.

"Oh, shoot, Nixon, you'd be out of your mind worse than you are already not to go to Michigan, not to see what it's like to sexually turn on women you may never see again the rest of your life but who will always remember the way you looked at them when you handed them a sex toy," O'Brien said, relenting in her own selfish desire to get her pal back in town. "So just tell me what you need and I'll send out your stuff right away."

And Frannie mailed everything, from a pair of long underwear in case the Michigan weather turned ugly, to Connie's camping clothes, a cookstove, and her hiking boots. And then Connie had to bravely call Sabrina and tell her daughter that she would not be able to baby-sit during the coming weekend because she would be en route to one of the largest women's music festivals ever held in the United States of America.

"You're going to the Lakeside Women's Festival?" Sabrina asked in a tone of voice that was not even close to being soft and quiet.

"Yes, I am."

And the conversation went downhill from there, until Connie made up an excuse to hang up, told Sabrina to call Jessica if she had any questions, and promised to send the kids something from the trip.

Then Burt Reynolds called, yelped like a puppy when he

heard about the road trip, and asked innocently if he could somehow manage to meet her at a wayside, or maybe in her tent. Connie was flattered but filled him in quickly with the facts of a festival that surely did not disdain men but disallowed them from joining in on the women-only adventure. It's just for females, she told him. It's an oasis of safe, woman-driven openness. It's apparently a place bordered by a private lake where an entire community is erected every June. It's a self-contained, volunteer-orchestrated womb of life. A female Nirvana with music, camping, food, demonstrations and more laughter and fun than some women experience the rest of the year. It's a terrific spot for Diva's to set up shop for a week with a captive, sexually deprived, understimulated, ready-to-feel-good, all-woman audience.

And driving through a very long and heavy rainstorm with baby Sara, teenager Meredith, and the constant whistling of highway wind through the back window that never quite shuts, Connie Franklin Nixon—nurse extraordinaire, mother to three would-be goddesses, kisser of Burt Reynolds, follower of her list of dreams—rides out this portion of the sort-of-welcome storm of her life with as much abandon as she can muster for a woman who thought she would be home packing boxes, picking out a new couch and worrying about osteoporosis.

And as she drives she holds on to the slips she keeps dragging out of her pocket as if they are the only things keeping her from jumping out the window and running back the way she has just come.

The drive to female Nirvana takes two days and requires a one-night stay along the Interstate near Toledo. The kids—especially Sara who has just turned 22 and wants to see the inside of as many bars as possible before she gets back to her New York apartment—suggest a night out, but Connie cracks the for-real whip she's taken to carrying with her—pink and black with a deep red handle—and makes them work out a plan for setting up camp, the mobile Diva station, and a schedule for the week-long festival. She promises both her charges time off for fun and thinks, the entire time that she is speaking, that running a portable sex-toy store is not unlike running a ward of a hospital—except it may be a lot more fun.

Connie Franklin Nixon has never been to an all-women's festival in her entire life. She's never ridden through three states with two 20-something, openly wild women. She's never commanded a trailer filled with sex toys, eaten Chinese take-out while huddled over makeshift plans for a booth display, or had a man call her on her cell phone and talk dirty while she is driving a van as her companions sit in the backseat and play strip poker.

This is what Connie thinks about as she hugs her pillow in the double bed with the crappy mattress, next to Sara and Meredith. Her traveling companions have fallen asleep to the constant hum of a hotel air conditioner while Connie, restless, her mind a buzz of extraordinary ideas for a kick-ass booth at the festival, rolls over for the eighth time with the certainty that none of what awaits her was drafted onto the pages of her list of dreams even when she thought she was ready to hibernate in her house more than 400 miles away in Cyprus, Indiana.

Or maybe, just maybe, every single thing was right there on all those years of pages and she just never bothered to notice.

———

Incredulous.

Remarkable.

Unbelievable.

Jaw-dropping.

Connie, Sara, and Meredith are visually and emotionally awestruck. They are creeping through a superbly organized maze of womankind that snakes its way inside a forest on an unmarked dirt road a good 30 miles from a town so small it is not even on a map. They have driven through Detroit, east and north from Flint, and have been following a road lined for miles with women sleeping in ditches, waving flags, singing to each other, cooking over portable grills, and holding each other's hands and babies as they wait for the main gates to open.

Diva's display and sales pass allows them to enter the festival a day early so they can set up their portable shop and their own camping area, and prepare for the estimated five to eight thousand women who are expected to pass through the gates of the festival during the next 48 hours. Already it looks as if half of those thousands are camped and eager to get inside, and the three women—the Diva Sisters, as they have taken to calling themselves—are stunned. Sara has been crying since they hit the dirt road.

"This is so beautiful it's shocking," Sara mumbles as Connie drives slowly past campers, trailers, women leaning against their backpacks, and several buses jammed with camping gear and a lovely assortment of women. Meredith is hanging out the back window, passing out Diva-labeled condoms and shouting, "Come see us at the Diva booth," while Connie wonders how this kind of thing could have been going on for the past 30 years without her knowing a thing about it.

"Oh, my God," she whispered when they first saw the lines, the women. The tangle of energy seemed to rise from the snake of female humanity waiting patiently for the gates to their own personal heaven to open. "I had no idea something like this existed, that women came together like this had no idea."

Women waiting not for hours but for days and—after Sara jumped from the van to walk alongside and hug women and to help Meredith pass out more condoms and Diva brochures—she reports back that there are no arguments, no testy women, no one worried about being so far back in line. Sara reports that she can feel not one ounce of negative energy.

And passing through the gate is only the beginning.

"Welcome to a new world, a woman's world, a view of life as it could be," the festival registrar tells Connie as she places a plastic bracelet on her wrist, explains the logistics, and asks Connie where she intends to work for her festival shifts during the week.

"I'm working at Diva's," Connie says.

"Is this your first time?"

"Yes."

"Oh, honey, what took you so long?"

Connie wants to haul out her wallet and show her the photographs of her three daughters, her two grandchildren, her nurse's credentials, her insurance cards, and then pull down her pants to show her stretch marks and varicose veins. But the woman addressing her is about 65. She probably knows exactly what took her so long. So Connie just smiles and enters a world that is run and managed and has been perfected over the years by women who have a vision for a universe where tolerance, acceptance, openness, and sharing are standard fare.

Everyone does several volunteer shifts in the kitchen, garbage patrol, transportation, day care—whatever they can do, the festival worker tells her. No men are allowed on site, except the few from the local community who come at night to pump out the portable toilets or to drop off fresh produce, and their arrival in womanland is announced with a very loud horn. There are special teams, which Connie signs up for, of trained professionals who can intervene for everything from medical to mental mishaps. There is no crime. No one is hungry. When a woman with a baby showers, the stranger behind her holds the baby. Women sing spontaneously as they wait in line for vegetarian meals. Old friends hug under trees and help each other change flat tires. If a shift is short of help there are immediately 25 volunteers. There are sections for women with children, women who do not drink, women who want to party until the sun rises over the outhouse, women who are in wheelchairs, women who want to camp in total quiet, women who want to sit around the campfire with other old-timers.

Meredith, who has known about this festival for years, and has attended smaller events, tells Connie and Sara about the three women who started the festival back in the late '60s as a way for women musicians and artists to flourish in their own space. "They wanted to create a safe haven for women, a place where women could come together at least once a year and be totally free of any male influences or pressures. And the festival has grown steadily, improved and sustained the women who attend it during the rest of the year," she tells them. "And my mom was here for the first 15 years and brought me when I was a baby."

Meredith ain't no baby now, Connie knows, as they back up a trailer, haul out and erect a major tent, set up the Diva Sisters' base camp, and then drive the van and trailer alongside

of the lake, past waving women and towards the craft and retail area where they spend almost eight hours creating a Diva
haven and retail shop for the hundreds of women who they
expect to visit them starting the very next morning.

"Exhausted," Connie declares that night as the three
women collapse in webbed camping chairs and sip the wine
Sara made them buy before they left civilization. "I feel as if
I've just been transported to a foreign land and that my entire life has been a lie. *And* I'm exhausted."

"Wait," Meredith cautions. "By this time tomorrow night
the ground will be humming. There will be women camped
all over the place and you will see and feel even more than
you do now."

Sara has been sitting and sipping without speaking for a
good 30 minutes. She's staring into the fire, drinking her
wine and occasionally looking up into a sky that is littered
with stars that can only be seen from a remote location in the
summer in the state of Michigan. Connie thinks Sara is seconds away from jumping onto her chair and leaping right
into the sky.

"Think about what you were doing a week ago," Sara says
when Connie and Meredith finish their discussion about
what is about to happen for the next seven days. "I'd been
staring at my college diploma and wondering what in the hell
I am going to do with the rest of my life, when I ran into
Kinsey at the coffee shop."

"And . . . ?" Meredith asks.

"Most women would have hesitated," Sara tells her Diva
Sisters. "They would have mentioned the rent payment, or the
need to find a real job, or they would have offered a frightened
laugh. Why is it that 'no' is often our first response—well,
the response most likely to come first when someone asks us

something that society has conditioned us to think is not correct? How did that happen?"

Connie looks up at Sara and sees a woman who is younger than all three of her daughters and perhaps wiser than all of them put together. She sees someone she has learned to trust in just the span of a few days. She sees a young woman of remarkable intelligence who dresses like a Joni Mitchell groupie, loves to drink before 10 A.M., has probably never turned down an offer for fun in her life, has a shiny college degree and a pierced nose and eyebrow, and who believes that she can turn the world on a dime if she wants to.

"It happens because we just let it happen," Connie tries to explain as the wind picks up and makes the smoke change direction so that she has to cover her eyes. "It's so easy to think that you are going to be different and live your life in a way that honors all your dreams and then, well, shit happens and most of us become ordinary."

"You don't seem ordinary," Sara says, waving her hand through the smoke as if she can feel it slide through her fingers.

"What?"

"Connie," Sara says, sitting up. "You could be my grandma, really, and here we are, drinking Pinot Grigio, sitting by a fire in the middle of nowhere, and we're about to turn on thousands of women. You said 'yes.'"

"This time," Connie admits. "But I almost didn't come. I had this plan just like other people have and I was terrified to veer off it."

And she fingers the scraps of paper in her pocket and ushers out her life story for her Diva Sisters, a parade of haste, a warning from the hinterlands, a saga of happenings

that overtook her world and gave her just a few regrets but
not enough opportunities.

Meredith scoots her chair towards the fire. She looks
right at Connie and smiles.

"Jessica tells me all kinds of stories about you, do you
know that?" she tells Connie.

"What?"

"Don't tell her I told you this, but her stories . . . well,
Connie, you may have looked at yourself as a 'no' woman,
but you totally inspired Jessica to start this business, to be
her own woman, to rock the world with more than just a vibrator."

Connie can't speak. She holds out her glass so that Sara
can fill it again and then she says very softly, "What?"

"Really," Meredith assures her. "Jessica's told me stories
about how hard it was when you decided it was better to be
alone than to be with a man who gave you nothing but a fishing anchor. She watched you—hell, don't we all watch our
mothers?—and she may have slipped away, but she really
never went anywhere, Connie. I think you've probably said
'yes' more than you think you have."

Connie closes her eyes. She struggles to remember
something. There is a faint glow towards the back of her
wine-woozy mind. She sees herself curled up on the old
couch, divorced, cramming past 1 A.M. for some stupid-ass
nursing certification that she needed so she could make another $1.50 an hour—$1.50 which meant the difference between having and not having dance lessons, a tank or two of
gas a month, and a pair of shoes for Jessica's birthday that
otherwise would have been a laughable request.

"Mom"—Jessica's young voice echoes in Connie's
mind—"I know what you're doing."

Connie turns to see Jessica at 15, proud, growing into her

beautiful blonde self as if she knew all along where she was going, walking towards her at 1 A.M. on a November morning with her t-shirt pulled down over her knees and her hair sticking up as if she's just had her finger inside an electrical box.

"What?" Connie asks.

"I know you stay up like this to study so you can get that raise," Jessica tells her.

"You do what you have to do."

"But is this what you want to do?"

Sitting by the fire with her eyes still closed, Connie looks at her daughter and sees years past that moment, maybe towards a night when she is sitting by a campfire and figures something out, maybe in a week when something else new and wonderful gleaned from this week has magnified and jumped into her heart, maybe something she remembers about another moment that is as reassuring as this very conversation, the moment of remembering, the new knowledge of the past becoming present, becoming now.

"Yes," Connie told Jessica. "I want to give you the world, honey, you know that, and sometimes giving you the world, or something extra, or maybe just the basics, is not always easy, but it's my choice. Yes, Jessica, it's what I want to do and what I want to do this very moment, right now, the second you are standing there in your underwear and t-shirt."

Slowly, Connie opens her eyes, and she looks through the flickering crimson and gold flaming arms of the fire.

"So many people never live in the present and keep reaching back," she tells Meredith and Sara. "There's lots of stuff back there to pull out, but I think some of us, some of us who are lucky, we learn not to apologize all of the time. I've made tons of mistakes and many of them with Jessica. It's silly, really, to think that you would make the same choices now that you made back then. Look back right now, both of you, and think about some dumb-ass thing you did."

Both women laugh.

"It could have been something you did yesterday or a month ago but the bottom line is that you are not the same person this second as you were even a day ago," Connie, the head Diva Sister, assures them, trying to reassure herself as well. "I sure as hell would never have said yes to this adventure ten years ago, or even a month ago, but sitting here right now, I can't imagine saying no to anything."

"Anything?" Meredith asks with a dirty laugh, as if she is about to propose something way, way off the beaten path.

"Yes," Connie shouts boldly into the chilly, star-filled Michigan night air. "Yes, yes, and yes again."

Connie's voice carries like a wild seed in a March wind and women camping along the edge of the lake hear her yesing into the wind and they spontaneously join in chanting from one campfire to the next—"yes" and then "yes"—until there is a chorus of yesness reverberating throughout acres of land, out into the fields, back through every single camping loop and towards the gate by the dirt road where sleepy guards are holding steamy cups of hot coffee to stay awake until morning. "Yes!"

And each woman who chants "yes" thinks of something or someone to say yes to.

A lost lover.

One missed chance.

Tomorrow's question.

A lusty rendezvous.

Postponed dreams.

Third and fourth chances.

That one time something or someone wonderful may

come back around again because she is ready. Now she is ready.

Change . . . please, now, change.

And just yes, just yes, to this one moment, a chorus of women, ready, wanting, eager, to be, to try, to never settle, to be together, to navigate for these few precious days into a place of glorious companionship, learning, yearning—into a tide that will tug them into a sea of *yes* with or without a well-worn list of dreams.

An endless, bountiful sea of yes.

Nineteen

22. *Stop doubting yourself—for God's sake, you save people's lives for a living.*

Josie has a slight limp, a very loud voice and absolutely no inhibitions, so when she says, "I'm 62 years old and I don't believe I have ever had an orgasm," at least forty women within a 75-foot radius hear her and turn suddenly in the direction of her voice as if they have been shot in the face.

Sara and Meredith cannot move. It is barely noon and they have worked like ravenous dogs for three hours. They greet. They sell. They explain. They laugh. They hug. They start all over again and the astounding stories, just two hours into their Diva festival week, are stories that have already made them weak in the knees.

And there limps Josie.

"What the heck is this?" she demands, picking up a lively looking black-and-silver instrument with a curved end and a couple of buttons that fits like it was made to nestle into the palm of her hand and only her hand.

Connie looks quickly at her Diva Sisters, then steps forward. She wants to leap over the counter, grab Josie in her arms, rock her like a baby, and whisper in her ear, "It's never too late." But instead she moves along the side of the Diva counter, which is actually a string of portable tables arrayed with sex toys, gently puts her arm around Josie and says, "Come over here for a second."

The second lasts a good 20 minutes as Connie quietly explains how a hand-held G-spot vibrator works. Josie stands silently, not moving, listening with such attentiveness that Connie bumps her shoulder against the woman once to make certain she is still breathing.

"Most women never have an orgasm by vaginal penetration," Connie explains, as if she has been demonstrating sex toys her entire life.

Josie looks into Connie's eyes and then quickly looks away, not because she is embarrassed, but because her mind is focused on the magical black instrument that could, just could, take her to a place she has never been before.

"There is this wonderful soft spot just inside of your vagina, not more than an inch or two, called the G-spot, which ironically is named after the man who discovered it— as if such a discovery is possible by a man," Connie explains, remembering the details of her Diva sex-toy class from

Meredith perfectly. "And this little instrument is designed to stimulate that wonderful spot and hopefully give you the orgasm you've been searching for."

"How do I find the spot?" Josie asks in a barely audible whisper.

"That's the fun part," Connie answers. "You get to play around with this. You will find it, believe me, and while you are looking you may find a few other places that get you flying as well."

Josie abruptly covers her face. Nurse Nixon emerges quickly.

"What is it, sweetheart?" Connie asks.

"This is suddenly so embarrassing, and I rarely get embarrassed."

"I'm a woman, and I also happen to be a nurse, so don't be embarrassed," Connie says, putting her arm around Josie.

"I don't even know where my clitoris is."

Holy hell.

Connie wants to cry. She wants to storm a stadium filled with men who are grabbing themselves in the crotch area and yell, "What the hell have you been *doing*?" She wants to line up the hundreds and hundreds of women she expects to see during the next seven days and tell them all at one time, "You can do this. You can let go. You can be sexually satisfied with a partner or with yourself. Let me show you how. You never have to worry or wonder again."

"Oh, sweetheart," Connie manages to tell Josie, "lots of women have never been sexually satisfied and I can walk you through this if you won't feel embarrassed. Can you listen for just a moment? You don't even have to look at me. Is that okay?"

Josie squeezes her eyes shut and nods and then Connie

takes her on a verbal tour of her own body. She walks Josie
down her own breasts, she waltzes her down her stomach
and towards her vagina where Connie, Nurse Nixon once
again, explains the ins and outs of every inch, every fold,
every mound that lies in a place that has been foreign territory for Josie.

"See?" Connie asks gently.

"I think so."

"Do you want to try one of these?" Connie asks, touching the edge of the black-and-silver vibrator.

Josie smiles. Her smile is a trillion-candle light in the
middle of nowhere, dawn in the spring desert, the light of
early winter before nightfall, and she nods and then asks
Connie to take her back to the table and to show her every
single thing that she might consider purchasing that could
squeeze into her backpack.

Josie leaves 45 minutes later, having spent $349.55. She
hugs Connie for so long that three other customers come
and go, and then she promises to report back before the end
of the week, after she has a chance or many chances, she
says, winking, to try out her Diva delights.

And Connie sighs and once again wants to cry. She wants
to cry for every single woman at the festival, in the state, in
the country, in the entire world who has never been able to
feel the release of her sexual power and energy. She wants to
cry for Josie and for every lost soul like Josie who has already
paraded into the Diva booth. She wants to cry for herself, for
having given up on something that she is just beginning to
realize is a very important and wonderful and necessary part
of life. And she wants to cry, too, for remembering that she
hesitated, that she questioned coming to the festival, that
she was so consumed by drifting through her list she might

have missed the entire point of the list even as she focused
on #22, which is propelling her through her day like a wild
rocket.

And the parade of women galloping towards the Diva
display is seemingly endless.

The customers come and they go. They ask questions
and they say things, they tell the Diva Sisters things they have
never before been comfortable telling anyone—ever.

The stories are astounding. The stories are heartwarming.
The stories are a litany of longing, loss and heartache. They
are beautiful and powerful. They are funny and terribly sad.
Occasionally there is a story of hope. Sometimes there is a
sexual success story.

——*No one told me I could feel something like this.*

——*My friend wanted to show me but I was too embarrassed.*

——*My husband says it's my fault. He says I am frigid.*

——*Sex has never lasted more than five minutes and that's been
for 26 years.*

——*I went into a sex-toy store once and there were men behind
the counter. They laughed at me and I slapped the first one I could
reach and ran out the door.*

——*I had no idea things like this existed. Show me. Show me
now. Please. Can you hurry up, because my friend won't be back at
the tent for a few more hours?*

——*My daughter needs this shit. Give me one of these and this
one and I love this one. I'm getting her all of this and I don't care
what it costs or what it says. Wrap it up. She will not go through what
I went through. She will not.*

——*I've been using sex toys for five years. Do you have any job
openings?*

——*If you start sex-toy parties you will put Tupperware out of
business in three weeks.*

All of this in just the first day and that evening the Diva

Sisters proudly call Jessica, who is flabbergasted by their success but quickly agrees to ship more products to Flint, and then tells her mother she is proud, says, "I love you" three times during the phone conversation, while Sara and Meredith slump on folding chairs, exhausted and humbled by the scope and importance of what they are doing.

"Mom," Jessica asks, "are you doing okay?"

Connie is so tired she could lie down on the portable table and sleep while the vibrators whirl in her ears. She is thinking about her deep bathtub in Cyprus and a cold glass of wine and someone rubbing her feet and how in God's name she is going to sleep on the ground for seven more nights, but she pauses before she answers. Connie looks over at her Diva Sisters, who are talking quietly, mostly with their hands, and at the women in the booth next to them who have quickly become her friends, and she funnels back through the day to Josie and Cara and Susan and all the other women who may now have a shot at sexual happiness be-cause of Diva's, because she is there, because she has done something that just might be very close to remarkable.

"Honey, I'm frigging bone-tired but I don't remember ever feeling like this in my entire life."

"Like how?"

"Satisfied. Totally exhausted but satisfied and powerful and as if I've changed more lives in one day than I did all those years on the surgical unit or sloshing through some stupid-ass meeting or kissing the rear end of yet another 29-year-old doctor who had no idea how to tie up his own damn pants."

Jessica laughs so loud that Sara and Meredith can hear her, and then she suggests that it must have been a pretty damn good day for Connie to feel what sounds like euphoria.

"I get what you do now, Jessica," Connie told her. "I see

something now. I only glimpsed it when I was in New York, but I get it in a whole new way now that sexually repressed women are weeping in my arms and begging for Diva products and advice."

"Advice?"

"I'm trying."

"Mother, maybe you should take some of the products back to the tent with you," Jessica suggests. "Do you have a clue what you are talking about?"

"Sort of."

"What do you mean 'sort of'?"

"Meredith gave me the crash course, remember? And every time there is a break we play with the toys."

"It's not quite the same," Jessica suggests.

"Honey, the tent is a little crowded and this is not, let me repeat that, NOT something I want to discuss with my daughter, who happens to be my employer," Connie says forcefully, turning her back to her Diva Sisters.

Jessica laughs, which disarms her mother.

"What is so funny?"

"Think back, say, three weeks ago, Mom," Jessica says. "Could you have even imagined this conversation?"

"Hell no," Connie says, starting to laugh, too. "Three weeks ago I was a different person."

"Me too."

"Two miracles," Connie suggests. "Remember what I told you when you were little?"

"Which time, Mom?"

"There's always something," Connie reminds her. "That's what I told you."

"I'm realizing that more than ever," Jessica says, wondering as she does so what the next something might be. "Mom . . ."

"What, baby?"

"Thanks."

"For what, sweetheart?"

"For everything. Thanks for everything."

Connie cannot speak. Connie Franklin Nixon, nurse to the masses, senior citizen sexual goddess instructor to thousands, kisser of Burt Reynolds, keeper of the list of dreams, grandmother of two—and soon to be three—and lusty seeker of unprovoked passion, simply cannot utter one single word.

"It's okay, Mom. Did I tell you that I love you?"

Connie whispers, "I love you too, baby," just before Jessica hangs up and a line of women, short, tall, young, old, single, married, heterosexual, homosexual, bisexual, transsexual, asexual, white, black, religious and non-religious, spiritual and not-so-much, from every imaginable neighborhood and pattern of life in the United States, Europe, New Zealand, Canada, China and even Indiana continue their parade into the tent that covers the Diva Sisters and their products that Connie has lined up and filled with batteries in a spot for testing she lovingly calls "the playpen."

Three days of almost total sunshine, one rainy morning, a night spent laughing during a campfire with new Diva clients— women who are unafraid to tell their life stories, an assortment of female humanity that would make Eve jealous and rock with gratitude—following eight concerts, three workshops, after Connie's first group shower in 44 years, discussions about everything from cheap sex to how the United States totally screwed up the Gulfshore disaster, countless moments of quiet introspection while walking back and forth from the campsite to the Diva display ... and Nurse

Nixon gets her first voluntary call to duty as a member of what is affectionately known at the Lakeside Festival as the Marauding Mothers.

It is 1:21 A.M. on Thursday morning. Connie thinks she is dreaming when she hears a gentle voice so close to her ear she can almost feel the breath against her cheek.

"Connie. Connie Nixon. The nurse. We need you."

Sara and Meredith, awash in young dreams that have been sautéed with very long and delicious Margarita party trimmings, do not budge.

Connie answers "yes," and only then remembers suddenly that she is in a tent in the middle of Michigan, peddling sex toys, and not rolling over in her old double bed in Cyprus, Indiana.

"Connie, we have a crisis and we need you STAT."

Without thinking, Connie's nursing feet move as if they have been set on fire with a blowtorch. She pulls on her sweatpants, a light jacket, and the ever-handy fanny pack filled with everything from a tweezers to a secret dose of Demerol that she has kept within arm's reach almost every day for the past 30 years. She unzips the tent, steps into the low beam of several flashlights and sees the faces of three other women who quickly identify themselves. A surgeon, a physical therapist, and a volunteer guide.

New faces. New lives. Exploring a whole new world. People who are not like me but who are like me, Connie thinks as she remembers her list and is suddenly seized with the reality of what she is living, what is happening, what she is about to do.

The four women speak quietly, outlining what has happened and what needs to happen next. All are professionals who normally operate in a vision of protocol and now the women stretch that protocol miles from their office and hospital doors, over mountains, through rivers and across the very lake that a woman just threw herself into hoping that she would sink to the bottom, be sucked through a drain-pipe and into the Shawassee River, then out into Lake Huron where she would drop to the bottom and be lost forever as close to Buffalo as possible.

The woman's physical injuries, as reported to them by her friends, appear minor. Scrapes, a possible sprained ankle from a major flip over a downed and very waterlogged tree and, most important, an admission from the woman that she has not taken her anti-depressants for three days.

The women do not judge, they do not hesitate, but they immediately appoint Connie as the Marauding Mother in charge, which is definitely not a problem for Connie.

The four Marauding Mothers come together with a plan in less than five minutes and are quickly guided to their pa-tient by the guard who then stands back and lets the profes-sionals take over.

Following a fast physical injury assessment, a handful of Band-Aids, the removal of wet clothes, a move to the patient's warm trailer and her eager agreement to crawl into her sleeping bag, Connie nods twice to her fellow Marauders and they slip from the trailer and stand guard outside the door. They will stand there all night, the following day, and for a month if that is what is needed.

Connie doesn't talk at first. Instead, she sits on the bed and slips her hands under the woman's neck so that her head is resting on Connie's legs.

"Tell me," Connie says, rubbing the side of the woman's face, moving her hands to massage the tight muscles in the back of her head. "It's fine now, really, talk to me."

The woman, a medium-sized kindhearted mother of three from a city not far from the very Buffalo she wanted to see from the bottom of the lake, mingles her tale with a deluge of tears that do not stop for the next 35 minutes. Connie runs her fingers from the wet edges of the woman's eyes, down her cheeks and back again, without hesitation, as she listens to a story she has heard all too often before.

She's tired and lonely.

The side effects of her medication have buried her libido, her slim waistline, her ambitions for a second career.

Once, maybe just this once, she wanted to be away from the confines of a medication that set her free in some ways but held her captive in so many others.

She felt safe at the festival and then, before she could turn back, before she could retreat into a world that would remain clouded but as sane as she might ever know, it was too late. Just too goddamned late.

"I thought if I could just float away that so many people would be happy and not have to worry about me anymore," she tells Connie as she curls against her, weeping. "One tiny part of me watched what I was doing, it was as if I was split into two pieces and one piece was watching from the banks of the lake as I went further and further, but the water felt so good and so I ran faster, and then I fell and I guess someone saw me go under."

Going under, Connie thinks as she listens. Another woman going under. Another woman seduced by the softness of the sea, the waves of life on the other side, the destructive forces of a world that assumes a position and expects you to sit the exact same way it does.

Connie rocks the woman like a baby and cries with her as a friend. Connie Franklin Nixon lifts the weight of a woman's world into her own arms as she moves the woman—someone who could be any woman—back and forth, shifting and sifting her burdens of life from one side to the next.

"I know, I know," Connie whispers into the woman's hair as she bends over her.

"I'm so sorry for all of this mess," the woman sobs back.

"Don't be sorry, honey, it is what it is."

And the woman cries until her own lake is empty and, when Connie asks her if she will take her medicine now, if she will promise to take it every day for the rest of her life, the woman answers, "Yes, I will." And Connie rolls her over, tucks the sleeping bag up around her shoulders, hands her a glass of water, one magic blue pill, and then leans over to kiss her in the soft tender spot just below her left eye.

Outside Connie makes certain there will be someone with the woman throughout the night, and every second of every day of the week, and then she reports back to the Marauders.

The Marauding Mothers are restless then. They need to decompress and the physical therapist invites them into her trailer where she warms coffee, spreads out crackers and cookies, and agrees with Connie and the surgeon that what happened this evening will not be passed on to the woman's home territory, the life she left behind, the already thick file that can now be accessed by everyone in the world because there are so few sacred ground rules left, so few moments of privacy, such little compassion for the bent and broken.

"It happens here sometimes like this," the guide says, her tiny fingers barely able to touch around the coffee cup. "Women feel so safe here, so warmed by the energy that is around them, that they feel as if they can sustain themselves without the armor they have to wear every other day of their lives."

"Wouldn't it be something," the surgeon muses, "if it was really like that, if we could create this kind of funky vacuum where this woman could just float free and not worry?

And all the pressures of the real world were not so magnified?"

"It's like that here in many ways," Connie shares. "This is my first time here but I can't remember a place or time when I have ever felt more free, more safe, more relaxed."

"Well, aren't you the dildo lady?" The guide laughs. "That would make anyone relaxed and at ease, for crying out loud."

"Yes," Connie laughs back. "But I'm so busy making everyone else a satisfied customer that I can't use the products myself."

The women dip into a conversation bordered by sex and lust and love. It is just one more link in Connie's seemingly unending chain of physical love that started with the unexpected discovery of her daughter's box in the garage. The Marauders hold nothing back. Camouflaged by the last hours of darkness, and with a simple battery-powered light, they play a sophisticated game of Spin the Bottle. They share their sexual pains and joys as if they have known each other for an eternity.

There is a story of lost love, a tale of one woman finding that it really was another woman she loved, Connie's buried passions, and the common curse of middle age—a long marriage tethered by familiarity, responsibility, and the unnerving idea that lust is something for the children to inherit.

The women laugh, they withhold nothing, and their stories wage like a friendly war as they tackle the menaces of menopause, the miracle of masturbation, and the wonderment of the very bold conversation they are sharing as the caffeine rips through them like a long blade of excellent fire.

"This," Connie says as she notices a feather of light bending over the far side of the lake, "is exactly what I was talking about, what, three hours ago."

The women smile because they know too.

"This entire night is a gift," the surgeon agrees. "In a week I'll be back yanking out gall bladders and keeping an insane schedule that includes ferrying the kids to day camp, office hours, and a husband who still doesn't get this shared-chores idea, and I'll lean back into this night as if it were a Christmas gift that I have wanted my entire life."

The guide, who in her real life is a stockbroker and a member of the community symphony orchestra, tells them that she has been to the Lakeside Festival for 12 years in a row and that she takes dozens of photographs of the women she meets and strings them together each year into a collage that she keeps right above her computer. She says that she uses the collage as a reminder that she is not alone, that the women who touch her life for this one week each year keep her sane the rest of the year, and that without this female tonic she might go mad.

"It just gives me hope," she tells the Marauders. "It lets me know that my thoughts and ideas about openness and tolerance and lifestyles are not insane. And I never feel lonely or abandoned or like a freak because I think that all people—not just women—should be who they are, who they know they are in their hearts and souls."

The women raise their coffee cups after that and they cannot stop. Their stories flow like the underground river that could have pulled the drowning woman to Buffalo. The physical therapist talks about the woman sitting on a rock at the far corner of the hiking trail that circles the entire lake who was totally naked and unafraid to expose her double mastectomy for the first time since she had had the operation five years ago.

"She told me that she had stopped everything significant and meaningful in her life because her body had changed so much," the therapist tells them. "She said she'd been a dark ball of cancer, a dead end on the highway of her own life even though she has been in remission since the operation, and then 18 women had hiked past her, stopped to say hello, and no one even batted an eye when they saw that she was breastless."

Breastless.

Depressed.

Suicidal.

Alone.

Divorced.

Married.

A lesbian.

An abandoned heart.

An unclaimed soul.

A woman with excessive sexual desires.

A woman with marginal sexual desires.

It didn't matter. Hardly anything mattered except the common threads of the bonds that women can share and celebrate openly and without hesitation at a festival. A festival where a woman could throw herself into a shallow lake, hoping for a quick traverse to the muddy bottom of another lake hundreds of miles away, and experience a resurrection in the arms of a group called the Marauding Mothers who will look the woman in the eye unblinkingly for eight hours straight, and act as if she is sane and lovely without hesitation or judgment.

And Connie Franklin Nixon was thinking that maybe it really was her list of dreams that brought her to this spot, to these lovely moments, to a place where she had to erase ". . . people who are not like you" from her list because suddenly the common, miraculous denominators of all lives were sitting all around her.

Then the sun would not be stopped.

The guard pulls them from the trailer 3.1 hours into a conversation that would be remembered for years. Pulls them from the trailer with one more cup of steaming fresh coffee and an exchange of phone numbers and email addresses, and after Connie had agreed to do the follow-up assessment with the drowning woman twice a day for the rest of the week.

The guard pulls them from the trailer as most of the camp still sleeps, except an armful of women who know when to rise early and look at the sky, blazing like the furnace of hell which they know is really the archway into another day of heaven.

An archway that finds the Marauding Mothers starting a Friday they will remember for the rest of their lives with a display of feminine majesty that includes the cry of a loon, the ricochet of waves across an eager lake, blissful morning coolness and the soft heartbeat of thousands of women who are drowning together in a place that they wish with all of their hearts, souls, minds, bodies, and spirits that they will never have to leave.

Never.

twenty

14. *Maybe sex. Something meaningless. Just sex. A man's hand on my face, my breast. Not caring what happens next. Over and over again. Sex. I can't even believe I just wrote this. It's a HUGE dream. Sex. My list. SEX. This one is a big maybe. But I wrote it down. I can't even believe I knew how to spell it.*

The night before the festival ends is a crashing wave of reality that most women refuse to accept.

Bags are packed. Coolers are emptied. Women won't put out their campfires. A good three hundred of them are swimming at midnight. A group of food freaks, including three internationally renowned chefs, have cooked up a feast with seven days of leftovers. There is a pool of coffee, beer, wine, and soda, and the last three bottles of vodka in all of southern Michigan are stashed at the edge of the lake. World-famous singers, women who would be mobbed to death anywhere else, are wading in the water, hugging women who are just like them but who are not famous and cannot sing a single note. This night, if the Lakeside Women's Festival women were in charge of the world, would never end.

Diva's remaining products, about three dozen of them, are lying like dying twigs in the near-empty trailer. The tables have been stacked. The signs, folded and then folded again, look like lost babies on an international flight as they rest in the empty abyss of the van. Meredith has disappeared into the arms, the tent, the heart, the life of a brassy firefighter from New Jersey who sings in a rock band on the weekends, writes children's books, and has an eight-year-old son. Sara is one of the swimmers. She's also made a name for herself this past week as the wild and wonderful and open young thing from Diva's who put on a lovely red-studded dildo harness over her clothes and boldly demonstrated how to use it during a last-minute sexual power workshop that was attended by a whopping 328 women.

And Connie . . .

Connie is alone. She is sitting in the large stand of pine trees less than a block off the trail leading to the beach where the other women are swimming, eating, talking and postponing unnecessary reality as long as possible. She has the last bottle of Diva-purchased wine tucked against her right leg, a heart that is as light as winter's first snowflake, and a yawning desire to soak in the scents and scene of these last hours of her remarkable past week as long as possible.

The women, the freedom, the fun, the laughter, the openness, the scenery, the food, and even the hours and hours of work, which were some of the most positive and powerful moments of Connie's life have already nested inside of her soul, a new and very permanent part of every breath she takes.

Thoughts of leaving Lakeside in the morning, driving back to New York, and what might happen following that, are left to drift like a slow-lifting kite towards a sky that is filling with the promise of a northern light show and a half moon after a week-long festival.

It happens to be Sunday, which is as cosmic to Connie as her very presence in a place that has turned into a working wonderland for her, and close to the hour when Connie used to sit in her bedroom rocking chair and work on her list of dreams.

Connie laughs out loud, takes a sip of wine, and focuses on her list. The list that she left buried under her tidy cotton underwear in her travel bag back at Jessica's when she packed in what seemed like 12 minutes for a camping trip to Michigan, but that she has memorized. She thinks of this camping trip with two virtually unknown women who quickly became friends, comrades, and sisters.

Sara, with her hippie hair and face and clothes emerges with an embraceable heart and a knack for relating to customers and keeping the books that has Connie and Meredith whispering about her potential future as a Diva employee, or possibly the head of some new training division. Meredith, with her brassy mouth and strident views of sexuality, reveals herself as a kindhearted Diva Sister who is an organizational whiz, an extreme risk-taker, and someone you can count on when everyone else has turned you down or packed up early to leave town.

Me, Connie wonders; what do they think about me? A grandma nurse who can be bamboozled into selling sex toys

first in Manhattan, of all places, and then who agrees to
throw herself into a van that is pulling a trailer halfway across
the country?

A woman who had a hell of a good time. A really good
time, and who does not want it to end.

"Should it end?" Connie whispers off the edge of her
wineglass. "Does it have to end?"

Connie's questions hover close to her as she imagines
what she would write on her list now. This Sunday. This moment when she has passed through some kind of invisible
barrier of change. Right here on the edge of the lake, when
the sounds of her several hundred new friends roll up through
the thick bed of pine needles and right into her heart. Just as
the summer stars begin to dance, and the dry red wine seems
to cascade through her veins, Connie tells herself to be honest, to be as open as the women who laid open their hearts
and lives to her during the week, across a table filled with
sexual devices that proved to be a wonderful bridge.

Be honest, Connie Franklin Nixon.

And the first thing she thinks about is sex. Not making
love. Just sex. Hot #14. The very idea of sex. Sex and more
sex rides itself to the top of her Lakeside Sunday list as if it
were the queen of the world, the madam of everything, the
keeper of secret gems and hidden treasures. And Connie
tells herself that it's about time. It's about damn time,
Connie.

Her hands drop, and she balances her glass of wine
firmly on her left knee, and her other hand digs into the
earth at a place where Connie tells herself she has started
over. Started over from a well-chosen path, from a place of
sometimes-regret, from a spot on earth that was a familiar
road, a predictable journey, a hand-drawn map that needed a

major overhaul, a wise choice once that was destined for re-
discovery, a life that had turned a corner and forgot to look
over a shoulder.

Not going back is fine.

Not going back but occasionally visiting might be best.

Not going back but remembering so you don't see the
same view twice.

Not going back so you can turn a new page, write a new
chapter, develop an entire new list.

Not going back so you stretch and grow and see yourself
in a light that you never knew existed.

Not going back so that you can fly. *Fly.*

The wine, now that the bottle is nearly empty, is the
medication of the Goddess of Lakeside Fun and Connie
wants to kiss this goddess on the lips as she kicks off her tennis shoes and runs her feet through the pine needles and the
earth that is rich and fragrant with a patch of heat from a
long summer week. Heat from wanting. Heat from needing.
Heat from waiting too goddamned long.

Not going back. Never back to the abandonment of
youth, of married life, of sex by design, of limping towards a
tryst that was over before it began, of assuming the position
and expecting to be taken care of, of waiting for a second
player to ride onto the scene and create magic as if it was impossible for that to happen when a table was set for one,
when the real world never waited, when it was possible to be
the rider in charge of destiny.

Starting over.

The words "starting over" roll from Connie's mouth as
she breathes in the scents of a summer night and says the word
"sex" over and over again. She says it slowly and then louder
and then she whispers it to herself, gives herself permission

to say it often and one more time after that, and to have it
again and again.

The word "sex" becomes a small pillar that drives itself
to a place deep down into Connie's own sea. She becomes a
swimmer on the shore of her own lake, diving with the pillar
between her teeth, deeper and deeper, to the lock she placed
on her sensual and sexual self the night her would-be lover
John left her with a credit card and a bracelet that still sits on
her wrist like a chain.

A goddamned chain.

Her chain.

A chain she embraced for so many long, long years.

Connie bends at the waist as she reaches her lock, swimming as if her life depends on it. She bends and she takes
her teeth, her lovely, perfect, straight teeth that she has
bleached and brushed and taken care of for 40-plus years
since she had braces and vowed she would always have fine
teeth. Connie puts her teeth on the chain from John and she
smiles. Connie smiles and then she runs the metal links over
her lips as if she is kissing the bracelet. She kisses it, runs her
tongue over its fine, expensive edges, and she lingers there
as if she is a lover and she does not want the moment to end,
as if she is in charge and she will let go whenever the hell she
wants to let go, as if she knows exactly where she is going.

The metal slips under her tongue and touches her perfect, white teeth. She runs the thin and long edges against
the backside of her lip and one tiny edge catches there, on
the precise spot where a lover might bite her, might dig in
and ask for more, might stop and wait for an answer that will
only come with a movement of hands and legs, the tilt of a
neck.

Connie stops and feels the taste of iron, blood—her

blood—and she thinks of it without hesitation as her sexual communion. She bites a bit harder and feels a trickle of that very blood move against her lip and she closes her lips to kiss it, to accept it, to own it, and then she stops.

She stops and she listens to the wind balance itself. She listens to women, free and fast, diving and laughing and running. She hears singing and the clang of silverware and laughing in every single direction. When she concentrates, the vibrations of the water and the night sky and the small edge of wind bring her individual conversations that make her smile so wide that she almost loses her grip on the bracelet.

Almost.

But Connie is in charge. She will not let the bracelet slip from her lips until she wants the bracelet to slip from her lips. She will let go only when she is ready. And she is not ready just yet.

She closes her eyes and sees the pages of her list of dreams, dreams buried under her cotton underwear, disappear under a wave of passion that crushes her and takes her breath away. It is a wave of longing and long-forgotten passion and lust for what she knows is hers, should have always been hers, will now be hers for the rest of her life.

And she almost lets go then when her chest heaves and she feels the weight of her longing move through her entire body as if someone else is inside of her and moving like a lover would move. Moving with the rhythm of Connie's very breath and along every inch of her skin until she feels as if she is owned and wanted and almost to an orgasmic place of release, but she still does not let go.

The light June breeze stops and Connie bites into the bracelet with her four front teeth, dipping her head, lowering her torso and thinking one thought—sex.

Just sex.

And then she moves her head up fast and hard. Fast and hard because she wants it now and the bracelet holds on, trying to keep her chained, keep her still, keep her quiet, but Connie pulls harder and the bracelet cannot stop her. Nothing can stop her. No one can stop her. Connie feels the bracelet stretch and then it pops. A sound of metal giving way and sliding pieces of a jeweler's branding escaping from its long-held and terribly controlled position.

Connie Franklin Nixon, Diva Sister of the world, sexpert to hundreds, a vibrating maker of lists, drops the broken bracelet from her teeth into the palm of her hand. And she never opens her eyes.

She does not open her eyes as she takes the bracelet and throws it over her shoulder where it lands in the dark of the night on a tree branch 30 feet in the air. Where it lands and where it will stay for the next four years until a young woman searching for a way to find romance ponders that thought under a tree, looks up, finds the glistening and slightly tarnished band, takes it back to a small town in Ontario, melts it down and forms a gold necklace out of it that will one day catch the eye of a man she will love the very second he touches her neck, just there, just below the small curve of the beautiful gold necklace.

And then Connie laughs and she sighs as a woman might sigh with lingering pleasure after terrific sex.

Fantastic, wonderful, lovely, and frigging terrific sex.

twenty-one

1. *Stop being afraid.*

6. *Take yourself to confession. Make the penance easy.*

Jessica will kill them, slaughter them like easy prey after a long drought that has made them thirsty enough to lose their minds, make rash decisions, not be accountable for their thoughts and especially their actions.

Thirty-three minutes into the ride back to New York, Sara asks what many normal people might think would be a simple question.

"Connie, how far is it from here to where you live in Indiana?"

The distance is a tiny blip on the map. The span from one finger to the next. Fifty miles here and then fifty miles there. Right down this way past the Interstate, across the top here and then down just a thumb or two, Connie explains, pointing with her finger while Meredith drives and tries really hard to keep from laughing because she knows.

She knows what they are about to do.

"Let's just go," Meredith suggests. "We're close. We worked our asses off this week. It would take, what—one part of a day? Maybe one extra day at the most? What do you think?"

Sara does not hesitate. She says, "I'm in," without taking a breath, so Connie, who knows exactly how to get there from Eastern Michigan, thinks about telling Meredith to turn left on Highway 12.

Connie hesitates for seconds and realizes that a month ago she would have hesitated for minutes. She is still a little afraid, just a little, but when she thinks about #1 she tells herself if she cannot knock #1 off the list she may as well throw the whole damn thing out the window so it can blow all over the freeway.

"What the hell," Connie shrugs as if this is something that she does all the time, twice a week, without blinking.

"Are you sure?" Meredith asks, smiling.

"I'll call Jessica," Connie answers, feeling cocky, still riding the high from addressing #14 in a way that is beyond huge. "I'll just leave a message on her machine and tell her we might be a day or two late. Will that screw anything up for Kinsey?"

"Not really," Meredith replies. "I think I had the day off anyway so I could crash because I knew we were going to be wiped out after this week-long adventure. Kinsey is in between gigs. He's cool. Good to go. He's our man."

Wiped out? Connie thinks. Wiped out, my ass. Who's tired? I feel as if I could fly. I want to fly. But, I'll play dumb. I'll say I *had* to stop home. I'll figure this out. I'll make this work with Jessica. Leave it up to me.

Connie calls immediately, praying for an instant, as she is dialing, that Jessica will not be there. And she is not.

"Honey, it's Mom. We are exhausted and I really need to stop at home and get my bills and check on some things, so we may be at least a day late. I hope this isn't too much for you. Call me. We should get into Cyprus before 5 and I'll make certain the girls don't look under your old twin bed."

Sara and Meredith cannot stop laughing and, when they hit Highway 12, Meredith turns right, and not left, and the Diva Sisters have a good five-hour drive to discuss the thrills and spills of living in a place like Cyprus, Indiana. There's the handful of stoplights, cheerleading tryouts, the mid-summer citywide picnic, a battle over sewers on the south side of town, neighbors who lean over fences that are actually painted white to share coffee and wine, sixteen people of color, a singing waitress at the midtown coffee shop, and not one sex-toy store.

First, however, Connie needs to notify O'Brien, who picks up the phone on the first ring and screams as if she has been slashed with a surgery instrument when she hears that Connie and the Diva gang are cruising into Cyprus. Not only will she be home and available in five or six hours but the hospital crew is scheduled for its monthly Monday night binge at her house and how cool if Connie could make it.

"Come to my house," Connie suggests. "I have my Diva Sisters with me, but you will have to be in charge of the food and drinks and I have no clue about what the house looks like."

"Your house is as fine as it has always been," O'Brien

says. "The mail is on the table, the newspapers are stacked
up against the dishwasher, and the damn real estate agent
keeps calling me because you will apparently not return her
calls."

"Shit."

"What does that mean?" O'Brien asks.

"Well, I have been a bit busy and I never checked phone
messages this week, which is like a miracle, and I am way behind on my bright idea to begin showing the house next
week."

O'Brien snorts and reminds Connie that it's her house
and her life and if she is not ready, because she has been busy
selling sex toys and not cleaning out the rest of the garage,
all she has to do is tell the real estate agent.

"Tell her what?"

"Tell her you will get back to her when you're ready."

"Ready."

Connie thinks "ready" is a funny word on this particular
Monday. She thinks she may need to put a wedge into whatever idea, or plan, or thought had formed her decisions before she took off like a wild cannon shot, before she yanked
the gold bracelet off of her wrist, before she felt the hands
of life embrace her in a way that was not so much holding as
a caress.

"We'll talk tonight, baby," Connie promises her old
friend. "What time are you expecting the mad bomber crew
to arrive?"

"By 7. I'll have them start at my house because I won't be
able to get ahold of all of them. I'll bring the food. Stop and
pick up some drinks and warn those two young things what
they are about to get themselves into."

"Like they don't know," Connie says as she hangs up and
wrestles with the idea of her soon-to-be surprise homecoming.

Wrestles with how to explain to her hospital friends what she has been doing for the past few weeks, rehearses it in her mind and decides quickly, as her traveling companions also wrestle with the radio dials, where to stop for coffee and what it might look like in a place called Indiana, how absolutely comedic her description of the last three weeks might sound to someone who knew her just a month ago when she was wiping up the floor outside the day room on her hospital floor with a surgery gown.

"Oh, well," she practices in her mind, "I just flew off to New York after I discovered that my daughter is a sex-toy entrepreneur and then we ended up in New Orleans and, yes, we saw the damage from the flood waters everywhere we went but the French Quarter looked beautiful, alive. And, well, then I met this man who tried to shut down the manufacturing side of the sex-toy business, those dildos and what-not, and he got a crush on me because, oh, as you can see, I got a wild new haircut in New York from this woman I met on the airplane. Then right after that Burt Reynolds, oh, the man, who looked like Burt Reynolds, kissed me, not just once either, and then we had to get back to New York. Then this woman, here she is, it's Meredith—the other one, Sara, has just a few piercings and tattoos, and Meredith, she's the punky-looking one—she asked me if I would help out at the store and then after she trained me very quickly in the use and care and feeding of sex toys, well, after that I almost had no choice but to help out with this road trip where we went to the Lakeside Festival—I am sure you've all heard about it. It was quite a week and you have no idea how many women are sexually unsatisfied and we sold tons and tons of products and did demonstrations and many of the women came back to tell us they had tried the products and that they work perfectly and now here we are for just a quick visit before we head back to New York, and . . ."

And, what?

Connie's question hangs in the warm air of the van for a good 50 miles before they stop for gas and Sara wonders if there is a U-Haul dealership in Cyprus where they can unload what is left of their product line and drive back to New York without the trailer. The question hangs for more miles after that, when Connie drives and her two assistants fall asleep in the back seat cuddled up in each other's arms and snoring softly as if they are in their own beds, which makes Connie think about women.

She thinks about how safe and wonderful it is to be able to lie curled around someone you care about who also cares about you. Meredith and Sara have managed to slip out of their seatbelts and are lying on the bench seat behind her, Meredith against the back of the seat and Sara in front of her, curled against her as if they have done this a hundred times before.

Connie glances at them, sleeping like babies, and thinks that their very position defines the wonderment of female friendship. There is nothing evil or insane or sick or sexual about what they are doing. There is only their even breath, an occasional movement of a leg or elbow as the van rattles over a bump, and the miraculous notion that these two women have swiftly bonded like blood sisters over shared time, space, and a common cause.

It's beautiful. Simple. Lovely. Wonderful.

Connie thinks about the parade of female humanity that passed before her during the past week. An assortment of women of every shape and size, of every conceivable sexual preference, from places and professions throughout the world, with views and ideas and ideals that stretch out in a multitude of directions, with absolutely nothing in common and everything in common.

She finds herself wondering if she showed her own daughters, her Jessica, Sabrina and Macy, the true joys and wonderment of female friendships.

Was I open enough? Did they see me laugh and act with abandon with my own girlfriends? Was I too damn stuffy? Did the divorce change everything and not necessarily for the good? Should I have been a better example? Was I too strict? Not strict enough?

The questions flash by like road signs, one after another; questions Connie has already asked herself so many times the words fall from one part of her brain and into the next in almost rehearsed action. But she still wonders.

And she wonders about the example of her own mother. Did she ever lie against the backseat of a car with her head in her best friend's lap, laughing out the window, down some long highway in the hinterlands of Illinois? Did she pull over for a hamburger and a beer? Did she sit for hours in the town café smoking the cigarettes that eventually killed her while she talked about sex, men, and more sex?

The Diva Sisters roll and rotate as Connie maneuvers through her memories, pausing when she remembers Lydia, the woman who lived next door to them when she was growing up and who was almost always in the kitchen when Connie came home from school. Connie's mother—who never worked outside of the home, who believed in all things traditional and Catholic, who had dated and slept with only one man her entire life, who slipped a book on menstruation and sexual intercourse under her pillow and never spoke about it, who loved to drink cheap wine on Friday nights with the guys before her father's poker games and who then retreated silently to the kitchen, who cried like a baby when Connie told her she was getting a divorce, who was always there but who seemed to always have something to say that she never could quite say—her mother told her once that she loved Lydia.

It must have been menopause, Connie thinks as she passes through a long stretch of nothingness just above the Indiana border. She remembers her mother crying at odd moments and, once, waking during a storm to find her drinking coffee at 2 A.M. and doing crossword puzzles at the kitchen table while lightning flashed against the side of the house and exposed the tired eyes of her mother who suddenly looked ill, sad and terribly lonely. Connie remembers standing there and then looking up to see Lydia moving in her own kitchen across the yard as if she were putting away dishes.

"Can't sleep?" Connie asked.

"No. I just can't sleep, sweetheart."

"Maybe you and Lydia should just hang out, Mom. It looks like she's up too."

Her mother smiled. It must have been a secret, Connie thinks now, a secret that the two women were meeting in the middle of the night for coffee, for comfort, maybe a glass of port wine, for whatever it was that they fed each other.

"I was just over there," her mother confided. "Sometimes we wake up and when we can't sleep we come to the kitchen, turn on the light and then she comes over here or I go over there."

Connie looked at her mother and then she looked across the yard and into the kitchen where Lydia was now standing with her hands on her hips, not moving, apparently looking out of the back window and into the black spaces that now filled up her own yard.

"Is Lydia your best friend, Mom?"

Connie's mother had smiled. Her face grew still and she

rested her chin on the top of her hands, which were rolled into little balls. She shifted her legs under the table and then she closed her eyes.

"I love Lydia," she answered. "She's the best friend I've ever had. I just love that woman. I don't know what I would do without her."

Lydia's kitchen light went out then and Connie's mother got up, set her cup on the counter, and said, "Come on, baby, the storm is almost over. I'll tuck you back into bed and maybe we can both go back to sleep."

It wasn't until this moment, driving past cornfields, tiny burgs that would fit into the left finger of New York City, sleeping Divas on the back seat, toward a potentially uproarious welcome-home party, the new and enlightened uncertainty of the future, that Connie knew her mother had friends, loved them, and had showed Connie how it was done and how she'd got it, most likely way before Connie got it.

The storm, Connie thinks, has really just begun.

Meredith has been in every room, touched every piece of furniture, opened cupboards, sat on the couch, walked through the garage, examined all of the photographs on the wall outside of Connie's bedroom and, without asking, started to unthaw a small turkey that she discovered when she opened up the freezer in the back of the garage.

"What the hell are you doing?" Connie asks her, laughing at the absurdity of cooking a mini-Thanksgiving dinner on a wonderful summer evening when the hospital gang will be arriving soon with so much food they will never be able to eat it all.

"Half of the turkey is the smell," Meredith tells her,

working some kind of microwave-water-back-to-the-microwave magic on the turkey.

"The smell," Connie echoes, hands on hips, watching Sara move her shoulders into the couch the exact way Sabrina used to do. "You're making a turkey dinner for the smell."

"Well, we can eat the damn thing and then pack sandwiches, if we ever leave, to eat in the car and you have not seen me around a turkey and, Connie, this house and your pre–sex-toy life, it's just so Rockwellish that I am compelled to do this."

Rockwellish.

Connie knows what Meredith means and she likes it. She likes that her backyard touches her neighbor's backyard and that they often share a hose, garden utensils, a half-ass power mower. She likes that she can wave to people from her front window and that she had a turkey in her freezer. She likes that in this moment there are people in her house, women filling up all the quiet spaces with talk and energy and laughter and life—wonderful, noisy, wild life. She likes that her couch is worn so thin in the places that matter— where a rear end bumps against a cushion, where elbows rest on extended arms and feet graze like lazy cows against fabric that has been discontinued so long that no one could find its name in a file if they tried. She likes it too that there are hints of a life past the worn exteriors that have rumbled through the walls and floors and often out the back windows when no one was looking, or when her three girls *thought* that no one was looking. She likes the house, what happened here—mostly—and that someone from the big city who grew up in apartments, rattled around in buses and in the subway, and who understands the peace of a place that is simple and familiar would feel comfortable enough to go through her underwear drawer and freezer.

And yet.

Yet, nothing feels the same. There is no urgent need to stay in Cyprus, to clean out the garage, to march back to the hospital to say hello to everyone who will not be at this evening's party. There is no yearning from the center of her uterus to stay staked to the corners of her house, of her plan, of any damned list that she may have worked on for the past 30-plus years and this throws Connie into a near tailspin. A tailspin that she disguises with activity.

She opens the mail, tosses a bag of chips and a cold beer at Sara, tells Meredith to let it rip and to throw down plates and chill any white wine she finds, and to make herself so much at home that she wants to buy the place. Connie talks on about O'Brien, about her own pre-dildo life as a head nurse, as a manager, as someone who is destined for a new career as a medical consultant, as someone who is totally confused at the moment about her immediate destiny in spite of all the planning and lists and who does not want any-one, except maybe O'Brien, to know about these confusing aspects of her life.

The turkey-thawing adventure works; the house quickly smells like a holiday and Sara and Meredith ask for a personal tour of the room that was once Jessica's and, when they get inside, Meredith, the kick-ass, no-holds-barred woman of the world, yanks her cell phone out of her pocket and calls Jessica.

She calls Jessica, which makes Connie want to run screaming from the house because she expects the old Jessica to answer the phone, the girl-woman who up to a few days ago had kept her professional identity a secret, the quiet loner, the control freak of the century, the emotional riptide roller-coaster kid. But instead someone else answers

Meredith's call. Someone who Connie can hear laughing during a conversation that is a one-sided cliffhanger.

All from Meredith:

"Yeah, it's kind of retro in an Indiana-virginal sort of way."

"No way? The window?"

"Mothers always know, honey. She *knew*."

Connie shakes her head. She knew about the window and the ladder under the trees and the party on the one freaking Friday night her girls were ever left alone when they were teenagers.

"Under the mattress. How clever! Do you want me to look?"

Meredith motions for Sara to get off the bed and to lift up the mattress, which Connie can verify has not been moved or flipped or turned for at least ten or more years. Not since the weekend she went through the house in a manic relay that had her cleaning as if she had just been knighted by Martha Stewart. A weekend from hell, as her children would surely remember it—the grand weekend from hell.

Meredith motions for Sara to lift up the bed and to fish around with her hands. Connie can't stand it and she starts pulling back the covers and lifting the far edge of the bed so that she can slip her fingers between the mattress and the box spring. What could possibly be under the mattress? What other Jessica secrets has she yet to uncover?

Connie finds two magazines that make her laugh out loud. A *Playgirl* and a *Playboy*. She holds them out for Meredith and Sara to see.

"Magazines, huh? Just like the movies, Jess. Seems as if your sexual ambiguity started right here in this house."

There's more, Jessica says. *The beginning of everything,*

Meredith mouths to them as they keep looking and finally Sara finds it wedged between the metal frame and the side of the box spring.

"Oh, my God!" Sara exclaims, grasping the ancient vibrator in her hand as if she has just discovered a cure for some horrid social disease. "It's a little baby vibrator."

Well, shit, Connie thinks as Sara drops it into the palm of her hand. Just shit. She stands there, imagining where Jessica must have purchased it, probably at some roadside joint between Indianapolis and Cyprus during a funky car trip with her girlfriends. How brave of her, Connie thinks. How damn brave.

Without thinking she says out loud, "I should have bought this for her."

"What?" Meredith and Sara say at the same time.

"I should have given her this. She probably bought it from some sleazy guy who sold them from the back of a trailer."

"My mother bought one for me," Meredith shares as they all sit on the bed staring at the small vibrator in Connie's hand as if it may speak at any moment. "It freaked me out at the time but it worked like a dream."

"Hey," Sara says, crossing her legs and pushing her skirt under her ankles, "you weren't the same person back then as you are now, Connie. I would have freaked if my mom had given me something besides a slap across the face if I even said the word 'sex.' "

"It was a different world, really, think about it," Meredith says without hesitation. "My mom was an old hippie chick and I was raised in this wonderful way that allowed me to embrace all of my self—including the sexual parts. I know I was like one in a million."

Meredith and Sara decide to wrap up the vibrator and

carry it back to New York, where they will start a personal
sex-toy museum in the corner of the Diva store. Connie
drops the vibrator into Sara's hand and when they leave the
room she stretches out sideways on the bed and tries to
imagine herself back when Jessica must have purchased what
was probably her first sex toy.

Worried.

Overworked.

Scared.

Lonely.

Impatient.

Mostly broke.

Trying hard to be everything to everyone.

And apparently frigid as hell.

"It was a different world," Connie says out loud just as
the doorbell rings, holding onto each syllable as she says it
so that she can convince herself with her own words. "And I
was a different person. Totally different. I have to forgive myself. I have to."

Then Connie rolls off Jessica's old bed, kneels on the
floor, pulls the mattress back into its old well-worn position,
fixes the sheets for one of the Diva Girls and then skips, actually skips, into the kitchen excited as hell to witness the
look on O'Brien's face when she sees the wild hair and glowing eyes of a woman almost, sort of, and very nearly unleashed.

The sex-toy party doesn't start out that way. Not at all. Never
in a million years. Not even close.

There is first, and for a very long time, fun and friends
who gallop like wild ponies through the house embracing
the Diva Girls, sampling turkey, piling bags of chips and
homemade salsa and an assortment of other food a good foot

high onto the counter. There is a zipping hot coffeemaker, beer and wine for the nurses who do not have to get up until the beginning of the second shift, three cakes, a bag of freshly made cookies, a plastic container filled with fresh fruit, and an assortment of wonderful women that could probably find a cure for cancer, save the environment, hopscotch naked down at the town square, and party for a week without stopping if they didn't have kids, jobs, families, lives and several thousand other responsibilities.

When O'Brien shows up, Nurse Nixon leaps into her arms. O'Brien holds her without looking first so that she can feel her friend's heartbeat, move her hands across her shoulders and just feel her, right there, next to her. When she does pull away, never taking her hands off of her friend, O'Brien sees exactly what Connie thought she would see.

A woman unchained.

A heart that has risen from the dead.

A magical transformation that is as spiritual as it is physical.

A touch of fresh sensuality.

A wild-ass cannonball that has recently left its red-hot barrel.

Nurse Nixon grabs her friend, the woman she feels has permanently lodged herself into the left side of her heart, and they escape to the bedroom while Meredith and Sara pelt the other women—four nurses, three aides, a unit manager, one doctor, and a social worker—with tales of the Lakeside Festival, the traveling sex-toy store, and life in the big city.

Frannie O'Brien, with a lovely mouth the size of Cincinnati, is almost speechless. Almost.

"Girl," she says as Connie sits in her rocking chair and

O'Brien positions herself on the bed across from her. "What have you done with yourself?"

"Everything, it seems like, Frannie. I feel like I've been gone for, like, ten years. Everything looks different here."

"Sweetie, *you* look different. The hair, the swagger, the new attitude. Was this shit on your list? Was this the stuff you never wanted me to see? Sex-toy goddess? Kisser of men in swamps? Woman who attends infamous women's festival and rocks the world? Jesus."

Connie cannot imagine a time when she has not loved this woman sitting in front of her. She cannot imagine what it would be like to not do this, sit and talk and open herself up so that everything beyond her ribs is exposed. She cannot imagine that she would be who she is right this moment—a wild, unhinged woman who thought she knew exactly where she was going and who has instead taken an almost magical turn into uncharted territory. A woman who knows nothing and who also knows everything.

"Frannie, I think I am having the time of my life."

"It looks like it. You are glowing in the dark. Think of the money you're saving on lightbulbs, for God's sake."

"It's a bit bizarre, Frannie, but I feel like I've done more in the past two weeks than in the past three years."

"It's not more, it's just different. Have you stopped to think that you may have used up this part of your life— Cyprus, the medical path you never really chose but you felt as if you had to take?"

"Damn it, I didn't want to get serious tonight, O'Brien, but it's clear—well, sort of clear—that I've grabbed onto something new and unexpected. I've had fun before—you know that because you've been there for most of it—but when I think of the word 'fulfilling' right now, working as a consultant and doing what I've done for most of my life makes me want to vomit."

"Not a good thing, babe," O'Brien whispers, taking her hand.

Taking her hand and then asking her to imagine the impossible. Imagine, O'Brien asks, never coming back. Imagine a shift in the wind that turns you around so you face a whole new direction. Imagine a life in a place you never imagined having a life before. Imagine that you could come back, that you could always come back and jump into the shoes you leave by the side of the door, but imagine then—imagine anything and everything else.

"You know," Frannie continues, "when you have a friend and they are, like, dating or married to this huge asshole and you just can never bring yourself to tell them?"

"All the time. Me, for instance."

"Yes, you, but—ready for this now?"

"Sure. Hit me, Frannie."

"I sort of thought that way about you taking this job and moving but not really moving and plodding along on the damned list of yours as if it were some kind of religion."

Connie looks at her friend and her heart leaps like one of those Irish dancers who never move their bodies, only their feet. It lurches, and then stands till.

"You're kidding!"

"No."

"Wow."

"You were living, you *are* living—but some of those things on that Sunday list of yours, well, they were simple things, places and people and magic moments that would be over soon like a carnival ride."

"Well, Frannie, I hate to say this, but up yours. You never said one word. Why? And not everything is quick. Recapturing

Jessica has not been quick and I have not had sex yet, but I am thinking about it, which is more than I have done in a very long time."

Frannie does not let go of her friend's hand. She smiles and tells her that the list was real, it is real and it is still very important. She tells Connie that to have said something would have been to negate all those years of dreaming and wishing and wondering what it might be like the minute she could actually do something about it. It would have been crossing out *your* list and inserting *my* list, she tells her.

"Your list?" Connie asks. "You have a list?"

"Christ, baby, we all have a list. Some of us write it down and some of us don't write it down. Number one on my list is to get the hell out of here when the man retires. You know that. We've talked about all of this but it just hasn't lined up like your list. It's my list. It's not like yours. I just want you to see that it's just dandy if the list changes because you are changing right along with it."

Connie pushes herself to the edge of the seat so that she is inches from O'Brien's face.

What else? She wants to know what the hell else is on O'Brien's list.

Grandchildren. Paris in the dead of winter. A break from the weary world of the insane but then going back, always going back to help those people. More time like this. One last dance with her ill brother. A painting class. More grandchildren. A ton of free time to volunteer. Brandy at 11:30 A.M., just before lunch.

All things Connie knows but, line them up, and they become a list.

A list of dreams.

"What happens is that my list changes," O'Brien shares. "That's why I don't write it down. It is as unfaithful as a male

movie star. You kept yours so close, so tight, it was unthink-
able for you to move off-center."

"Maybe. But it changed a bit from here to there."

"Just maybe?"

"Would you have told me all of this if I hadn't found the
box and gone to New York like a madwoman?"

"Eventually. I figured something else would have happened. Something unexpected to throw you off-course.
Something to show you more choices. Maybe not, though. I
think this is like some great chance. What happened to you is
cosmic. A kind of lovely slap in the face. We get slapped like
this all of the time but most of us don't pay attention and
then the moment is lost. You, Connie, baby, have chosen to
feel the slap."

Connie laughs big-time. A surge of fear and fun runs
through her mixed in with something almost narcotic that
feels cleansing and just this side of insane.

"Honey, I have no idea what I'm doing," Connie admits.
"I have been winging it for the past two weeks."

"What else is new? You've been winging it since I've
known you."

Winging it is exactly what happens next as Sara pounds
on the door and then pushes it open without waiting for a yes
or no response. Sara, who is standing in the door with her
arms full of left-over Diva products and the most devilish
smile Connie has ever seen on her young face, begs them to
come into the living room.

"What?" Connie asks as if she doesn't already know.

"We are having a sex-toy party. And we want you to help
demonstrate."

O'Brien drops to one knee, and then the other, laughing
so hard she is certain she will wet her pants.

Connie cannot move. Out in her living room are women

who have vaulted through her life, in a mostly professional, sometimes fun, always kind and generous manner but who, to the best of her recollection, have never discussed sex toys in a group setting.

"What?" Sara demands, trying very hard to be patient.

"Are you all drunk?" Connie wants to know.

"Mostly just me and Meredith. Everyone else is just curious as hell. Really. They just want to know."

O'Brien lifts up her head and looks at Connie, raises one eyebrow in that Well-are-you-going-to-do-something-about-this? way, and then Connie gets up slowly.

"Do we know how to do this?" Connie asks Sara, who is weaving and about to drop three vibrators, a couple of dildos, two harnesses and a handful of cherry-flavored condoms. Turning and thinking that what will happen next may be the penance, the #6 that she has been hoping to cross off of her damned list.

"Just do what you've been doing all week, Connie. The crowd will love you."

Frannie O'Brien is off the floor and out the bedroom door before Connie can move, screaming, "I cannot wait to see this!" and Connie smiles at her lovely assistant Sara, bends over to pick up everything she has dropped, and doesn't even bother to turn and look at her old rocking chair as she marches like a true Diva Sister towards what she's pretty sure will be the first-ever sex-toy party held in Cyprus, Indiana.

twenty-two

This is the beginning. My list. It is way past time and I may never have done this if it were not for my mother and her list of dreams and our reconciliation. So here I go. Only two. It's just a start on this late spring night while I pretend to work. While I open myself up. While I begin my own list of dreams . . .

1. Take down your wall. Not brick by brick but all at once. Hurry. There is a world waiting for you, Jessica. Get over it. Get going.

2. Forgive yourself. Dare to forgive yourself and before this night has ended do something your mother would tell you to do.

The constant movement of New York does not slow during an early summer rainstorm. Jessica has shifted her chair so she can lean against the sill where she has opened the window. Rain has always been her antidote. Her salve. An expensive bottle of dry white wine. A pony ride in spring. Her mother's breath against her sleepy face on a late Sunday morning. All the bills paid at the end of the month. The one thing that she seemingly cannot resist.

Besides work. Besides her restless need to command her

life and the lives of the people who stack themselves up against her left leg. Sometimes excessive. Always compulsive. Driven to the edge, around the corner, and back again.

It is 10:15 on Monday night and after she has wrestled with party planning for the release of the new Diva products, marketing releases, and a work schedule that may soon have to include new employees, a three-city expansion plan, and a nagging not-enough-sleep-food-or-drink headache, she learns that there is a Diva sex-toy party going on in the living room where she used to watch old "Charlie's Angels" movies and eat Doritos, do her damn chemistry homework, irritate as many people as possible with her sarcastic comments, and plot the beginnings of a small woman-owned business that eventually turned into Diva's.

Jessica Franklin Nixon has started her own list of dreams. A list inspired by the movement of her mother, by her own restless heart, by the notion that she must live as she encourages her clients to live. She has imagined her mother's list, has heard selected portions of it during the past two weeks since her mother has not so much barged into as collided with her life, and she thinks on this gorgeous rainy night that it is time, way past time maybe, for her to follow her mother's example. Two items, she thinks, is a great place to start.

Jessica turns to open the window even more, hoping to catch a trace of rain on her face, to feel the wind blowing in off the ocean all those blocks away, and because she hears voices. Men and women laughing. Feet dancing across the wet sidewalks. The drifting rumble of voices from the bar across the alley, a hip place for single city business people who are addicted to the world they inhabit during the day, a world they love, a world they can hardly bear to leave, a place that is more familiar than their own kitchen walls or their living room couch.

Jessica leans in, pushes her face against the screen, hoping to feel the soft rain on her face, and feels the window pop.

"Damn it!" she yells, missing the falling screen by half an inch as she tries to grab it. "Oh, no—"

"Oh, no—" not because a warm shower hits her hair and face and arms and neck when she leans out to watch the screen drift in the wind like a heavy kite, but "oh, no" because the screen is plummeting directly at a man who is standing just under her window with a book on top of his head to keep it dry.

"*Move!*" she screams and without hesitation the man moves forward to see who is screaming and the screen falls at his feet.

Right at his feet.

"Oh, thank God," Jessica shouts down to him from her window, which is only a story and a half above the level of the sidewalk. Just high enough maybe to have someone lose an eye from a falling screen or get a concussion or be maimed with a screen rash for the rest of his life.

"I'm so sorry," she yells down, leaning from the waist as far as she can go. "Are you okay?"

The man smiles. Then he laughs, and he does not stop looking up at Jessica.

"This happened to me last week," he tells her. "I swear to God, three blocks from here, walking home late like this and another damn window fell right in front of me."

"You're kidding," Jessica says, incredulous, and as if she has known this man for years and can fall into an easy conversation at the drop of a screen. "Can I get you something?"

He looks at her as if he can't believe what she's saying. He's got a suit jacket slung over his arm, his tie is undone, his hair is tied up in a ponytail and he looks, well, he looks happy in spite of his second near-death experience in seven days.

"Come have a drink with me and I won't sue you."

"What?"

"You heard me. Whatever you're doing can wait, for crying out loud. It's what, going on 11, you almost killed me, I like the sound of your voice and maybe this is one of those cosmic events that brings people together."

Jessica takes one of those long pauses, as if she is in a play and has forgotten her lines, a pause that is one part a "holy shit" pause, another part a "he could sue me" pause, and finally a tiny, soft speaking pause that makes her chest rise just a bubble with excitement and she wants to say, "What the hell." What the hell because of what she has just written on her brand-new list, and how swiftly it is already happening, and how maybe, maybe, if she does not lean over the ledge again and say yes, everything will be the same as it was and that will not be good, not at all.

He waits. The ponytail man waits in the pattering rain and she can see his white smile, and that he is slender like a marathon runner, and that he has moved the hand with the book in it to his hip and she suddenly wonders what he is reading.

"First tell me what you're reading," she hears herself saying.

His laugh is a swell that bursts like a riptide in the rain. His laugh tells her instantly that he holds nothing back, that he knows how to let it go, that he is unafraid, that he is a risk-taker, and she likes everything she hears.

"Hillary Clinton's book, for the third time. I want her to be the first woman president. I want to work for her."

Now, Jessica knows she should go down. She knows that she should laugh into the warm June rain and turn off the lights very quickly and grab something off one of her shelves and run down the steps to meet this man who she almost nailed with a falling screen. She knows that this would very quickly erase #2 right off the list she has just—JUST—started.

She should.

But Jessica hesitates. She's close to just running out the door but the queen of control does not have this encounter written down in her appointment book. She's got a good two hours of work left and he could be a mass murderer, or not.

Jessica Franklin Nixon hedges her bets. She is in the middle of the fence, on the very windowsill of her life, and she pauses.

She pauses.

She thinks of choosing the man or the not part. She thinks about how it felt when she finally said, "I love you" to her mother. She thinks about lists and dreams and the fragile, wild opportunities of chance.

"Can I meet you in the bar, right there, in a few minutes?" she asks him, pointing towards the rendezvous. "I'll be the one with a wet head."

"Yes," he calls up to her. "Please come. Really. Even if you don't like Hillary. Come anyway."

This time Jessica laughs and it is as if she has never heard the sound before. The light swift movement of air from her lungs, the sound of fun, the sound of life seems suddenly unfamiliar to her. A part of her wants to scramble right out the window, just like the old days, when she met her boyfriends next to the garbage cans alongside the garage by the house where her mother has kidnapped half of her staff and is now holding them for an unknown ransom.

"I will," she promises. "Give me 15 minutes to close up."

He smiles and she doesn't move.

"By the way," she adds. "I'm already volunteering for Hillary."

Screen Man touches his finger to his wrist where most

people would wear a watch, says "Fifteen," and turns to stride across the street and into the bar.

And Jessica sits down. She doesn't turn off the lights or lock the window or make any sudden move to leap across her door-desk and head to the bar that she has been listening to ever since she opened her store and started working late at night with the window open.

Jessica—woman of the world, professional sex-toy entrepreneur, asexual, bisexual, nothing sexual, sex addict wannabe—panics.

"Jesus, what am I doing? What am I thinking? Why did the damn screen fall? Who is this guy? What are the chances?"

The word "chances" bounces off her throat like she has been punched by a wild boxer and she takes the word and holds on to it as if the entire building has just been flooded and the word is her only way out. Her life raft. Her list of dreams. A chance. Number two.

Chances.

Chances.

Chances.

The chance of a lifetime. The chance to know. The chance to find out. The chance to dance through a conversation. The chance to flirt. The chance to dismember the borders of a man who may not really have any borders. The chance to open my eyes for the first time in my life and see what my mother has been telling me I need to see.

Jessica puts one hand on her heart and covers it with the other. She forms a cross, a sign of hope, a marker of light on her own chest, and she lets herself think of her mother now, her new mother. The kisser of swamp men, and the new queen of the women's festival. The broad with a whip in her back pocket who has given Diva's a lurch into a place that Jessica did not even know existed a few weeks ago. Her mother, who she'd partially dismissed, who she wonders now if she ever knew, who has unexpectedly transformed herself into a woman . . . a woman . . .

"A woman . . ." Jessica says out loud. "She showed me how to be a woman."

And WWMD?

What Would Mother Do? A screen drops on a man's head and passion of the physical sort beyond tireless hours of work is nonexistent in my life. I work too much. The necessity for the sexual side of my own life has been denied. I can sell advice about sex but I have not been able to cross some border that I built, a wide canal of frigidity. But I started my own list. My own damn list that may be identical to the list my mother created.

What the hell, Jessica says, stopping the chain of wretched thoughts that is dragging itself through her mind, and not through a place where it can vibrate her into ecstasy.

What the hell.

Jessica spins her chair around so that she is sitting with her face as close to the window as possible. She can see the soft lights from the bar where Screen Man is waiting for her, the darkened line of windows from the neighboring businesses, the wet June sky and a parade of cars that seems to be endless in Manhattan, no matter what hour of the day it is.

Jessica gets up and leans out into the rain. She has a hundred rain memories that start with her father in a fishing boat and move to picnics outside, her mother running through the backyard in her bathing suit in early April, camping in the dunes when the road was swept away, a college night on a drenched rooftop, and this night. This moment.

Now.

Jessica thinks of just now. She thinks of what she might

never have again if she doesn't turn off the lights, hide the money bag instead of depositing it three blocks away at the bank, slam the window and then run as fast as she can into the bar and into a conversation and who the hell knows what else with a man who is reading a book she has almost memorized and who refuses to cut his hair and who probably knows what to do with every single thing that she sells in a store that has for just this night taken up enough pages in her own play of passion.

She shakes her head and water flies everywhere and Jessica leans into the New York night further, further than she has leaned into any night in a very long time, and she waits for the rain to run down her face and cruise across her breasts and trickle down to the top of her not-so-expensive slacks.

And finally, Jessica Franklin Nixon makes a decision. It's a long-time-coming kind of decision that has risen inside of her like a spring tide, slowly—receding and then growing bolder until there is nothing to do, absolutely nothing to do but surrender. Surrender already to her own list of dreams. To her life. To *now*.

She decides to let go. Tonight for starters and maybe every night. Maybe.

She decides that she may never be just one person, may never be attracted to just men or women, maybe will fall in love with Screen Man and marry him before tomorrow's nightfall. She decides that whatever happens in the bar tonight will not be a mistake but an adventure.

It will be a chance.

A chance to feel. A chance to walk off the edge of the windowsill and into the arms of whatever or whoever catches her—a simple, wild, wonderful, miracle of a chance.

Then she moves like a bullet. She dances across the floor, turns out lights, slams the window, hides the money, and does not think of anything else except the man waiting at the bar and the warm summer rain on her face, and what she might have missed by waiting so goddamned long to seize this kind of chance.

To live her own list.

twenty-three

1. Stop being afraid.

In Ohio, rumbling across I-90 just as the lawn-encrusted suburbs of Cleveland start appearing everywhere, Connie has second, third and fourth thoughts. It is the first time in her life that she is truly terrified. Sara is driving, and Connie has her knees lodged up against the back of the front seat so that she can write in her portable planner, and suddenly she feels as if she is being pressed up against a brick wall in a space that only has room for something the size of a cheap box of wine.

Meredith, who is busy reading a stack of magazines and newspapers Connie dragged along from her kitchen counter, turns to ask Connie a question and sees that she is as white as her running socks.

"Babe, Connie, hey, are you okay?"

Connie has a snake wrapped around her throat. A very large truck driver is sitting on her chest. A band of monkeys with yellow stripes that run from their long noses to the tip of their pointy asses are pulling on her hair. Her feet are on fire and long flames of red and white and gold are moving towards her arms and face and are poised to rip down her throat like a wildfire if she opens her mouth.

When Connie does try to open her mouth she discovers her jaw has been wired shut. Her hands have turned to ice and she cannot dislodge them from their tight grip on Sara's headrest. Connie Franklin Nixon cannot remember how to speak. Is she Spanish? German? Did she grow up in Argentina? If she did speak what would she say?

"Get off the freeway!" Meredith yells to Sara. "Exit! Just get off."

Sara looks in the mirror and sees that Connie has turned to stone. Meredith has one hand on her arm, a place of human contact, a touch of reality, and has moved across the bench seat to be right next to her.

When Connie looks up, she sees that she is in the parking lot of a restaurant. But where? There is a huge green garbage dumpster in front of the van, a string of cars on the other side, and a warm hand on her arm. She still cannot speak. The weight on her chest has left her breathless. Everything is hazy, as if someone has turned her over, poured a load of smoke and fog into her body and mind, slammed the door shut, and run like hell from the scene of the crime.

"Listen, Connie, it's Meredith, we are in Cleveland, just

off the Interstate and everything is going to be OK," she hears Meredith say. "Can you say something? Need a drink of water? Do you want to go to the hospital?"

"The hospital," Connie manages to whisper and then she begins to laugh.

Sara is standing outside the van window, just inches from Connie's face, and sees her laughing. Sara looks at Meredith as if she has just witnessed a flock of geese flying out the back window.

"The hospital," Connie says again, and then Meredith gets it.

"You're laughing at the word 'hospital' because that is who you were, that is what freaked you out, that is where you never want to go again the rest of your life. Is that right?"

Sara motions for Meredith to move over and roll down the window and then she puts her hands on either side of the door and leans in so that she is as close as she can get to Connie without sitting in her lap.

"Hey, Connie," she says softly. "It's okay. It's gonna be fine. We're going to take care of you. Take a breath."

Connie comes back slowly. She sees a soft shade of blue, the disappearing wings of the wild birds that have cluttered up her mind. She hears the lovely voices of her friends, her companions, her co-workers, her sex-toy assistants, and she feels safe and embarrassed as hell. She puts her face into her hands, hunches over and she tells Sara and Meredith that she thinks she just had a panic attack. She tells them she was reading through her notes, wondering if she had made all the necessary phone calls, locked the back door, reset the timer light on the dining room table, canceled the newspapers, given a list of stuff that needs doing to O'Brien, closed the garage door, left a message for the Realtor, and called her other two daughters.

"Not to mention," she says, straightening up, putting one hand on Sara's arm and one hand on Meredith's, "this sudden overwhelming feeling that I have no clue what I'm doing and that I should just stay the hell back in Cyprus where I belong."

"I thought so," Meredith says firmly. "You've been fidgeting since last night when your friends drank everything we had, bought every last sex toy, and told you they were jealous of your newfound profession. You also talked about the hospital."

"I'm a nurse, for crissakes."

"You *were* a nurse," Sara reminds her. "Maybe you can be an ex-nurse and be something else. A part of you will always be a nurse."

"Selling sex toys isn't what I had in mind," Connie admits. "I feel kind of like an ass. Like a kid who gets a bag of candy after a long fast, eats it all and then pukes into his own lap."

Sara and Meredith laugh. Meredith asks if Connie wants to go in to the restaurant and get some coffee, but Connie says she can't face the public yet, so Sara brings back three huge cups of coffee in paper cups and they sit in a circle in the empty back of the van to hash out Connie's nervous breakdown. There are no windows back here, just the cushion of sleeping bags and a soft tent bag and the loose structure of sharing, conversation and openness that has sustained the Diva Sisters since they left New York. It is a miracle of mixed generations, lifestyles and cultures that is astonishing and brilliant and so remarkably possible.

Connie looks at Meredith and Sara and smiles, imagining what her life would be without them, imagining the same way she imagined just hours before what her life would be like without O'Brien, Sanchez, McHenery, and everyone else who was at her house fondling Diva products, drinking coffee and wine and laughing until way past midnight.

And she decides to confess. What could be worse than what these two women have both just witnessed? Connie falls into the saving grace of two women, two of the most unlikely suspects she has ever had land in her life, and yet she feels the karma of their female presence, sees the arms that have already captured her as she was falling, erases their ages, their wild looks, the knowledge that she is old enough to be their mother, and she confesses.

Connie tells them about her list, how they were and are a part of it as #26, and they both listen, kind, young women warriors of the road who between them seem to have an arsenal of emotional and worldly experience stockpiled and ready to go at a moment's notice. Connie pulls a very wrinkled #1 from her pocket to show them and tells them that she has been scared since last night, and maybe for a very long time before that as well. Sara and Meredith listen, occasionally lean over to place a gentle hand on Connie's shoulder or leg, and they do what women do best, what other women know they do best, what women always need from each other.

They listen.

It is not just the list, Connie confesses. It's a fascinating and terrifying pause in life, this flying into the wind, this major leap in 15 directions when I thought I was headed in another, and this eating up of weeks of my time—the time of the list.

"When I first got back home, everything looked unfamiliar and distant," she says, creeping into the half-opened closet of her fears as if she may faint at what she sees. "A part of me wanted to run screaming from the house, from how I lived, from where I thought I was going. And then, as the evening wore on, I settled back into who I am, where I am supposed to be going, and I wanted to stay and yet . . ."

"Yet?" both Sara and Meredith say at the same time.

"Now, I'm scared I might miss something. I'm scared if I stick to the program, if I focus on my list as I had intended to do, an entire world might fly past me and I would have considered it only as a passing storm cloud and not as a chance, an adventure, something new to try."

"Anything else?" Meredith asks.

Connie is silent. She remembers moments like this from when she was a kid and she had to go to confession, had to walk up the endless aisle of her church and step behind a curtain and say things that even back then she thought were stupid and controlling, and how a part of her ever since has held something back. Held something back in a secret cave behind her heart and a narrow chasm that leads to the edge of her very lonely pubic bone. A cave that has seemed to crumble bit by bit since the day she discovered the plans for her daughter's sex-toy empire hidden in the box in the garage. Crumbled as she leaned into a daughter she feared she might never know. Crumbled as she tapped into her reserve of control and danced with swamp rats, learned how to charge up a vibrator, and reclaimed the luscious heart of her sexual self.

"I thought I knew where I was going, and what I wanted, and what was going to happen in three months," Connie says. "My whole life, since I divorced, has been about making certain I knew what might happen one day and then the day after that and well, hell, the uncertainty makes me feel a bit unsettled, even if I was excited about dancing through these next three months in an unstructured way. At the end, I knew exactly where I would be and how I would be living and what I would be doing."

This, Sara reminds her, makes no sense, given the trail she has followed for such a long time. Raising kids alone, running the hospital, a few quiet adventures here and there, landing on her feet no matter how hard the blowing wind was trying to knock her over.

"Connie, I am new at this sex-toy business too but you seem so damn *natural* when you are talking to people. And last night when you actually put on that harness in front of your friends and showed them what to do—well, good God, Connie, do you think that was the act of a woman who is *afraid*?"

Connie actually blushes. She blushes as she remembers how no one in the room would admit that they knew how to wear a harness that is used to hold a dildo, and how Sara and Meredith looked at her as if she were nuts when she held one out to them to demonstrate, and how she ended up standing on the coffee table in the middle of the living room demonstrating how to do *it,* and *it*—meaning numerous intimate sexual adventures with a partner—man, woman, or someone in the middle.

"Nurse Nixon, you look stunning!" O'Brien had bellowed.

"Knock it off," Connie told her. "This is serious business."

"Sex is always serious business," the doctor yelled back. "Connie, the world has suddenly turned on its end because of you."

"Me?" Connie shouted back from her perch on the table. "What did I do?"

"Look around, honey," the doctor said. "You may have just changed the lives of every single woman in this room. How's that for a powerful feeling?"

Connie had brushed it off, sold everything that the Diva

Sisters had set on the counter between the dining room and
the kitchen that had never seen the likes of this wild night,
and then even sold the harness she was wearing.

Uncertainty, she now tells Sara and Meredith, has suddenly frightened the living hell out of her. Maybe, she explains, I don't know who I am.

"Well, shit, Connie, it's been my experience in all of my
28 years," Meredith says, stretching out her legs so one falls
on either side of Connie, "that the heart of us stays the
same. You are still Connie, the nurse, mom, friend and all
that other stuff, but if we didn't evolve, if we don't leave ourselves open for chances and what we might become—minus
the heart stuff—what the hell would be the point of life?"

"Profound," Sara says, lowering her head.

"Listen," Meredith persists. "If you really want to know,
I had no clue that I'd be doing what I'm doing now, but I love
this and I have no idea what I might be doing next year or
when I'm your age but that's just dandy with me because I'm
pretty sure I know who I am."

There's something attractive, Sara admits, about safeness, about knowing what time the alarm clock will go off
every day and what time you will eat and that you will retire
in 32.5 years and get a pension and maybe take a cruise to
Hawaii and then go to Arizona or Florida every winter or to
the same cabin in the woods every July until the day you die.

"Sounds like hell," Connie tells her.

"Well, hell, yes, but a comfortable kind of hell."

"Look, Connie," Meredith finally says. "Knock it off.
You are just going back to New York to help us settle in at the
store, work the party, just a few things that I know Jessica
really needs help with. Do you have to question whether it's
your frigging destiny?"

Destiny? Connie cannot remember the last time she

heard that word. Destiny. It sounds horrid, old, crusty and
rotten. She pulls up her legs, laces her arms around her knees,
shakes off the last trace of the bird wings that brushed
against the exposed valves of her heart, and says, "No," just
as she tucks #1 back inside her pocket.

"No."

Connie sits in the passenger seat and she breathes in and
then out, and five minutes pass, and then an hour and she is
back inside chipping away at the sides of the cave and thinking that maybe she can work on the list and take occasional
detours. Then, when she thinks they may be driving like this
for the rest of their lives, she sees the blaze of lights that can
only mean New York City is close and, as they get closer and
closer to Manhattan, to a world that still seems like Disney-
land to her, she says another word.

Connie says, "Yes," and when she looks up they are
parked right outside of Diva's and it's almost the next day.

The rest of the week at Diva's is about as close to chaos
as Jessica can bear to be a part of, witness, stand next to,
and administer. The stunning success of the women's festival, the Diva Designs new product line party that is scheduled for Saturday, the sudden and very welcome return of
Sara—whom Jessica hires full-time on the spot—Meredith
and Connie, makes Jessica want to thank everyone within a
five-thousand-mile radius. Beyond the necessary flurry of
activity that needs to happen there is also this one new idea—
sex-toy parties for the masses—that seems to have swallowed
them all whole.

"You should have seen them," Meredith reports. "The
women are hungry in more ways than one for something like
this, and your mother was perfect."

"It was something I had hoped we could start maybe next year but now . . ." Jessica is thinking out loud. "Now? I am so overloaded I want to lie down and wake up back on that couch in Cyprus myself."

Connie stands speechless while Jessica, Geneva, Sara, and Meredith talk about her as if she is absent, a breathing mannequin, a fly who has come in on the backside of a dark pair of suit pants.

"It wouldn't be hard," Sara adds. "Even though the store here is comfortable and easy, there are still lots of women who just don't want to walk into a sex-toy store. They might talk about it, but doing it is something entirely different."

And they go on and on and Connie listens and then she slips into the stockroom and feels, once again, as if she wants a cigarette.

Then, later, there is also the massive bouquet of daisies that Connie notices—as if she could miss it—sitting on the end table in the corner of the living room of Jessica's apartment.

"Flowers?" she cries. "Can I read the card?"

Jessica wants to say no. She has her head buried in a stack of paperwork. She has managed to keep Screen Man a secret from her mother for one entire day. She's also managed to say yes to dinner with him at the same small bar which features a lovely assortment of bar food that at the time seemed delicious and non-threatening. Dinner, she told Screen Man, is about all she thinks she will have time for during the next week, month, or indeed the next 12 years of her life.

"Go ahead," Jessica says, surrendering to the inevitable as her mother glances down at the bouquet.

Hillary and I had the time of our lives. No more screening in my life. More drinks? Dinner? Do you want to move in?

Connie reads the card and smiles when she slips it back

inside its little envelope. She doesn't say anything. She waits. She stands right there and she waits.

"His name is Martin. I sort of had a date. He was standing under my window and a screen almost fell on his head. He's smart, sexy, and he loves Hillary Clinton."

Jessica details what happened, stays away from the simple idea of fate, and tells her mother without hesitation that she's attracted to him, his Hillary Clinton book, and his lovely ponytail.

"This is grand news, baby," Connie tells her. "I suggest you get him to a swamp as quickly as possible."

"*Oh, Mother,*" Jessica says in a tone of voice that is much louder than a kind response. "I'm not as fast as you are. I let him touch my hand. We may kiss in a month or two."

"Very funny."

"Speaking of funny, mother dearest, your personal stylist has been by and you apparently have a date for the party on Saturday night."

"Are you nuts? What are you talking about?"

"Mattie asked for an invitation for some guy who is a customer who she thinks you have to hook up with, someone she already mentioned to you, and I said, 'Why not?' and he's coming with her, but he's really coming with you."

"I don't have time for a date, for crissakes," Connie says, wondering how this could have happened. "I'm working, aren't I? And what a fine place to meet a man—while I'm handing out free Diva condoms."

"There will be plenty of time for flirting, Mother, don't worry."

"Worry?" Connie yells about a decibel higher than her daughter. "Worry? What? Me, worry? Jessica, have you stopped to think about everything that has happened during the past few weeks? Have you?"

Connie feels the soft wings of the same birds that flew into her chest on the drive home trying to work their way back inside of her but she fights them off with a surge of anger and honesty.

Without giving Jessica a chance to answer, Connie asks the big question.

"How long do you think I can keep doing this for you?"

Jessica has not bothered to have a prepared answer for this question. She has been juggling her mother from one day to the next, tossing her from her left hand to her right hand, off the back of her foot, down her back and right into whatever needs to be done or is happening at the moment and maybe, just maybe, even further than that. But to where? For how long? In what capacity?

Jessica looks at her mother, her blazing eyes firing questions, even after her mother has become silent. She balances for just a moment with one foot standing firmly in place as an employer, a maker of good decisions, a business leader, and the other foot planted just as solidly in the heart of a woman she calls Mother, new friend, a mentor of action and example. She chooses to stay in the middle, to hedge all of her bets, to pull wisely from both sides.

"How long do you *want* to keep doing this?" she fires back.

Connie freezes for a moment, and then she smiles.

"I should ground you for the rest of your life, young woman," she says, pushing the birds way back where they belong, clearing her mind, rushing forward while holding onto a major pause.

And there are still two questions hanging like an unanswered wedding invitation, an extended hand, a map with endless roads.

Jessica reaches out across the desk and puts her hand on top of her mother's. She longs to go to confession, she wants to ease the lines from her mother's face, and maybe from her own.

"Mom, listen," Jessica says slowly, not at all certain about what she is about to say, "just so you know, part of the time I have absolutely no idea what I am doing. None at all. When we went to New Orleans? Not a clue. The new employees? Sort of knew. The party? That's under control because it's easy. Expansion and sex-toy parties? I'm halfway there but not really and add to that this Screen Man Martin and you may as well start laughing."

"So, you are human?"

"Very, Mother. I don't have the answers to either of these questions right now but I can tell you that you came here at a time when I needed you more than ever and didn't even know it, and that spending these weeks with you, getting to know you, having you help me look at myself and who I am, and what I might be missing is, and continues to be, absolutely wonderful. And—"

And.

And Jessica tells her that she has been inspired to begin her own list of dreams. She holds out the beginnings of her own small list, tells her mother that her presence and her presents have moved into her life like an unexpected gift, and that is how she met the Screen Man, and why she now knows that risk is a pleasure that needs to be addressed every day.

Connie can feel her heart leap and begin a tango with itself. She puts her hands on Jessica's face, kisses her on the lips and whispers, "Thank you, sweetheart." And then she adds, "Does this mean I get a raise?"

"Actually, Mother, I think I should start paying you. You are working your ass off, for crying out loud. You deserve it."

"I'm torn," Connie admits. "This is an adventure. It's fun. I never in my wildest dreams imagined doing something like this, staying here, coming back from the festival . . . any of it, but here it is and what do I do?"

"What *do* you do?" Jessica asks her right back.

"My mother would say, 'Wait and see,' " Connie replies. "But I look back, towards Cyprus, and I miss it. A part of me really misses it."

"Is that so bad?"

"At some point it may affect your plans, where you are going. You rely on me now, and that's okay, but I was just getting used to looking out the window and seeing this expanse of free time, all the things I've been thinking about doing for such a very long time."

"Mom, you are a big girl now. You are in charge. You can come or go at any time. You can stay and work. Or go home. You run the show. You know that. You've always known that. Now you just have a few choices."

"In charge" is always a good thing to say to Connie Franklin Nixon. And she knows her wise daughter is right, and she knows she could come or go or leave in the middle, and she's thinking that if she leaves now she might miss something on this side of her life just as much as she might miss something on the other side of her life.

The Franklin Nixon women talk for a very long time. Jessica pushes back her books, her computer, her endless lists of tasks, and they go through an entire pot of coffee and they both get feisty. Connie stampedes Jessica with questions, with her own business-minded concerns, with the harsh realities of living with a relative for an extended period of time. Jessica throws her mother a bone. She talks about business chances, creating a new world of friends, exploring a side of herself and her life that might have been on her damn list anyway.

"Have you thought about that, Mother? Did it ever occur to you that this is part of your list of dreams? That sticking to a plan, one that you think is written in stone, might not be the best way to live?"

"I haven't had the time to line it all up like that but the thought has recently crossed my mind."

"Go get it," Jessica orders. "I know you have it with you."

Connie pulls her list of dreams, her imagined second half of life, her world of thoughts and wonderment and an occasional burst of passion and angst out of her bulging make-believe dresser—her suitcase—and carries it back to the table as if she is holding a carton of eggs.

"Tell me," Jessica urges, inching her chair forward so that she can put her arm around her mother.

"No one has ever read it and I don't want anyone to ever read it," Connie shares. "It's intimate stuff. Private, like a journal. And sometimes when I look at it, it makes me sad to remember who I was, what I was doing, where I was in my life when I wrote it. There are many, many versions and this new idea that the list already needs to be revamped."

"You were a good mom. I would have hated you along the way no matter what had happened, divorce or not, lifestyle or not. It's programmed into the genes of teenagers. You know that."

Connie knows and she sees herself pages beyond that. She sees herself wrapped up in a part of life that is as tantalizing as it is terrifying. She imagines out loud what it would be like to change everything. Everything. The house. The new condo. The job. Where she lives. Everything.

"It's not in the pages, huh?" Jessica asks gently, touching the side of Connie's list book.

"Not like that."

"Look again. Maybe you missed something," Jessica says, smiling.

Connie looks. Jessica politely gets up, makes yet another pot of coffee, slips into the bathroom to call and let Kinsey know she is going to be a bit late, and studies her own face in the mirror to give her mother a little time alone. When she looks in the mirror, Jessica sees the soft skin of her mother, matching eyes, three teeth that could have been moved back into place with braces, but three teeth that seem perfect to her anyway. When she lifts up her hair, pulling it behind her ears and then onto the top of her head, she sees that she does indeed look like her mother. She leans forward, hands on her head, belly against the cold sink, and she suddenly knows what she will look like when she is 58 years old, Connie's age.

Jessica stands there a very long time. She runs a parade of questions through her own mind, asking herself if she can really stand to work with her mother for an extended period of time, and answering with a soft, "Yes." She asks herself if her business, if Diva's could be more because of her mother, and she gets the same answer. She asks if she could use her mother in ways that she has not bothered to sit down and examine. Yes, again.

But live with her? Again? Now that she is a daughter, a friend, a boss but no longer a little girl? Not so much.

And then she knows what her mother will say. She knows exactly what her mother will say when she goes back to the living room/kitchen/dining room/office/bedroom. She knows what Connie will say and she wonders when other daughters get the mother-daughter connection. When do other daughters peer into their own eyes and see their mother's eyes? A shell that was designed by the womb of a woman, outlined with parts of her own self and then left empty, almost empty, for the girl-daughter to fill as she wishes? When does that girl, who becomes a woman, gaze into her own eyes and forgive and open her own heart and wander down a new trail that crosses beyond the hedges of just mother-and-daughter? When do other daughters not just lean in but stand straight so that the mother can lean too? When do they lift up their hair and see the cheekbones, the long ears, the sloping necklines, the rounded chin that graces the face of their own mother?

Jessica knows what her mother will say as she steps from the room, drops her hair back down to her shoulders, and rubs her eyes so that she can see, she can truly see.

"Maybe that page fell out," Connie says.

"Maybe it did," Jessica says, sitting back down and turning her chair so that she can plant her feet on either side of her mother.

"What did you find?"

"Piles of dreams, baby. All kinds of them and, as you already know, some of them are bursting into reality as we sit in this spacious apartment."

Jessica, the CEO, swings into action. She whips a quick plan out of an idea that has been floating between her and her mother since the moment her mother walked into her store. Jessica throws it out there, knowing already that her mother will catch it and accept it and that the plan, just like any plan or any list, might, could, or should change at any moment.

Connie will stay and help with the party.

She will help at the store.

She will, with Geneva's blessing, become a kind of administrative assistant while she is in New York, serving at the will and whim of the CEO. She will be worked into the schedule. She will sit in on some meetings. She will stay at the apartment unless her stay is extended and then she may, for reasons of personal, physical and mental safety, have to find alternative living space. She can offer her opinions on the progress of the business at any moment but her opinions and thoughts may be dismissed.

And of course she has the right to change anything Jessica has said at any given moment.

"Let's do a week by week," Connie says, agreeing to just that. "I'll stay through the party, try not to get in the way if and when you have any downtime or the Screen Man wants to come over, and then we'll just see. We'll just call this a nice extended visit for a while. I do have to make some decisions about the house, the other job, the condo."

"You know, Mom, you are still in charge. No matter where you are, or what you do, or where you go, you are still in charge."

Connie's laugh rips through the apartment like a wild breeze. She raises her arms, sets her list book on the desk, encircles her daughter—the CEO of Diva's—kisses her on the lips and says, "Just give me that lovely whip, sweetheart, and I'll show you who is in charge."

Just give Connie the whip.

twenty-four

4. Dance with a handsome man who doesn't care if you have a double chin, have to pluck your long facial hairs, or put on a girdle in order to get into the damn dress.

19. Moments with my daughters that are real and open and where all four of us can be who we are.

12. Take a deep breath and allow the two daughters who actually let you visit them to live their own lives. Accept their traditional choices. Maybe this one should be listed in two places. This is hard. Keep your mouth shut except to smile when you visit or they visit.

18. A fancy dress. Something formal and long that sits right at the tip of my breasts. A Cinderella dress—this is embarrassing, but sometimes when I dream I see this dress—slits up the side, beads. Maybe when I wear it I'll be someplace wild and wonderful.

Frannie O'Brien has just finished a release evaluation on a 15-year-old white female from a lovely suburb near Chicago who has already been pregnant, run away, had an abortion, been through two drug treatment programs, tried to steal her family's car and fortune, and has been asking for a sex-change operation for the past year and a half.

The girl cannot leave the hospital. She may be in the select care psychiatric unit for a very, very long time and this fact makes O'Brien want to weep not because the girl will be there, not because she needs to be there, but because she has to be there.

"Damn it," she says out loud, in her office. "This baby girl may be in the hospital for a very long time, but she'll get out. She will get out."

O'Brien believes everyone will get out. She stretches her psychiatric nurse's training and her severely enlarged heart across every single patient who is admitted to her hospital and, by the time they get to her unit, one of the best in the country, they have pretty much been everywhere else. Sometimes they get out. Sometimes they do not get out for a very long period of time and the reality of this often brings O'Brien to her knees and makes her pick up the phone to call Nurse Nixon—her friend, her muse, her listening ear.

And that damn Nurse Nixon is suddenly not available, and temporarily parked in a new harbor, and Frannie misses her so much her teeth ache and she has lost count of the number of times she has tried to call her only to remember that Connie is not at home and sorting through the junk in the garage. She is not walking the sand dunes, or skydiving, or taking a pottery class, or whatever in the hell was on her list of dreams, but she's in New York or New Orleans or New Something. And, as happy as O'Brien is for her sweet pal, that is exactly how unhappy she is for herself.

Right this second she fights the urge to call Connie's cell phone and tell her about this girl who wants to be a boy, and who is as messed up as any kid who has ever come into the unit, but she does not pick up the phone.

She does not. And then there is a knock on the door.

"What?" she bellows with the intonation of someone who has been interrupted and who very much does not like to be interrupted.

"I'm sorry, Frannie, but this came for you by some kind of special courier, a really cute guy in a gold truck. . . ."

O'Brien wants to laugh in spite of the interruption but she cuts off the lovely young secretary and asks for the package, and struggles not to utter, "What the hell," out loud. It's a letter from Nurse Nixon, and folded inside it is a sealed envelope.

> *Sweetheart,*
>
> *This is last-minute but you and Daniel have to come. I know you can get the time off of work. This is on me. I want you to be there. I want you to be with me. I want to have fun and I want to show both of you how much you mean to me and how much I appreciate everything you have done and still do for a fat-ass divorcée who occasionally hears her house singing. I will be at the airport. Bring something fancy to wear, drinking shoes, and not a damn thing else.*
>
> *Missing you like crazy.*
>
> *The Sex Queen*

Frannie rips open the envelope and two airplane tickets and a confirmed reservation for a Manhattan hotel fall out of the envelope and she cannot help it. O'Brien cries. She kisses the tickets, holds them against her heart, closes her eyes and imagines herself and Daniel in New York City and she keeps on crying.

O'Brien cries for a while and then she thinks it might be a really good idea to see when the tickets are for, and she is hoping for late July, or maybe even August, and she looks at the tickets and she sees that they are for Friday. That's the Friday that is two days from the Wednesday she is in the middle of and as she shuffles through the tickets in a state of near panic something else falls out that she missed. It's a

beautifully designed formal invitation embossed in gold letters on bright red paper.

> YOU ARE CORDIALLY INVITED TO THE RELEASE PARTY
> FOR DIVA'S DIVINE SIGNATURE PRODUCTS . . .
> JOIN US AS WE SALUTE THE SEXUAL REVOLUTION
> BY CREATING ONE OF OUR OWN.
> COCKTAILS AT 6 P.M.
> UNVEILING AT 7 P.M.
> DINNER AND DANCING FOREVER AND EVER.
> COME . . . ALWAYS COME . . . IF YOU DARE.

Oh, my God.

Frannie drops the tickets and invitation and puts her
hand to her face, covering her eyes. She has never been to
New York City. She has tried to go for years but schedules
and finances and kids and life have blocked her exit. O'Brien
knows where all the best restaurants are located, where to
go, what she would do if she even had one free day in a city
that has captured her imagination for years. It's been her
dream. It's been on her own list and she is overwhelmed.

"I am going to kick her ass," O'Brien growls as she
reaches for her phone to call her husband and she wishes
with all of her heart that she could see his face when she tells
him where they are going to be for the weekend and what
they are going to do once they get there.

"You want me to *what*?"

Connie asks this question of Jessica—who has a phone in
each ear and her computer running while she mouths directions to Sara, who is on the floor stuffing lovely blue bags
with free Diva products for Saturday's gala, and simultaneously

gives directions to Connie, who occasionally thinks that nothing will ever again surprise, startle, or shock her.

"You have to get to the airport in, like, one hour."

"What?" Connie shrieks at the news. "Why?"

"It was going to be a surprise but I, once again, need your help to facilitate what was going to be your surprise."

Jessica talks into one phone, hangs up the other one, and tells her mother that she was going to go to the airport but now, because of yet another glitch, she has to get back to the store and handle a massive shipment that they need for Saturday's party. Saturday being tomorrow. The day after today. Hours away.

"Who's at the airport?" Connie asks.

"Sabrina and Macy."

Connie is surprised, shocked, and startled, which startles her even more.

"How?" she manages to utter. "The kids?"

"They're coming alone, no husbands, a network of babysitters and they can only stay two days but . . ."

Connie grabs Jessica by the arm and finishes her sentence.

"But this is a huge event. It's not only a party for the products, dear daughter, but it's a celebration of your hard work, Geneva's hard work, and what a woman can do when she wants to. I'm proud to be a part of this, sweetheart, and now, with your sisters, O'Brien, and Geneva's family—the ones she dared to invite, flying in, too—how grand is this?"

"You guys are going to make me cry," Sara says, looking up from her sea of boxes and tissue paper.

"My mom will get lost on the way to the airport, Sara. Can you help her? Bring them back here. They can give us a hand. I have so much shit to do in the next 24 hours I'm thinking I might go blind."

Jessica blubbers, she is talking so fast, but Connie under-stands everything. Her daughters are staying around the cor-ner at a very sweet boutique hotel; she'll meet them back at the apartment in two hours; they can help with the packag-ing, phone calls, opening wine, whatever needs to be done and then they can walk to the store and have dinner across the street. Then Connie stops Jessica.

"That's enough," she says, pushing her daughter back into her chair. "I'm on it. Sara, we leave in ten minutes."

And they do, with Sara driving and Connie sitting back in wonderment as they whip past Central Park, join the horn-honking parade of cabs, businessmen and -women and a con-stant caravan of buses that remind Connie of absolutely nothing that she encounters when she drives in Indiana. Chicago maybe. Indiana never. Sara serenades Connie with her own family tales as they head across the bridge and join a line of cars at the tollbooth, and Connie fades.

Connie fades from where she is and into the worlds of her other two daughters. *Those girls*, as she has referred to them for the past ten years with O'Brien, and occasionally with Jessica. Those girls, who managed to finish college, marry fast, have babies and become, so Connie thinks, part of a world that she thought did not often match the rhythms of her own beating heart. A world that, in her mind, revolves mostly in one direction. A world, she once imagined, that would not allow them to travel to big urban wildernesses for the unveiling of their sister's sex-toy products.

"Was I wrong?" Connie asks Sara, who can usually pick up on her undisclosed thoughts and who now only imagines the question has something to do with the other daughters, the good girls, the ones with the babies and the lives that are so far south from anything Sara can imagine that she's actu-ally excited to be meeting them.

"Something about these two chicks we're picking up?"

"I used to wonder where I went wrong because they married and starting throwing out babies so fast, and then I just figured it was their lives, and yet I sometimes imagine it's because of the divorce, how much I worked, well, everything that I was and did that they did not want to be and do."

"But they did," Sara answers.

"What do you mean?"

"Connie, they both found men they claim to love, they got married, they had babies—they did everything you did, so apparently the divorce and whatever lectures you threw at them about what happened to you bounced through one ear and out the other."

"That's what I told them *not* to do."

"They were kids. What you said didn't matter. Have you asked them?"

"They seemed happy. I think they are happy, it's just that, well, I was hoping they'd be more like Jessica."

Sara laughs so loud she snorts and Connie reaches over to grab her a tissue and steers while she blows her nose—still laughing.

"What's so funny?" Connie demands.

"Connie, you can't have three of them the same. Imagine how crowded the sex-toy industry would be if what you wanted was true?"

"I just wanted them to know they had choices, that they could be and do anything."

"That's what they seem to be doing," Sara throws back. "Hey, it's probably a damn good thing I am coming along with you."

But they flew into Connie's arms screaming as if they had not seen her in years, kissing her face and lips, not letting go of her arms, shouting about how they were in New York, "without the damn kids or men," and looking as if they were on fire from the inside out.

"Mom," Sabrina said, "in a million years did you ever think we'd all be meeting here to go to the sex-toy launch for our sister and your daughter? Did you?"

"It was something I always prayed for," Connie said, feeling the skin of her daughters, her babies, the girls she never wants to let go of. "Of course not. It's more likely we'd all be at a Tupperware Party in Indianapolis."

"And Mom, Mom, have you tried any of the stuff she sells?" Macy asks, whisking her hair out of her eyes and then closing them as if she is remembering what happened the last time she used a Diva product. "It's all so remarkable. If I was not so bound up in my own work and daycare and everything I'd open a store for her in Indianapolis."

"I've thought the same thing, but my husband would shoot me," Sabrina chimes in. "That man has got to loosen up."

And their laughter ripples throughout La Guardia as the four women grab bags and race towards the car that Sara has parked illegally in a handicapped zone.

Then Connie grabs her own fingers to form praying hands because she has not had time to write from her list and slip them into her pocket but she knows exactly what would be on her slips today—everything having to do with dancing, everything having to do with letting go, everything having to do with allowing her daughters to live their very own lives.

Everything.

Connie is lacing up the back of a long black gown she snatched off the rack at a fabulous secondhand store with the help of Mattie, who she has come to realize could probably turn the world on end with one small hand, locate a lost contact lens in the middle of a gravel pit, and single-handedly direct traffic in the heart of a massive snowstorm.

The gown, which Connie decides has been pre-owned by an eccentric and very wealthy movie star, floats off her shoulders, plunges towards the middle of her breasts and makes her look magically gorgeous, miraculously slim, and utterly divine.

"Come hook me up, Jessica," Connie yells from the bathroom, hoping that her oldest daughter, who is near exhaustion and who has managed to regain her near-goddess-like attitude, will make it through the evening without toppling into her arms or on her own face.

Jessica is still in her bathrobe when she slips into the room, takes one look at her mother, and lets go of a very audible and loud sigh.

"Oh, Mother, you look beautiful! The dress is stunning. Mattie has turned your hair into a delightful hair garden. Oh, Mom . . . I'm trying to act like I know everything, Mom, but tell me something new, and bend over just a little bit so I can hook this up so those beautiful breasts don't flop into some-one's drink."

Connie lets Jessica finish, and then smooths down the backside of the dress, and then she turns to face her, puts her hands on her shoulders and says, "I feel really sexy."

Sexy.

Alive.

Ready to meet the press and handle them as Jessica has instructed.

Beautiful.

And even more sexy than that.

"Mother, you *look* sexy. I hope this guy can handle you. And I hope the swamp man doesn't find out. You are the perfect walking advertisement for Diva's. Beautiful. Ravishing, actually. Thank God I got your genes," Jessica tells her, laughing.

Then they hurry. Sabrina and Macy arrive while Jessica is in the bathroom, looking as if they have been living on the Upper East Side and dressing for formal events their entire lives. They are polished, wrapped, finished, and glowing from their toenails to the Mattie-styled hair that reeks of so-phistication and style. Sabrina comes in with a bottle of champagne and announces that it was sitting right outside the apartment door.

"Open the card," Jessica yells. "I'm at the mascara stage. Hang on."

Sabrina whistles, which almost makes Connie fall over. It's been a while, too long, since she heard her middle daughter whistle. Sabrina always whistled when she was happy, when she was walking to her bike or car, when some-thing magical was about to happen, and it is a sound, Connie realizes, that she has sorely missed.

"It's from the screen stud, Jessica. It says, *'This is your night, beautiful Jessica. Save the last dance for me. Congratulations.'*"

More whistling.

And then Jessica emerges from the bathroom in a whirl of blazing red and orders them to fill four glasses, with just a sip for the pregnant sister, as quickly as possible because Jessica is about ready to jump out of her skin, her dark nylons, and the red dress that she bought because it is not only provoca-tive and sexy but the color of passion. And she announces, as if no one has heard the news, that she is *all* about passion.

And Connie is about to faint.

Her three daughters. New York City. Lust and love and passion and profound moments everywhere she looks and her heart racing from one side of her life to the other to see them, just see them laughing, pouring the champagne, turning each other around to fix a hem, pull back a wisp of hair, dip a wet finger to the edge of an eye, literally jump with excitement.

And this night, with absolutely no room for a list pocket, Connie forces her list of dreams into an invisible place she has just sewn into the curve of her heart. A place for dreams, she tells herself, that are only dressed in love.

Connie takes her glass while her daughters toast Jessica, and she watches, but a part of her is not there. A part of her sees them sitting on the dining room table the time she caught them making chocolate chip cookies out of Play-Doh and real chocolate chips, and then throwing up because they thought they could actually eat them. Discovering Jessica and Sabrina tying Macy to the tree behind the garage at the moment, the exact moment, they are about to set fire to the bale of hay they have not so tenderly placed around the entire tree, so that they can burn her at the stake, and then rescue her. Connie takes a sip of the gloriously dry champagne and she sees her three girls huddled around a magazine they have discovered in the neighbors' garbage. It's *Playboy* and they are giggling and putting their hands over their own breasts to measure. She steps back to keep from crying as Jessica goes over the night's schedule, and reminds them of their jobs—Connie, woman handling the media; Macy, caterer patrol; Sabrina, security—and she remembers three high school and college graduations, two weddings, and the way the door sounded when each one of them left for a job, a new life, a place too far away. The door closing. Lives changing. Girls turned into women. A mother unleashed and the tangle in her heart—always wondering, wanting, needing to know if she'd done all she could.

And she sees them. Three incredibly beautiful yet totally different women. Jessica, with her drive for professional success and her sometimes and recently melting emotional distance. Sabrina, with her two babies, her life in the suburbs, part of her life dancing in place while she decides where she will turn next. Macy and her man and baby lurching, so she has just discovered, towards a possible new life and direction in California where the husband will work and Macy will finish graduate school.

All of this, Connie thinks, and what came before it, what is happening now, what will happen for the rest of our lives. In seconds, maybe just one second, Connie knows she could turn this evening into a Nixon-Franklin love fest. She could drop her eyes right now and cry for a week. She could tell them everything, every single fear and regret and ache and loss and joy and let them spread it out and give her an answer, their answer, their interpretation. She could tell them all together about the list and check to see if they are compiling their own. She could tell them about how she has felt her heart really fly during the past few weeks, and how just when you think you know, you really don't know anything.

But this is Jessica's night. It is her weekend, and her time, and wise Connie puts her arm on Sabrina's shoulder and she raises her shimmering glass into the air and she says she needs to offer up a toast before Frannie and Daniel appear in the horn-honking limo to whisk them away.

"Jessica, I want you to know how proud I am of who you are, what you are doing, and what you have accomplished," she starts. "But I want you to know too, Sabrina and Macy, that I am proud of you also and your choices and especially proud that you could be here, to share this night with your sister. You are all gorgeous, wise, and terribly sexy. And all three of you, each one of you, are a dream come true for me. This is to you—all three of you. I love you."

They touch glasses, sip the champagne and, before they

can finish, the horn summons them. The horn, and O'Brien, who runs screaming up the steps and into Connie's arms and then into the arms of "the girls," the women who have been a part of her life so long she thinks they are her daughters too. Frannie has also purchased a long black gown that is a breathtaking visual commentary on her dark skin, her gorgeous brown and very wide eyes, the generous figure she has never once apologized for but embraced her entire life. And when she sees Connie's black dress they both laugh, grab bags and notebooks and three daughters and descend on the Irishman like a lively feminine plague.

Nothing, really, could have prepared any of them for what they are about to be a part of, witness, and remember for a very long time. The smiling limo driver delivers them to a tall, chic building that stands as if it is guarding the Hudson River and the swirling mass of activity that spreads itself out on either side of the river's banks. There is a uniformed doorman, bright lights everywhere and three—count them, three—television remote trucks already setting up on the sidewalks.

Connie gulps and lurches for Jessica's arm as she looks up to see a gown-clad Sara waving like a madwoman from inside of the building.

"Three trucks already, Jessica?" Connie tries to whisper.

Jessica is smiling. She is not walking but appears to be floating. Her night has started, and she is into it.

"I was hoping for just one, Mother. This is so perfect. Things are going to go through the roof."

Meredith, Kinsey, Geneva and Sara have almost everything under control. Geneva, in her own red passion dress, looks as if she could, at that moment, have everything and everyone under control if she just snapped her fingers. She has a list in her hand, a pen sticking out of the top of her lively updo, and a partner who looks as if she would be able to catch anything or anyone that fell in between the cracks.

Besides the reporters, Geneva's family and an assorted and flamboyant jumble of friends invited by Sara, Meredith and Kinsey, it seems—from the list Geneva is holding—that the entire state of New York may be at the event. Politicians, representatives from what appears to be every organization ever formed, neighbors, business owners, manufacturing representatives, university professors, dozens of friends—hundreds of people are here.

"This many?" Connie shrieks as she walks into the building and is immediately overwhelmed by its elegance. Gleaming floors, a view of the river that will only escalate as the night lights rise, bobbing boats tied to the dock, soft lanterns blazing on the patio, linen tablecloths. No expense, it seems, has been spared, no detail overlooked. Cinderella would never want to leave this party.

Jessica does not even stop to answer questions but has locked arms with Geneva as they prepare their last few notes for their presentation and the magical unveiling of Diva's products that have been carefully arranged under layers of silk that match the hue of Geneva's and Jessica's dresses.

"Two hundred and fifty people?" Connie asks, to anyone who will answer. She looks like an Indiana doe who has just spotted her first headlight.

"Mother," Sabrina answers firmly. "There were more people at my wedding. Think of this as a large dinner party."

"This many people could make up an entire town," Connie falters.

"Well, tonight we are Diva Town, Connie," Kinsey declares, swishing past in a white tuxedo, a bright red shirt, and a tie in the shape of a sexual instrument, and moving so fast Connie can't quite make it out.

Diva Town it is as the jazz quartet sets up. Geneva and Jessica make certain everything is complete and ready and perfect and Connie quickly organizes her press packets, grabs a glass of white wine, waves off Macy, who asks her with an upturned thumb if she is okay, and stations herself near the entrance to meet, greet, and direct.

Later she will think that it made sense—sort of, way later when months have passed and people stop her on the street and three friends she has not seen in years send her framed copies of her photo on the cover of two magazines. Later when her feet stop aching and she realizes she may never be able to wear the dress again because of the wine stains and Jessica has taught her how to be gracious about interviews and story angles and why it made sense for Connie to be there and a major, not just a minor figure on a night when she would really have rather danced on the deck with those men—all of those men.

"And really," Connie will admit, "it was not horrible, but just a little scary until Sara leaned in and said, 'Connie, just be yourself, for God's sake,' and I was and it seemed to work."

But it started out shakily, with Geneva's family swooping in all at once, and then a car filled with friends, and before Connie could look up and see who in the hell Mattie was bringing with her she saw Burt Reynolds getting out of a taxi with Justin about the same moment Jessica saw Justin getting out of the taxi with Burt Reynolds and, thank goodness, *after* the Screen Man had arrived and was noshing at her elbow. Jessica's "holy shit" look matched Connie's and mother and daughter's eyes met and then they raised their shoulders at the same moment, as if they had rehearsed, and just let it all happen.

"Burt," Connie thought as he took her in his arms and

kissed her right in front of all three of her astonished daughters, and about three seconds after the guy she was supposed
to dance with, and eventually did, showed up.

There was no time for necking. Not a second as Connie
ushered the two southerners into the party just as a cameraman from some news magazine show galloped up to her and
asked who she was.

It wasn't a fatal mistake because Connie was just being
herself, as instructed by her personal advisor, 22-year-old
Sara Hanson, when she answered, "Oh, I'm just the mom.
My daughter, who is part owner, is over there."

And that is how it started.

"The *mother*?"

"You work there too?"

"You're a trained nurse?"

"A whip in your pocket?"

"Indiana?"

Before Connie could answer too many questions, she
raced across the lobby to Jessica, whispered in her ear, lifted
her head up to watch Jessica smile and then took her daughter and Geneva by the elbow, as if she were a grade school
teacher leading two girls off to the time-out corner, and almost flung them at the first cameraman.

But it didn't work.

Connie was way too sexy, the whole idea of a grandma
selling sex toys threw the reporters all right off the edge.
And so, Connie, after two more glasses of wine, agreed to
anything they wanted as long as Geneva and Jessica were included.

Anything, while the band played on and almost every one
of the 250 invited guests arrived, and Sabrina and Macy,
along with Meredith and Sara and Kinsey, worked the crowd
like professional entertainers, and the champagne seemed

endless and the city night sky exploded in a blaze of summer
glory—*anything* actually meant two instant on-camera interviews, a promise for two magazine stories, quotes in five
newspapers and a trade publication, and agreeing to consider one very strange but sort of cute offer from the man in
charge of the building, who watched the interviews and
wanted to take her golfing next Thursday at his uncle's private club in New Jersey.

Finally, the clang of silverware against the appetizer
plates sounded so beautiful to Connie it made her want to
weep. It was her cue to leave her media post and become
part of the crowd, a Diva fan, the mother of the bride, and
when the cameras sidled up to the edge of the platform
where Geneva and Jessica were making their presentation it
was suddenly Mattie with her alleged blind date who got to
Connie before Commissioner Michael Dennis. Mattie in-
troducing her friend Luke, a medium-sized blond-haired guy
to whom she could only say hello because the presentation
was about to begin.

Connie saw.

She most certainly saw the Screen Man lean into Jessica,
kiss the side of her cheek, and she saw Jessica's hand linger
on his shoulder while she pushed back her hair the exact
same way she had been pushing back her hair since it grew
out when she was 14 years old. Jessica pushing back her hair,
and showing herself and the world that she is in charge, and
walking arm in arm with Geneva to the small stage and the
table of soon-to-be-exposed Diva products.

Geneva is stunning, and Jessica does not skip a beat, and
just as they are about to whisk the cover off of the table,
Connie Franklin Nixon feels the familiar right hand of Frannie
O'Brien slip into hers and Connie thinks for a second that
she could be anywhere.

She could be in her damn garage, or at the new job, or slipping a pair of pruning shears through the back fence, or walking up Fifth Avenue. And as long as she can look up and see her daughters, touch O'Brien's hand, turn and see her Diva Sisters, spy two men who want to take her golfing, out to dinner, and who knows where else, she could give a rat's ass about the assumed protocol of her list of dreams because now she is in the middle of a very powerful and extraordinarily lovely dream.

Too fast, just too fast, the new products in their sleek red cases with ribbons and the coolest opening side-vents, invented by Justin, are passed around and photographed and Jessica has announced that Diva's will soon be franchised and marketed, and not just in the United States. Thank God O'Brien is there, and Daniel is next to her because Connie could very easily fall right over.

"Connie, this is so fabulous," O'Brien whispers as she raises a hand to wipe the tears off of Connie's face.

"It is something, Frannie. Who would have thought?"

Frannie laughs just a bit too loudly and Daniel squeezes her hand to try and keep her quiet, but there is no stopping Frannie. Especially if she is with Nurse Nixon.

Connie leans over to whisper as Geneva finishes the program—announces that the bar will stay open until 2 A.M., and the band will stay until 2:30 A.M.—and tells her best friend she thinks her heart is about to explode.

"I could die right now I'm so damn happy," Connie whispers. "This is beyond dreaming. It is."

"Jesus, baby, don't die before you sleep with one of these guys and can try out some of these products. I'll kill you if you die. You're supposed to try them all first and then call me."

It's Connie's turn to laugh and all three of her daughters

turn towards her because they know her sound. When they were little girls they knew if they heard that sound everything was good and when it was too quiet, as it often was, things were not so good. This night, the perfect evening, things were good. Very good.

When the music starts again Connie cannot move. She wants to stay right there until she figures out which way to turn next, but then there is another hand in hers. A man's hand, and when she opens her eyes there is Burt Reynolds and that's what she says.

"Hello, Burt."

"That must be the other guy's name. I'm Michael."

"Yes, darling, but you look exactly like Burt."

"And you, Connie, look absolutely fabulous."

Burt had the first dance but not all of them. Luke had several, and Daniel, and Frannie, and every single one of the daughters, and they drank wine and ate food blessed by the goddess of lust and love and when the summer moon had long since dipped behind the lowest possible building, the Diva Sisters and their saucy and spirited escorts finally—finally—left the party.

There was also kissing under the stars, and exchanges of phone numbers, and making Sunday brunch dates, and a feeling of rapture that wrapped around every single one of them that made this night one they would never forget.

And every single person, man and woman, who left—including the Diva Sisters—had a fabulous new sex toy nesting in the bottom of a purse, inside a tuxedo jacket, or riding in plain sight in a left or a right hand.

twenty-five

15. *Be my own boss. Lots of employee benefits. Hiring people I want to be with a lot. Free lunch all of the time. A clear view of a goal that includes the feelings, schedules and talents of the people who work for me. I like this one. Oh, yes. Hey, I'm in charge.*

33. *Go see more plays.*

The Chicago skyline in mid-summer is a towering mass of heat and steel and concrete. The city shimmers. Heat rises in swells that bounce from block to block, from building to building, from one corner of the city to the next. The Lake Michigan sea and its miles of sandy shoreline string themselves like wet pearls along the east edge of a city that seems to stretch from Wisconsin all the way into Indiana.

And it is fun, and wild, and sophisticated, and not so sophisticated, and not like any other city Connie has ever been to in her life, not even New York City. Concerts, dances, block parties, neighborhoods where it is still hard to find someone who speaks English, the smell of sizzling Polish sausage colliding with thick garlic-encrusted pizza, spontaneous gatherings on street corners where men and women congregate to smoke cigarettes, drink beer out of plastic cups from the local bars, and talk with their hands. . . .

Jessica has bounced into the back room of Diva's, where Connie has her head buried inside of a large cardboard box, and has simply said, "Mother, think about Chicago. I'll be back later." And Connie has been suddenly struck deaf and dumb, frozen in place.

Chicago, which is very close to Indiana. Chicago, where two grandbabies live. Chicago, which she thinks she can sometimes see on late winter nights in the reflection off the dunes when she is hiking in the frozen sand along the Indiana shores of Lake Michigan.

There is never much time to actually think about anything. There hasn't been much time at all since the explosion of business following the Diva launch party, and all the publicity, and the insane knowledge that women are beyond ready for everything that Diva's has to offer, and the phone calls for home parties, and the push to expand, and the appearance of the Screen Man at a variety of times and places, and two dates with the blond man Luke, and countless phone calls from Burt Reynolds, and this one thought, tiny and creeping so it eventually will form a much bigger thought, that *something has to change again.*

Something has to change because the Manhattan apartment is very, very tiny and Jessica cannot always go to Martin's house and—What if?—what if Connie wanted to have a sleepover, and the real estate agent is losing patience, and the condo is almost finished.

But first Chicago.

"Why?" Connie asks when Geneva shuttles into the office on her lunch break, which Geneva is certain will very soon become a long break as she gears up to move into Diva's fulltime.

"She hasn't asked you yet?"

"She just asked me to think about Chicago as she was flying out the door."

Geneva hesitates. Occasionally she wants to place her hands around her partner Jessica's lovely neck and squeeze it very hard.

"I hate this when she doesn't follow through. She was supposed to talk to you about the expansion days ago. We've got a lock on Los Angeles and Las Vegas but Chicago—well, I might as well talk to you so we can get this over with and get moving."

Moving indeed, Connie learns during the next 13 minutes, as Geneva shuts both of them in the storeroom with the expansion and franchise plans and talks about Chicago locations, and where they want to be by the end of December. The bottom line—right down there below stocking shelves, selling at the Manhattan store, training new staff members, cooking dinner, buying coffee, and playing with the idea of sex-toy parties for women over 40—is that they are hoping Connie can visit Chicago, meet with their real-estate broker, scout out store locations and consider managing that store which they hope to have open by September 15.

"Consider *what*?" Connie asks as if she has suddenly gone deaf for real.

"You heard me, Connie. It makes total sense to us, but it also has to make sense to you. What do you think?"

"Think? I haven't been thinking much. Living and working for sure, but there hasn't been much room for thinking."

Geneva snorts and throws back her head. She imagines Nurse Nixon not thinking and planning and working like a starving dog and she keeps laughing because Connie Franklin Nixon thinks all the time. Connie's a natural-born marketing and managing genius. She's tireless. She's fun. She's the reason Jessica drives herself like another starving dog. She's the example of a lifetime.

"Connie, knock it off. Listen, just call your pal or go take a walk or ring up that guy you've had lunch with three days in a row and see what comes up."

"How fast do you need to know?"

"Jessica was supposed to ask you days ago. We need to have someone in Chicago on Friday. Honest."

"Friday? You two babes are rich. *Friday?* What's your backup plan?"

"We were thinking of asking Sabrina. She might be ready to sell leather thongs. Or maybe O'Brien. Do you think she's ready for a career change?"

Connie pushes her head back, cracks her neck, and lets out a wad of air as if she really is smoking. She says, "You don't have a backup plan, do you?"

"Nope."

Connie reaches back. There's a silent pause in the sound of Sara and Kinsey verbally dancing with customers, the ringing phone, and the marching and sometimes merciless waves of city noise that penetrate through the concrete, steel and wooden walls like a restless, bored street gang. One moment, way back where Connie reaches, splashes into full view.

The girls are eight, five, and two and Connie is hanging on to a tiny shred of sanity by the tips of her fingernails. Daddy Roger is working second shift, huge chunks of overtime, and it's the heart of fishing season. Connie doesn't want to drink, or dance, or leave, or kill anyone. She doesn't want a moment of silence, or a trip to Paris, or a nanny from England. Connie wants something very simple.

She wants a choice.

It is 9 P.M. on a Thursday and she is working third shift and has not slept in 34 hours. Macy has the chicken pox, and she forgot to bake cookies for Jessica's choir concert party, and her ankles are swollen, and when she raises her arms above her waist her back hurts so much she drops to the floor, and the bathroom is filthy, and the grocery supply has dwindled and she just wants a choice.

Not a go or a stay choice. Not a want-babies or don't-want-babies choice. Not a married or not-married choice. Those choices Connie has already made.

Something awesomely simple.

A walk before bedtime. Looking into neighbor's windows. Kicking pine cones into the gutter. Waving to someone she knows. Watching the streetlights come alive as if there is a magic switch behind the oak tree on the corner.

A bath. Nothing fancy, just some hot water in the brown bathtub. No candles. Nothing but hot water and 20 minutes and maybe the ratty old blue washcloth.

The chance to read. Not a magazine but a book. An entire book. Stretched out. The window open. The phone off the hook and tucked under the pillow. Words and sentences and paragraphs and page after page after page.

A kiss on the neck. In that one spot. Behind her ear and down three inches where a wild nerve must have landed sideways. Lips, soft and then harder on that one spot. Then again and maybe one more time after that but just a little bit slower.

Lasagna, a salad, garlic bread and more than 27 minutes to eat it all. Someone else cooks. She sits and eats. Alone. Maybe one glass of wine. Make it two glasses of wine. Lots of cheese. No one spilling milk.

A phone call. Long and winding. Looking out the window. No place to go. The quiet sensations of time covering every word she utters.

She wants to knock off some of the items on her list. The growing list. The list that seemed to change as everything else seemed to change. Or not.

"Connie?" Geneva interrupts. "Are you still thinking?"

"I told you I wasn't thinking."

"You always think and you sure as hell are thinking right now. Where are you?"

"Oh, Geneva, I was long gone to a place I really don't want to see again. Back there, years ago when I had no choices and was saddled like a derby horse with all my directions and destinations predetermined. It wasn't so bad, but it was tiring. And, okay, sometimes it was an exhausting disappointment that seemed endless. Pretty damn tiring minus the good things mothers and women are only supposed to mention in public."

"I can imagine," Geneva offers. "I think my mother told me this same story about three thousand times."

"Choices are good," Connie admits.

Geneva just smiles.

"What the hell, Geneva. I need to go home, clear up some business, take a breath. And I'll go check out Chicago for you. But . . ."

"But what?"

"One step at a time. I'm just going. And then we'll see."

"We'll see? You sound just like a mom."

"I am a mom."

"I have a *but* too, Connie."

Connie grits her teeth, closes her eyes, says nothing.

"There's no time to go to Indiana. You need to fly into Chicago on Friday and work all day and part of the evening. You would also have a meeting Saturday with the broker, a few more appointments—especially if you see something you like—and fly back here Saturday night late on the red-eye. Maybe early Sunday if you really want to stay, but you must be back here Sunday by early afternoon."

"Why?"

"We have to make a decision by Monday afternoon."

"You jackasses," Connie says.

"But it's a choice," Geneva throws back at her without hesitation.

Connie hesitates only to look at Geneva. To look at her and her ease in negotiations, her sure sense of self and direction, her knowing exactly what Diva needs and that Connie can and will most likely make up her mind before the end of the conversation.

"I need to go pack," Connie says as she smiles and gets up immediately and playfully whacks Geneva upside the head.

Just like a mom.

Connie prayed for a woman. She prayed just as she imagined the airplane might be dipping towards Cyprus as it descended into the Windy City. She leaned against the window, felt her nose freeze instantly, and wondered what she might be missing at this very second.

O'Brien halfway to work. The staff at her new place

of employment locked in their mandatory Friday morning weekend-assessment meeting. Her next-door neighbor wondering how in the hell much longer he would have to cut her grass. Her real-estate agent leaving yet another message and driving past her house yet another time. The cute guy at the corner gas station wondering why she never rushed in any more for black coffee on the way home from work. The way she had the stoplights in town timed so she never had to stop if she was going 32 miles per hour. The stretch of maple trees in front of the library that she took leaves from every single season of the year just so she could be near not only the leaves but her beloved library. The wild summer art festival—when? Next week maybe—damn, that filled the center of Cyprus with working artists, live music, a food fest and a chance to see everyone she hadn't seen since the last festival.

Comfortable, countable, reliable, predictable things and people and places and Connie threw a kiss to all of Cyprus and continued praying for a female real-estate agent in Chicago as the plane swooped towards O'Hare.

Maybe in a month, or next year, or when she got to collide on a more intimate level with Michael or Luke or whomever she was with when she totally let her sexual self snap—it might not matter whom she was discussing the new sex-toy store with. And it didn't matter either that she had sold plenty of products to men.

Or did it?

Connie rushed at herself with the lingering "why" question about her wanting to spend the next day and a half with a real-estate broker who was a woman and knew it made absolutely no sense. Maybe it was because she was so close to home. Maybe she was afraid of running into someone she knew from the hospital, as unlikely as that scenario appeared. Maybe she was just a big, middle-aged baby who was slouching back towards a very comfortable position. Maybe she should just shut up, and give it up, and get off the plane and see what happens.

It was a man dressed in a thousand-dollar suit, with brilliant white teeth, hair trimmed three seconds ago and, if she guessed correctly, Connie determined he must be about 15 years old. There he was holding up a white sign that said NIXON and greeting her with a lively, "Hello, how was your flight?"

And they were off and Connie was totally disarmed by his professional manner and by the way he answered every single question she asked without raising an eyebrow. They stopped immediately in the airport coffee shop to lay out the day's plans, and the night after that, and whatever of the next day and night they might need as well.

Well, there.

Connie drew a line, imaginary and deep, so she thought, as they moved from the baggage area and walked across the concourse to the coffee shop. She would be Connie Franklin Nixon, spokesperson for Diva's, potential store and regional manager, possible executive board member, and not another person for the entire time she was with Jason Belmont. Not a mother or ex-wife or sex-starved nurse-in-transition. Not a wild kisser of swamp men or dancer until 3 A.M. in Manhattan. Not a dream-list devotee. Just Nixon, like the sign the broker held at the airport, assistant to the sex-toy stars, planner of the future, progressive woman of the universe.

She threw herself into her exhilarating but demanding job while shrugging off her almost physical attraction to Chicago, and she acted as if she were about to hire a new staffing assistant back at the Cyprus hospital. She wanted to know Jason Belmont, and why he was the chosen real-estate broker guru, and what he could do that no other broker could do, and how long it would take him to do it.

Contacts. Negotiating skills. A law degree. Obvious charm. More contacts. A way to steer clear of controversy— even for sex-toy stores. Even for high-end sex-toy stores. Determination. Research, and once again, contacts. Knowledge, not just of the city but the suburbs, too.

"How much controversy are we expecting in Hinsdale, Burr Ridge, Naperville or a place called Wrigleyville?" Connie asks over coffee.

"It could be a disaster with protests at the planning-commission level, or it could be a piece of cake if it's done right," Jason explains. "It's not like you want to put in a pizza parlor or a religious goods store, although I have to tell you these days either one of those could cause some kind of disastrous mess in the neighborhood."

"What? Like a religious reaction to pepperoni?" Connie replies, straying quickly from her straight woman disguise. She simply cannot help herself.

Jason laughs and tells her that her approach will probably work well in Chicago, even in some of the upscale suburban neighborhoods they are ready to attack.

"If you know your business like I know my business, we should knock them all dead today, Connie," he says enthusiastically. "Jessica told me you would probably run for mayor by the end of the weekend, so let's go to it."

"Fine, Jason, but just so you know, Diva's is planning on a piece of cake, a swift and controversy-free lease agreement, and it would be perfect if our selection included an option to purchase," she says. "The women of Chicagoland are waiting and Jason, if you disappoint them, imagine what that would feel like."

Jason did not want to imagine. He wanted to succeed and at the tender age of 34 he was totally disarmed by this New-York-by-way-of-Indiana woman who seemed to know this part of Illinois, her business, and herself very, very well.

Connie started taking notes on the way to the car and didn't stop all day long. Jason knew his territory and what to do to make that work for his customers. He knew the direction Diva's wanted to take but he didn't know the potential customers like Connie knew the potential customers. He had mapped out a vigorous day of touring, meetings, and more touring that was not scheduled to end until 8 P.M. when he took her to dinner at her hotel and where he expected to finish every single task he had outlined for the day.

He wanted to know more as they drove from the airport into the heart of the city, stopping at locations he had mapped out along busy thoroughfares, close to mass transit drops, and in hip, funky sections before they strayed towards the suburbs. By 3:30 P.M. they had visited 12 potential locations, rejected all but two, and Connie had a sense that they needed to venture out a bit more into the fingertips of the suburbs, not the hands or wrists or elbows, just close enough so the women could get to them quickly, and without making an excuse, and close enough too for the city girls who would be equally embarrassed to have to drag themselves out to the burbs.

"Brilliant," Jason says. "I have two places that might be perfect. There are places in the city, you know that, but this part of Illinois is such a changing, dynamic world. I think I understand what you might be getting at."

What she is getting at, Connie wants to tell him, is that women want, deserve, and need sex just as much as men need it, and they don't want to have to purchase their appliances at old fading warehouses next to the interstate.

"I've read a little bit about the seemingly sudden explosion of sex-toy stores," Jason confides as they spin off of the Eisenhower Expressway and take the side streets towards Elmhurst and then down to Oak Brook. "Maybe it's the ripple effect from *Sex and the City* or something but everyone is surely more willing to talk about it now."

"Justin, I suppose it was just a matter of time before someone like Jessica or the women who have already opened up stores said, 'What the heck are we waiting for?' " Connie explains. "Imagine, if you can, what a nice woman, say, like me, would feel like buying a toy from some tattoo-covered guy in an alley somewhere."

Jason laughs and tells her he has been to every sex-toy store within a hundred-mile radius of downtown Chicago.

"And?" Connie demands.

"It's an interesting blend of the tattoo man and smaller boutiques that have tried hard to set a new standard, and there are several places over in Boy's Town, where the gay men hang, and close to Andersonville where the gay women hang," he shares. "It totally makes sense to have a store, a chain of them, that caters to women. Just women. Something upscale and comfortable."

"That's what Diva's is trying to do but, of course, men are always allowed too," Connie says as they pull up in front of an empty store next to a busy shopping area. "This, for example, might not work because someone going in here could run into someone coming out of that children's clothing store."

"But," Jason argues, "it also might work. You know, kind of the one-stop shopping theory. You get your kids some new underwear, pick up groceries over there, and then slip in here and pick up a new vibrator for later in the day."

"You're probably right, Jason," Connie says, laughing.

"Part of the idea is to make it seem, like it is, that it's perfectly normal to do what needs to be done to be sexually satisfied, to feel good, to make certain that your sexual self is as nourished as every other part of your self."

Jason does not want to get out of the car but he sees their contact standing inside of the store they are about to visit. He knows they should get out but the conversation, this particular assignment, and this woman who could be his mother, are a swirl of excitement that he finds beyond interesting.

"Shouldn't we go in?" Connie asks.

"I talked to a lot of women too," he admits with his hand on the door. "Friends, my sister, the woman I'm dating, my boss, who is a woman, and I can tell you that every single thing you say is correct. I think the store will be packed the day it opens and every day after that."

Connie looks at him. She looks at him and thinks about all the mothers her age who have tried hard to raise men like Jason. Thoughtful. Open. Smart. Up to this point very non-sexist. She wonders what his dinner conversations might have been like, what his father did, how he came to be sitting in this car in a parking lot with Nurse Nixon and searching the suburbs of Chicago for a location for a sex-toy store. She really wants to know.

"Jason, will you tell me your story over dinner?"

"My story?"

"Yes. How you came to wear that fancy suit and paddle to this point in your life."

"Business first," he says, shaking his finger at her. "Once we get this down to two or three locations you can throw the light on me and I'll talk, but there isn't much to say."

"Liar," she shoots back, getting out of the car.

And, as she says it, Connie Franklin Nixon looks and

sounds not only professional but as if she already knows the entire story.

Jessica calls three times during the day and Connie calls her four times. By 7:30 P.M. they have decided on three potential locations, all in the suburbs, and all in areas where customers can buy a bottle of wine, a new blouse, or toys for the kids and eat a bagel within shouting distance of the new Diva's store.

"Lighting?" Jessica asked during the first call.

"Minor renovation and design work?" she asked during the second call.

"Options, legal problems, purchase plan?" she asked during the third.

Jason, Connie explained, had everything covered and then some. And the choice, they all agreed, would be simple once she and Jason sat down and laid out everything on a flat surface, called Jessica and Geneva before midnight—they hoped—and then drove back to the store one more time on Sunday and met with whoever was handling the lease agreements.

"It could take most of the day," Jason warns as they head back towards Connie's hotel. "I know you have a mid-afternoon flight, and we can work around that. And one more thing."

Connie turns as he pulls into the parking lot of a brewery/restaurant not far off the freeway, two blocks from her hotel. *One more thing*, she thinks, could probably be the title for a movie made about her life. She's been hearing "one more thing" for weeks now, which is exactly how she ended up here in Illinois with Jason and his white teeth.

"Your call, Jason," she tells him. "Buy me a glass of wine and I'll give you anything you want. I'm beat."

"I'd love to have my mother join us for brunch before we head back to Eastbrook tomorrow morning," he admits, somewhat shyly.

"Your mother?"

"Indulge me. She wants to ask you something and I think Eastbrook is where we will end up."

"Buy me the wine and I'll answer your question," Connie says as she swings her very tired legs from the car and walks into the restaurant.

Brunch, so it seems, is on for 11 A.M. at a very old, very cool, very good restaurant that has been catering to Chicago food aficionados since 1942, just miles from Eastbrook and, interestingly, not very far from the condo where Jason's mother lives with another woman.

"One more thing," Connie says out loud, as her head hits the pillow that night, and she falls asleep dreaming about absolutely nothing and too exhausted to remember to glance at her list of dreams.

One more thing.

Classy, beautiful, and totally fun, Christine Belmont meets them at the back table carrying a tray of Sunday morning mimosas and looking just as Connie imagined the mother of suave Jason Belmont might look like.

The conversation roars from point A to point Z so rapidly that Connie feels as if she has been rammed by a wild, but very nice, diesel truck. Christine, at 54, is embracing the word "change" in every aspect of her life and, now that Jason has helped free her from her house mortgage by selling her home, she has moved in with her best friend and is interested in making one more change.

"I'd like to work for you," Christine confesses to Connie.

"Really?" Connie says softly, trying hard not to swallow her entire glass and realizing that one more thing really meant two more things.

"I've been an assistant art director for over 25 years and I need a change so bad the veins in my face hurt."

"What were you thinking?"

"The new store. Anything having to do with the new store, the next one, or the one after that."

"Sex toys."

"I like to think beyond sex toys. More like, empowerment tools for women. It's about damn time someone opened up a place like this. If you close your eyes and listen for just a second you'll hear the weeping sounds of women all over this area crying because they did not get any again last night. . . ."

Christine Belmont hesitates for just a second and then finishes her sentence.

"Or what they did get was so exhaustingly horrid they shouldn't have bothered."

Jason does not turn away during the conversation. Apparently he has heard this particular discussion, and no doubt other discussions, richer and racier, many, many, times before.

"Do you have first-hand knowledge about this?" Connie asks Christine, throwing on her manager's hat.

"I did, but not anymore."

"The best friend, the new life? What? If it's not too personal," Connie asks.

"Nothing's too personal for my mother," Jason says first, not even close to blushing.

"And aren't you glad, son?" Christine asks as she launches into her own personal quest to discover her sexual identity, to be able to feel, to be, to experiment.

"When Jason told me about this account something snapped inside of me," Christine goes on. "I was one of those women who went to those joints, and dated five thousand men, and then discovered that my sexual power could only come from myself. I had to own it, take charge, and that's exactly what I did and what I would love, let me repeat that, *love* to do for other women who are waiting, for all those voices I hear crying in anguish right this moment."

Jason just sits and smiles. He takes a bite out of his omelet as if this kind of thing, a conversation with his mother and a client about the sexual powers of women, happens on a regular basis, which it most likely does.

Christine wants to know about plans for the store, who Connie intends to hire to work there, when it will open and, she throws in, she has talked to absolutely no one about Diva's and she is ready to go whenever Connie is ready to hire her.

"Let's get the location," Connie says, turning to Jason. "Let us do that first and then someone will be back here soon—I am not sure who that will be—to interview, get the design going, and finalize all the plans. Before then, you can get me your résumé, anything we might need."

Christine has it in her bag, pulls it out, slides it across the table and around the toast and asks why Connie isn't going to manage the store before Connie has a chance to take a breath.

"First the location, then the staff," Connie says, lying through her teeth and right into her coffee, which is, of course, very dark.

The store location was the easy part. By the time the

plane left, Jason and Connie and Jessica, via a flurry of phone calls, all agreed that Eastbrook would be the community—either the store attached to a new and very hip development or a restored home in the center of the town.

Connie's location, however, was something totally undecided.

twenty-six

Jessica's list

3. Sex. Wild, wonderful . . . did I say wild and wonderful sex?

Connie's list

14. Maybe sex. Something meaningless. Just sex. A man's hand on my face, my breast. Not caring what happens next. Over and over again. Sex. I can't even believe I just wrote this. It's a HUGE dream. Sex. My list. SEX. This is a big maybe. But I wrote it down. I can't even believe I knew how to spell it.

Jessica knew what would happen.

Connie knew what would happen.

And everyone who knew them knew it was about damn time.

Michael Dennis called first. He did not beg or whisper or assume anything more than just the notion that he would like to come back to New York, dance again, hold her hand in public, tell her the rest of his story, and spend the entire day with her and do it all on purpose, with absolutely nothing else on the schedule but that one thing.

To see Connie.

No meetings or plant tours or tuxedos or phone calls or someplace else to be but right there.

He also said please.

Martin asked next.

Could Jessica possibly spare even one half a day? Maybe a very long night in between Chicago plans, Los Angeles, general Diva madness, staffing problems, her mother, sisters, Geneva, and the rest of her heartbreaking schedule that barely left time for a hug.

Could she?

Could she please?

Connie held her breath when Michael called, a soft, sweet pause that made her smile, made her remember the moment she kissed Burt Reynolds while the sounds of the swirling swamp waters serenaded them, and how her lungs filled and then emptied into her throat. Remembered how she moved into him and how her entire body paused moments after that.

Paused and then stopped. Stopped moving and thinking and worrying and wondering, and then just simply wanted. Wanted to jump over #14 and into #3000. Connie wanted.

Wanted Burt.

Yes. Connie said, Yes, Michael, come on Wednesday and I will meet you at Diva's and we'll take it from there. Do not bring a tuxedo, or a schedule, or anything from the past. Bring Michael, she said. Just bring Michael, and his smile, and his open heart, and the way he stands next to me, and the electrifying charge I feel when he touches me.

Yes.

Connie said yes.

Jessica hesitated. She dropped her eyes into her robot-like planning machine and tried not to have a nervous break-down. Chicago loomed. Los Angeles loomed. Las Vegas loomed. Manhattan loomed. Her world was a blazing sunrise of possibilities and where was the Screen Man in all of this? Where was Martin?

The pause was much longer than Connie's. It hung in the air like a hot city breeze that was trapped between one river and the next. Birds did not fly. People walked slower. Some bars ran out of ice-cold beer. People walked around without shirts on and spoke to themselves as if they were delirious.

Martin was delirious.

Infatuation-like delirious and he had to find out about all of Jessica Franklin Nixon. All of her.

Please, he said again during the hot pause. During the pause while Jessica shifted and remembered how she felt the last time when sex turned into a garden of passion that con-sumed her and made her sleepless and wild and able to see images and people and predict the future. How she felt when she was on fire from the inside out, and when birds spoke to her, and she could suddenly understand 15 languages, and thought she surely could discover a cure for cancer, and walk naked across a thin wire strung from one tall building to the next.

Jessica fingered her schedule and she saw this one open-ing. It was a small hole in her world of time. A wedge into a place that had been sealed shut. A vault of improbability and she said one word. And as she looked at the schedule she wrote down her #3.

Well.

Martin put his hand on his head where the screen would

have hit him and that was all. He did not breathe or squirm or imagine anything but the next sound he might hear from the telephone. Jessica's voice. He loved to listen to her soft, firm, commanding, sometimes flippant voice.

Well, she said again.

And then she plunged. Jessica plunged into the real and sometimes sultry world of Divaness. She placed her hands on the edge of the desk and she said his name first.

Martin.

And then again.

Martin.

Wednesday evening. Meet me at Diva's and we'll take it from there.

Jessica said yes.

And Martin danced with the imaginary screen on his head and he hung up quickly before Jessica could change her mind.

Burt Reynolds flew fast. Martin danced fast and then it was Wednesday. No one slept on Tuesday. Martin, Jessica, Michael and Connie tossed and turned and walked and wrote and ate and drank and they wondered.

And there were hours of imagining. Wonderful, glorious imagining.

Everyone wondered and imagined and placed their hands on their hearts and breasts and in that one sweet spot below the waist and wondered some more.

There were few plans after that. Just a lively hurry to get there. A hilarious, almost simultaneous mingling and meeting at Diva's that caused Sara and Meredith to whisper like high school girls in the storeroom while the couples swayed and talked and laughed at the improbability of the meeting at Diva's. For one insane moment they considered sharing a late dinner but Michael, the Swamp Man, came to his senses and said that he had dinner reservations that he did not want to miss, and there was the exit line.

The excuse to get on with it.

And they did.

Connie did not want to eat dinner or walk or dance or know anything more than she already knew at that moment about Michael. She wanted to rip his shirt off the second he closed the door to his suite. She wanted to feel every inch of his body and not think about anything else but that moment and what his skin felt like under her fingers. Connie wanted. She simply wanted, and as she left Diva's with her hand in Michael's she decided that for now, for this night, for what might happen, that was all that mattered.

She wanted.

Jessica danced from one foot to the next. Sex had not been that far removed from her, but making love, that was a long, long time ago, and she hesitated.

She hesitated and Martin saw it and he stepped forward. He stepped forward, and he took her hand, and he smiled, and he bit his tongue lest he say something inappropriate like "I love you," and he didn't whisper or promise or push. He just took her hand.

Jessica stopped dancing then and she lifted the keys for the door out of her pocket and she threw them behind her back so that they smashed into the door of the storeroom where she knew her prized employees were huddled, listening and smirking and laughing and whatever else they might be doing. She threw away the keys and she stepped forward, and just before she did that she made sure she grabbed her very large briefcase.

Martin said my place and Jessica said no.

Mine.

Because she knew her mother was not coming back that night.

Then they left and after that they hurried and kissed on the street and while walking and in the lobby and pretty much every other place imaginable.

And in the morning, when Connie thought of her list, she smiled.

And in the morning, when Jessica thought of her list, she smiled.

They both laughed for a very, very long time and loved, absolutely loved, the way they felt when they knew the numbers from their list had indeed become a glorious and lustful reality.

twenty-seven

31. Sign the final house papers.

32. Pick out all the extras for the condo. Stop procrastinating.

1. Stop being afraid. (Here I go again.)

I t's possible. Connie leans her lovely blonde head towards the wall and decides to rest it there. She is thinking that if it happened once it is very possible that it may happen again. Why not? Why the hell not? After this past month, and part of the one before it, is anything not possible?

Her house could speak again. Connie knows that if it happened once, even if the electrical problem was fixed, it is very possible that it may happen again. The trapped whispers and sighs and yearnings of her entire family could leak out into the palm of her hand. They could leak out and filter down her arm and back into her heart where they belong.

"Come out," she whispers seductively with her lips touching painted plaster. "Speak to me. Please."

Nurse Nixon has returned to the Franklin Nixon homestead. She has shuttled back to Indiana with her bulging suitcase, her new wardrobe, more than enough Diva supplies to last her the next 20 years, a new face, new hair, choices times one hundred, and a deep and throbbing desire to stand in place for just a few moments, breathe quietly, search for the answers to the unlimited questions she must address, and simply let the past few months settle into some kind of solid and recognizable form.

If such a thing is even possible.

Not to mention there is a stack of mail to choke a well-maintained physical trainer, a yard that looks as if it is eating itself, unpaid bills, a list of people who want to see her house, condo papers to finalize, a new job to consider, phone calls, the last purging of the house. And an uncontested fight to get and keep #1 off of her list of dreams.

And this one looming and terribly immense deadline. She has one week. Seven days to make yet another decision because the Diva Sisters need to know if she wants to manage the Chicago store, if she's in, if she wants to keep moving in this direction, plunge full-time into the lovely world of Divaness, manage the staff, sit on the executive board, help with the Midwest expansion plans, the ever-increasing demand for sex-toy parties—or lurch back towards whatever is left of her prior life.

How Connie wants the silent walls to speak to her.

How she wants to wake up the band that has gone into hibernation inside of the kitchen walls.

"Frannie, I need a break from my break," she told

O'Brien the morning she decided it was time to get on an airplane and head west. "I need to lie down on my ratty couch for more than an hour, process what has happened, and make some pretty heavy decisions."

"Get home," O'Brien ordered. "Don't do anything rash yet—well, anything more rash than you already have. We'll make believe we're back at work together and plotting the takeover of the entire health care industry."

"I've missed you."

"Ditto, baby," Frannie shared. "Slink back here and I'll help you ease into your decisions."

Ease?

Where's the ease? Connie wants to know. The love is everywhere and now it is up to her to find the ease or make ease out of what suddenly seems like a pile of chaos. Sex toys, Michael, all these daughters she feels as if she has just gotten to meet for the very first time, the choices she moaned and begged and yearned for not so long ago, and the calm stint she thought she had designed for herself during her three-month retirement.

Where to start?

Connie willed herself into practicality and savaged through the first two days back in Cyprus as if her entire body were on fire. She mowed the lawn and answered calls, checked in at the old hospital and the new medical facility, let Sabrina and Macy know she was back from New York, but nothing more than that, and then she made a list of everything else that she needed to finish.

Another list, but this one was not as dreamy as the totally tattered pages she had attacked during the past couple of months.

By Wednesday morning the house was as good as it was going to get for a real-estate showing, as long as no one looked too closely in the garage where she was careful to tuck Jessica's box of Diva plans into a well-hidden position, and Connie had assigned herself the task of disappearing for most of the day while a series of eager purchasers pawed their way through the house.

Michael thought a nice solution to her numerous problems would be to move to New Orleans and open a Diva store there that would not only help the faltering economy of Louisiana, which continued to stumble from being washed out to sea, but would also help to keep his personal economy right where it needed to be.

"Like you need any help," Connie retorted, bragging before he had a chance to do it himself.

"At least think about it," he told her.

"What? Because I only have to make a thousand decisions by the end of the week?"

"No, because we are so good together."

"Michael, we just met."

"Connie, remember when you couldn't even say the words 'sex toys'?"

"Barely."

"You slept with me."

"I did?"

Michael's laugh was a wink away from being totally irresistible. It was one of the many, many things she liked about him, but on her list of things to do this week, *get tied down in a serious and lasting relationship* wasn't really that close to the top. He knew it too, but Michael also knew about lost chances and being too afraid to try something because of something else that was still lodged in your memory bank. Something that needed to be permanently erased or ignored, like a bad dream.

"Here's what I do know," he had explained before he left

New York on what turned out to be not just a one-day, but a three-day visit. "I am totally attracted to you. You are fun, and sexy, and sweet, and smart, and I don't want to let go of that, Connie. Call me a sap but I could fall right in love with you."

Love.

Connie did not totally freeze because her left eye twitched, but she was as close to freezing as possible. It was a number, two numbers, actually, on her list of dreams that she was not quite ready to shift into her front pocket.

"You just like me because my daughter owns a sex-toy store," she had finally managed to say.

And they left it there, just like that, blowing in the wind that drifted from Cyprus to the swamps and back again. Just there, with talk of a visit back to New Orleans, and one to Chicago, and another to Cyprus, and long phone calls, and Connie thinking about him when she should be thinking about five thousand other things, and remembering the night, and the two after that, in his suite, and the mornings, and the terrific shower, and the lunch they never ate, and wondering how for the love of God she had lived so long without *it*.

Without sex and lust and passion.

And that was the question, she knew, the real question she had to answer in the days she had to pick through the sides of her life back in Cyprus, Indiana. And as hard as she knew the excavation process might be, she also knew that it would be a journey that could prove to be fascinating, fun, and not anything like the days she thought she would be having when she pored through her list of dreams.

The list. The leather book was now resting back in the lap of the rocker and she remembered to pick it up and stick it inside of her underwear drawer minutes before the real-estate agent drove up, as she headed back towards the old hospital, the new nursing facility, and out to see the condo that might be hers eventually.

Or not.

O'Brien was waiting for her not so patiently at the hospital where a parade of morning catastrophes had made her want to jump from the same window she constantly kept her patients from imagining as a jumping-off point.

Connie had made the obligatory trudge through her old unit, past the administrator's office, through the break room and back towards O'Brien's unit where they sat in O'Brien's office and looked at each other like two extremely happy but slightly confused women.

Rolling through her visit to the hospital, Connie explained that coming back was like stepping into a time-warp machine. Everything suddenly seemed old and long ago. Connie flashed back with O'Brien to all the moments when someone they were working with departed for a new position, or some portion of a new life, and how that change would throw them and everyone they worked with into some kind of introspective place of wondering.

Wondering if they should be making a change. Wondering why they stayed. Wondering what would happen if they made a change. Wondering what was beyond the large entrance doors to their world.

"I don't miss this," Connie admitted. "It's like suddenly entering a strange land. I had no idea I would feel this way."

"It's old stuff, Connie. You were ready to leave this place a long time ago. It's good to know for sure, don't you think?"

"Yes, but what if I feel the same way when I get over to the new job? What if I walk in and want to vomit and feel as if that world is just as old?"

Frannie looked at her friend and smiled. She smiled and asked her why she was suddenly so afraid. So weary. So unsure.

Connie didn't have to hesitate to answer. She had everything planned. She had her list. She knew where she was going. There was a mild plan that could have been altered here and there and, when she looked up, she could see where she was going.

"Jesus, Connie, you need to stop for a second."

"I know," Connie said, dropping her head and running her hands through her hair. "I feel like I ran into a wall that wasn't supposed to be there while I was going as fast as possible."

Frannie reached across the table and put her hand on Connie's arm. She said she had an idea. A little idea.

"What?" Connie asked.

"First of all, none of this is bad," O'Brien offered. "This is all good stuff. Choices, chances, places, new people. I bet it was all on your list but maybe it looked a bit different to you. But it's also a lot to digest, and there isn't a lot of time, which really has never mattered in the past."

"So?"

"What did we always do, what have we done for years when we needed to be, or settle or solve or just act stupid?"

Connie smiled and sat back up.

"The lake and dunes. Can we go?"

"Yes, baby. We have to go. I'm the psych nurse here and it's part of your rehabilitation plan."

First, Connie agreed to go visit the medical complex

where she was scheduled to start work as a consultant in just a few weeks. Act like you are going to go there all the time, like it's your job, and see how you feel, O'Brien advised. Then she was to spend part of a day at the new condo. Walk the neighborhood. Think about living there, turn around when she was pulling out of the driveway to go someplace and see the house, the condo, that part of her life. Sit in the yard. Look out the windows. And then back to the old house. The one with the stuff in the garage. The one guarding her list of dreams.

"We'll go Friday after I'm done with work," O'Brien told her. "I'll call and see if we can get a cabin. We'll do the whole thing. Stop for a fish fry, get our wine, pull in late and sit in the dark while we watch the waves for a while. Then we'll get to it."

And you, O'Brien, Connie thought as she got up to start on her assignments with hearty resolve, how could I ever live without you?

They always stop at the Wind Drift Café, a small corner joint blocks from their favorite motel and cabins that they had discovered ten years ago and had claimed as their own oasis, more than a port in the storm, a lively, down-to-earth pub and restaurant that served whitefish so fresh O'Brien swore to God every single time they ate it that her plate was still moving.

Their Northern Indiana Cheers never changed and that, of course, was part of the charm. The Friday night waitress, Mary, would probably die serving french fries; the bartender, Bruce, would do likewise, serving his five millionth old-fashioned to one of the crusty local guys; and the owner, a saucy redhead who was pushing 80 and had been flirting with O'Brien's husband Daniel since the day she met him, always treated them like empresses.

"I'd sure as hell miss this place," Connie admitted, diving into her tart cole slaw, a kind of Midwestern must-have salad that is a mandatory part of a traditional Catholic, old-school Friday night fish fry. "Do you know that I've driven up here a few times by myself just for this fish, and to gab with all these wonderful people?"

"Me, too," O'Brien confesses. "I actually drove up the weekend you were in New Orleans because Daniel was wrapped up with work and I needed to breathe some of this lake air."

"Hey," Connie says brightly, reaching across the tartar sauce. "If Daniel dies, or runs off with the meter maid, and things don't work out with the Swamp Man, I'm going to marry you."

O'Brien doesn't flinch.

"Another mixed marriage?" she jokes. "If my mother isn't dead by then she'll die on the spot. Another white family relative will push her over the edge. And, oh, yeah, we couldn't hold the reception here by the lake because we'd have to get married in a foreign country, what with the same-sex issue and all, which is a very perfect reason for moving to Canada, if you ask me."

They joke, but both women know they could live together in a second and that, no matter what Connie decides to do with this lively middle section of her life, they'll always make time for the Wind Drift, these quick getaways, and each other. Those facts are without question. Everything else is hanging fire or, at the very least, smoldering lightly.

Connie loves the ebb and flow of the conversations at

the restaurant where people listen in on each other's discussions and then add what they think, buy you a drink and ask if they can eat your leftover bread without hesitation, guilt, or a second thought.

"There is some of this in Chicago and New York," Connie stresses as they force themselves to leave so they can catch the sunset. "It's easy to get seduced by a city but really, nothing's like the Midwest, and the open charm that seems to pour from just about every place and every person."

"Write that down," O'Brien urges. "We need to keep tabs to help you make your decisions."

"The decisions," Connie says, faking self-strangulation with her hands as they get into the car. "The dreaded decisions."

Frannie has managed to book a room at a small, old-fashioned-looking hotel right on the edge of the Indiana Dunes State Park that is deceiving on its faded exterior because the rooms have been gutted, fitted with new floor-to-ceiling windows, private decks, and new interiors that are small but as charming as anyplace they have ever stayed. Their favorite cabin, a rustic number right in the park, was swallowed up weeks ago during the rush to be near water in the middle of summer.

But first the requisite and very quiet drive down a road they had discovered years ago. It parallels a private patch of land leading out to what they call their ocean but what is actually the south end of Lake Michigan. The road is not on any map, and had probably been designated for abandonment, but has been lost in some kind of unique paper shuffle. And there it is every single time they make their homage—a narrow strip of asphalt that curves around a field, past a very old farmhouse, and ends abruptly behind a stand of sturdy pine trees that holds fast in the rising white sands that stretch for miles in either direction, and shifts just as much as the rest of the world around it.

Glorious solitude.

A lively summer breeze.

The still-warm summer sand.

A sun dropping like a slow rock.

The soft swooshing sound of bird wings.

Not another person in sight.

And wise O'Brien running back to the car for a special bottle of wine, two sturdy plastic glasses and a flashlight, before the sun turns the corner.

"Connie," O'Brien finally says after she has opened the wine and passes a glass to her friend. "Guess what?"

"What, honey?"

"This is that Australian stuff you were drinking the night you heard the house talking."

"Really?"

"I put a whole case in the car."

"Are we expecting company or is this going to just be a wild, drunken weekend?"

"Just us, just for us and for the hours of talking, and because I couldn't lift the damn thing out of the trunk by myself."

Connie laughs and takes a sip and swears to God she immediately hears what sounds like a gaggle of singing sailors. She looks at O'Brien, who hears it too.

"What the hell?"

They turn towards the sound and see a long irrigation pipe sticking up, right into the wind, that Connie guesses immediately is whistling and echoing because their bodies have blocked some portions of the lake breeze.

"Shit," they both say, laughing at once.

"It was on the list," Connie says next.

"What?"

"A case of dry red wine. Or buying some really expensive wine. It was on my list of dreams."

Connie brings the glass to her lips, takes a sip, and holds the wine inside of her mouth for a very long time before she swallows it. When she does, she tastes the rich tannins of a wine that likes to bite and slap taste buds on the way down. She filters a drop of earth, a pinch of the sky, a hint of lemon, and feels the breath of a baby on her neck, the wine floating towards her bloodstream, a warm ache at the very tip of her pubic bone.

"It is on the list."

"It was pretty expensive, you know. I think you wanted it to be expensive."

"Anything over ten bucks is expensive."

"Thank God," O'Brien says, feigning a fainting spell. "I just made it—this was twelve bucks a bottle and there was no discount for the case. This is a big deal, baby."

A big deal, Connie repeats, as they launch into a conversation that will take them through another bottle of wine and into the slice of darkness that they can actually see riding across the lake on waves that get longer with each gust of wind. A big deal, as they shift their hips, lean into each other. O'Brien lights up one of her damn cigarettes and Connie grabs one and smokes it too and then puts it out after three puffs because she finds it as disgusting as sucking on a dirty sock. A big deal, as they talk about the list and life.

The list and life.

Think about it, O'Brien orders. Think about what is on your list, and what you have done the past few months, and what you could do in the next few months and all the months after those.

The sex and lust. New York. New Orleans. The convertible. Connie almost has the list totally memorized and when she realizes what Frannie is getting at she swallows her entire glass of wine and holds out her cup for a refill.

"You've been doing it all along," O'Brien says. "I don't know what you are so worried about."

"I didn't think of it like that," Connie admits. "I had this plan, this way I thought everything was going to happen, how I wanted it to happen, and then everything became unexpected, wild, and, well, wonderful in a sometimes confusing way."

"Jesus, it sounds like hell."

They both laugh at everything. Sitting in the sand at midnight. Dancing in New York. Kissing men in swamps. Breakfast at the Algonquin. Selling sex toys. Diva-ing it up in Cyprus with women who are already so grateful they have sent Connie thank-you letters. The box in the garage. New hair. Men looking twice. More than a stretch of time. Worrying about one goddamn thing after another at their age.

Everything.

Every single thing.

And the wild notion that in order to live the list of dreams Connie not only needs to get rid of #1 but acknowledge that everything, even the almighty list, needs to change.

Connie lets the wind dance along the short edges of her hair when she turns and puts her face into the breeze. She closes her eyes and imagines a life without this—without moments of pause and pleasure, moments of wondering, the warm length of a good friend's back nestled against your own back, wine dripping down your throat like melted gold, choices dancing within arm's length like kites coming down from a high wind, knowing people in a way you never realized they existed, rising like a feather to meet your lover's kiss.

It's all there.

It's all here.

It's never been anywhere else.

"Unexpected choices," O'Brien tells her, close to the last glass of wine. "They seem to be the best kinds of choices."

"I thought I was so cool," Connie admits. "I thought I was open and that I knew my daughters, knew who they were, knew where I was going, knew that sex was a minor chord in my life that I had decided to skip right over, knew how long to idle before the light turned green—everything. What the hell was I thinking?"

"Claiming your sexual self and giving other women the chance to do the same thing is a pretty big deal," O'Brien replies. "You've lived an entire new life in just a couple of weeks. Just think what the next couple of years might be like. Think of that list as your diving board, baby."

And, Connie adds, I still have to make just a few major decisions while a mess of people in my life hold their breath.

Oh, shit, Frannie says, pulling her friend up from the sand, there will always be a big decision and one after that and then just when you think you can see where the road stops, there's a new frigging highway or a detour that will drive you nuts because you think—heavy emphasis here on the word "think"—you like the road just the way it is.

"I still need a decision in, like, 24 hours," Connie complains.

"You'll get one, baby, and believe me, it will be a complete surprise to someone."

"Maybe lots of someones," Connie shouts back, as the

wind dances down her neck and bounces off the back of her legs and she races O'Brien to the car, gets her toe stuck under a log, and falls flat on her face.

"Get up, Nurse Nixon," O'Brien shouts. "This is not an omen."

They could have used two more cases of wine, and another week, but they only had until very early Sunday morning when Frannie had to get back to fill in during the second half of first shift and when Connie had to make her blessed call to New York so that about fifty people could get on with their lives.

No pressure, Connie joked most of the day on Saturday while they hiked up the beach and back around the dunes hiking trail, fought the urge to check their cell phones, lingered over a very long lunch at the restaurant two bluffs over, and then simply sat on their porch, exhausted, sunburned, and totally not ready to face an early-morning drive back to reality.

They had giggled away the remainder of Friday night, slept with the windows and door wide open, and woke early when a seagull walked into the room and then could not remember where the door was.

"Jesus," Connie said, jumping from the bed with her pillow as a shield. "O'Brien, help me, there's a bird on your suitcase."

Frannie jumped up, screamed—which made the bird go to the bathroom on top of her suitcase—and then simply ran towards the bird with her red T-shirt flapping behind her and the poor bird took off and probably alerted every bird on the lake that a couple of strange women were at the dunes and to be on the lookout.

"Go figure," Connie said, suddenly longing for a cup of coffee like she had never longed for coffee before.

"See?" O'Brien said. "Something else unexpected. This is your fault, Nurse Nixon. Now that you have learned how to fly at a new altitude, you sexy bitch, even the birds want you."

The laughter could have woken the people across the lake and set the tone for a day that Connie thought had brought her inches closer to some necessary decisions.

Before their walk to the café for dinner, and what would end up to be a night when they stayed to close the joint, played poker with two guys from Bloomington named Hank and Dan, let some babe from Chicago buy them tequila, and had dessert at midnight, they had a very brilliant talk on the now-birdless porch.

On the porch, with the sun filtering through a wild stand of birch trees and a beach so white it looked as if someone from the linen store had placed a series of sheets on the ground for miles. The hotel manager, who drifted past and waved when she saw them, came back moments later with two cold beers and a wish for a happy night.

And what about that happy life?

"Connie," O'Brien finally said. "Let's just do this. Let's have a quick triage, access the damage, the possibilities and then walk to dinner, which you are buying, by the way."

Connie was way ready, and so they started.

They started simple. The Swamp Man cometh. And he lingereth in Connie's mind. Terrific, wonderful sex which she hoped to have again—but a long-term, serious relationship? Not so much. Not yet. Those numbers on the list needed to simmer. She wanted to dance the rumba with the entire band, waltz with her new decisions, feel the power of her newly acquired sexual self in a way that did not limit her.

"Like a swinger?" O'Brien asks.

"No, sweetie. Like a woman who doesn't want to make the same mistakes she made the last time. Great sex does not a relationship make. I'm pacing myself this time. Michael's a terrific man but I can't leap like that. I just can't do it."

See how easy this is, Frannie offers. Next.

The new job?

Connie hesitates. She could do the job, she could fill up the time, manage an entire medical universe, do the paperwork and still have time to play, but something happened when she went to the facility. Something telling.

"My heart sank," she admits. "I could feel it fall into a memorized pattern of familiarity and when I left, my breathing changed. Honest to God. I felt better when I left and I never turned around. Not once."

"Well, that pretty much answers all the other questions then, doesn't it?"

"No."

"Give me the rest of your beer if you are going to toy with me like this," Frannie says. "What do you mean *no*?"

"Since we got here this idea has been swaying back and forth inside of me. It's like taking a recipe and shifting around the ingredients and making something sort of the same, but totally different."

Frannie, impatient as hell, grabs the beer out of her hand.

"The absolute most powerful, wonderful time I had, well, besides making love with Burt Reynolds, was talking to women about the toys, not just selling them, but here in Cyprus when we had the mini-Diva-sex-toy party, well, shit, Frannie, I loved that," Connie confesses.

"It showed, baby. And this means?"

"Let me skip ahead just a second. I love the condo. I'm

not ready to leave Cyprus, but I can't stay there now like I would have, like I might have, if I kept the new job."

Frannie leans over and gives her a hug. "This is good news so far, keep going."

Connie's short stint in the Diva world showed her that women were more than ready to move beyond the sexual limits they had accepted in their own lives. More than ready to rip open their sexual selves the way they had ripped open everything else. But sometimes, Connie had learned, they were not quite ready to do that in a store, or in public, or with someone they did not know or trust.

"Sex-toy parties," Connie said. "That's what I should be doing. Designing programs, and putting together a traveling van, and workshops, and intimate gatherings where women can look up and see someone with wrinkles and a few miles under their belt, have them explain how a dildo works, how to turn on a vibrator, and then share a slice of cake and a cup of coffee while their friends play with the toys. I have tons of ideas, including a big one that we have to call them something besides toys."

Frannie O'Brien thinks Connie is a genius.

Even now, Connie can't stop herself. She talks about parties that are not only instructional but also fun. Parties where talking about sex is made to seem normal and important and lively and not at all like something that should not be right there on the front of the plate. O'Brien can see that her friend is on fire but she's impatient and she cuts her off.

"So you're saying . . ."

"Let that other woman Christine run the Chicago store. She's absolutely perfect. I'm right here. I'll hop on Jessica and Geneva's board, work on the training manual, travel for them and design an entire package of party plans, instructions, you name it."

"Whooo, baby."

"I'll keep the condo for now, get out of the house with the singing walls, travel, and make a whole new list of dreams."

"Was it the beer?"

Connie brushes her off.

"What do you think?"

"I think sex has been very good for you and it sounds like you are going to make it very good for lots and lots of other women as well," she says, slightly taken aback by the plan but not surprised that Connie would do more than consider it.

"And guess what, baby?" Connie asks, leaning in to grab her beer back. "I'm going to need an assistant and I know you can retire early if you want to."

O'Brien roars with laughter as if she had just figured out how to do it.

"The Irishman would have a heart attack," she says, snorting. "Can you see us, driving through town with boxes of sex toys in the car, throwing out condoms at a parade, giving an in-service at the women's club and then flying off to Las Something for a plastics convention?"

Connie says yes.

She can see it all, absolutely every single moment.

She can see it because she finally sees herself moving like wind, holding onto her Sunday list of dreams, moving with them as her dreams change, changing herself, not being so tied to a number that she misses the sunset.

Yes, she can see that, yes, she can, and then she grabs Frannie O'Brien by the hand, spins her around the tiny deck and launches into a discussion about sexual satisfaction in rural women as compared to urban women and the two women, friends, sisters, and females who know when it's time to start moving and stop talking, head towards the café where Connie works the crowd and wonders, even after the tequila, how many women could fit into the Wind Drift on a Sunday afternoon for a Diva sex-toy party.

Connie's Latest List of Dreams

The 48th revision

1. Stop being afraid.

2. Let go. Stop holding on to things so tightly. Loosen your grasp. Be honest.

3. Get rid of SHIT. Start with the garage.

4. Dance with a handsome man who doesn't care if you have a double chin, have to pluck your long facial hairs, or put on a girdle in order to get into the damn dress.

5. Stop setting the alarm clock.

6. Take yourself to confession. Make the penance easy.

7. Recapture Jessica. Find Jessica. Hurry, Connie, but start slowly. Find your baby.

8. Do something with your damn hair. Everyone looks the same after 47. Take a deep breath and hand the scissors to someone else, for crissakes.

9. Imagine what it might be like to fall in love. It's a place to start. Look up the word in the dictionary first. Get over it.

10. Buy a convertible. Something flashy. Red or blue. Put the top down and drive someplace without thinking. Just get in the car and take off.

11. Watch all the movies you have clipped out of the review section for the past—what?—thirty years.

12. Take a deep breath and allow the two daughters who actually let you visit them to live their own lives. Accept their traditional choices. Maybe this one should be listed in two places. This is hard. Keep your mouth shut except to smile when you visit or they visit.

13. A span of time to indulge myself in any damn thing I want. Eat. Drink. Be merry time. Turn off the phones. Maybe lie about what I'm doing. Minutes. Seconds. Hours. Days.

14. Maybe sex. Something meaningless. Just sex. A man's hand on my face, my breast. Not caring what happens next. Over and over again. Sex. I can't even believe I just wrote this. It's a HUGE dream. Sex. My list. SEX. This one is a big maybe. But I wrote it down. I can't even believe I knew how to spell it.

15. Be my own boss. Lots of employee benefits. Hiring people I want to be with a lot. Free lunch all of the time. A clear view of a goal that includes the feelings, schedules and talents of the people who work for me. I like this one. Oh, yes. Hey, I'm in charge.

16. Really good wine. I want to go into a store that has removed all of the price labels and just buy whatever kind of wine looks fabulous. Just buy whatever in the hell I want to buy, without worrying about how much it costs.

17. Another camping trip. Don't call me crazy. I loved camping when I was a kid. I want to resurrect the old tent and do it. Fires every night. Burnt hamburgers. Cold mornings. Whiskey in my coffee cup.

18. A fancy dress. Something formal and long that sits right at the tip of my breasts. A Cinderella dress—this is embarrassing, but sometimes when I dream I see this dress—slits up the side, beads. Maybe when I wear it I'll be someplace wild and wonderful.

19. Moments with my daughters that are real and open and where each of us can be who we really are.

20. Time in New York City. This city scares me but I dream about it. I want to walk on the streets, sit in a café, meet people at a bar. New York City. I want to own the damn place.

21. Start sleeping naked again.

22. Stop doubting yourself—for God's sake, you save people's lives for a living.

23. Tell the people you love that you love them. Do it more.

24. Take a painting class—start with oil and then try watercolors. If this is a success—meaning no one laughs too loud—take a pottery class.

25. Write more thank-you notes—real notes, not email. Let people know. Even for the little things.

26. Mix up your friends. Do this with intention. Younger, older, whatever. Not just the ones who are convenient.

27. Buy your own damn books. Stop sharing. You can afford this. Don't wait until they are out in paperback, either.

28. At least think about the possibility of love—this is a biggie. Maybe this one should take up a couple of pages. Right now this is a blink of a dream. Maybe it's more of a nightmare.

29. Look at yourself naked—physically and psychologically and spiritually. Figure out how to salute what you see. Shit—this has been on the list, I think, since it started.

30. Drink wine before noon and anything else you want. Stop trying to figure out who made all these senseless rules anyway. Stop following the rules.

31. Sign the final house papers.

32. Pick out all the extras for the condo. Stop procrastinating.

33. Go see more plays.

34. Take an Italian cooking class without worrying about all the damn calories in pasta.

35. Call all those people in your address book who disappeared—even those jackasses from high school. A call does not a reconnection make. Find out whatever happened to everybody.

36. Enough. Stop writing—Connie—Stop writing and start doing something.

37. Make certain the list changes. Give yourself that option. Keep some. Throw some away.

Epilogue

Nurse Nixon's Easy-Reference Diva Sex Dictionary

In order of importance here is what you need to know right this second. Read this in the bathroom if you have to, but this is a one-two-three quick study for a handful—pardon the pun—of sex terms that will get you going and coming.

DIVA—In numerous countries this word means goddess and that's exactly what it should always mean to you.

VIBRATOR—A Diva's best friend. Vibrators are battery- or electric-powered divine devices that can be used to stimulate any area of your body. Think below the waist. Think fast motion. Think wonderful. They come in all shapes and sizes. Some are camouflaged as lipstick tubes, one plugs into your car lighter, one looks like a brush. Get a bigger purse and get going.

G-SPOT—There's a lovely and lively group of nerves resting an inch or so inside of your vagina, and some nosy doctor whose last name began with a G made mention of this as a potential hot sexual spot. We think it was a woman named Gloria and she would tell you that not every woman goes into orbit right there but, just in case, there are a number of G-spot toys and we think you should try every single one just to make sure.

DILDO—This is an artificial penis or if you don't like the word "penis," or the object itself, just think that this is something that would do what a penis does if you did like one. Tall, short, curved, bumpy, with batteries, without. Pink. Purple. White. Black. If you can imagine it, and thank heavens Diva's has a great imagination, we have probably already designed one just for you. This is definitely in "the more the merrier" department.

LUBRICATION—This is not your mother's baby oil, baby. Lubrication is used to help make your sex life easier, faster, longer. It comes in lovely jars and bottles and, like those dildos, it comes in lots of varieties. Tons of flavors. Slippery and not so slippery and slippery in the middle. You can use it on the real penis, the make-believe one, other sex toys, your fingers, someone else's fingers. Believe the Diva Sexpert on this one. Lube is to die for.

HARNESS—A harness, as you know, holds things in place, just like a bra, and there is absolutely nothing like a fine, comfortable, attractive bra. Don't look now but a harness is used to hold a dildo in place so you can do whatever you want with it. They mostly come in leather, with cool buckles and loops, and there's something powerful . . . oh, never mind.

PLEASURE BALMS—These sweet sex accessories are used to heat up a particular area on the body and to help bring a little fun into the bedroom, barn or bowling alley—wherever you plan to do it, women. They are sweet, often scented, tasteless if you prefer, and include powders, lotions and talcs that can be sprinkled, patted, placed or gently rubbed anywhere you can possibly think of on the human body.

MASTURBATION—Divas have a right to own every part of themselves . . . even their sexual parts. Masturbation means taking care of yourself sexually. Touching, using Diva toys, exploring a lovely fantasy. Sigh. It's a healthy activity. Loving yourself in all ways is number one in a Diva's world. Self-satisfaction begins at home and remember, you and only you are responsible for your sexual satisfaction.

ROLE-PLAYING—Whips, chains, blindfolds, dressing up as Jane and Tarzan . . . whatever you think might float your boat is included in this category. Some people like to control and others like to be controlled. Fantasy is, and always will be, an important part of sex and if you feel safe and everyone in-volved agrees—Diva, darling—you don't have a thing to lose.

VIDEOS AND BOOKS—Don't underestimate your mind's connection to your body and what a sexy book or video might do to make you a well-rounded woman. Diva's has a huge selection of books, manuals, and videos that can be used to turn up the heat a notch on your sex life. Books and videos, just like those vibrators and dildos, come in a variety of tem-peratures and textures. Hot, hotter, and hottest.

SEX TOYS—This is not your grandma's toy store but it should have been. Sex toys include everything from a fine bottle of wine to a great sexy movie and back around again to every-thing else in your dictionary. When someone says, "Do you want to play with my toys?" and you gave away your Barbie dolls a long time ago, you will now know exactly what board game they are talking about.

Connie's Calming Sex Tips for Real Divas

1. Relax. Do this any way possible. Have a drink. Let your mind run through a sea of tall grass at the edge of a very lovely blue ocean. Turn off the lights. Take a bath. Shut off every other light in your world except the one that shines on your sexual self. Relaxing means letting go and letting go is a very, let me stress that, very important part of waltzing without tripping while you enjoy sex.

2. Have one extra glass of wine. It can't hurt and hopefully, within minutes, you will have forgotten you even had the damn thing.

3. Look at yourself. Not your face, sweetie, your self. If you have never laid down on a floor and held up a mirror to view your own vagina and its surrounding territory this is a good time to start. If you are giving driving directions to someone else it really helps to know the map.

4. Talk to another woman. Sexual experiences vary—no one understands that like a Diva Sister—but women know. We do and sometimes a sex-laced conversation can help you get answers, liberate your fears, and let you know that you are not alone.

5. Make sex a priority. What could be more important? Write it in your planner if you have to. Think about it—is changing the oil on time or reseeding the backyard really as important as feeling good?

6. Remember, if you do the same thing in the same place at the same time—something will wear out. Even sex can get boring—I know that's hard to believe—if you do it the same way day after day, week after week. . . .

7. Read. The Internet and bookstores are filled with lively sex manuals and books and really, the best place to start is at a Diva store because we have had the pleasure, and I mean pleasure, of reading them all and we know which book can harm you and which book can help you.

8. Start out slow, sweetheart. You do not have to turn into a porn queen the first day you decide to get on with it and get it on. Slow may mean something as simple and as lovely as a kiss behind the neck, three undone buttons instead of one, or a very early dinner and lights out.

9. Sex can be anything you want it to be. Liberating. Fun. Wild. Quiet. Something you do alone or with a partner. It can be simple or complicated. Putting everything and everyone else, and what they say about sex, out of your mind and just falling into it will often result in the most wonderful sexual moment you have ever had.

10. Never be afraid to ask for help. A bottle of lubrication, a quick call to your Diva rep, a suggestion from your partner or a call to a Diva Sister may make all the difference. Remember, we want you to be happy just as much as you want to be happy.

Kudos from Connie's Clients

"My girlfriend had a surprise Diva's Decadent Delights Party for my 55th birthday, and at first I almost died of embarrassment, but then the party started and everyone relaxed, and by the end of the party Connie had changed my life and the lives of all 12 of my friends. We have booked six more parties. We are very happy women."
—BETH W., INDIANAPOLIS

"I am 44 years old and thought I knew everything. What an ass I was. Connie and her assistant have kick-started my life, not just my sex life but every aspect of my life. I feel powerful, whole, and as if I have just discovered a part of myself that has been missing since the day I was born."
—JESSICA S., RACINE, WISCONSIN

"I took my mother to Diva's in Chicago and Connie was there. She took one look at my mother, dismissed me, and took my mother into a private room where she showed her everything, talked to her, and answered all her questions. The next day my mother called me weeping. She told me that she had just had her first orgasm. Now I cannot stop crying."
—KENDALL D., CHICAGO

"When I was in college I was date-raped. Sex after that was horrid and I finally gave up. My friend took me to a sex-toy party and Connie was demonstrating the toys and she made me feel as if sex was a gift I could give myself and that I was in charge and I believed her. It took me 23 years but my life is back in my own hands now."
—JACKIE L., CLEVELAND, OHIO

"My sister turned 60 last week and I threw her a sex-toy party. Oh my God. I had no idea. We had a few drinks and Connie was so open and real, and so much like us, that no one held back. I'm going to start working for Diva's. I want to change the world like Connie changed mine."

—GLORIA B., CEDAR RAPIDS, IOWA

"When I read about this I knew I had to meet Connie and see what Diva's was all about. It has been a long time coming, if you pardon the pun. I am a sex therapist who has been looking for a safe, clean, open, and free place to send my female clients for a very long time. I highly recommend Diva's, all their services, and especially Connie's fabulous parties."

—DR. JOYCE P., LOS ANGELES

"I grew up on a small farm in a very rural part of Idaho. My family belonged to a religious group that is still dominated by men. Women, we were told, are here to have babies. When I read about Diva's I went to the website, and while at first I was shocked, I very quickly got over it. This store and attending one of Connie's classes, called "Erasing the Past—Sex as a Gift," absolutely changed my life and will now change the lives of my daughters. Thank you. I can't say it enough. Thank you, Connie and Diva's."

—MARY C., SALT LAKE CITY, UTAH

"You think when you get older that you know everything and then sometimes you just settle. I would have settled sexually and in many other areas of my life if my friend had not invited me to one of Connie's parties. I am free. I am just getting started. I am 71 years old."

—BETSY P., AUSTIN, TEXAS

"Just when I thought my wonderful life could not get any better I waltzed into Diva's when I flew into Las Vegas and I stayed three hours. I thought I was happy. Now I am REALLY happy."

—JILL N., SANTA FE, NEW MEXICO

About the Author

Kris Radish is the author of six books. Her Bantam Dell novels *The Elegant Gathering of White Snows, Dancing Naked at the Edge of Dawn* and *Annie Freeman's Fabulous Traveling Funeral* have been on bestseller and Book Sense 76 Selection lists. She also writes two weekly nationally syndicated columns.

She travels frequently throughout the country speaking about women's issues, the value of female friendships and the importance of personal empowerment, as well as the necessity for laughter, a terrific glass of wine, lying quietly in the summer grass, embracing kindness, following the path in your own heart and no one else's, and having fun at all costs.

Kris lives in Wisconsin with her partner, a teenaged daughter—whom she sees when the gas tank is empty, a college son—who shows up when it's time to wash clothes, and where she is cruising through menopause on her Yamaha 1100 Classic VStar, her Trek bicycle, a treadmill, a pair of orange-laced walking shoes, a chlorine-blocking swimsuit, a gallon of calcium, about 100 notebooks for her novels, short story, poetry, and journalism ideas and a case of cheap wineglasses.

She is also working on her fifth novel, *Searching for Paradise in Parker, PA*, which Bantam Dell will publish in 2008.

If you loved Kris Radish's

the Sunday List of Dreams,

you won't want to miss any
of her acclaimed titles.
Look for them at your
favorite bookseller's.

And read on for
an early look at
Kris's next novel

SEARCHING FOR
PARADISE
IN PARKER, PA

coming soon from
Delacorte Press

Addy hits the wall ...

Addy Lipton has been nurturing a wild desire for a good twenty-two months to drive her 1998 dark blue Toyota Corolla right through the closed garage door of the lovely two-story white brick and cedar home she shares with a man she vaguely remembers marrying a very long time ago.

The Toyota has not been inside of the garage since 1992 and the last time she opened the kitchen door leading into the garage, and stepped inside of what she now calls "The Kingdom of Krap," was just days before her milestone fiftieth birthday and very close to two years ago. Addy had opened the door to set a bottle of wine in the cool garage so it would chill before her sister showed up to help her celebrate. She placed it next to the bag of dog food left over from Barney the black lab—who had passed without a doubt into doggie heaven in 2001—and then dared to look into the bowels of the garage where she had not bothered to gaze for a very long time.

"What the hell," she said out loud as she raised her eyes and wondered if she had suddenly been transported to a used appliance store.

The garage, totally her husband Lucky's disgusting domain, was crammed to high tide with refrigerators, a couple of dishwashers, three dryers, an assortment of machines that must have been something workable at one time when they could actually be plugged in and turned on, and—from what she could see—about 15 dead microwaves.

"Lucky, Lucky, Lucky," she said through a jaw that was as tight as a rusted dishwasher bolt, scanning past the machines and having a *moment*. A moment of desperation, wonderment, tepid fury, and astonishment at what not only her assumed half of the garage, but her entire life in halves and quarters and eighths and sixteenths had become.

"A garage filled with crap that my husband will use with his goofyass friends, not to fix, but to spread across each other's lawns like teenagers," Addy told herself, turning slightly in the kitchen doorway to see two piles of old bowling balls, a stack of wire coat hangers, a lawnmower that she knew for a fact did not start, and the back end of a 1951 Chevy that Lucky had been working on since he found its decaying hulk sticking out of his uncle's old shed and dragged it home when their son was a baby. Nineteen years. The car had not moved, or turned over, or gravitated to the local restored antique car parade, for nineteen years.

Addy reached down and picked up the wine bottle, telling herself that she would not now wait for her sister, that she would open the bottle immediately and drink it warm. Warm, like everything else in her life. Nothing hot or cold or spicy but every damn thing seeming to sit right in the middle as if waiting for something, someone, anything to push it off to one side.

After the bottle was empty and her sister Helen—Hell as she was aptly named—stole her away for a birthday dinner where Lucky actually managed to show up on time, and she was back home again, Addy could not stop thinking about the damn garage, which as a birthday gift to herself she began calling The Kingdom of Krap.

And the garage drove her crazy with wondering.

Wondering what else might be stored behind ragged cardboard boxes and the mountains of junk Lucky and his ridiculous friends scavenged from behind stores and each other's garbage piles.

Wondering how a section of the house and her life had gotten so out of control.

Wondering what would happen if Lucky spent half as much time with her as he did with his obsessive collecting and make-believe restoration projects.

Wondering why she was somehow content to sit and simply observe as her marriage seemed to drift off to a place where she could barely see the outlines of what it used to be.

Wondering if she was really prepared to spend the next thirty to forty years—if the family genes held up—lurking at the edge of her garage, of her life.

And that's when she started wondering what it might feel like to drive the car right through the door.

She imagined it first as an accident. Something that she did as she bent down to grab the papers and books and piles of third-grade projects that she needed to grade for school the following day. Addy would close her eyes during recess duty or a staff meeting and see herself reaching backwards just as her foot fell off the brake and hit the gas pedal while the car was in first gear.

The car would lurch forward like a large stone that had been pried loose after much pushing. It would jump just as she turned to see the front end of the little Toyota crash an inch below the handle in the middle of the door and then she would see the old Chevy buckle, the dishwashers spread as if Moses were driving the Toyota, and coat hangers fly like thin birds who have just seen a large dog advancing upon them.

Sometimes this vision got her through a particularly tough day. One of those days when a sick third grader would vomit first on himself, and then on the girl in front of him, and then, on the way out the door, on Addy. A day when the principal would drag a mother into the room who didn't like a comment on a paper composed by one of her students that was obviously written by the mother who had forgotten that third graders do not usually know how to spell words that she has to look up in the dictionary. A day when her son might call her from his dorm room and whine about money, or the pressures of his measly part-time job, or the fact that his mother would not give him five hundred dollars to go on a spring break trip to Florida so he could drink cheap booze until his brain swam.

More times than she cared to remember, Addy had actually edged the Toyota inch by inch up the driveway until she felt the front bumper kiss the garage door. She'd put the car in neutral and then imagine the whole scene all over again—flying pieces of the wooden door diving past her window, rocketing wedges of metal, years of precious scavenging being pummeled by the foreign car Lucky sold parts for but hated to recognize as a superior model.

But she never did it.

She never did more than nudge the door. Never bothered to tell Lucky she had harbored an overwhelming desire to flatten his hobbies, his haven, his Krappy land of fun and freedom. Never told her sister, never mentioned it during the after-work pizza-and-beer gatherings, never told her friends at the YWCA, never asked her son Mitchell what he thought of the mess in the garage, never did more than simply think about ramming her automobile from the edge of her world right into the center of her husband's.

Until today.

It is April 1 in Parker, Pennsylvania, and everywhere else on Addy's side of the Equator and Addy thinks that if she did it today, she would have an excuse. She would plow through the garage door in second gear, which she has also imagined during the past twenty-two months, and try hard to make it through the crap and into the backyard. She could blame it on the date. "I was just going to dent it a little and say April Fool's," she'd tell Lucky. Lucky, she imagined, would either laugh or rush to check on his favorite bowling ball.

There is also the menopause excuse, which would be a lie because Addy is dancing lightly on the brim of menopause—that joints-aching, two-periods-in-one-month, fifteen-extra-pounds-last-year, occasionally-crying-when-she-looks-at-Mitchell's-baby-photos place—but not in real menopause, which of course would be all of the above times one thousand. She is thinking of saying it had been a hot flash or a fast-beating heart or the ridiculous urge to shift with her elbow instead of her hand. Lucky, she knew, was terrified of the word "menopause." Simply to say it out loud might just be enough to throw him into a state of forgiveness.

It is 6:48 P.M. and Addy has plunged into the place of wanting so badly that she has her hand on the gearshift and her mind set on ramming through the door. Addy is exhausted from the pre–spring break tests, from her college son's absent but seemingly ever-present presence, from a marriage that has not so suddenly turned into something that feels and looks and tastes more like a business partnership that a union of two people in love and lust forever and ever.

Sitting in the car, with the tires hovering over the long cracks in the asphalt driveway, Addy this very moment wants lots of things.

She wants to ride a pony and to sleep in.

She wants to do tequila shots with her sister in Mexico.

She wants to spend the rest of Mitchell's college money on a total house makeover.

She wants to go to Italy before she needs to wear trifocals, which is one focal away.

She wants Lucky to initiate a conversation that has nothing to do with "stuff" and everything to do with "them."

She wants to come home, swing open the garage door, and pull her car inside.

She wants to lie in bed naked with all the magazines and books and television clickers on the floor and talk, just talk, with Lucky, just Lucky, for hours and hours and hours.

She wants to make people laugh—really, really hard and for a very long time.

Addy has one hand on the steering wheel and the other on the gearshift and the car is in first gear. She is trying to decide if she should back up and start the garage-door-bashing procedure from the backside of the curb or from where she is right this moment. Her mind is as light as a third-grade song. She pauses to place her right hand over her heart because she is surprised she is so calm, so ready, so eager. And when she feels her heart beating softly, true, regular, and as it always has, she decides that she would like to back up about twenty-five feet, shift into second, and then hit the door with an intoxicating burst of speed.

Addy turns to make certain an unseen object has not bounced into the driveway while she has been idling at the lip of her decision. As she turns, she feels the seat next to her under her right hand, notices the last glow of an early spring sunset between the two houses at the end of the cul-de-sac, thinks that her training class at the Y is paying off because her neck no longer aches when she twists sideways, and then she stops at the back end of the basketball hoop.

Addy revs the Toyota. She takes in a huge breath, a long-remembered yoga movement, and she closes her eyes.

Closes her eyes to remember the moment, the months of imagining, the abyss she must now cross to take her someplace, anyplace, through the broad barriers of a life that is a garage, a receptacle for dumpage and stagnation, and just as she raises her head and shifts, Lucky is there.

Lucky Lucky.

His head is dipping towards her as if it is a ball that has just passed through the bottom of the ragged edges of the almost-abandoned basketball net.

Addy can feel her heart bounce from her chest, crash through the windshield, and slam against the very garage door that she had hoped to have pushed apart—now.

"Gezus, Addy, I've been waiting for you for like an hour," Lucky shouts, pulling open her car door.

"What?" she asks him, unable to move, wondering already when she will be able to drive through the door now that her plan has been interrupted.

"Honey, you are not going to believe this."

"Try me."

"Ready?"

"Yes," Addy yells. "YES."

"We're going to Costa Rica."

"What?"

"I won the company sales incentive prize."

"You're kidding?"

"No. Costa Rica. Do you teach that in third grade?"

Addy slowly shifts the car into park, sets the brake, turns the key into the off position, shuts off the lights, and swings her legs out of the car right in between Lucky's legs.

"Yes," she says, as she gets up and follows Lucky into the house.

And as she passes the garage door she touches it lightly like lovers touch when they don't want anyone else to see.

what I should have said to Addy . . .

Man oh man. I practiced for like an hour on how to tell her about the trip but then when the car pulled up and I saw her just sitting there, doing who the hell knows what women do when they sit in a car and stare, I lost it.

"Lucky," she would have said if I had told her that the thought just disappeared into some black hole behind my eyebrows, which she has been after me to trim for God's sake, men in Parker do not trim their eyebrows, "Write it down."

But I didn't.

Now I remember when it's too late. Which is pretty much how my system has been running for a while now.

"Honey," I wanted to say, "I never told you this because I wanted it to be a surprise but some of those nights when you thought I was out farting around I was working the phones in my office because I wanted to win this trip . . . for you."

There was more.

I wanted to see her walking down the beach in her bathing suit and then have one of those dinners right in the sand by the water for just two people with champagne and watch her read for about five hundred hours in a row by the pool, because she'd rather read than eat, but I got so excited when she pulled up and then I got impatient, which is another one of my many life curses, and I just ran outside and told her.

And what I really should have said to Addy disappeared.